Praise for Jedediah Berry's *The Manual of Detection*

"From the classic tropes of the detective procedural, this debut novel weaves the kind of mannered fantasy that might result if Wes Anderson were to adapt Kafka. . . . [Berry creates] the feeling of inhabiting a strange and haunting dream, with its own persuasive logic and somnambulant pacing." —*The New Yorker*

"A wryly cerebral take on noir fiction." —*Financial Times*

"This novel seems to take its inspiration from the works of Kafka, Italo Calvino, Borges and Angela Carter, with perhaps a dash of Terry Gilliam for good measure. Berry sets up a neat literary game and plays it through to the end with a great deal of wit and aplomb. A handsomely designed book, *The Manual of Detection* is a distinctively surreal whodunit." —*San Francisco Chronicle*

"[Berry] defies many mystery novel conventions, but adventurous readers who stay with his strange and fabulous debut work will be handsomely rewarded. . . . *The Manual of Detection* might not follow the detective-fiction manual, but there is nothing mysterious about the appeal of this inventive, outrageous and often amusing dream-within-a-dream." —*The Wall Street Journal*

"Chapter by chapter, scene by scene, [*The Manual of Detection*] felt like a lost collaboration between the *Barton Fink*-era Coen brothers and David Lynch while he was collecting his thoughts for the first half of *Lost Highway*. . . . An eerie and unusual delight, employing the conventions and plotting of mystery novels in ways that are resonant of many predecessors, but haven't been done quite like this before." —*Las Vegas Weekly*

"[Berry] dares the reader to preemptively figure out the crime at its center by making his meta-novel just what the title implies. . . . A fun meditation on the relationship between perception and reality." —*TimeOut New York*

"A literary romp that parcels out clues and motifs with dazzling abandon . . . The prose snaps with smart imagery, and with tableaus both wondrous and inexplicable. This is monstrously impressive stuff." —*The Valley Advocate*

"Berry takes a peculiar and highly appealing course in this novel, painting a world that is drenched in anonymity and absurdity. He grounds his writing in the kinds of details that bring the world to life while simultaneously creating a surreal air of mystery." —Bookotron.com

"An unlikely sleuth anchors an unlikely investigation in Berry's fantastical melding of Kafka, Hitchcock and *The Man Who Was Thursday*. . . . Berry's debut is a boldly inventive deconstruction of Cartesian metaphysics, the criminal justice system and the well-oiled detective story."
—*Kirkus Reviews*

"Berry has created a wonderful and fantastic world, a vintage mystery seen through a hall of fun-house mirrors. . . . A remarkably auspicious debut."
—*Booklist*

"Take everything you think you know about classic pulp-noir detective fiction, turn it sideways and look at it through a hall of mirrors. . . . All this rich texture, delivered with deadpan style and combined with the twisty story's fast pace, makes for an immensely satisfying read."
—*BookPage*

"Berry's ambitious debut reverberates with echoes of Kafka and Paul Auster. . . . This cerebral novel, with its sly winks at traditional whodunits and inspired portrait of the bureaucratic and paranoid Agency, will appeal to mystery readers and non-genre fans alike." —*Publishers Weekly*

"The plot's bursting with as many twists and surprises as you could hope for. . . . It steams along the smooth rails of Berry's neatly constructed sentences, barreling round each well-cambered turn with barely a judder."
—*London Review of Books*

"Great fun and very clever. My comparison? Flann O'Brien's *The Third Policeman*—which is about as good as it gets." —*The Observer*

"Berry's work is reminiscent of the coolest young American novelists—Michael Chabon, Jonathan Lethem, Glen David Gould—in its sheer delight at how genre writing can be reinvigorated and reimagined. *The Manual of Detection* makes the weird, fantastical world of the unconsciousness seem comically logical—like its subject, it is a dream."
—*Scotland on Sunday*

"I was impressed, besotted, and transported by *The Manual of Detection*. Such a great book! Surprising and completely satisfying, with mythic images and precise sentences. I wish I'd written it, but I'm almost as happy just to have read it."　—Karen Joy Fowler, author of *The Jane Austen Book Club* and *Wit's End*

"Inventive, atmospheric, and fiendishly delightful. If you've ever fallen under the spell of Borges, Ray Bradbury, or Angela Carter, I urge you to acquire your own copy of *The Manual of Detection*."
　　—Kelly Link, author of *Magic for Beginners* and *Pretty Monsters*

"Jedediah Berry knows magic. *The Manual of Detection* combines the intricacy and thoughtfulness of Borges and Kafka with the page-turning excitement of a detective thriller. I couldn't put it down, and when I reached the end, I immediately wanted to read it again, to try and figure out how he'd done it. This novel is a master puzzle, with all the show-stopping elements of a flock of doves flying out of a magician's sleeve. It made me laugh, thrill, think, and wonder."
　　—Hannah Tinti, author of *The Good Thief*

"A tingling masterpiece of elegant noir and storytelling verve—full of sizzling oddballs, sparkling villains, and knock-out femmes fatales. The story unfolds with a knife-thrower's accuracy, and like the Manual says, 'with a corpse around the next corner.'"
　　—Maria Flook, author of *My Sister Life* and *Lux*

"In this richly imagined, genre-defying work, our hero's search for truth is subverted by consciousness that can itself deceive, by perception that cannot be trusted. *The Manual of Detection* establishes Berry as a wholly original, brilliant new voice in fiction."
　　—Sabina Murray, author of *Forgery, A Carnivore's Inquiry*, and *The Caprices*

"I feel like I found the thesis Encyclopedia Brown wrote after he grew up and went to Hogwarts. Except that in parts it's like the movie *Brazil*. I don't know whether there's a plan for a sequel, but I want more."
　　—Alexander Chee, author of *Edinburgh*

ABOUT THE AUTHOR

Jedediah Berry's short fiction has appeared in numerous journals and anthologies, including *Best New American Voices* and *Best American Fantasy*. He lives in Northampton, Massachusetts, where he works as assistant editor of Small Beer Press.

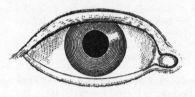

The Manual

of

Detection

JEDEDIAH BERRY

PENGUIN BOOKS

PENGUIN BOOKS
Published by the Penguin Group
Penguin Group (USA) Inc., 375 Hudson Street, New York, New York 10014, U.S.A.
Penguin Group (Canada), 90 Eglinton Avenue East, Suite 700, Toronto,
Ontario, Canada M4P 2Y3 (a division of Pearson Penguin Canada Inc.)
Penguin Books Ltd, 80 Strand, London WC2R 0RL, England
Penguin Ireland, 25 St Stephen's Green, Dublin 2, Ireland (a division of Penguin Books Ltd)
Penguin Books Australia Ltd, 250 Camberwell Road, Camberwell,
Victoria 3124, Australia (a division of Pearson Australia Group Pty Ltd)
Penguin Books India Pvt Ltd, 11 Community Centre,
Panchsheel Park, New Delhi – 110 017, India
Penguin Group (NZ), 67 Apollo Drive, Rosedale, North Shore 0632,
New Zealand (a division of Pearson New Zealand Ltd)
Penguin Books (South Africa) (Pty) Ltd, 24 Sturdee Avenue,
Rosebank, Johannesburg 2196, South Africa

Penguin Books Ltd, Registered Offices:
80 Strand, London WC2R 0RL, England

First published in the United States of America by The Penguin Press,
a member of Penguin Group (USA) Inc. 2009
Published in Penguin Books 2010

3   5   7   9   10   8   6   4

PUBLISHER'S NOTE
This is a work of fiction. Names, characters, places, and incidents either are the product
of the author's imagination or are used fictitiously, and any resemblance to actual persons,
living or dead, business establishments, events, or locales is entirely coincidental.

THE LIBRARY OF CONGRESS HAS CATALOGED THE HARDCOVER EDITION AS FOLLOWS:
Berry, Jedediah.
The manual of detection / Jedediah Berry.
p. cm.
ISBN 978-1-59420-211-7 (hc.)
ISBN 978-0-14-311651-6 (pbk.)
1. Private investigators—Fiction.   2. Femmes fatales—Fiction.
3. Criminals—Fiction.   I. Title.
PS3602.E76375M36 2009
813'.6—dc22
2008044753

Printed in the United States of America
DESIGNED BY MEIGHAN CAVANAUGH

Contents

ONE

On Shadowing

The expert detective's pursuit will go unnoticed, but not
because he is unremarkable. Rather, like the suspect's
shadow, he will appear as though he is meant to be there.

L est details be mistaken for clues, note that Mr. Charles Unwin,
lifetime resident of this city, rode his bicycle to work every day,
even when it was raining. He had contrived a method to keep his umbrella open while pedaling, by hooking the umbrella's handle around
the bicycle's handlebar. This method made the bicycle less maneuver-
able and reduced the scope of Unwin's vision, but if his daily schedule
was to accommodate an unofficial trip to Central Terminal for unofficial reasons, then certain risks were to be expected.

Though inconspicuous by nature, as a bicyclist and an umbrellist
Unwin was severely evident. Crowds of pedestrians parted before the ringing of his little bell, mothers hugged their children near, and the children
gaped at the magnificence of his passing. At intersections he avoided eye
contact with the drivers of motor vehicles, so as not to give the impression
he might yield to them. Today he was behind schedule. He had scorched
his oatmeal, and tied the wrong tie, and nearly forgotten his wristwatch,

all because of a dream that had come to him in the moments before waking, a dream that still troubled and distracted him. Now his socks were getting wet, so he pedaled even faster.

He dismounted on the sidewalk outside the west entrance of Central Terminal and chained his bicycle to a lamppost. The revolving doors spun ceaselessly, shunting travelers out into the rain, their black umbrellas blooming in rapid succession. He collapsed his own umbrella and slipped inside, checking the time as he emerged into the concourse.

His wristwatch, a gift from the Agency in recognition of twenty years of faithful service, never needed winding and was set to match—to the very second—the time reported by the four-faced clock above the information booth at the heart of Central Terminal. It was twenty-three minutes after seven in the morning. That gave him three minutes exactly before the woman in the plaid coat, her hair pinned tightly under a gray cap, would appear at the south entrance of the terminal.

He went to stand in line at the breakfast cart, and the man at the front of the line ordered a coffee, two sugars, no cream.

"Slow today, isn't it?" Unwin said, but the man in front of him did not respond, suspecting, perhaps, a ruse to trick him out of his spot.

In any case it was better that Unwin avoid conversation. If someone were to ask why he had started coming to Central Terminal every morning when his office was just seven blocks from his apartment, he would say he came for the coffee. But that would be a lie, and he hoped he never had to tell it.

The tired-looking boy entrusted with the steaming machines of the breakfast cart—Neville, according to his name tag—stirred sugar into the cup one spoonful at a time. The man waiting for his coffee, two sugars, no cream, glanced at his watch, and Unwin knew without looking that the woman in the plaid coat would be here, or rather there, at the south end of the concourse, in less than a minute. He did not even want the coffee. But what if someone were to ask why he came to Central Terminal every morning at the same time, and he said he came for the coffee, but he had no coffee in his hand? Worse than a lie is a lie that no one believes.

When it was Unwin's turn to place his order, Neville asked him if he wanted cream or sugar.

"Just coffee. And hurry, please."

Neville poured the coffee with great care and with greater care fitted the lid onto the cup, then wrapped it in a paper napkin. Unwin took it and left before the boy could produce his change.

Droves of morning commuters sleepwalked to a murmur of station announcements and newspaper rustle. Unwin checked his ever-wound, ever-winding watch, and hot coffee seeped under the lid and over his fingers. Other torments ensued. His briefcase knocked against his knees, his umbrella began to slip from under his arm, the soles of his shoes squeaked on the marble floor. But nothing could divert him. He had never been late for her. Here now was the lofty arch of Gate Fourteen, the time twenty-six minutes after seven. And the woman in the plaid coat, her hair pinned tightly under a gray cap, tumbled through the revolving doors and into the heavy green light of a Central Terminal morning.

She shook water from her umbrella and gazed up at the vaulted ceiling, as though at a sky that threatened more rain. She sneezed, twice, into a gloved hand, and Unwin noted this variation on her arrival with the fervency of an archivist presented with newly disclosed documents. Her passage across the terminal was unswerving. Thirty-nine steps (it was never fewer than thirty-eight, never more than forty) delivered her to her usual spot, several paces from the gate. Her cheeks were flushed, her grip on her umbrella very tight. Unwin drew a worn train schedule from his coat pocket. He feigned an interest in the schedule while together (alone) they waited.

How many mornings before the first that he saw her had she stood there? And whose face did she hope to find among the disembarking host? She was beautiful, in the quiet way that lonely, unnoticed people are beautiful to those who notice them. Had someone broken a promise to her? Willfully, or due to unexpected misfortune? As an Agency clerk, it was not for Unwin to question too deeply, nor to conduct anything resembling an investigation. Eight days ago he had gone to Central Terminal, had even purchased a ticket because he thought he might like to leave town for a while. But when he saw the woman in the plaid coat, he stayed. The sight of her had made him wonder, and now he found he could not stop wondering. These were unofficial trips, and she was his unofficial reason; that was all.

A subterranean breeze blew up from the tracks, ruffling the hem of her coat. The seven twenty-seven train, one minute late as usual, arrived at the terminal. A pause, a hiss: the gleaming doors slid open. A hundred and more black raincoats poured all at once from the train and up through the gate. The stream parted as it met her. She stood on her toes, looking left and right.

The last of the raincoats rushed past. Not one of them had stopped for her.

Unwin returned the schedule to his pocket, put his umbrella under his arm, picked up his briefcase, his coffee. The woman's solitude had gone undisturbed: should he have felt guilty for being relieved? So long as no one stopped for her, her visits to Central Terminal would continue, and so would his. Now, as she began her walk back to the revolving doors, he followed, matching his pace to hers so he would pass only a few steps behind her on his way to his bicycle.

He could see the wisps of brown hair that had escaped from under her cap. He could count the freckles on the back of her neck, but the numbers meant nothing; all was mystery. As he had the previous morning, and the seven mornings before that, Unwin willed with all the power in his lanky soul that time, like the train at the end of its track, would stop.

This morning it did. The woman in the plaid coat dropped her umbrella. She turned and looked at him. Her eyes—he had never seen them so close—were the clouded silver of old mirrors. The numbered panels on the arrival and departure boards froze. The station announcements ceased. The four second hands on the four faces of the clock trembled between numbers. The insides of Unwin's ever-wound wristwatch seized.

He looked down. Her umbrella lay on the floor between them. But his hands were full, and the floor was so far away.

Someone behind him said, "Mr. Charles Unwin?"

The timetables came back to life, the clocks remembered themselves, the station resumed its murmuring. A plump man in a herringbone suit was staring at him with green-yellow eyes. He danced the big fingers of his right hand over the brim of a hat held in his left. "Mr. Charles Unwin," he said again, not a question this time.

The woman in the plaid coat snatched up her umbrella and walked away. The man in the herringbone suit was still waiting.

"The coffee," Unwin began to explain.

The man ignored him. "This way, Mr. Unwin," he said, and gestured with his hat toward the north end of the terminal. Unwin glanced back, but the woman was already lost to the revolving doors.

What could he do but follow? This man knew his name—he might also know his secrets, know he was making unofficial trips for unofficial reasons. He escorted Unwin down a long corridor where men in iron chairs read newspapers while nimble boys shined their shoes.

"Where are we going?"

"Someplace we can talk in private."

"I'll be late for work."

The man in the herringbone suit flipped open his wallet to reveal an Agency badge identifying him as Samuel Pith, Detective. "You're on the job," Pith said, "starting this moment. That makes you a half hour early, Mr. Unwin."

They came to a second corridor, dimmer than the first, blocked by a row of signs warning of wet floors. Beyond, a man in gray coveralls slid a grimy-looking mop over the marble in slow, indeliberate arcs. The floor was covered with red and orange oak leaves, tracked in, probably, by a passenger who had arrived on one of the earlier trains from the country.

Detective Pith cleared his throat, and the custodian shuffled over to them, pushed one of the signs out of the way, and allowed the two to pass.

The floor was perfectly dry. Unwin glanced into the custodian's bucket. It was empty.

"Listen carefully, now," said Detective Pith. He emphasized the words by tapping his hat brim against Unwin's chest. "You're an odd little fellow. You've got peculiar habits. Every morning this week, same time, there's Charles Unwin, back at Central Terminal. Not for a train, though. His apartment is just seven blocks from the office."

"I come for the—"

"Damn it, Unwin, don't tell me. We like our operatives to keep a few mysteries of their own. Page ninety-six of the *Manual*."

"I'm no operative, sir. I'm a clerk, fourteenth floor. And I'm sorry you've had to waste your time. We're both behind schedule now."

"I told you," Pith growled, "you're already on the job. Forget the fourteenth floor. Report to Room 2919. You've been promoted." From his coat pocket Pith drew a slim hardcover volume, green with gold lettering: *The Manual of Detection*. "Standard issue," he said. "It's saved my life more than once."

Unwin's hands were still full, so Pith slipped the book into his briefcase.

"This is a mistake," Unwin said.

"For better or worse, somebody has noticed you. And there's no way now to get yourself unnoticed." He stared at Unwin a long moment. His substantial black eyebrows gathered downward, and his lips went stiff and frowning. But when he spoke, his voice was quieter, even kind. "I'm supposed to keep this simple, but listen. Your first case should be an easy one. Hell, mine was. But you're in this thing a little deeper, Unwin. Maybe because you've been with the Agency so long. Or maybe you've got some friends, or some enemies. It's none of my business, really. The point is—"

"Please," said Unwin, checking his watch. It was seven thirty-four.

Detective Pith waved one hand, as though to clear smoke from the air. "I've already said more than I should have. The point is, Unwin, you're going to need a new hat."

The green trilby was Unwin's only hat. He could not imagine wearing anything else on his head.

Pith donned his own fedora and tipped it forward. "If you ever see me again, you don't know me. Got it?" He snapped a finger at the custodian and said, "See you later, Artie." Then the herringbone suit disappeared around the corner.

The custodian had resumed his work, mopping the dry floor with his dry mop, moving piles of oak leaves from one end of the corridor to the other. In the reports Unwin received each week from Detective Sivart, he had often read of those who, without being in the employ of the Agency, were nonetheless aware of one or more aspects of a case—who were, as the detective might write, "in on it." Could the custodian be one of those?

His name tag was stitched with red, curving letters.

"Mr. Arthur, sir?"

Arthur continued working, and Unwin had to hop backward to escape the wide sweep of his mop. The custodian's eyes were closed, his mouth slightly open. And he was making a peculiar sound, low and whispery. Unwin leaned closer, trying to understand the words.

But there were no words, there was nothing to understand. The custodian was snoring.

———

OUTSIDE, UNWIN DROPPED HIS coffee in a trash can and glanced downtown toward the Agency's gray, monolithic headquarters, its uppermost stories obscured by the rain. Years ago he had admitted to himself that he did not like the look of the building: its shadow was too long, the stone of its walls cold and somehow like that of a tomb. Better, he thought, to work inside a place like that than to glimpse it throughout the day.

To make up for lost time, he risked a shortcut down an alleyway he knew was barely wide enough to accommodate his open umbrella. The umbrella's metal nubs scraped against both walls as the bicycle bumped and jangled over old cobblestone.

He had already begun drafting in his mind the report that would best characterize his promotion, and in this draft the word "promotion" appeared always between quotation marks, for to let it stand without qualification would be to honor it with too much validity. Errors were something of a rarity at the Agency. It was a large organization, however, composed of a great many bureaus and departments, most of them beyond Unwin's purview. In one of those bureaus or departments, it was clear, an error had been committed, overlooked, and worst of all, disseminated.

He slowed his pace to navigate some broken bottles left strewn across the alley, the ribs of his umbrella bending against the walls as he turned. He expected at any moment to hear the fateful hiss of a popped tire, but he and his bicycle passed unscathed.

This error that Pith had brought with him to Central Terminal—it was Unwin's burden now. He accepted it, if not gladly, then encouraged by the knowledge that he, one of the most experienced clerks of the fourteenth floor, was best prepared to cope with such a calamity. Every page of his report would intimate the fact. The superior who reviewed the final version, upon finishing, would sit back in his chair and say to himself, "Thank goodness it was Mr. Charles Unwin, and not some frailer fellow, to whom this task fell."

Unwin pedaled hard to keep from swerving and shot from the other end of the alley, a clutch of pigeons bursting with him into the rain.

In all his days of employment with the Agency, he had never encountered a problem without a solution. This morning's episode, though unusual, would be no exception. He felt certain the entire matter would be settled before lunchtime.

But even with such responsibilities before him, Unwin found himself thinking of the dream he had dreamed before waking, the one that had rattled and distracted him, causing him to scorch his oatmeal and nearly miss the woman in the plaid coat.

He was by nature a meticulous dreamer, capable of sorting his nocturnal reveries with a lucidity he understood to be rare. He was unaccustomed to the shock of such an intrusive vision, one that seemed not at all of his making, and more like an official communiqué.

In this dream he had risen from bed and gone to take a bath, only to find the bathtub occupied by a stranger, naked except for his hat, reclining in a thick heap of soap bubbles. The bubbles were stained gray around his chest by the ashes from his cigar. His flesh was gray, too, like smudged newsprint, and a bulky gray coat was draped over the shower curtain. Only the ember of the stranger's cigar possessed color, and it burned so hot it made the steam above the tub glow red.

Unwin stood in the doorway, a fresh towel over his arm, his robe cinched tight around his waist. Why, he wondered, would someone go through all the trouble of breaking in to his apartment, just to get caught taking a bath?

The stranger said nothing. He lifted one foot out of the water and scrubbed it with a long-handled brush. When he was done, he soaped the bristles, slowly working the suds into a lather. Then he scrubbed the other foot.

Unwin bent down for a better look at the face under the hat brim and saw the heavy, unshaven jaw he knew only from newspaper photographs. It was the Agency operative whose case files were his particular responsibility.

"Detective Sivart," Unwin said, "what are you doing in my bathtub?"

Sivart let the brush fall into the water and took the cigar from his teeth. "No names," he said. "Not mine anyway. Don't know who might be listening in." He relaxed deeper into the bubbles. "You have no idea how difficult it was to arrange this meeting, Unwin. Did you know they don't tell us detectives who our clerks are? All these years I've been sending my reports to the fourteenth floor. To you, it turns out. And you forget things."

Unwin put up his hands to protest, but Sivart waved his cigar at him and said, "When Enoch Hoffmann stole November twelfth, and you looked at the morning paper and saw that Monday had gone straight into Wednesday, you forgot Tuesday like all the rest of them."

"Even the restaurants skipped their Tuesday specials," Unwin said.

Sivart's ember burned hotter, and more steam rose from the tub. "You forgot my birthday, too," he said. "No card, no nothing."

"Nobody knows your birthday."

"You could have figured it out. Anyway, you know my cases better than anyone. You know I was wrong about her, all wrong. So you're the best chance I've got. Try this time, would you? Try to remember something. Remember this: Chapter Eighteen. Got it?"

"Yes."

"Say it back to me: Chapter Eighteen."

"Chapter Elephant," Unwin said, in spite of himself.

"Hopeless," Sivart muttered.

Normally Unwin never could have said "Elephant" when he meant to say "Eighteen," not even in his sleep. Hurt by Sivart's accusations, he had blurted the wrong word because, in some dusty file drawer of his mind, he had long ago deposited the fact that elephants never forget.

"The girl," Sivart was saying, and Unwin had the impression that the detective was getting ready to explain something important. "I was wrong about her."

Then, as though summoned to life by Unwin's own error, there came trumpeting, high and full—the unmistakable decree of an elephant.

"No time!" Sivart said. He drew back the shower curtain behind the tub. Instead of a tiled wall, Unwin saw the whirling lights of carnival rides and striped pavilions beneath which broad shapes hunkered and leapt. There were shooting galleries out there, and a wheel of fortune, and animal cages, and a carousel, all moving, all turning under turning stars. The elephant trumpeted again, only this time the sound was shrill and staccato, and Unwin had to switch off his alarm clock to make it stop.

TWO

On Evidence

Objects have memory, too. The doorknob remembers
who turned it, the telephone who answered it. The gun
remembers when it was last fired, and by whom. It is for
the detective to learn the language of these things, so that
he might hear them when they have something to say.

Unwin's damp socks squelched in his shoes as he dismounted in
front of the broad granite facade of the Agency's office building.
The tallest structure for blocks around, it stood like a watchtower between the gridded downtown district and the crooked streets of the old
port town.

South of the Agency offices Unwin rarely dared to travel. He knew
enough from Sivart's reports of what went on in the cramped taverns
and winding back lanes of the old port's innumerable little neighbor-
hoods to satisfy his curiosity. Occasionally, when the wind was right,
he would catch a scent on the air that left him mystified and a little
frightened, and tugged at him in a way he could not easily have explained. He felt as though a trapdoor had opened at his feet, revealing
a view onto something bottomless and unknowable—a secret that
would remain a secret even at the end of the world. A moment would
pass before he could place it, before he knew where the scent had come

from. Then he would shake his head and chide himself. Seeing it so rarely, he often forgot that it was there: the sea.

He brought his bicycle with him into the Agency lobby, where the doorman allowed him to keep it on rainy days. He could not bear to look at the clock on the wall behind the front desk. His lateness, Unwin knew, would necessitate a second report for the benefit of his supervisor. It was Mr. Duden, after all, who had only recently filed for the presentation of the wristwatch—and did Mr. Duden not expect him to continue to exhibit the virtues that the wristwatch both acknowledged and embodied?

As for this so-called *Manual of Detection,* good sense dictated that he refrain from reading any part of it, including the page ninety-six to which Detective Pith alluded. Whatever secrets the *Manual* contained were not intended for Charles Unwin.

Only one dilemma remained. How to explain his presence at Central Terminal that morning? The coffee story would not do: a blatant falsification, brought to dwell perpetually in the Agency archives, a stain in the shape of words! Yet the truth was hardly appropriate for an official report. Best, perhaps, to write around that hole in the story and hope no one noticed.

The elevator attendant was a white-haired man whose spotted hands shook when he moved the lever. He brought the elevator to a halt without glancing at the needle over the door. "Floor fourteen," he said.

On the fourteenth floor were three columns of twenty-one desks each, separated by clusters of filing cabinets and shelving. On each desk a telephone, a typewriter, a green-shaded lamp, and a letter tray. The Agency neither prohibited nor encouraged the use of personal decorative flourishes, and some of these desks flaunted a small vase of flowers, a photograph, a child's drawing. Unwin's desk, the tenth in the east row, was free of any such clutter.

He was, after all, the clerk responsible for the cases of Detective Travis T. Sivart. Some argued, though never too loudly, that without

Detective Sivart there was no Agency. The point was perhaps only somewhat overstated. For in bars and barbershops all over town, in clubs and parlors of every grade, few topics could generate more speculation than Sivart's latest case.

The clerks themselves were by no means immune to this fervor. Indeed, their devotion was of a more personal, indwelling nature. In newspapers Sivart was "the detective's detective," but on the fourteenth floor he was one of their own. And they did not need the newspapers for their morsels of information, because they had their Unwin. During the processing period, his fellow clerks would quietly note the drawers he frequented, the indices to which he referred. The bolder among them would even inquire into his progress, though he was always certain to give some vague and tantalizing reply.

Some of those files—in particular The Oldest Murdered Man and The Three Deaths of Colonel Baker—were discussed in clerical circles as paragons of the form. Even Mr. Duden alluded to them, most often when scolding someone for sloppy work. "You like to think your files stand up to Unwin's," he would proclaim, "and you don't even know the difference between a dagger and a stiletto?" Often he simply asked, "What if Unwin had handled The Oldest Murdered Man that way?"

The theft of that three-thousand-year-old mummy was one of Unwin's first cases. He remembered the day, more than fifteen years earlier, that a messenger delivered Sivart's initial report in the series. It was early December and snowing; the office had fallen into a hush that seemed to him expectant, watchful. He was still the newest employee on the floor, and his hands trembled as he turned Sivart's hurriedly typed pages. The detective had been waiting for his big break, and Unwin had silently waited along with him. Now here it was. A high-profile crime, a heist. Front-page news.

Unwin had sharpened pencils to steady himself, and sorted according to size all the paper clips and rubber bands in his desk drawer.

Then he filled his pen with ink and emptied the hole punch of its little paper moons.

When he finally set to work, he moved with a certainty of purpose he now considered reckless. He tweaked organizational rubrics to accommodate the particulars of the case, integrated subsequent reports on the fly, and casually set down for the first time the identities of suspects whose names would recur in Agency files as certain bad dreams recur: Jasper and Josiah Rook, Cleopatra Greenwood, the nefarious biloquist Enoch Hoffmann.

Did Unwin sleep at all that week? It seemed to him that Sivart's progress on the case depended on his ability to document it, that the next clue would remain obscured until the previous was properly classified. The detective produced notes, fragments, threads of suspicion; it was the clerk's job to catalog them all, then to excise everything that proved immaterial, leaving only the one filament, that glowing silver thread connecting the mystery to its only conceivable solution.

Now he could remember nothing of his daily existence in those weeks except the accumulation of pages beside his typewriter and of snow on the windowsills, then the surprise of a fellow clerk's hand on his shoulder at the end of the day, when all the desk lamps but his own had been extinguished.

Unwin disliked hearing mention of his old cases, this one in particular. The Oldest Murdered Man had grown into something beyond him, beyond Sivart, beyond even Enoch Hoffmann, the former stage magician whose mad will had been the cause of it all. Every time someone spoke of the case, it became less the thing it was: a mystery put to rest.

For twenty years Unwin had served as Sivart's clerk, sequencing his reports, making sense of his notes, building proper case files out of them. He had so many questions for the man, questions about his philosophies of detection and the finer points of his methods. And he especially wanted to know more about The Man Who Stole November Twelfth. That case represented the end of an era, yet the detective's notes on it were unusually reticent. How exactly had Sivart seen through Hoffmann's ruse? How had he known it was Tuesday and not Wednesday, when all others in the city trusted their newspapers and radios?

If Unwin had ever passed the detective by chance in the halls of the Agency offices or stood beside him in the elevator, he did not know it. In newspaper photographs, Sivart appeared usually at the edge of a crime scene, a raincoat and hat hung in the gloom, his cigar casting light on nothing.

UNWIN WAS SOOTHED BY the harmonies of an office astir. Here a typewriter rang the end of a line, a telephone buzzed, file drawers rumbled open and closed. Sheaves of paper were tapped to evenness against desktops, and from all quarters came the percussive clamor of words being committed eternally to crisp white expanses.

How superb, that diligence, that zeal! And how essential. For none but the loyal clerks were permitted to dispatch those files to their place of rest, the archives, where mysteries dwelled side by side in stark beauty, categorized and classified—mysteries parsed, their secret hearts laid bare by photographs, wiretaps and ciphers, fingerprints and depositions. At least this was how Unwin imagined the archives to be. He had never actually seen them, because only the underclerks were permitted access to those regions.

He removed his hat. On the rack by his desk, however, another hat was already set to hang. It was a plain gray cap, and beneath it a plaid coat.

She was seated in his chair. The woman in the plaid coat (she was not, at that moment, in the plaid coat, yet somehow, astonishingly, she was no less she) was seated in his chair, at his desk, using his typewriter by the light of his green-shaded lamp. She looked up as though from a dream, forefinger paused over the Y key.

"Why?" Unwin wanted to ask, but then her eyes were on him and he could not speak; his hat was glued to his hand, his briefcase filled with lead. That feeling seized him—the feeling that a trapdoor had opened at his feet and that the slightest of winds could push him in. But it was not the sea that dizzied him; it was the clouded silver of her eyes, and something on the other side of them, just out of sight.

He walked on. Past his desk, past the clerks whose typewriters went silent in midsentence at his approach. He knew how he must appear to them—addled, shaky, unsure: not the Unwin they knew, but a stranger with Unwin's hat in his hand.

He did not know his destination until he saw it. Few besides Mr. Duden himself ever approached the door to the overclerk's office. The glass window, of the opaque kind, was uncommonly so. Before today Unwin had only glimpsed the door from afar. Now he set his briefcase down and raised his fist to knock.

Before he could, the door swung inward and Mr. Duden, a round-headed man with colorless hair, said quickly, "Pardon me, sir, there seems to have been a mistake."

Unwin had never been "sir." He had always been "Unwin," and nothing more.

"Yes, begging your pardon, Mr. Duden, there has been a mistake. I arrived several minutes late today. I shall spare you the details, since all of them will go into my report, which I would like to begin writing immediately. From this I am prevented, however, by the presence of another person at my desk, using my typewriter. Measures had to be taken, no doubt, because I am so late to work."

"No, begging your pardon, sir, you aren't late at all. You just don't . . . That is, I was informed that—how to put it?—that you'd been promoted. And while of course we're pleased that you'd think to come down here to visit your old colleagues, sir, it is against Agency policy for . . .

well, for a detective, you know, to communicate directly with a clerk, without the intercession of a messenger."

"Agency policy. Of course." Already this was the longest conversation he had ever had with his supervisor, except for an exchange of memoranda regarding the allotment of shelf space among the occupants of the east row that had transpired some three years earlier, but that was not, strictly speaking, a conversation at all. So it was with great hesitation that Unwin asked, "But you and I may speak freely, may we not?"

Mr. Duden glanced about the room. No one was typing. Somewhere a phone rang unheeded, then succumbed to the general silence. Mr. Duden said, "Actually, though I am the supervisor of the fourteenth floor, I, too, am—technically speaking, that is—a clerk. So this conversation is, you see, against Agency policy."

"Then I suppose," said Unwin, "that we should terminate the exchange, in keeping with policy?"

Mr. Duden nodded with relief.

"And I'm to find my new desk elsewhere in the building?"

It pained Mr. Duden to say, "On the twenty-ninth floor, perhaps. Room 2919, according to the memo I received."

Of course, an interoffice communication! With such a missive as his guide, Unwin could follow the trail back to its source and settle the matter in person. Though to ask for a memo directed to his superior would be rather unorthodox, Mr. Duden believed that Unwin outranked him now, so he could not refuse the request. But then, to take advantage of his superior's confusion would be to employ the very misunderstanding he wished to dispel. Imagine the report he would have to write to explain his actions: the addenda and codicils, the footnotes, the footnotes to footnotes. The more Unwin fed that report, the greater would grow its demands, until stacks of paper massed into walls, corridors: a devouring labyrinth with Unwin at its center, spools of exhausted typewriter ribbon piled all around.

Mr. Duden saved him from that fate, however, when he produced the memo for Unwin's perusal without being asked.

To: O. Duden, Overclerk, Floor 14
From: Lamech, Watcher, Floor 36

An employee under your Supervision, Mister Charles Unwin, is hereby promoted to the rank of Detective, with all the Rights, Privileges, and Responsibilities that position entails. Please forward his Personal Effects to Room 2919, and proceed according to Protocol in all regards.

The bottom of the memo was adorned by the Agency's official seal, a single open eye floating above the words "Never Sleeping."

Unwin folded the paper in half and slipped it into his coat pocket. He saw that Mr. Duden wanted it back, to keep it for his records, but the overclerk could not bring himself to ask for it. It was better this way—Unwin would need to incorporate the memo into his report. "I assume that the woman at my desk," he said, "whose name I have not learned, will carry on with my work, the work I have been doing for the last twenty years, seven months, and some-odd days."

Mr. Duden smiled and nodded some more. He would not say her name.

Unwin returned the way he had come, avoiding the eyes of his co-workers, especially those of the woman seated in his chair. He could not help glimpsing the plaid coat, however, hanging where his own coat should have been.

IN THE ELEVATOR three men in nice suits (black, green, and navy blue) were speaking quietly among themselves. They regarded Unwin's arrival with scrupulous indifference. These were bona fide detectives, and Unwin did not have to be a detective himself to recognize the fact. He stood with his back to them, and the elevator attendant hopped off his three-legged stool and closed the door. "Going up," he announced. "Next stop, floor twenty-nine."

Unwin mumbled his request for the thirty-sixth floor.

"You're going to have to speak up," the attendant said, tapping his own ear. "What floor is it that you want?"

The three detectives were silent now.

Unwin leaned closer and repeated, "Thirty-six, please."

The attendant shrugged and threw the lever. No one spoke as the needle rose past fifteen, sixteen, seventeen, but Unwin knew the detectives were watching him. Were these three in communication with Detective Pith? He had been watching Unwin for some time, long enough to know that he went every morning to Central Terminal. And if he were watching, others could be watching, too—and not just while he was at the office. Unwin felt as though the Agency's unblinking eye had turned upon him, and now there was no escaping its gaze.

It might have been watching that morning eight days before, when Unwin first saw the woman in the plaid coat. He had woken early, then dressed and eaten and left for work, failing to realize until he had descended to the street and gone partway to work that most of the city was still sleeping. He could not continue to the office—it would be hours yet before the doorman would arrive with his ring of keys—so Unwin had wandered in the near dark while delivery trucks idled at storefronts, and streetlamps winked out overhead, and a few seasoned carousers shuffled home, arms over one another's shoulders.

It seemed like a dream now: his passage through the revolving doors of Central Terminal, the cup of coffee from the breakfast cart, the schedule plucked from the racks by the information booth. All those trains, all those routes: he could purchase a ticket for any one of them, he thought, and let himself be borne from the city, let the reports pile up on his desk forever. The mysteries assigned to Sivart now were hollow compared to those of earlier years. The Rook brothers had gone into hiding after November twelfth, and Cleopatra Greenwood had fled the city, and Enoch Hoffmann had performed with quiet precision the cardinal feat of magicianship and caused himself to disappear. The city thought it still needed Sivart, but Unwin knew the truth: Sivart was just a shadow, and he himself a shadow's shadow.

So it was that he found himself standing at Gate Fourteen with a ticket for the next train into the country, no clear plan to return, checking his wristwatch against the four-faced clock above the information booth. Even to him his behavior seemed suspicious: a clerk rising early, acting on whims, purchasing a ticket for a train out of the city. What kind of motive would anyone from the Agency assign to such behavior? They must have pegged him as a spy or a double agent.

Perhaps this promotion was not an error, then, but a test of some kind. If so, he would prove himself above suspicion by maintaining that it was an error, could only be an error. He would prove that he wanted his job, that he was nothing if not a clerk.

He had not boarded the train that morning after all, had not gone into the country. The sight of the woman in the plaid coat had stopped him. She was a mystery to him, and mystery enough to keep him from leaving. So long as she was there each morning, he would wait with her, and so long as no one appeared to meet her, he would return to work: that was the unspoken bargain he had struck with her.

Still, these detectives in the elevator were watching him—intently, he felt. He tapped his umbrella against the floor while humming a few bars of a tune he knew from the radio, but this must have looked too calculated, since humming and umbrella-tapping were not among his usual habits. So instead of tapping, he used his umbrella as a cane by gently and repeatedly shifting his weight onto it and off it again. This was a habit Unwin could call genuine. But employed as a distraction, it seemed even to him a very suspicious-looking contrivance. He had not read a word of *The Manual of Detection*, while these detectives probably knew it front to back, knew even the rationale behind Samuel Pith's assertion that operatives must have secrets of their own.

The attendant brought the elevator to a halt at floor twenty-nine, and the three detectives brushed past, then turned. The one in the black suit scratched a rash above his collar, glaring at Unwin as though he were somehow the cause of it. The one in green hunched bulkily, a dull, mean look in his half-lidded eyes. Navy blue stood in front, his mustache a crooked line over his lip. "That's no hat to wear to the thirty-sixth floor," he said.

The other two chuckled and shook their heads.

The attendant closed the door on the detective's thin scowl, and again the needle climbed upward. From above came the creaking of machinery; steadily the sound grew louder. When the door was opened at last, a chill wind escaped from the elevator shaft to play about Unwin's ankles. His socks were still damp.

The corridor was lit by yellow light fixtures shaped like upended tulips, and between them were doors without transoms. At the opposite end of the hall, a single window permitted a rectangle of gray, rain-ribboned light.

"Thirty-six," the attendant said.

In the memo Lamech had identified himself as a watcher. That title was unfamiliar to Unwin, but the intricacies of Agency hierarchy could not be entrusted to just any employee. There were clerks innumerable, with underclerks beneath them and overclerks above, and then the detectives, those knights-errant upon whose work so much depended, while everywhere at once scurried the messengers, lower in status, perhaps, than even the underclerks but entrusted with special privileges of passage, for their words, on any particular day, could originate in the highest halls of the Agency offices. And dwelling in those halls? What shrewd powers, with what titles? On that, Unwin did not care to speculate, nor do we now, except to this extent: on the thirty-sixth floor, behind doors marked by bronze placards bearing their names, the watchers performed what duties were entrusted to them.

The seventh door on the right (Unwin counted thirteen to a side) bore the name he was looking for. Unlike all the others, this door was ajar. He knocked gently and called through the opening. "Mr. Lamech?"

No response. He knocked harder, and the door swung inward. The room was dark, but in the column of light from the hall Unwin saw a broad maroon rug, shelves of thick books with blue and brown spines, a pair of cushioned chairs angled toward a desk at the back. To one side was a great dark globe, and before the window loomed a bald and massive globelike head. On the desk a telephone, a typewriter, and a lamp, unlit.

"Mr. Lamech," Unwin said again, crossing the threshold, "I am sorry to have to bother you, sir. It's Charles Unwin, clerk, floor fourteen. I've come about the matter of the promotion. I believe there may have been some kind of error."

Lamech said nothing. Maybe he did not wish to speak with the door open. Unwin closed it and approached. As his eyes adjusted, he began to discern a heavy-featured face, shoulders wide as the wide-backed chair, big unmoving hands folded over the desk.

"Not your error, of course," Unwin amended. "Probably a transcriptionist's typo or a bad connection on one of the older lines. You know how things get when it rains, sir. Fits of static, the occasional disconnect."

Lamech regarded him wordlessly.

"And it has been raining on and off for days now. Fourteen days, in fact. More rain than we've had in quite some time."

Unwin stood before the desk. "It's a matter of poor drainage, sir. Bound to interfere with the lines."

He saw that Lamech's telephone was in fact unplugged, the cord left dangling over the edge of the desk. The watcher said nothing. The only sound was the rain against the window—the cause, Unwin supposed, for all his talk about the weather.

"Unless you protest," Unwin hazarded, "I'll just switch on your desk lamp for you. That way I can show you some identification, which I'm sure you want to see before bothering with any of this. Wouldn't want to waste your time. And you can't trust anyone these days, isn't that right?"

He tugged the cord. The lamp, identical to the one on Unwin's own desk twenty-two floors below, made a puddle of pale green light over the desktop, over Unwin's outstretched hand, over the seated man's gray crisscrossed fingers, and over his heavy gray face, from which a pair of bloated, red-flooded eyes glared out at nothing.

Corpses were nothing new to Unwin. Hundreds of them populated the reports entrusted to his care over the years, reports in which no detail was spared. People poisoned, shot, gutted, hanged, sliced to ribbons by industrial machinery, crushed between slabs of cement, clobbered with skillets, defenestrated, eviscerated, burned or buried alive, held underwater for lengthy intervals, thrown down stairs, or simply kicked and pummeled out of being—the minutiae surrounding such incidents were daily fare, so to speak, to a clerk of the fourteenth floor. Whole indices, in fact, were organized according to cause of death, and Unwin himself had from time to time contributed new headings and subheadings when an innovative murder necessitated an addition or expansion: "strangulation, unattended boa snake," was one of his, as was "muffins, poisonous berry."

A man so thoroughly versed in the varieties of dispatchment might, then, regard with unusual ease the result of an actual murder, in this case a man whose neck had been bruised by strangulatory measures, tongue emitted as a result of smotheration, eyes bulged almost clear of the skull, result of the same.

Unwin yanked his hand from the light and took several steps back-

ward, tripped over the edge of the rug, and fell into one of the thickly
cushioned chairs, the softness of which did nothing to diminish his
revulsion. In each dark corner, Unwin could almost see a killer crouched,
waiting for an opportunity to strike. To move from where he sat would
have brought him closer to at least one of them.

So he remained motionless, briefcase clutched in his lap, seated as
for a proper meeting with Mr. Lamech. This meeting went on for some
time, with only the weather having anything to say, and the weather
spoke only of itself.

THREE

On Corpses

Many cases begin with one—this can be disconcerting,
but at least you know where you stand. Worse is the corpse
that appears partway into your investigation, complicating
everything. Best to proceed, therefore, with the vigilance
of one who assumes that a corpse is always around the next
corner. That way it is less likely to be your own.

A knock at the door shook Unwin from his stupor. How long had
he been sitting there? Long enough for his eyes to adjust to the
light, for him to see that he was quite alone with Lamech's corpse.
If someone were going to leap out and kill him, he would have done
it by now.

A second knock at the door, louder this time. He should have left
as soon as he saw the corpse, should have cried out, or even run into
the hall and fainted. That would have made his role in the matter obvious: he was the unlucky discoverer of a horrendous crime. But what
would they think when he answered the door and said, "Please, come
right in. And look, there's a dead man at the desk. Strange, isn't it?"

He could squeeze himself behind the end of the bookshelf, but that
would make for a poor hiding place. When he was found cowering there,
the suspicion against him would only increase. If he waited a little longer,
maybe, the person at the door would give up and go away.

Unwin waited. There was no more knocking, but he heard the sound of a woman's voice. "Mr. Lamech?"

The body, then. He would have to do something with the body. He went to stand behind Lamech's chair and gazed down at the broad, blank scalp. From this angle it looked as though there was nothing wrong with the man. He was only very tired, had eased back into his chair for a brief nap. He did not even smell as Unwin imagined a corpse would smell. He smelled like aftershave.

Still, Unwin could not bring himself to touch the dead man. He took hold of the chair and rolled it slowly backward. Lamech's big hands drifted apart as they slid over the surface of the desk, but his fingers stayed rigid. Then the arms dropped suddenly, and the upper half of the body fell forward. Unwin had to yank the chair back to keep the man's head from striking the edge of the desk. The chair creaked under the slumped weight of the corpse.

The woman knocked again, so loudly this time that everyone on the floor must have heard.

"One moment!" Unwin shouted, and the woman let out a little *oh!* as though she had not really expected an answer.

With his foot on one leg of the chair to keep it in place, Unwin heaved against the body with both hands. It bowed deeper and the spine emitted a series of popping sounds that made him recoil. He closed his eyes, held his breath, and pushed again. This time the body slid off the chair and tumbled soundlessly into the dark beneath the desk.

In the most commanding tone he could muster, Unwin called for Lamech's visitor to enter.

The woman wore a black dress with white lace around the collar and cuffs. The dress was very fine, but of a style Unwin had not seen worn in the city for ten years or more. In her hands she clutched a small purse, also strangely old-fashioned. Her hair was bound up in a black lace cap, still damp from the rain. She was perhaps ten years older than Unwin, and very beautiful—*a real stunner,* Sivart might have written.

She was also the most tired-looking woman Unwin had ever seen. She gazed warily into the room, the shadows beneath her eyes so dark that Unwin mistook them at first for an exotic sort of makeup.

"Please come in," he said.

She came forward with dreamlike hesitancy, always about to stumble, somehow remaining miraculously on her feet.

"Mr. Lamech," she said.

He sat down, relieved that she did not know the watcher by sight, but the tip of his left shoe made contact with the body under the desk, and he had to cough to conceal his alarm.

"I know this isn't how things are done here," she said.

Unwin's stomach tightened. Had he given himself away so quickly?

"I know I'm supposed to request an appointment," the woman went on, "and then someone informs me who will be handling my case. But I couldn't wait, and I couldn't see just anyone. I had to see you."

So it was she who had broken the rules. Unwin cleared his throat and gave her a stern look. Then, to demonstrate his generosity, he gestured for her to sit.

She gazed at the thick cushion, her eyelids drooping. "I mustn't," she said. "I would fall asleep in an instant." Just the thought of sitting down appeared to overwhelm her; she squeezed her purse and closed her eyes for a long moment.

Unwin rose from his seat, thinking he might have to catch her. But she steadied herself, blinked several times, and said, "I'm something of a detective myself, you see. I figured out that you are Sivart's watcher."

Unwin knew as she said it that she was right. Lamech had been Sivart's watcher, just as he was Sivart's clerk. Now he was all three of them at once: clerk by appointment, detective by promotion, watcher by mistake.

"My name is Vera Truesdale," she said, "and I'm the victim of a terrible mystery."

Unwin sat down again, knowing he would have to play along for now. He had left his briefcase beside the other chair, so he opened the uppermost desk drawer and found what he was looking for: a pad of notepaper. He set this in front of him and took up a pencil.

"Proceed," he said.

"I arrived from out of town about three weeks ago," Miss Truesdale said. "I'm staying at the Gilbert Hotel, Room 202. I have repeatedly asked to be moved to a room on a higher floor."

Unwin resorted to shorthand to get it all down. "Why do you want to be moved?" he asked.

"Because of the mystery," Miss Truesdale said. Her voice had taken on an impatient edge. "If I were staying in a room on a higher floor, they might not be able to get in."

"Who might not be able to get in?"

"I don't know!" Miss Truesdale nearly shouted. She began to pace the short width of the room. "Every morning I wake up surrounded by . . . odds and ends. Empty champagne glasses, bits of confetti, roses. Things of that nature. They're scattered over the floor, over *my bed.* It's as though someone has thrown a party in my room. I sleep through it, but I don't feel that I do. I feel as though I haven't slept in years."

"Champagne glasses, confetti, and . . ."

"Long-stemmed roses."

". . . and roses, long-stemmed. Is that all?"

"No, that isn't all," she said. "The window is open, and the room is freezing cold. There's a dampness to everything, a terrible, cold dampness. I can hardly stand it any longer. I'm sure I'll lose my mind if this continues." She opened her eyes very wide. "Maybe I already have lost my mind. Is that possible, Mr. Lamech?"

Unwin ignored her question—surely Lamech would not have known the answer either. "I'm certain we'll be able to help you," he said, but then set down his pencil and pushed the notepad away. He was already out of his depth. What more was a watcher expected to do?

"You'll send him, then," Miss Truesdale said.

At a loss, Unwin opened the appointment book on Lamech's desk. He flipped through the pages until he found the present date. There Unwin's own name was penciled in for a ten o'clock meeting. He glanced at his watch. Lamech had intended to speak with him in just a few minutes.

Miss Truesdale was still waiting for an answer.

"We'll send someone," he said.

She did not seem content with that, and her knuckles turned white as she squeezed her purse again. She was about to speak but was interrupted by a creaking sound that came out of the wall beside the bookshelf. She and Unwin both followed it with their eyes. He imagined a monstrous rat crawling up behind the wainscoting, led by its infallible nose toward the enormous cadaver that Unwin had hidden under the desk. The creaking sound rose nearly to the ceiling, then stopped, and a little bell on Lamech's desk chimed twice.

"Aren't you going to get that?" Miss Truesdale asked.

Unwin raised his shoulders as Mr. Duden often did in moments of displeasure. "I'm afraid I must ask you to leave now," he said. "I have an appointment, one that was scheduled in the usual way."

She nodded as though she had expected this all along. "The Gilbert, Room 202. You won't forget, will you?"

He wrote that down at the top of the notepad, repeating aloud, "The Gilbert, Room 202. Now, you try to get some rest, Miss Truesdale." He rose and showed her to the door. She went willingly, though she seemed to have more to say. He avoided her eyes and closed the door before she could speak again, then waited, listening. He heard her sigh, heard her irregular footsteps retreat down the hall, then the rush of air as the elevator door opened and closed.

The bell rang again.

He went to the wall and felt it with the palm of his hand. The surface was cool to the touch. He put an ear against it and held his breath. From the building's unseen recesses came a low keening sound, as of wind trapped in a tunnel or air shaft. What could be hidden there? Unwin recalled something Sivart had written about the manor of Colonel Baker, in the case reports chronicling that wretched man's three deaths: *It's more secret passageways than real passageways, and every looking glass is a two-way mirror. I had to shake the hand of a suit of armor, if you can believe it, to open the door to the library. The old guys are suckers for the classic stuff.*

Could the same be said of Mr. Lamech? Unwin went to the bookshelf and began to search. The books were identified only by roman numerals and alphabetical ranges; reference works, perhaps, for some vast and intricate discipline. He did not need to comprehend the subject to find what he was looking for: one volume, the spine worn at the top from frequent handling. He pulled it forward, and immediately a panel in the wall flew open, revealing something like a miniature elevator car. Inside was an envelope of brown paper, about a foot square, with a note attached.

Taking it, Unwin felt he was crossing a boundary that had long separated him from the world that was the subject of his work. But here was a note, so brief that he read it in the instant he saw it.

Edward,

Here is your special order. I didn't peek. But if you want my advice, you'll let sleeping corpses lie.

Kisses
Miss P.

That the Agency should employ a dumbwaiter came as a surprise. It was his understanding that every communication, no matter how trivial, was to be conveyed by messenger. The operator of the switchboard could not even connect one employee to another—Agency bylaws dictated that the telephones were for external calls only. So what manner of special order could this be, to have arrived in the office of a dead man by such extraordinary means?

The envelope was heavy, unbending, and unsealed. Might Lamech have been planning to present this to him when they met? Unwin slid one finger under the flap of the envelope and tilted it open.

Inside was a phonograph record. Unlike those he had seen for sale in music shops, it was pale white, almost translucent, and at its center was the Agency's open-eyed insignia, the spindle hole serving as pupil. Looking closer, he saw a series of letters and numbers imprinted between the groove of the lead-out. The three-letter prefix, TTS, was one he had seen on every report to cross his desk in twenty years, seven months, and some-odd days. It stood for Travis T. Sivart.

The bell rang again, and the dumbwaiter sank toward the place from which it had come. Unwin closed the panel. He felt he was a clerk again: composed, prepared to carry on, engrossed by the facts of the thing and not the thing itself. He returned to Lamech's desk, tore off the page of notes from his meeting with Miss Truesdale, and put that in his pocket.

He glanced at the telephone. Why had the cord been left unplugged? Unwin reinserted it into the base of the phone, then switched off the green-shaded lamp.

The phonograph record, he knew, was evidence from the scene of a crime, and to take it would be to commit another. But a moment later Lamech's door was closed, the elevator on its way back to the thirty-sixth floor, and the record inside Unwin's briefcase, snug beside his copy of *The Manual of Detection*.

How to account for this splendid misconduct?

When it came to Sivart's cases, it should not surprise us to learn that Unwin's sense of stewardship might extend even to covetousness. If the chosen clerk of "the detective's detective" is to come upon a file—however strange in form—that is by all rights his to review, register, and archive, is he to leave it and walk away, as though Sivart's latest case never existed? Another file, perhaps, Unwin could have forsaken. But even that minor report would have come to haunt him, in those moments before dusk when the city is enveloped in shadow.

Unwin had known few such evenings; he hoped for no more. When the elevator arrived, he told the attendant to take him to the twenty-ninth floor. He wanted to inspect his new office.

ON THE TWENTY-NINTH FLOOR, another long hall, another lone window at its end. But in place of the carpeting of the thirty-sixth, here was a buffed surface of dark wood, so spotless and smooth it shone with liquid brilliance. The floor gave Unwin pause. It was his personal curse that his shoes squeaked on polished floors. The type of shoes he wore made no difference, nor did it matter whether the soles were wet or dry. If the shoes contained Unwin's feet and were directed along well-polished routes, they would without fail sound their joyless noise for all to hear.

At home he went about in his socks. That way he could avoid disturbing the neighbors and also indulge in the occasional shoeless swoop across the room, as when one is preparing a breakfast of oatmeal and the oatmeal wants raisins and brown sugar, which are in the cupboard at the other end of the room. To glide with sock-swaddled feet over a world of glossy planes: that would be a wondrous thing! But Unwin's apartment was smallish at best, and the world is unkind to the shoeless and frolicsome.

He could not remove his shoes with the elevator attendant looking on. Unwin's two extra trips this morning were suspicious enough, though the little man gave no indication that he thought anything of it. So Unwin walked resolutely from the elevator and pretended not to hear the commotion for which he was responsible.

The doors here were more numerous and more narrow than on the thirty-sixth, and in the absence of plaques, names were painted in black over opaque glass windows. From within the offices came the steady patter of typewriters, while here and there voices muttered hushed inscrutables. Was it only Unwin's imagination that the voices quieted at his advance?

Room 2919, halfway down the hall, was not unoccupied—the window glowed with amber light. Unwin touched the glass. The name inscribed there had been scraped away, and only recently: black flecks of paint still clung to the frame.

He became suddenly aware of a spatial concurrence. His new office, at the middle of the east side of the twenty-ninth floor, was situated directly above his old desk on the fourteenth and directly below Lamech's office on the thirty-sixth. If a hole were drilled vertically down the building, a penny pushed off Lamech's desk would, on its descent toward Unwin's desk twenty-two floors below, fall straight through Room 2919.

He was still standing there when the door behind him opened and the detective with the thin mustache and navy blue suit stepped into the hall. He was about to light a cigarette, but when he saw Unwin, his pale lips went taut with a smirk. "I told you they wouldn't go for that hat on the thirty-sixth floor," he said. "Actually, it isn't well regarded here either."

"I'm sorry," was all Unwin could think to say.

"Okay, you're sorry. But who are you?"

Unwin's identification was in his coat pocket, but it was the identification of a clerk who did not belong on this floor. So along with the badge, he presented the memo from Lamech. The detective snatched them both, glanced at the badge, jabbed that back at Unwin, then read the memo slowly. "This isn't addressed to you," he said, and stuffed it into his own pocket. "I better confirm it with Lamech."

"I believe that Mr. Lamech doesn't wish to be disturbed."

"Not by some kidney-foot clerk, maybe." The detective snickered. "And this is the guy they got to replace Travis."

Unwin opened his mouth to protest but closed it once he understood what the detective had said. He, Unwin, was replacing Detective Sivart? He had neither the training nor the disposition required for the job. He was a clerk—a fine one, to be sure, and respected among his peers for his shrewd demeanor, his discerning eye, his encyclopedic knowledge of the elements of a case. He was tenacious in his way, insightful when he needed to be—but only into things already written down. He was no Sivart. And what had happened to Sivart, that he could need replacing?

The detective pointed at him with his unlit cigarette. "I'll be watching you, neighbor," he said. He removed the handkerchief from his jacket pocket and used it to polish the outer knob of his office door, then the inner knob, too. When he realized that Unwin was watching him, he snapped, "I am an enemy to messiness in all its forms," then stuffed the handkerchief back into his pocket. He threw the door closed behind him. The name on the glass was Benjamin Screed.

Unwin tucked his umbrella under his arm and turned back to 2919. So this had been Sivart's office, and now he was meant to occupy it. Meanwhile, the woman in the plaid coat had taken his place on the fourteenth floor. Did that make her his clerk? How would she busy herself until he filed his first report? At this rate she could be waiting for a very long time.

FOUR

On Clues

Most everything can be divided into two categories: details and clues. Knowing one from the other is more important than knowing your left shoe from your right.

Room 2919 was small and windowless. At the center of the office was a desk, its surface covered with balled-up sheets of typing paper. The lamp was on. Seated with her head slumped over the back of the chair was a round-faced young woman, thick red hair bound up with a pin at the top of her head. Crooked small teeth were just visible between her parted lips. Her plump, short-fingered hands were limp across the keyboard of the typewriter.

Was it Unwin's fate to go from one office to another discovering a fresh corpse in each of them? No—this woman was not dead. He saw now the soft rise and fall of her shoulders, heard the sound of her snoring. Unwin cleared his throat, but the woman did not stir. He drew closer, peering over the desk to see what she had been typing.

Don't fall asleep. Don't fall asleep. Don't fall asleep. Don't fall asleep. Don't fall asleep. Don't fall asleep.

The phrase was repeated over half the page, but at last she had written:

Don't fall asleep. Don't fall asleep. Don't fall

Unwin removed his hat and cleared his throat again.

The woman twisted in her chair and shifted her head from her left shoulder to her right. Her hair tumbled free of the pin that held it in place, and a few strands stuck to her lipstick. The light from the desk lamp flashed in her eyeglasses but did not wake her. She began to snore more loudly.

Unwin reached over and pressed the typewriter's carriage release. The platen flew to the end of the line with a clatter, and the bell sounded high and clear. The woman woke and sat straight in her chair. "I don't know any songs for this," she said.

"Songs for what?"

She blinked behind her glasses, which were too big for her girlish face. She could not have been much older than Unwin was on his first day at the Agency. "Are you Detective Unwin?" she asked.

"Yes, I'm Unwin."

She rose and swept her hair back up on her head, fixing it in place—not with a pin, Unwin now saw, but with a sharpened pencil. She said, "I'm your assistant, Emily Doppel."

She straightened her blue woolen dress, then began clearing the crumpled pages off her desk and into a wastepaper basket. Her hands were shaking a little, and Unwin thought he should leave the room and give her the chance to recover, but she spoke quickly and without pause as she worked, so he was unable to excuse himself. "I'm an excellent typist, and I practice as much as I'm able," she said. "I've studied the Agency's most important cases, and I'm not averse to working extra hours. My greatest fault is my susceptibility to unpredictable bouts of deep sleep. The irony of my condition, in light of the Agency's foremost motto, is not lost on me. But the work I've done to make up for my weakness has strengthened my resolve beyond normal expectations. I apologize in advance for the snoring."

All that remained on her desk—aside from the typewriter, telephone, and lamp—was a shiny black lunch box.

Emily came around the desk and reached to take Unwin's hat, but he held tightly to the brim. She clutched it and tugged until he relented, then she brushed off the trilby and hung it on the coatrack.

She stood very close, and the room felt suddenly small for them both. He could smell her perfume in the air: lavender. She reached for his briefcase, and he drew it against his chest, shielding it with both arms.

"It's okay," she said, her smile revealing her crooked teeth. "That's what I'm here for."

So his assistant knew what she was here for, even if Unwin did not. But what to do with her? Were he at his desk on the fourteenth floor, he might have been able to think of something. There were always labels to be typed, folders to be sorted: alphabetically, in chronological or reverse-chronological order. But Unwin took pleasure even in those minor tasks and would not soon have parted with them.

He freed one arm from his coat and transferred his briefcase to the other hand while Emily slipped the coat off and away and hung it below the hat. She had also taken possession of his umbrella without his seeing how it was done.

"I have a lot of work to do," he said.

She folded her hands in front of her. "I'm prepared, of course, to hear all about our case, assuming you've already been contacted by your watcher."

"I have . . . conferred with the gentleman," Unwin said.

There was a knock at the door, and Emily opened it before Unwin could stop her. In the hall stood a man in a crisp white shirt and yellow suspenders. His age was unapparent: the unkempt blond hair belonged on the head of a boy of thirteen, but he entered the room with the unhesitant calm of someone much older. He was holding a shoe-box-size package wrapped in brown paper.

"Messenger for you, sir," Emily announced, as though Unwin were not in the room with her.

Unwin accepted the package and unwrapped it while the two watched. Inside was an Agency identification badge for Charles Unwin, Detective. Beside it was a pistol. Unwin snapped the box shut. "Who sent this?"

"That information is not within the bounds of my message," said the messenger, running his thumbs along the undersides of his suspender straps.

Unwin had parlayed with messengers before. He found them, on the whole, a rascally lot, prone to twist the rules governing their profession to their own advantage. This one was clearly no exception.

"Can you tell me when it was sent?" Unwin tried.

The messenger only looked at the ceiling, as though to acknowledge the question would shame them both.

"Are you free to take a message, then?"

With that, Unwin knew he had snared the man. Messengers were obliged to deliver only what they were given, whether packages or words, but they had to take a message whenever asked. This one let go of his suspenders and sighed. "Spoken or typed?" he asked.

"Typed," said Unwin. "Emily, you told me you are an excellent typist."

"Yes, sir." She returned to her typewriter and loaded a fresh sheet of paper bearing the Agency seal. She held her hands suspended over the keys and tilted her head a little to the left. Her eyes went unfocused, as though she were gazing into some distant, tranquil place.

Unwin began, "To colon Lamech comma Watcher comma floor thirty-six return from colon Charles Unwin comma capital C capital L capital E capital R capital K comma floor fourteen comma temporarily floor twenty-nine return.

"Now for the body of the text. Sir comma with all due respect comma I must request your immediate attention to the matter of my recent promotion comma which I believe has been given in error point."

Emily's typing was confident and somewhat brash—she threw the carrier to each new line with a flourish, as one might turn a page of exquisite piano music, and her fingers danced high off the keys at the end of each sentence. Her style lent Unwin even greater resolve.

"As you may know comma I am solely responsible for the case files of Detective Travis Tee point Sivart point. Naturally comma I hope to return to that work as soon as possible point. If you are unable to reply to this message comma I will assume that the matter has been settled comma as I would not wish to trouble you any further than is necessary point. I will of course make sure that you receive a copy of my report point."

Emily plucked the page from her typewriter, folded it into thirds, and slipped it into an envelope. The messenger put it in his satchel and left.

Unwin wiped his brow with his shirtsleeve. The messenger would go directly to Lamech's office on the thirty-sixth floor and discover Lamech dead. That relieved Unwin of the responsibility of reporting the fact himself.

"A clerk," said Emily thoughtfully. "It's the perfect cover, sir. Criminals will naturally underestimate a common clerk, never suspecting that he could be their undoing. And you already look the part, if you don't mind my saying. Since your subterfuge must prevail within the Agency, as well as without, I assume this is an internal affair. No wonder you're the one they got to replace Detective Sivart."

Emily rose from her chair and gestured toward the back of the room. Her nervousness was gone now—her virtuoso performance at the typewriter had restored her confidence. "Sir," she said, "allow me to conduct you to your private office."

There was a door behind the desk, painted the same drab color as the walls—Unwin had failed to notice it before. Emily led the way into a room sunk in greenish gloom. Its dark carpeting and darker wallpaper gave the impression of a small clearing in a dense wood, though it smelled of cigar smoke.

The single window offered a much better view than those on the fourteenth floor. Through it Unwin could see the rooftops of the tightly packed buildings in the old port town and beyond them the great gray splotch of the bay, where smoke from ships mixed with the rain. This was the view Sivart would have turned to gaze upon while writing up his case notes. Down there, near the water, Unwin could just make out the dilapidated remains of Caligari's Carnival, which had served for years as Enoch Hoffmann's base of operations. Strange, Unwin thought, that the detective could see the lair of his adversary from the comfort of his own chair.

But then, Hoffmann had not been heard from in a long time—not once in the eight years since The Man Who Stole November Twelfth—and the carnival was in ruin. Could it be that Sivart was gone as well? Unwin remembered discovering, in some of the detective's reports, inklings of plans for retirement. He had been careful to excise them, of course—not only were they extraneous, they were tendered gloomily, when a lull between cases put Sivart in a dour mood. They appeared with greater frequency after November twelfth, and Unwin supposed he was the only one who knew the toll that case had taken on Sivart. *I was wrong about her,* he had written, meaning Cleopatra Greenwood. And it was true—he had been.

Sivart's plan involved a home in the country somewhere and the writing of his memoirs. Unwin had been surprised at the detail of Sivart's description: a little white cottage in the woods, at the north end of a town on a river; a slope covered with blackberry briars; a tire swing; a pond. Also a trail that led to a clearing in the woods. *A nice place to take a nap,* he had written.

Unwin knew that Sivart might never have found his way to that cottage. Something terrible could have happened—why else a corpse on the thirty-sixth floor?

As though sharing in Unwin's thoughts, Emily said, "There's no official explanation regarding his disappearance."

"Is there an unofficial explanation?"

Emily frowned at that. "Sir, there is no such thing as an unofficial explanation."

Unwin nodded, swallowing against the dryness in his throat. He would have to be careful with his words, even when speaking to his assistant.

Emily switched on the desk lamp, and now he could see a wooden filing cabinet, chairs for visitors, empty bookshelves, and a decrepit electric fan in the corner. He set his briefcase on the floor and sat down. The chair was too big for him, the desk absurdly expansive. He put the box containing his badge and pistol next to the typewriter.

Emily stood before him, her hands clasped behind her back, waiting. What would she do once she perceived that his clerk's identity was not a cover? The scent of her lavender perfume, mingled with that of Sivart's cigars, tickled Unwin's nostrils, made him dizzy. He tried to dismiss her with a polite nod, but Emily only nodded in reply. She had no intention of leaving.

"Well," he said, "I trust you have undergone standard Agency training, as well as any training requisite to your particular position."

"Of course."

"Then you can tell me what I might expect from you at this time?"

She frowned again, only now the look was darker, more wary. Unwin understood that his assistant had been looking forward to this day, her first on the job, for a long time. He risked disappointing her. It would be dangerous, Unwin thought, to disappoint her.

She changed her mind about what was happening, though, and appeared suddenly pleased. "You're testing me!" she said.

She closed her eyes and tilted her head back, as though to read something imprinted on the backs of her eyelids. She recited, " 'On the first day of a new case, the detective shares with his assistant whatever details he feels the assistant ought to know. Typically this includes important contacts and dates, as well as information from related cases called up from the archives.' "

Unwin sat back in the enormous chair. He thought again of that corpse upstairs, bloated with mystery. He felt as though the thing had crawled onto his back and would drag him into the grave with it if he did not throw it off. What was the case Lamech had meant for him? Whatever it was, Unwin wanted nothing to do with it.

He said, "I see that you have a subtle mind, Emily, so I can trust you. As you suspected, this is an internal affair. The case before us, number CEU001, concerns the very reason for my presence here. Our task is simple: to find Detective Travis T. Sivart and convince him to return to his job as quickly as possible." He was forming a plan even as he spoke it. With Emily's help, perhaps, he could pretend to be a detective just long enough to bring Sivart back to the Agency. Then *he* could make sense of the watcher's corpse, of Miss Truesdale's long-stemmed roses, of the phonograph record he had found in Lamech's office.

Emily was all business now. "Clues, sir?"

"No clues," Unwin said. "But then, this *was* Sivart's office."

Emily checked the filing cabinets while Unwin searched the desk. In the top drawer, he found, forwarded according to Lamech's demands, his personal effects: magnifying glass for small type, silver letter opener presented to him upon the completion of his tenth year of faithful service to the Agency, spare key to his apartment. The second drawer contained only a stack of typing paper. Unwin could not resist: he withdrew several sheets and rolled one of them into the typewriter. It was a good model, sleek and serious, with a dark green chassis, round black keys, and type bars polished to a silvery gleam. Thus far the typewriter was the only thing Unwin liked about being a detective.

"Empty," Emily said, "all empty." She had finished with the filing cabinets and was moving on to the shelves.

Unwin ignored her and checked his margins, adjusted the left and right stops (he liked them set precisely five-eighths of an inch from the edges of the page). He tested the tension of the springs by depressing, only slightly, a few of the more important keys: the E, the S, the space bar. They did not disappoint.

He pretended to type, moving his fingers over the keys without pressing them. How he wanted to begin his report! *This,* he might start, and lead from there on into *morning,* yes, *This morning, after having purchased a cup of coffee,* but no, not the coffee, he could not start with the coffee. How about *I*? From *I* one could really go anywhere at all. *I am sorry to have to report* would be nice, or *I was accosted by one Detective Samuel Pith at Central Terminal,* or *I am a clerk, just a clerk, but I write from the too-big desk of a detective,* no, no, *I* would not do at all, it was too personal, too presumptuous. Unwin would have to leave *I* out of it.

Emily was standing in front of him again, out of breath now. "There's nothing here, sir. The custodian did a thorough job."

That gave Unwin an idea. "Here," he said, "let me show you an old clerk's trick. It's something of a trade secret among the denizens of the fourteenth floor."

"You have done your homework, sir."

He was happy for a chance to impress her, and perhaps to win her confidence. "In an office as busy as the one on the fourteenth floor," he explained, "a document occasionally—very occasionally, mind you—goes astray. It is lost under a cabinet, maybe, or accidentally thrown out with someone's lunch. Or, as you have just reminded me, cleared away by the overzealous custodian."

Unwin opened the lid of the typewriter and gently prised loose the spools of ribbon. "In cases such as those," he went on, "where no carbon copy is available, there is only one method for recovering the missing document. Impressed upon the surface of the typewriter ribbon, so faintly that only close examination under a bright light will reveal them, are all the letters it has ever marked on paper. This ribbon here is only slightly used, but Sivart must have done some work with it."

He put the ribbon into Emily's hands. She drew a chair closer to the desk and sat down, while Unwin angled the lamp to provide her with the best possible illumination. She held a spool in each hand and stretched the ribbon between them, her big glasses shining in the lamplight.

Unwin removed the paper he had just rolled into the typewriter and took a pen from his briefcase. "Read them to me, Emily."

She squinted and read, " 'M-U-E-S-U-M-L-A-P-I-C-I-N-U-M.' Muesum Lapicinum? Is that Latin?"

"Of course not. The first letter on the ribbon is the last Sivart typed. We'll have to read it backward. Please proceed."

Emily's nervousness returned (better that, Unwin thought, than her suspicion), and her hands shook as she continued. Twenty minutes later those hands were covered with ink. Unwin typed a final copy, separating the words where he imagined spaces ought to be.

Wednesday. I'm putting aside my designated case in favor of something that's come out of left field, even though it's probably a load of bunkum. As for protocol, stuff it. I think I've earned the right to break the rules now and then, assuming I know what they are. So, clerk, if you ever see this report, may it please you to know I've been contacted by atypical means—over the telephone for cripes sake—by a party previously unbeknownst to me, to whom I am apparently beknownst. I mean, he knew my name. How did he get my number? I don't even know my number. He said, "Travis T. Sivart?" And I said, "Okay." And he said, "We have much to discuss," or something of that bodeful ilk.

He wants me to meet him at the cafe of one of our finer civic institutions. Maybe Hoffmann's behind it. Maybe it's a trap. One can hope, right? Thus concludes my report for the day. I'm off to the Municipal Museum.

Once he had read the report twice, Unwin handed it to Emily. She read it and asked, "Could the telephone call have had something to do with The Oldest Murdered Man?"

Unwin ought to have guessed that she would be familiar with Sivart's cases, but to hear his own title spoken aloud by someone he had only just met—someone not even a clerk—caused him to shudder. Emily seemed to take this as discouragement and lowered her eyes.

Still, he had to consider the possibility that Emily was correct, that the telephone call did have something to do with the ancient cadaver in the museum, with the case consigned to the archives thirteen years ago. He thought of the note to Lamech he had found in the dumbwaiter: *Let sleeping corpses lie.* What if the Miss P. who had offered that advice meant *that* corpse, *that* file?

It did not matter. All Unwin had to do was find Detective Sivart, and now he knew where Sivart had gone. He picked up his new badge and rubbed its face with his sleeve. In the burnished Agency eye he could see his own distorted reflection. *Charles Unwin, Detective.* Who had inscribed those words? He took the clerk's badge from his jacket pocket (no gleaming frontispiece there, only a worn, typewritten card) and replaced it with the detective's. That, at least, would help him if he encountered Screed again. And the gun? The gun went with his old badge into the desk drawer. The gun he would not need.

Emily followed him to the outer office. He took his coat, hat, and umbrella from the rack, waving off her assistance.

"Where are you going?" she asked.

"I'm off to the Municipal Museum," he said, but the situation seemed to call for some words of encouragement, so he adapted something he had seen in Agency newspaper advertisements. "We have a good team here, and the truth is our business."

Emily said, "But we haven't rehearsed and codified any secret signals, for use in times of duress."

He glanced at his watch. "I'll let you choose something, if you think it's necessary."

"You want me to come up with something right now?"

"It was your idea, Emily."

She closed her eyes again, as though better to see her own thoughts. "All right, how about this? When one of us says, 'The devil's in the details,' the other must say, 'And doubly in the bubbly.' "

"Yes, that will do nicely."

Still she squinted behind those enormous lenses, out of worry or irritation or both. Unwin would have to find something for her to do, an assignment. The phonograph record in his briefcase was a Sivart file of some kind and could be of some use to him in his search. He said, "I have a job for you, Emily. I want you to find a phonograph player. The Agency must have one somewhere."

He did not wait to see if this was enough to placate her, and turned to go. His hand froze on the doorknob, however, at the sound of movement on the other side of the door. A shadow loomed in the window, but no knock came. An eavesdropper. Or worse: they had already found Lamech's body and come to question him.

Unwin cautioned his assistant with a nod and set his briefcase down. The interloper was tapping the glass now, very lightly, as though to send a secret signal of his own. Unwin raised his umbrella saberwise over his head and threw the door open.

The man on the other side toppled backward onto the floor. Black paint spilled from a bucket in his hand, splattering over his clothes, his chin, and the polished wood floor. He held his paintbrush over his head, to protect himself from the anticipated blow.

Unwin lowered his umbrella and looked at the freshly painted words on his office window. DETECTIVE CHARLES UN, it read, and that was all it would ever read, because the painter stood, stabbed his brush into the bucket, and walked back toward the elevator, muttering.

Detective Screed's door opened. He saw the puddle of paint, saw the black boot prints that trailed down the hall. He yanked the hand-kerchief from his jacket pocket as though to begin cleaning the mess but put it to his forehead instead. He slammed his door closed again.

"Emily," Unwin said, "send a message to the custodian, please."

He stepped over the paint and went down the hall, his shoes squeak-ing. Other office doors opened, and other detectives peered out at him. Among them were the two he had seen in the elevator with Detective Screed. Peake was the name on one door, Crabtree the other. They shook their heads at him as he passed, and Peake—still scratching the rash at his collar—whistled in mock admiration.

FIVE

On Memory

Imagine a desk covered with papers. That is everything
you are thinking about. Now imagine a stack of file
drawers behind it. That is everything you know. The trick
is to keep the desk and the file drawers as close to one
another as possible, and the papers stacked neatly.

Unwin pedaled north along the dripping, shadowed expanse of
City Park. There were fewer cars on the street now, but twice he
had to ride up onto the sidewalk to pass horse-drawn carriages, and a
peanut vendor swore at him as he swerved too close to his umbrella-
topped stand. By the time Unwin arrived at the Municipal Museum,
his socks were completely soaked again. He hopped off his bicycle and
chained it to a lamppost, stepping away just in time to avoid the spray
of filthy water raised by the tires of a passing bus.

The fountains to either side of the museum entrance were shut off,
but rainwater had overflowed the reservoirs and was pouring across
the sidewalk to the gutter. The place had a cursed and weary look
about it—built, Unwin imagined, not to welcome visitors but to keep
secrets hidden from them. He fought the urge to turn around and go
home. With every step he took, the report he would have to write
explaining his actions grew in size. But if he were ever going to get his

old job back, he would have to find Sivart, and this was where Sivart had gone.

Unwin angled his umbrella against a fierce damp wind, climbed the broad steps, and passed alone through the revolving doors of the museum.

Light from the windowed dome of the Great Hall shone dimly over the information booth, the ticket tables, the broad-leafed potted plants flanking each gallery entrance. He followed the sound of clinking flatware to the museum café.

Three men were hunched over the lunch counter, eating in silence. All but one of the dozen or so tables in the room were unoccupied. Near the back of the room, a man with a pointed blond beard was working on a portable typewriter. He typed quickly, humming to himself whenever he had to stop and think.

Unwin went to the counter and ordered a turkey and cheese on rye, his Wednesday sandwich. The three men remained intent on their lunches, eating their soup with care. When Unwin's food came, he took it to a table near the man with the blond beard. He set his hat upside down next to his plate and put his briefcase on the floor.

The man's stiff beard bobbed while he worked—he was silently mouthing the words as he typed them. Unwin could see the top of the page curl upward, and he glimpsed the phrases *eats lunch same time every day* and *rarely speaks to workfellows.* Before Unwin could read more, the man glanced over his shoulder at him, righted the page, and frowned so that his beard stuck straight out from his face. Then he returned his attention to his typewriter.

Despite all that Unwin had read of detective work, he had no idea how to proceed with this investigation. Whom had Sivart met with, and what had transpired between them? What good did it do to have come here now? The trail might already have "gone cold," as Sivart would have put it.

Unwin opened his briefcase. He had sworn not to read *The Manual of Detection,* but he knew he would at least have to skim it if he were going to play at being a detective. He told himself he would read only enough to help him along to the first break in the case. That would come soon, he thought, if he only knew how to begin.

He turned the book over in his hands. The edges of the cloth were worn from use. *It's saved my life more than once,* Pith had said to him. But Unwin had never even heard of the book, so he was sure the Agency did not wish for non-employees to learn of its existence. Instead of setting the book on the table, he opened it in his lap.

THE MANUAL

OF

DETECTION

A Compendium of Techniques and Advice
for the Modern Detective,
Representing Matters Procedural, Practical, and Methodological;
Featuring
True Accounts of Pertinent Cases
With Helpful Illustrations and Diagrams;
Including an Appendix of Exercises, Experiments,
and Suggestions for Further Study.

FOURTH EDITION

He turned to the table of contents. Each chapter focused on one of the finer points of the investigative arts, from the common elements of case management to various surveillance techniques and methods of interrogation. But the range of topics was so broad that Unwin did not know what to read first.

Nothing in the index seemed entirely appropriate to his situation, except perhaps one entry: "Mystery, First Tidings of." He turned to the corresponding page and began to read.

> The inexperienced agent, when presented with a few promising leads, will likely feel the urge to follow them as directly as possible. But a mystery is a dark room, and anything could be waiting inside. At this stage of the case, your enemies know more than you know—that is what makes them your enemies. Therefore it is paramount that you proceed slantwise, especially when beginning your work. To do anything else is to turn your pockets inside out, light a lamp over your head, and paste a target on your shirtfront.

The iciness that had settled in Unwin's wet socks climbed up his legs and began melting into his stomach. How many blunders had he already committed? He read the next few pages quickly, then skimmed the beginnings of those chapters that dealt with the foundations of the investigative process. Every paragraph of *The Manual of Detection* read like an admonishment tailored specifically for him. He should have developed an alternate identity, come in disguise or through a back door, planned an escape route. Certainly he should have remained armed. In one case file after another he had seen these techniques used, but detectives employed them without any apparent forethought. Was Sivart really so deliberate? Everything he did—whether throwing someone off his trail or throwing a punch—he did as though the possibility had only just occurred to him.

Unwin closed the book and set it on the table, set his hands on top of it, and took a few deep breaths. The man with the blond beard was working quickly now. Unwin saw the phrase *habits suggesting a dull but potentially dangerous personality, empty or clouded over,* and then, just as he typed it, *if he is in contact with the absentee agent, he does not know it.*

Maybe he had stumbled into a lucky spot after all. Unwin got the man's attention with a wave of his hand.

The man turned in his seat, his beard a pointed accusation.

"Begging your pardon," Unwin said, "but are you the person who met here with Detective Sivart recently?"

The typist's frown deepened, his eyebrows drooping even as his beard rose an inch higher. He ground his teeth and said nothing, then plucked the page from his typewriter, stuffed it into his jacket, and rose from the table with his fists clenched. Unwin straightened, almost expecting the man to come at him, but he walked past Unwin's table and stomped off to the very back of the room, where a pay phone was mounted to the wall. He lifted the transceiver, spoke a number to the operator, and dropped a dime into the slot.

The three men at the lunch counter had turned from their bowls of soup. They looked on with tired expressions. Unwin could not tell if they were suspicious of him or thankful for the reprieve from the man's typing. Unwin nodded at them, and they swiveled back to their lunches without a word.

He took up the *Manual* again. His hands were shaking. He fanned the pages, breathing in the scent of old paper, and caught a whiff of what might have been gunpowder. He could begin to count the things he had done wrong, was perhaps even now adding to the list, but he still did not know where to begin.

"He still does not know where to begin," said the man on the telephone.

Unwin turned. Had he heard correctly? The man with the blond beard stood with his back to the room, one arm resting on top of the telephone, his head bent low. He spoke quietly, then listened and nodded.

Unwin took a deep breath. This was his first hour in the field, and already his nerves were getting to him. He turned back to his book and tried to focus.

"He is trying to focus," said the man at the telephone.

Unwin set down the *Manual* and rose from his seat. He had not misheard: somehow the man with the blond beard was speaking Unwin's thoughts aloud. His hands shook at the thought; he had begun to sweat. The three men at the lunch counter swiveled again to watch Unwin walk to the back of the room and tap the man on the shoulder.

The man with the blond beard looked up, his eyes bulging with violence. "Find another phone," he hissed. "I was here first."

"Were you speaking about me just then?" Unwin asked.

The man said into the receiver, "He wants to know if I was speaking about him just then." He listened and nodded some more, then said to Unwin, "No, I wasn't speaking about you."

Unwin was seized by a terrible panic. He wanted to run back to his seat or, better yet, back to his apartment, forget everything he had read in the *Manual,* everything that had happened that day. Instead, without thinking, he snatched the telephone out of the man's hand and put it to his own face. He was still shaking, but his voice was steady as he said, "Now, listen here. I don't know who you are, but I'd appreciate it if you'd keep to your own affairs. What business is it of yours what I'm doing?"

No response came. Unwin held the receiver to his ear, and he heard something, a sound so quiet he could barely tell it from the prickle of static on the line. It was the rustling of dry leaves, or sheets of paper, maybe, blown by a mild wind. And there was something else, too—a sad warbling that came and went as he listened. The cooing, he thought, of many pigeons.

He set the telephone back in its cradle. The man with the blond beard stared at him. His jaw was moving up and down, but he made no sound. Unwin met his eyes for a moment, then returned to his table, sat, and hurriedly began to eat his sandwich.

One of the men at the lunch counter got off his stool. He wore the plain gray uniform of a museum attendant. His white hair was thin and uncombed, and his dark eyes were set deep in his pale face. He shambled toward Unwin, breathing through his whiskers while crumpling a paper napkin in his right hand. He stood in front of the table and dropped the napkin into Unwin's hat. "Sorry," he said. "I mistook your hat for a wastepaper basket."

The man with the blond beard was on the telephone again. "He mistook his hat for a wastepaper basket," he said. But as the museum attendant left the café, he knocked into the table where the man with the blond beard had been sitting. A glass tipped and spilled water on the papers stacked beside the typewriter. The man with the blond beard dropped the receiver and came running over, cursing under his breath.

Unwin took the napkin out of his hat; something was written on it in blue ink. He uncrumpled the paper and read the hastily scrawled message. *Not safe here. Follow while he's distracted.* He stuffed the napkin into his pocket, gathered up his things, and left. The man with the blond beard was too busy shaking wet pages to notice him go.

THE MUSEUM ATTENDANT GRABBED Unwin by the arm and directed him north into the first of the museum galleries. The name on his pin was Edwin Moore. He leaned close and spoke into Unwin's ear. "We must choose our words carefully. You especially. Everything you say to me I must spend precious minutes unremembering before I sleep. I apologize for waiting as long as I did to intercede. Until I heard you speak, I thought you were one of them."

"One of whom?"

Moore breathed worry through his whiskers. "I cannot say. Either I never knew or I have purposefully forgotten."

Their route took them through the halls of warfare, where empty suits of mail straddled horse's armor empty of horses. Gold and silver weapons gleamed in their cases, and Unwin knew them each, knew the slim-bladed misericord, the graceful rapier, the double-barreled wheel lock pistol. They were all in the Agency's index of weapons, though the pages dedicated to such antiquated devices were less useful than those covering the more popular implements of the day: the pistol, the garrote, the cast-iron skillet.

Moore looked in Unwin's direction as he spoke but would not meet his eyes. "I have been an employee of the Municipal Museum for thirteen years, eleven months, and some-odd days," he said. "I always follow the same path through these corridors, altering my course only when necessary, as when a lost child begs my assistance. I like to keep moving. Not to see the paintings, of course. After all this time, I no longer see the paintings. They may as well be blank canvases or windows onto white sky."

A dull but potentially dangerous personality, the man with the blond beard had typed, *empty or clouded over.* Was it Moore he had been describing? What sort of man worked to forget everything he knew? Doubtless he was a little mad. Unwin, mindful of the commandment to choose his words carefully, chose none for now.

Soon they came to a broad, circular chamber. Unwin knew the place. Light entered through a small window at the top of the domed ceiling, entombing in gray light the coffin of glass on a pedestal below. The Oldest Murdered Man was surrounded by schoolchildren, out on a field trip. The more brave and curious among them stood close, and some even pressed their faces to the glass. Unwin and Moore waited until their chaperone, a stooped young man in a tweed coat, counted the children and shepherded them away. Once the patter of their feet had receded, the only sound was that of the rain on the window high above.

They went closer, the squeaking of Unwin's shoes echoing in the vast room. A plaque set in the floor at the base of the pedestal declared, TO DETECTIVE TRAVIS T. SIVART, WHO RETURNED THIS TREASURE TO ITS

RIGHTFUL PLACE OF REST, THE TRUSTEES OF THE MUNICIPAL MUSEUM EXPRESS THEIR UNDYING GRATITUDE.

The Oldest Murdered Man lay curled on his side, his arms folded over his chest. His flesh was yellow and sunken but intact, preserved by the bog into which he had been thrown, all those thousands of years ago. Had he been a hunter, a farmer, a warrior, a chieftain? His eyes were not quite closed, his black lips drawn back over his teeth in an expression that suggested merriment rather than terror. The hempen cord with which he had been strangled was still twisted around his neck.

"I always found the name imprecise," Unwin said. "He may be the first victim of murder we've discovered, but surely he wasn't the first man to be killed by another. He may even have been a murderer himself. Still, he is our oldest mystery, and an unsolved one at that. We have the weapon, but not the motive."

Edwin Moore was not listening. He looked at the ceiling while Unwin spoke. "I hope there is enough light," Moore said.

"For what?"

The sun, though partly obscured by clouds, crested the window at the top of the dome, and the room suddenly brightened.

"There we are," Moore said. "Did I tell you that I always keep to the same route when making my rounds? That is why I reach this room at the same time every afternoon. There was a woman, I think. She wanted to draw my attention to something, to this. Who was she? Did I only dream of her? I try not to notice things, Detective. I know a story or two. I know the days of the week. That is enough to help eclipse the rest. But look, look there. Can you fault me for noticing that?"

Moore pointed at the glass coffin, at the dead man's parted lips. Unwin saw nothing at first, just the grim visage that Sivart had described, in his reports, as *a sad sorry face, laughing because it has to—a face you'd like to buy a drink.* Then he noticed a glinting at the back of the man's mouth, like that of the gold lettering on *The Manual of*

Detection. He knelt, using his umbrella for balance, and drew as close to the corpse as he could bear. He and the mummy peered at one another through the glass. Then the light shifted, and the dead man gave up his secret.

In one of his teeth, a gold filling.

Unwin dropped his umbrella and jerked upright, tripping over his own feet as he backed away from the mummy. He had the odd impression that his breath had escaped with his umbrella and gone skittering over the floor with it, out of reach. He needed them both, but he could not go and fetch them. He was still standing only because Edwin Moore was propping him up.

Let sleeping corpses lie, the note in the dumbwaiter had read. The gold filling twinkled in the mouth of the Oldest Murdered Man, and to Unwin it was as though the corpse were silently laughing at him. The implications extended deep into the Agency archives, all the way down to Unwin's own files. He said it aloud as he realized it: "The Oldest Murdered Man is a fake."

"No," Moore said. "The Oldest Murdered Man is real. But he is not in this museum."

Footsteps at the edge of the room caused Unwin and Moore to turn. The man with the blond beard stood in the doorway, his portable typewriter in his hand.

"We must continue," Moore whispered. "I've never seen that man before, but I don't like the looks of him."

Unwin was standing on his own now. "He was in the café not ten minutes ago," he said.

"No time to argue," said Moore. He picked up Unwin's umbrella and pressed it into his hands. They left the way the schoolchildren had gone, through an arched doorway and into a dim hall between galleries.

"Please understand," Moore said. "I tried hard to forget the whole thing. Succeeded, perhaps, many times. But every day there is the tooth again, the filling. And that woman, who keeps insisting that I see it. It itches at my brain. The filling may as well be set in my own head. I need to forget about it. Knowing much of anything is a danger to me. I need you to fix your mistake."

"My mistake?"

"Yes. I did not want to be the one to break it to you, Detective Sivart. But the corpse you retrieved from *The Wonderly* the night you first confronted Enoch Hoffmann—it was the wrong corpse. A decoy." Moore looked sad as he spoke, his breath whistling through bunched whiskers. "He tricked you, Detective. He tricked you into helping him hide a dead body in plain sight."

"Whose dead body?"

"Either I never knew—"

"Or you've purposefully forgotten," Unwin said.

Moore seemed surprised to have his sentence finished for him, but he took Unwin's arm without comment and guided him from the corridor. They passed through rooms of medieval paintings. Knights, ladies, and princes scowled from their gilded frames. Then a lighted place: shards of pottery on marble pillars, urns of monstrous size, miniatures of long-dead cities. Moore moved faster and faster, dragging Unwin on while the man with the blond beard followed. They caught up with the schoolchildren in a room of statues. These were of men with elephants' heads, the wise and quiet gods of a strange land sequestered in one dim and narrow gallery. Jewels glinted in the shadows, and the air was heavy and warm.

"Not my mistake," Unwin said at last.

Moore glared at him. "If not yours, whose?"

"You called Sivart a week ago. You must have met with him and forgotten. You showed him what you showed me. What did he do when you told him? You have to remember. You have to tell me where he went."

"But if you're not Sivart, then who are you?"

Those weird, elephant-headed gods fixed Unwin with their impassive eyes, and he found he could not speak. *I am Sivart's clerk,* he wanted to say. *I am the one who set down the details of his false triumph. It is my mistake, mine!* But they would trample him when they heard, those elephant people, and gore him with their jeweled tusks, strangle him with their trunks. *Remember,* they said to him, in a dream he could not entirely wake from. *Try this time, would you? Remember something.*

"Chapter Elephant," Unwin said.

"What was that?" Moore asked. "What did you say?"

"Chapter Eighteen!" Unwin corrected himself. He took *The Manual of Detection* from his briefcase and flipped through the pages, searching for Chapter Eighteen, for the chapter Sivart, in the dream, had told him to remember.

Moore's whole body was trembling, and the snowy hair on his head shook with each wheezing breath. He stared at the book in Unwin's hands. "*The Manual of Detection* has no Chapter Eighteen," he said.

Some of the schoolchildren were ignoring the exhibits now. They gathered instead around these two men, who were possibly the strangest things they had seen in the museum.

Unwin flipped to the last pages of the book. It ended with Chapter Seventeen.

"How did you know?" he asked.

Moore leaned forward, his face contorted, his eyes terrible. "Because I wrote it!" he said, and collapsed.

SIX

On Leads

Follow them lest they follow you.

I've got just enough to go on, Sivart had written in his first report on the theft of the Oldest Murdered Man. *That's what makes me nervous.*

On the night of the heist, a museum cleaning woman had spotted an antique flatbed steam truck, color red, lurking under the trees behind the Wonders of the Ancient World wing. In her thirty-seven years of employment, she told Sivart during questioning, she had seen many strange things, had seen the portraits of certain dukes and generals turn their eyes to watch her as she mopped, had seen the marble statue of a nymph move its slender right leg two inches in the moonlight, had seen a twelve-year-old boy rise sleepily from the settee of an eighteenth-century boudoir and ask her why it was so dark, and where his parents had gone, and whether she had a sandwich for him. But never had the cleaning woman seen anything so strange as the steam truck, which had the smokestack of a locomotive and the hulking demeanor of a story-book monster.

A thing like that tends to stick out, so it wasn't too hard to track it down. Caligari's Travels-No-More Carnival was closed up for the night: nothing on the midway but the smell of stale popcorn. I found the truck parked beside a pavilion near the boardwalk and pressed my thumb to the smoke-stack over the engine. Still warm.

I thought I'd have a peek inside, but somebody was coming from the docks, and I had to scram. The tent flap was hanging open by the entrance, so I wrapped myself in that and hoped nobody would spot my hat. In the end, though, I couldn't help but risk a look.

What I saw was a tall fellow with one very odd mug. It looked like it was made out of clay, all pocked and pale, but his eyes were bright green. He peered into the cab, his breath fogging up the glass. Then he sighed and walked on.

I came out in a hurry, meaning to get out of there, and nearly walked straight into a second man. The weird thing, clerk? It was the same guy I'd just seen go in the opposite direction. Turns out this model of goon comes in sets of two.

He called to his brother, and they got hold of me quick, then gave me a very professional roughing over. Our walk down to the pier was less than romantic. A rusting smuggler's ship, The Wonderly, *was docked down there. The whole thing reeked, like maybe they'd just raised it off the filthy bottom of the harbor.*

The man in charge was a squat little fellow in a rumpled gray suit. The Man of a Thousand and One Voices is more impressive in the carnival posters, with his face lit green by hocus-pocus. In the flesh he looks more like an accountant who's had a bad day and stumbled into the wrong part of town. He was shaking his head, looking sad about the whole thing. I was sad about it, too, and I let him know, in so many words.

We talked for a while. His real voice (if that's what it was) sounded soft and high-pitched, like a kid's. He explained how the Oldest Murdered Man

had been the carnival's main attraction for years, that they had been search-
ing for the mummy for a long time. "I'm only bringing him back home,"
he said.

"Why the boat, then?" I asked.

Enoch Hoffmann grinned. "The boat is for you," he said, and that's
when his two buddies threw me into the cargo hold.

The story of the detective's escape—how he found the corpse on
board, commandeered a lifeboat, and rowed it ashore through the
night—was in the newspapers the next morning. Agency representa-
tives returned the Oldest Murdered Man to the museum that day, amid
shouted questions and the popping of flashbulbs.

But if the mummy was not in the museum now, where was he? And
whose corpse was here in his place?

WITH HELP FROM SOME of the schoolchildren, Unwin carried
Moore into a back room. The place served as a holding area for pieces
of exhibits on their way into or out of the museum. Objects that might
have seemed momentous in the galleries languished here like junk-sale
leftovers. Paintings leaned in piles against the walls, sarcophagi gathered
dust in the corners, marble statues lay half buried in packing material.
The children put Edwin Moore on a worn blue chaise longue, and he
lay with his arms over his face, shivering and mumbling.

"Is he a knight?" one of the children asked.

"He's an artist," another one said.

"He's a mummy," insisted a third.

Unwin corralled them back into the museum and set them in line
behind their chaperone, who had failed to notice them leave. The children waved good-bye, and Unwin waved back. When they were gone,
he walked partway down the hall and peered around the corner. He did
not see the man with the blond beard.

From his sickbed Moore called out for water. Unwin searched

through the crates and found a bowl, dark clay with a black crisscross pattern around the exterior. It was, he supposed, ancient, priceless, and difficult to drink from, but it would have to do. He filled it from the drinking fountain in the hall and carried it to the chaise longue with both hands.

Moore sipped the water, spilling some onto his jacket. Then he lay down and sighed, but immediately began to shiver again. "There is no keeping it back," he said. "I had bound it so tightly, it came undone all at once."

"You did meet with Sivart," Unwin said.

"Yes, oh, yes." He took his arms from his face; it was as white as his hair. "But I never should have spoken to him. He left here in a passion. I thought he would chew his cigar in two. And you! Who are you?"

Unwin considered showing the man his badge, then thought better of it. "I'm Charles Unwin, Agency clerk. My detective's gone missing, and I'm trying to find him. Mr. Moore, you have to tell me where he went."

"Do I? I have already remembered too much, and they are sure to come for me now." He gestured for the bowl of water, and Unwin raised it to his lips. He drank, coughed some, and said, "Not even the Agency wants every mystery solved, Mr. Unwin."

Unwin set the bowl aside. "I'm not trying to solve anything," he said.

Moore's gaze appeared focused now, and the color was returning to his face. He looked at Unwin as though seeing him for the first time. "If you are Sivart's clerk, then you ought to know where he went. The sight of the gold tooth left him baffled. He needed information, the most reliable he could find." He added quietly, "Whatever the price."

Some of the places mentioned in Sivart's reports were as foreign lands to Unwin—he came upon their names often enough to be convinced of their existence, but it was preposterous to think he could reach them by bicycle. For him there were two cities. One consisted of the seven blocks between his apartment and the Agency office building. The other was larger, vaguer, and more dangerous, and it intruded upon his imagination only by way of case reports and the occasional uneasy dream. In a shadowy corner of that other city was a certain taproom, an unofficial gathering place frequented by the enterprising, the scheming, and the desperate. Sivart went there only when every supposition had proved false, when every lead had dead-ended. And because the place rarely had any direct bearing on a case, Unwin usually excised its name from the files.

"The Forty Winks," he said.

Moore nodded. "If you insist on tracking him down, Mr. Unwin, then I suggest you work quickly. I fear I've started the timer on an explosive, but I do not know when it will go off." He rose suddenly from the chaise longue. He was light on his feet and seemed a little giddy.

"What about the woman you mentioned?" Unwin asked. "The one you said showed you the tooth?"

Moore grimaced and said, "I took you at your word when you said you aren't trying to solve anything."

Unwin clenched his jaw. Without thinking, he had started asking questions he did not want to ask. After this, he thought, he would have to put down *The Manual of Detection* for good.

"This way, then," Moore said. "There is a back door—that will be the safest route."

The exit was no taller than Unwin's waist. It was blocked by empty crates, so they worked together to move them aside. The door opened onto the park. Here the trees grew thickly about the back of the museum, and the path was matted with oak leaves, orange and red. Unwin crouched to go through and opened his umbrella on the other side.

Moore bent down to look at him.

"Tell me one thing," Unwin said. "Is it true, what you said? That you wrote *The Manual of Detection*?"

"Yes," said Moore. "So take it from me—it is a bunch of rubbish.

They should have asked a detective to write it. Instead they asked me, and what did I know?"

"You weren't a detective?"

"I was a clerk," Moore said, and he closed the door before Unwin could ask him anything else.

HE RODE SOUTH THROUGH the city, his umbrella open in front of him. He ignored the blare of horns and the shouts of drivers as he wove through the midday traffic, keeping his head tucked low.

He passed the narrow green door of his own apartment building, then the grime-blackened exterior of Central Terminal. There he caught sight of Neville, the boy from the breakfast cart, standing just out of the rain, smoking a cigarette.

At the next block, Unwin veered east to avoid the Agency offices. He did not want to risk seeing Detective Screed again, or even his own assistant, not yet. The noise of the traffic receded as the cast-iron facades of warehouses and mill buildings rose up around him, rain pouring in torrents from their corniced rooftops. Unwin's arms and legs were shaking now, but not from the exertion or from the cold. It was that dead face he had seen behind the glass in the museum. He felt as though it were still mocking him with its awful gold-toothed grin. The thread, the one that connected mystery to solution, that shone like silver in the dark—Sivart had picked the wrong one, and Unwin had strung it up as truth. What did the false thread connect?

In the old port town, Unwin slowed to navigate the winding, crowded streets. Business carried on in spite of the rain, with deals being made under awnings and through the windows of food stalls. He felt he was being watched, not by one but by many. Was there something that marked him as an employee of the Agency? An invisible sign that the people here could read?

He pedaled on, easing his grip on his umbrella. The rain fell softly now. In the maze of old streets that predated the gridding of the city, he passed timbered warehouses and old market squares cluttered with the refuse of industry. Machines—the purpose of which he could not guess—rusted in red streaks over the cobblestone.

The crowds thinned. From chimneys, crooked fingers of smoke pointed at the clouds. Barren clotheslines sagged dripping over the street, and a few windows glowed yellow against the day's persistent gloom. Unwin quickened his pace, his memory of Sivart's descriptions serving as map, and came at last to the cemetery of Saints' Hill, a six-acre tangle of weeds, dubious pathways, vine-grappled ridges, and tumble-down mausoleums.

The Forty Winks was beneath the mortuary, a low-slung building of crumbling gray stone at the southeast corner of the block. He had half hoped that the place did not really exist, but the chipped steps leading from the sidewalk down to the basement level were real enough. He chained his bicycle to the cemetery fence, under the eaves of the building.

From the top of the stairs, he could hear the smacking of pool balls, the clinking of glasses. He could still go home, if he wanted. Sleep off the day and wait for the next one, hope that everything would right itself somehow. But a window level with the sidewalk creaked open, and someone looked up at him, wrinkling his nose as though trying to catch Unwin's scent. A pair of wide, reddish brown eyes blinked behind the glass.

"In or out?" the man called from below.

It was too late to go back. Unwin descended the stairwell, collapsing his umbrella just enough to make it fit. At the bottom of the steps was a slow drain, cigarette butts floating in the puddle that had formed. Unwin pushed the door open with the tip of his umbrella, then stepped over the water and into the Forty Winks.

The tables were lit only by candles, while the bar, on the cemetery side, had the benefit of several windows near the ceiling, through which a greenish light dribbled over bottles of liquor. Most of the bottles were arranged on shelves in a tall, oblong cabinet, its door gaping.

Not a cabinet, Unwin realized. A coffin.

Near the entrance, two men sat with their hats in front of them, speaking close over a guttering candle. At the back of the room, an electric bulb with a green glass shade hung low over the pool table. Two other men, very tall and dressed in identical black suits, were in the midst of a game. They played slowly, taking a great deal of care with each shot.

Sivart was nowhere to be seen. Unwin took a seat at the bar and set his briefcase in front of him. The man who had spoken through the window cranked it shut, made a show of dusting off his hands, and hopped down from the barrel he had climbed to reach. He ran a hand along the bar as he approached, sweeping up a folded newspaper. "Newsman says there's foul play at the Agency," he said. "An internal affair, they say. The eyes up top suspect one of their own."

A single black curl made an upside-down question mark in the middle of the man's forehead. This was Edgar Zlatari, the caretaker of the cemetery and its only gravedigger. So long as no one was in need of burying, he served drinks to the living. He was someone who knew things, a collector of useful information.

"New faces bring new woes, that's what they say," Zlatari went on. "What about you? You call your troubles by name? Or maybe they call you by yours?"

Unwin did not know how to reply.

"Leave your tongue on your pillow this morning? What's your line, friend?" Zlatari cast a suspicious look at the briefcase, and Unwin slipped it onto his lap.

"Okay, tight-lips. What'll it be, then?"

"Me?" Unwin said.

The bartender looked around, rolling his eyes. He smelled of whiskey and damp earth. " 'Me?' he says. That's a laugh."

The two at the table snickered, but the men at the pool table were unamused. At the sight of this, Zlatari's grin vanished. "Come on, pal," he said to Unwin. "A drink. What do you want to drink?"

There were too many bottles stacked in that coffin, too many choices. What would Sivart have ordered? A hundred times the detective must have named his drinks of choice. But Unwin had stricken them from the reports, and now he found he could not remember even one. Instead the response to Emily's secret phrase came uselessly to mind: *And doubly in the bubbly.*

"Root beer," he said at last.

Zlatari blinked several times, as though maybe he had never heard of the stuff. Then he shrugged and moved away down the bar. On the wall beyond the register was a tattered velvet curtain. In the moment Zlatari drew it aside, Unwin glimpsed a tiny kitchen. A radio was playing back there, and he thought he recognized the song—a slow melody carried by horns, a woman singing just above them, voice rising with the swell of strings. He was sure he had heard the tune somewhere before and had almost placed it when Zlatari pulled the curtain closed behind him.

Unwin shifted on his stool. In the mirror he could see the men at the booth behind him. One tapped his hat excitedly as he said, "Have I got a story!" and the other man leaned forward to listen, though the man with the story told it loudly enough for everyone in the room to hear.

"I saw Bones Kiley the other night," he said, "and we were just talking business, you know? Then suddenly, out of nowhere, he started talking *business*. So I said to him, 'Wait, wait, do you want to talk about *business*? Because if it's *business* you want to talk about, then we shouldn't be talking about business, because there's business and there's *business*.'"

"Ha," said the other man.

"So then I asked him, 'Just what sort of business are you in, Bones, that you want to talk about *business*?'"

"Ha ha," said the other.

"And Bones gets serious-looking, kind of screws up his eyebrows like this . . ."

"Ha."

". . . and he looks at me with his eyes squinty, and he says in this really deep voice, 'I'm in the business of blood.' "

The other man said nothing.

"So I said to him," and the man with the story raised his voice even higher as he finished his story, " 'The business of blood? The business of blood? Bones, there is no business but the business of blood!' "

Both men laughed and tapped their hats in unison, and the candle flickered and flared, making their shadows twitch on the uneven stone wall.

While the man with the story was telling it, the two at the pool table had set down their cue sticks. Identical faces, lips pale gray, eyes bright green: Unwin wondered if these could be the Rook brothers, Jasper and Josiah, the twin thugs who had aided Enoch Hoffmann in the theft of the Oldest Murdered Man, and in countless other misdeeds during the years of his criminal reign. *The worst thing that can happen,* Sivart often wrote, *and the other worst thing.*

Shoulder to shoulder the two approached, leaning toward each other with every step. It was said that the Rooks had once been conjoined, but were separated in an experimental operation that left them with crippled feet—Jasper's left and Josiah's right. Each wore two sizes of boots, the smaller on the side of that irrevocable severance. This was the only sure way to tell them apart.

The twins stood over the table with their backs to Unwin, obscuring his view of the men seated there. He felt a great heat coming off the two, drying the back of his neck. It was as though they had just come out of a boiler room.

"My brother," said one in a measured tone, "has advised me to advise you to leave now. And since I always take my brother's advice, I am hereby advising you to leave."

"Yeah, who's asking?" said the man who had told the story.

"In point of fact," said the other, in a voice that was deeper but otherwise identical to his brother's, "my brother is not asking, he is advising."

"Well, I don't know your brother," said the man with the story, "so I don't think I'll take his advice."

In the silence that followed, it seemed to Unwin that even the dead in their graves, just behind the wall where the mirror was hung, were waiting to hear what would happen.

One of the twins licked the tips of his thumb and forefinger and leaned over the table. He pinched the candle flame, and it went out with a hiss. From the dark of the booth came a muffled cry. Then the two men walked to the door with the storyteller between them, his feet kicking wildly a few inches above the ground. They deposited him outside, facedown in the puddle over the slow drain. He lay slumped amid the floating cigarette butts and did not try to pick his face up out of the puddle.

The brothers returned to the back of the room. One chalked his cue stick while the other considered the table. He took his next shot, sinking one ball, then another.

The man still in the booth blinked, his eyes not yet adjusted to the change in light. He put his hat on and went outside. After a moment's hesitation and a glance back into the bar, he lifted his friend out of the puddle and dragged him up the stairs.

Zlatari came out from behind the curtain, muttering as he went to close the door. Once he was back behind the bar, he uncorked the bottle in his hand and slid it across to Unwin.

The two men at the back of the room had finished their game, and were seating themselves side by side at the booth nearest the pool table.

One of them nodded at Zlatari, and Zlatari raised his hand and said, "Yes, Jasper, just a moment."

Eight years had passed since the names Jasper and Josiah Rook had appeared in Sivart's reports—like Hoffmann, the twins had gone into hiding following the events of The Man Who Stole November Twelfth. There were times when Unwin had hoped to see them come back—but only on paper, not in the flesh.

"Well," Zlatari said to him, "it's your lucky day. We're about to play some poker, and we need a fourth."

Unwin raised one hand and said, "Thank you, no. I'm not very good at cards."

Josiah whispered something into Jasper's ear—it was Josiah, according to Sivart's reports, who served as counsel, while Jasper was generally spokesman. The latter called to Unwin, "My brother has advised me to advise you to join us."

Unwin knew enough to know he had no choice. He took his bottle and followed Zlatari to the table, seating himself at the gravedigger's right. The Rooks regarded him unblinkingly. Their long faces, molded as though from the same mottled clay, could have been lifeless masks if not for the small green eyes set in them. Those eyes were very much alive, and greedy—they caught the light and did not let it go.

Zlatari dealt the cards, and Unwin said, "I'm afraid I don't have much money."

"Your money is no good here," said Josiah, and Jasper said, "To clarify, my brother does not mean that you play for free, as the expression may commonly be interpreted. Only that we do not play for money, and thus yours is literally of no value at this table."

Zlatari whistled and shook his head. "Don't let Humpty and Dumpty here spook you, tight-lips. That's just their version of gentlemanly charm. Mine is traditional generosity. The bank will forward you something to start with. And like he said, we don't play for money at this table. We play for questions."

"Or rather," said Jasper, "for the right to ask them. But only one question per hand, and only the winner of that hand may ask."

Unwin did know a thing or two about poker. He knew that certain combinations of cards were better than others, though he could not say for sure which beat which. He would have to rely on poker-facedness, then, which he knew to be a virtue in the context of the game.

"Ante is one interrogative," said Zlatari.

Unwin placed a white chip beside the others on the table and examined his cards. Four of the five were face cards. When his turn came, he raised the bet by one query, though under the guise of hesitancy. Then he traded in his single non–face card and received another face card, a king, in its place. A handful of royalty, then. What could be better? Minding his poker face, however, he made sure to frown at his hand.

There ensued a whirl of bets, calls, and folds, until finally only Unwin and Josiah were still in the game. Josiah set his cards on the table, and Jasper said for him, "Two pair."

Unwin revealed his own cards, hoping that someone would interpret.

"Three kings," Zlatari said. "Tight-lips takes the pot and keeps his nickname for now."

Unwin tried not to look pleased as he claimed the pile of chips. "I may ask my question now?"

"Sure," said Zlatari. He seemed cheerful at the Rook brothers' loss.

"But you just asked it," said Josiah, "and now you are down one query." As he said this, he blinked for the first time since they had started playing, though it was less a blink than a deliberate closing and reopening of the eyes.

"Shouldn't you have told me the rules before we started?" Unwin said.

"The laws of the land are not read to us in the crib," was Josiah's reply. "And you just expended another query, though you are allowed only one."

"It was rhetorical," said Unwin, but he tossed aside the two chips anyway.

Zlatari said, "Hell, we should be fair to the new guy," and he told Unwin how to trade up: two queries for a single inquiry, two inquiries for a perscrutation, two perscrutations for a catechism, two catechisms for an interrogation, and so on.

Unwin's next hand did not look to him as strong as the first, and he folded early, assuring himself there were better cards to come. Worse hands followed, however, and the other players directed their questions at one another, ignoring him. He listened carefully to their answers, but they were of little use because he hardly understood the questions. He heard names he did not recognize, references to "jobs" that were "pulled" rather than worked, and a lot of talk that sounded more like code than speech.

Zlatari asked, "Would putting the hat on the uptown bromides win dirt or be a fishing expedition?"

"A few rounds of muck could show ghost," was Josiah's reply.

At the end of the next hand, it was Jasper who threw in enough chips for a perscrutation and said to Zlatari, "Tell me about the last time you saw Sivart."

Zlatari shifted in his seat and scratched the back of his neck with grimy fingernails. "Well, let's see, that would have been a week ago. It was dark when he got here, and he did a lot of things he doesn't usually do. He was nervous, fidgety. He didn't ask me any questions, just took a seat in the corner and read a book. I didn't know the man could read. He stayed until his candle burned down, then left."

The Rooks appeared dissatisfied with the account. Apparently a perscrutation was a rather weightier kind of question and required a more thorough disclosure. Zlatari drew a breath and went on. "He said I might not see him again for a while. He said that Cleo was back in town, that he had to go and find her." Zlatari glanced at Unwin when he said this, as though to see if it meant anything to him. Unwin looked down at his chips.

Cleo could only be Cleopatra Greenwood, and Unwin had long ago come to fear—even loathe—the appearance of her name in a report. She had first come to the city with Caligari's Traveling Carnival and for years was one of Sivart's chief informants. But to file anything regarding her motives or aims was to risk the grueling work of retraction a month later. Mysteries, in her wake, doubled back on themselves and became something else, something a person could drown in. *I had her all wrong, clerk:* how many times had Unwin come upon that awful admission and scurried to fix what had come before?

The others were waiting for Unwin's next bet. His winnings were largely depleted, so he traded an inquiry for two queries but quickly lost both. The Rooks, as though sensing that Unwin would soon leave the table, turned their attention on him. Jasper used a query to learn his name, and Josiah spent an inquiry to ask what kind of work he did.

Unwin showed them his badge, and the Rook brothers blinked in tandem.

Zlatari's brow wrinkled behind his question-mark curl. "Well," he said, "it wouldn't be the first time I've had an Eye at my table. Detective Unwin, is it? Fine. Everyone's welcome here." But on this last point he seemed uncertain.

Unwin lost and lost again. All the questions came to him now, and he gave up answers one after another. His opponents were disappointed at the spottiness of his knowledge, though Zlatari licked his lips when Unwin told what he knew about Lamech's murder, about the bulky corpse at the desk on the thirty-sixth floor, its bulging eyes, its criss-crossed fingers.

Zlatari dealt new hands, and Unwin's was unremarkable: no face cards, no two or three of any kind. His beginner's luck had run out. This would be his last hand, and he had learned so little.

Zlatari folded almost immediately, but the Rook brothers showed no sign of relenting. They eagerly took up their new cards and just as eagerly counted out their bets. Unwin was going to lose. So he said to Zlatari, "A two, three, four, five, and six of spades: is that a good hand?"

Again that slow, sleepy blink from the twins.

"Yes," said Zlatari. "That is a good hand."

The brothers tossed their cards onto the table.

Unwin set his own cards facedown and collected his winnings, quickly, so they would not notice how his hands were shaking. He traded in all his chips, which was enough, Zlatari told him, for the most severe sort of question the game allowed. The inquisition would be answered by everyone at the table.

Unwin looked at each of them carefully. The Rooks were silent, imperious. But their questions had revealed that they, like him, were looking for Sivart. And Sivart was looking for Greenwood. So Unwin cleared his throat and asked, "Where is Cleopatra Greenwood?"

Zlatari looked over his shoulders, as though to make sure no one else had heard, even though the bar was otherwise empty. "Hell!" he said. "Hot stinking hell! You want to bury me, Detective? You want us in the dirt today? What's your game, Charles?"

Josiah whispered something in Jasper's ear, and Jasper said, "Those questions are out of turn, Zlatari. You're breaking your own rules."

"I'll break more," Zlatari said. He flicked his hands at Unwin. "Up, let me up!"

Unwin got to his feet, and Zlatari shoved past, knocking chips off the table and onto the floor. "You get your answers from them," he said, "but I don't want to know what they are. I've got enough graves to dig without having to dig my own." He went muttering to the farthest table and sat facing the door, twisting his mustache between thumb and forefinger.

The Rooks were still in their seats. Unwin sat back down and tried not to look directly at those green, unblinking eyes. He felt again the strange heat of the two men, dry and suffocating. It came over the table in waves; his face felt like paper about to catch.

Jasper took a card from his jacket pocket. Josiah gave him a pen, and Jasper wrote something and slid the card across the table.

Unwin's nose tingled with the scent of matchsticks as he read what Jasper had written: *The Gilbert, Room 202.*

Without having to look, he knew it was the same address written on the piece of notepaper in his pocket. Unwin had already met Cleo Greenwood, then. She had called herself Vera Truesdale and told him a story about roses in her hotel room.

He put the card in his pocket and stood up. He had asked only one question, and the Rooks had answered it—was he not entitled to a second, since there were two of them at the table? There were plenty of questions on his mind: about the identity of the corpse in the Municipal Museum, the meaning of Cleopatra Greenwood's visit to the Agency that morning, whether any of it meant that Enoch Hoffmann had come out of hiding. But the Rooks were looking at him in a way that suggested their business was concluded, so he stood and gathered his things.

At the door Zlatari grabbed his arm and said, "The price of some questions is the answer, Detective." He glanced back at the Rooks, and Unwin followed his gaze. They might as well have been a pair of statues, the original and a copy, though no one could have said which was which.

"I suppose you saw Cleo Greenwood since she got back to town," Zlatari said. "Heard her singing at some joint a little classier than this one. Maybe she looked at you from across the room. Time stopped when you heard her voice. You'd do anything for her, anything she asked, if only she asked. Am I right? Or maybe you imagined all that. Try to convince yourself that you imagined all that, Detective. Try to forget."

"Why?"

"Because you'll always be wrong about her."

Unwin put on his hat. He would have liked to forget, forget every-thing that had happened since he woke up this morning, forget even the dream of Sivart. Maybe someday Edwin Moore could teach him how it was done. In the meantime he had to keep moving.

He went to the door and hopped over the puddle on his way up the stairs. The Rooks' red steam truck was parked down the street—he was surprised he had failed to notice it before. It was just as the cleaning lady at the Municipal Museum had described it all those years ago: red and hunched and brutal-looking. Had he fallen into his files, or had his files spilled into his life?

He hurried to his bicycle, wanting to be as far from the Forty Winks as possible by the time the Rooks understood the extent of his poker-facedness. When they flipped over his last hand, they would see various numbered cards there, none of them concurrent, and of four different suits.

SEVEN

On Suspects

They will present themselves to you first as victims, as
allies, as eyewitnesses. Nothing should be more suspicious
to the detective than the cry for help, the helping
hand, or the helpless onlooker. Only if someone
has behaved suspiciously should you allow
for the possibility of his innocence.

An empty hat and raincoat floated at the center of the diagram in
Unwin's mind. Beside them was a dress filled with smoke. A pair
of black birds with black hats fluttered above, while below lay two
corpses, one in an office chair, one encased in glass. The diagram was
a fairy tale, written by a forgetful old man with wild white hair, and it
whirled like a record on a phonograph.

The rain fell heavily again, and Unwin pedaled against the wind.
These were unfamiliar streets, where unfamiliar faces glared with seeming menace from beneath dripping hats. A small dog, white with apri-
cot patches, emerged from an alley and followed him, barking at his
rear tire. No amount of bell ringing could drive it away. When it
rained like this, these city dogs were always lost, always wandering—the
smells they used to navigate were washed into the gutters. Unwin felt
he was a bit like one of those dogs now. This one finally left him to

investigate a sodden pile of trash at the corner, but once it was gone, he found that he missed it.

His umbrella technique worked best over short distances and at reasonably high speeds. Now he was soaked. His sleeves drooped from his wrists, and his tie stuck to him through his shirt. If she saw him like this, Cleopatra Greenwood would laugh and send him on his way. That she knew something was a certainty—she always knew something, was always "in on it." But what was she in on? Why had she come back to the city now?

Even after all his work at maintaining consistency, Unwin knew that a careful examination of the Agency's files would reveal perhaps a dozen versions of Cleopatra Greenwood, each a little different from the others. One of them, at the age of seventeen, renounced her claim on her family's textile fortune and ran off to join Caligari's Traveling Carnival. The carnival, in the autumn of its misfit life and haunted by odd beauties and ill-used splendors, made of the girl a sort of queen. She read futures in a deck of old cards and suffered a man with a handlebar mustache to throw daggers at her.

During one performance a blade pierced her left leg, just above the knee. She removed the dagger herself and kept it. The wound left her with a permanent limp, and the blade would appear again in many of Sivart's reports. When she found him in the cargo hold of *The Wonderly*, that night out on the bay, it was already in her hand.

I'd been trying to remember something I'd read about escaping from bonds, Sivart wrote. *It's easier if you're able to dislocate certain bones at will, but that's not in my job description. I was about as useful as a jack-in-the-box with his lid glued shut. So I was happy to see her, even though I didn't know what she was doing there.*

"I'm going to help you get what you came for," she said. *"And you're going to get me out of here."*

So she was in trouble, too. She was always in trouble. I wanted to tell

her she could do better than old twiddle-fingers back there, but I still needed
her to cut those ropes, so I played nice and kept it to myself.

We found the crate with Mr. Grim inside and carried it to a lifeboat.
It was tough going, she with her limp and me with sore feet, but with a
pair of ropes to lower them we managed to get corpse and crate down
onto the dinghy. She sat at the prow and rubbed her bad knee while I
rowed. It was dark out there on the water, no moon, no stars, and I could
barely see the seven feet to her face. She wouldn't tell me where she would
go after this. She wouldn't tell me where I could find her. Truth is, I
still don't know where she stands. With Hoffmann? With us? She seems
like a good kid, clerk, and I want to trust her. But maybe I'm getting
her wrong.

For years, over the course of dozens of cases, Sivart was never sure
whose side she was on, and neither was Unwin, until the theft of November twelfth, when Sivart caught her red-handed and did what he
had to do.

If what Edwin Moore had said was correct, then it might have been
Greenwood who made the switch that night and tricked Sivart into
returning the wrong corpse to the museum. And if Sivart had failed to
get the truth out of her, what hope did Unwin have? He was no threat
to her; he was nothing at all: DETECTIVE CHARLES UN, as it said on his
office door.

Ahead of him a black car rolled from an alleyway, blocking his route.
Unwin braked and waited. No traffic prevented the car from taking to
the street, but it stayed where it was. He tried to look in at the driver;
all he could see was his own reflection in the window. The engine let
out a low growl.

What would the *Manual* have to say about this? Clearly, Unwin was
meant to be intimidated. Should he pretend that he was not? Act as
though this were all a misunderstanding, that he was only a little em-
barrassed by so awkward an encounter? No such cordiality was forth-

coming from the driver of the vehicle, so he dismounted and walked his bicycle to the opposite side of the street.

The vehicle sprang from the alley and came straight at him. Unwin leapt back as it rolled onto the curb. Two steps farther and he would have been pinned against the brick wall. In the driver's window, distorted by streaks of rain, his own reflection again.

Unwin mounted his bicycle and pedaled back across the street. He tried to keep calm, but his feet slipped from the pedals, and he wobbled. He heard the screech of the car's tires as it turned in the street, its engine roaring as though it sensed its prey's weakness. Unwin regained control and slipped into the alley from which the car had come. Then the beast was behind him, filling the narrow passage with its noise. He pedaled faster. The car's headlights glared, turning the rain into a solid-seeming curtain. He thought he could reach the far end, but on the street beyond, the car was sure to overtake him.

He held his umbrella behind him as he emerged, and the wind tore it open. With his free hand, he yanked the handlebar to the left. The umbrella gripped the air, and the bicycle veered sharply onto the sidewalk, teetering at the gutter's edge.

The car dashed directly into the street, nearly colliding with a taxicab. Unwin did not stop to look. He was off and pedaling again, head ducked low over the handlebars, rainwater sloshing in his shoes. Then a second car, identical to the first, emerged from the cross street and halted in the intersection, blocking his escape. Unwin did not stop—he had forgotten how. He collapsed his umbrella and hefted it on his forearm, cradling it like a lance.

The driver's door opened, and Emily Doppel poked her head over the roof. "Sir!" she said.

"The trunk!" Unwin cried.

Emily got out and raised the trunk lid, then stood with arms open. Unwin hopped off, and the bicycle soared straight to his assistant, who lifted it into the air with surprising strength and dropped it into the trunk. She tossed him the keys, but he tossed them back.

"I don't know how to drive!" he said.

She got back into the driver's seat just as the other car halted beside them. Detective Screed stepped out. He spit his unlit cigarette into the street and said, "Unwin, get in the car."

"Get in the car!" Emily screamed at him.

Unwin got in beside Emily and closed the door. She threw the vehicle into gear, and his head snapped against the seat back. In the rear window, he saw Screed run a few steps after them. Then the detective stopped, bent over, and put his hands on his knees. The man with the blond beard was standing beside him, his portable typewriter in his hand.

"Where did you get this?" Unwin asked.

"From the Agency garage," she said.

"The Agency gave you a vehicle?"

"No, sir. It's yours. But under the circumstances I didn't think you'd mind."

Emily drove with the same gusto she put into her typing, her small hand moving quickly between the wheel and the gearshift. She rounded a corner so fast that Unwin nearly fell into her. Her shiny black lunch box tipped over between their seats, and its contents rattled.

How had his assistant found him? She knew he had gone to the Municipal Museum, but she could not have learned of his trip to the Forty Winks unless she spoke to Edwin Moore—or to other contacts of her own.

"I shadowed Detective Screed," she said, as though guessing his thoughts. "I knew he was up to no good when I saw him slink out of the office."

She took a winding route through the city, using tunnels and side streets Unwin had never seen. He felt the cold now, felt the dampness of his clothes against the seat. He took off his hat and squeezed the water out of it, took off his jacket and tie, squeezed those, too. The address on the card was still legible; he gave it to Emily, and she nodded.

"Did you find a phonograph?" he asked.

Emily's cheeks turned red. "I fell asleep," she said, keeping her eyes on the road.

Unwin opened the heating vents and settled back into the seat. They were headed uptown now, and through the gray drifts of rain to the north, beyond the farthest reaches of the city, he could see green hills, distant woods. Had he been there once, as a child? He seemed to remember those hills, those woods, and a game he played there with other children. It involved hiding from one another; hiding and then waiting. Hide and wait—is that what the game was called? No, it involved seeking, too. Watch and seek?

"Screed thinks you're guilty of murder," said Emily.

Unwin remembered his conversation with the detective on the twenty-ninth floor, how he had given Lamech's memo to him. Screed must have gone upstairs soon after. He probably found the corpse before the messenger did.

"What do you think?" Unwin asked.

"I think you're going to clear your name," she said. Her cheeks were still red, and there was something very much like passion in her voice. "I think you're going to solve the biggest mystery yet."

Unwin closed his eyes as the air from the vents slowly warmed him. He listened to the sound of the windshield wipers sweeping over the glass. Watch and follow? Hide and watch? Follow and seek?

Maybe he was confused. Maybe he had never played a game like that at all.

IT WAS DARK WHEN UNWIN WOKE, and his clothes were dry. Through the passenger window, he saw a low stone wall. Behind it a copse of red-leafed maple trees dripped in the light of a streetlamp. He was alone. He reached down and found his briefcase by his feet, but his umbrella was gone.

He opened the door and clambered out onto the sidewalk, jacket and tie over his arm. The air from City Park was cool and smelled of soil, of moldering things. A row of tall buildings stood opposite, the light from their windows illuminating shafts of rain over the street. Emily was gone. Had she finally seen through his facade and abandoned him?

A man in a gray overcoat emerged from the park with two small dogs on leashes. He paused when he saw Unwin, and both the dogs growled. The man seemed to approve and let them go on growling. A minute passed before he pulled them away down the block.

Unwin put on his tie, slipped into his jacket and buttoned it. He considered hailing a taxicab—not to take him to the Gilbert Hotel but to take him home. No cars moved on the block, however, and now he saw Emily, coming toward him from across the street. Her black raincoat was cinched around her waist, and she walked with one hand in her pocket. She did not look like a detective's assistant. She looked like a detective.

Without a word she handed him his umbrella, took the keys from her pocket, and opened the trunk. Together they lifted the bicycle out, and Unwin set it against the lamppost.

"Everything's set," Emily said. "There's a little restaurant in the back, but Miss Greenwood isn't in there. You'll have to go straight to her room. I've already spoken to the desk clerk. No one will stop you from going up."

Unwin looked across the street and noticed the sign over the door from which she had come. The cursive script was lit by an overhanging lamp: *The Gilbert*.

"You've done great work, Emily. I think you should take some time off now. Lie low, as they say."

Emily stood with him under his umbrella. She moved in very close and reached a hand up to his chest. He felt as he had that morning, in the office on the twenty-ninth floor—that the two were shut in together, without enough space between them. He could smell her lavender perfume. She was unbuttoning his jacket.

Unwin stepped away, but Emily held to his jacket. Then he saw why. He had put the buttons in the wrong holes, and she was fixing his mistake. She undid the rest of the buttons, then straightened the sides and refastened them.

When she was finished, she closed her eyes and tilted her head back, lifting her face toward his. "Those closest to you," she said, "those to whom you trust your innermost thoughts and musings, are also the most dangerous. If you fail to treat them as enemies, they are certain to become the worst you have. Lie if you have to, withhold what you can, and brook no intimacy which fails to advance the cause of your case."

Unwin swallowed. "That sounds familiar."

"It ought to," she said. She opened her eyes and patted his briefcase. "Don't worry, I put your book back where I found it. And I only took a peek. I think that page is especially interesting. Don't you?"

Emily closed the trunk and went around the car. He followed her with the umbrella, holding it over her head until she was inside. She rolled down her window and said, "There's something I've been wondering about, Detective Unwin. Say we do find Sivart. What will happen to you?"

"I'm not sure. This may be my only case."

"What about me, then?"

Unwin looked at his feet. He could think of nothing to say.

"That's what I thought," Emily said. She rolled up the window, and Unwin stepped aside as she pulled away from the curb. He watched the car veer down a street into the park and vanish among the trees, heard its gears shifting. When it was gone, he walked his bicycle across the street to the hotel, found an alleyway beside it, and left it chained to a fire escape.

Not until he had entered the hotel lobby and exchanged nods with the desk clerk did he realize that Emily had admitted to knowing his reason for coming here, even though he had never mentioned Miss Greenwood's name.

THE WOMAN WHO HAD introduced herself as Vera Truesdale answered her door on the second knock. She wore the same old-fashioned dress, black with lace collar and cuffs, but it was wrinkled now. Her hair was down, wavy and tousled. There were streaks of white in it that Unwin had failed to notice that morning. In the room beyond, the little lace cap lay folded on the pillow, and a black telephone was sunk in the folds of the untidy bed.

Her red-rimmed eyes were wide open. "Mr. Lamech," she said. "I didn't expect you to come in person."

"All part of the job," Unwin said.

She took his coat and hat, then closed the door behind him and went into the kitchenette. "I have some scotch, I think, and some soda water."

What had he read in the *Manual*, about poisons and their antidotes? Not enough to take any chances. "Nothing for me, thanks."

Unwin glanced around the room. An unfastened suitcase lay on a chair, and her purse was on the table beside it. In Lamech's office she had said she arrived in the city about three weeks ago—that much may have been true. But in a corner of the room, on a table of its own, was an electric phonograph. Had she brought this with her, too, or purchased it after she arrived? A number of records were stacked beside it.

She came back with a drink in her hand and pointed to one of the two windows. Both offered dismal views of the building beside the hotel, an alley's width away. "That's the one that's always open in the morning," she said, "even though I lock it at night."

The window gave out onto the fire escape. Unwin examined the latch and found it sturdy. He wondered how long he could get away with this impersonation. Miss Greenwood might already have found him out and was only playing along. He would have to take risks while he still could.

"Do you mind if I put something on the phonograph?"

"I suppose not," she said, nearly making it a question.

Unwin took the record from his briefcase and slid it out of its cover. He set the pearly disk on the turntable, switched on the machine, and lowered the needle. At first there was only static, followed by a rhythmic shushing. Then a deeper sound, a burbling that was almost a man's voice. The recording was distorted, though, and Unwin could not make out a word.

"This is horrid," she said. "Please shut it off."

Unwin leaned closer to the amplifier bell. The speechlike sound continued, stopped, started again. And then he heard it. It was the same thing he had heard on the telephone at the museum café, when he snatched the receiver from the man with the blond beard.

A rustling sound, and the warbling of pigeons.

Miss Greenwood set down her drink and came forward, nearly catching her foot on the rug. She lifted the needle from the record and gave Unwin an angry, questioning look. "I don't see what this has to do with my case," she said.

He put the record back in its sleeve and returned it to his briefcase. "That sleepiness routine disguised your limp this morning," he said.

She flinched at the mention of her injury. "I read the late edition," she said. "Edward Lamech is dead. You're no watcher."

"And you're no Vera Truesdale."

Something in her face changed then. The circles under her eyes were as dark as ever, but she did not look tired at all. She picked up her drink and sipped it. "I'll call hotel security."

"Okay," Unwin said, surprised at his own boldness. "But first I want to know why you came to Lamech's office this morning. It wasn't to hire Sivart. He went looking for you days ago."

That made her set her drink down. "Who are you?"

"Detective Charles Unwin," he said. "Edward Lamech was my watcher." He showed her his badge.

"You're a detective without a watcher," she said. "That's a unique position to be in. I want to hire you."

"It doesn't work that way. Detectives are assigned cases."

"Yes, by their watchers. And you don't have one. So I wonder what you're working on, exactly."

"I'm trying to find Detective Sivart. He went to the Municipal Museum, but you know that. Because it was you, wasn't it, who showed that museum attendant the Oldest Murdered Man's gold tooth?"

She considered this with obvious interest but did not reply. "What time is it?" she said.

He checked his watch. "Nine thirty."

"I want to show you something, Detective." She led him back to the doorway but did not open it. She pointed to the peephole and said, "Look there."

Unwin leaned in to look, then thought better of turning his back on Cleopatra Greenwood. She took a few steps away and opened her hands, as though to show that she was unarmed. "I trusted you enough to let you in, didn't I?"

He hesitated.

"Hurry," she said, almost whispering. "You'll miss it."

Unwin looked through the peephole. At first he had only a fish-eyed view of the door across the hall. Then a red-coated bellhop appeared with a covered tray in his hand. He set it on the floor in front of the opposite door, knocked twice, and went away. No one came for the food.

"Keep watching," Miss Greenwood said.

The door opened slowly, and an old man wearing a tattered frock coat peered into the hall. He had an antique service revolver in his hand and was polishing it with a square of blue cloth. He looked each way, and when he was satisfied that the hall was empty, he slid the revolver into his pocket. Then he picked up the tray and went back inside.

Miss Greenwood was grinning. "Do you know who that was?" she said.

"No," Unwin said, though the man did seem vaguely familiar. This game, whatever it was, was making him nervous.

"Colonel Baker."

"Now you're deliberately trying to rattle me," Unwin said.

"I'm trying to do good by you, Detective Unwin. You ought to realize by now that things are rather more complicated than you may have believed. Everyone knows that Colonel Baker is dead. Everyone knows that Sivart walked away victorious, case closed. Nonetheless, Colonel Baker is living across the hall from me. He orders room service every night. He likes a late dinner."

If not for the revolver, Unwin might have gone over there to prove that what Miss Greenwood had said was a lie. The Three Deaths of Colonel Baker was one of Sivart's most celebrated cases, and Unwin's file was a composition of the first order—no clerk could deny it.

Colonel Sherbrooke Baker, a decorated war hero, had become famous for the secret battlefield tactic that made him seem to be in two places at once. But in his later years, he was best known for his unparalleled collection of military memorabilia. In addition to several pieces of interest to historians of the ancient world, the collection contained numerous antique rifles and sidearms, some of which had belonged to the country's founding fathers. Others, experts agreed, were the weapons that had fired the first shots of various wars, revolutionary, civil, and otherwise. Few were allowed to study or even view these extraordinary items, however, for Colonel Baker spoke of them with pride but guarded them with something very much like jealousy.

In the colonel's will, he left all of his possessions to his son Leopold. But there was a stipulation: the colonel's precious collection was to remain in the family and remain whole.

A businessman who was not very good with business, Sivart had written of Leopold Baker. When the colonel died, his son was happy to accept the considerable sum his father had left him. He was less happy to learn that he had inherited the collection as well. All too vivid in Leopold's mind was the afternoon, as a boy of twelve, when he had interrupted his father's polishing to ask him to play a game of catch. "This," the colonel had told him, holding a long, thin blade before his eyes, "is the misericord. Medieval footmen slipped it between the plates of fallen knights' armor, once the battle was over, to find out who was dead and who was only pretending. Think of that while you sleep tonight."

The will contained no consequence for disobeying the colonel's wishes, so he was only three days in the grave when the auction commenced. Attendance was good, the hall filled with the many historians, museum curators, and military enthusiasts the colonel had spurned through the years. Once the bidding began, however, lot after lot was won by the same strange gentleman, seated at the back of the room with a black veil over his face. It was whispered through the hall that this was a representative of Enoch Hoffmann, whose taste for antiquities was by then well known. Leopold suspected it, too, but he was not displeased, for the stranger's pockets seemed bottomless.

At the end of the auction, the gentleman met with Leopold to settle their accounts. It was then that he pulled back his veil and revealed himself as Colonel Baker. The old man had not died, only faked his death to test his son's loyalty. The colonel declared his will invalid—he was very much alive after all—and reclaimed all that Leopold had thought was his.

That was when Sivart became involved. His report began: *The assignment was on my desk first thing this morning. Truth is, I'd expected it. A man plays a trick like that and word gets around. Word gets around enough, someone gets into trouble. To wit, the body of the colonel was discovered on the floor of his library early in the a.m., stab wounds eight in number. The weapon was the misericord from the colonel's own collection. The fallen pretender has been found out.*

My client? Leopold Baker, primary suspect.

It was the first time Sivart had been tasked with proving someone's innocence, and Unwin sensed that the job made him grumpy. Sivart took his time getting to the Baker estate, and his examination of the corpse was cursory.

Yes, he wrote, *dead.*

I told them to leave the body where it was and went for a walk. So many secrets in that place it gave me a headache. Through the trapdoor under the statue in the foyer, up a set of stairs behind a rack in the wine cellar, down the tunnel under the greenhouse. All this just to find a comfortable chair, probably the only one in the place.

That was in the colonel's study, which was where I found the whiskey, and also the first interesting thing about this case.

In the desk Sivart discovered the colonel's own writings about his military days. There the colonel revealed the secret behind the battlefield technique that had won him his glory. He seemed to appear in two places at once because he had a double, a brother named Reginald, whose identity was kept a secret from military command.

What almost got them caught was the matter of which hand to use when firing their weapons: Sherbrooke was left-handed and Reginald right-handed. A general noticed the discrepancy once, and Sherbrooke said, "In the trenches, sir, I am ambidextrous. In the mess hall, I use a fork." That made so little sense that it worked.

I took the whiskey with me and finished it before I could get back to the library. They'd left the body like I'd asked, though the coroner was getting prickly. I became intensely earnest with him, a tactic that usually works with men of his disposition. Is it wrong of me, clerk, to imagine sometimes that I am living in a radio play?

> Detective: Here, on the victim's right hand, between his thumb and
>   forefinger. What do you see?
> Coroner: Why, those are ink stains. What of them?
> (Arm thumps against floor.)
> Detective: Colonel Sherbrooke Baker was left-handed. Sinister, if
>   you will. Don't you think it strange that a left-handed man
>   would hold a pen with his right hand?
> Coroner: Well, I—
> Detective: And those wounds. The angle of the thrusts. Did your
>   examination reveal whether the killer was left- or right-handed?
> (Papers leafed through.)
> Coroner: Let me see. Ah. Ah! The dagger was held in the left hand!
> Detective: Precisely right, because Sherbrooke Baker is the killer, not
>   the victim. This body is that of Reginald, his brother.
> (Cue the strings.)

Reginald had learned of his brother's death and came to claim his rightful share of the loot, only to find the colonel still alive. The two men had not spoken in years, and neither was happy to see the other. Their estrangement, necessitated by the deception committed in their youth, was lodged deeply. Sherbrooke had reaped the majority of the benefits from their scheme, but this did not make him generous. The misericord was one of his favorite pieces, and he had always wanted an excuse to use it.

Sivart tracked the colonel to a hideout in an old fort in City Park. *He was half mad when we found him, and his retreat was quick. We lost his trail in the woods east of the fort. Then, an hour later, we got the report about the man in military uniform standing on the bridge over the East River. He'd jumped by the time I arrived.*

The final report in the case, a few days hence, was the shortest in the series.

A jacket washed up today, though with so many medals pinned to it, it's a wonder it didn't sink to the bottom and stay there. No doubt about whose it was. The Colonel had to die three times before it would stick. Leo's name is cleared, and I'm told that he's paid the Agency in full. Not a word of thanks from him, though, and my paycheck, I see, is in the same amount as usual.

"THE BODY WAS NEVER recovered," Unwin admitted, "but no conclusion could be drawn, other than the death of Colonel Baker. The case file is seamless, every clue set down in perfect detail. . . ." He trailed off, and saw in his mind the glint of gold in the mouth of the Oldest Murdered Man. He and Sivart had been wrong once; could they have been wrong again?

Miss Greenwood was watching him.

"The Oldest Murdered Man a fake," he said. "Colonel Baker alive despite three deaths. Is that what you're telling me, Miss Greenwood? And what about Sivart's other cases? You cannot dispute his success on The Man Who Stole November Twelfth."

"I'm sorry I lied to you," she said. "I did come to the Agency for help, but I knew what sort of reception I would receive if I used my real name. Please sit with me, Detective."

Unwin disliked the way she used his title. It sounded like encouragement. Still, he followed her back into the room. She moved her suitcase off the chair for him and sat down on the edge of the bed.

"I did look for Sivart when I first arrived in town," she said. "I needed his help. But by the time I saw him, about a week ago, he was shabby and a bit out of his head. It was here, in the lobby of the hotel. He said he couldn't stay. He said he'd seen something he couldn't believe."

"The gold filling," Unwin said. "I saw it, too. And Zlatari told me Sivart was at the Forty Winks about a week ago. He was reading something." Unwin heard in his mind a warning like a typewriter bell and stopped himself. He was giving information he did not have to give.

But Miss Greenwood only shrugged. "Probably his copy of the *Manual*. He was getting desperate."

"You're familiar with *The Manual of Detection*?"

"Know thy enemy," she said.

Unwin looked at his lap. Miss Greenwood was his enemy, of course. But now that they were speaking plainly, he found himself wishing it could be otherwise. Was this how Sivart had felt, each time he got her wrong?

She said, "I went to Lamech because I thought he would know what had happened to Sivart. I was concerned. Naturally, I was surprised when I found you sitting there."

"You hid it very well."

"Old habits," she said.

The telephone rang. It gleamed black against the stark white sheet and seemed louder for the contrast.

Miss Greenwood looked suddenly tired again. "Too soon," she said.

"If you have to answer it—"

"No!" she said. "Don't you answer it either."

So they sat staring at the telephone, waiting for the ringing to stop. Miss Greenwood swayed a little and breathed deeply, as though fighting off nausea. Unwin counted eleven rings before the caller gave up.

Miss Greenwood's eyes fluttered closed, and she fell back onto the bed. The quiet of the room was total. He could not hear the movements of the other hotel guests, could not hear their voices. Where was the noise of automobile traffic? He wished idly for any sound at all, for even a cat to call out from the alleyway.

Unwin rose from his chair and said Miss Greenwood's name, but she did not stir. He shook her shoulder—no response.

At a time like this, he thought, Sivart would take the opportunity to investigate. Perhaps he ought to do the same. He lifted Miss Greenwood's drink and sniffed it, but for what, he was not sure. The ice had nearly melted—that was all he could deduce. With his foot he raised the lid on her suitcase and saw that the clothes inside were neatly folded.

He brought the glass into the kitchenette, left it in the sink. Was Miss Greenwood, like his assistant, the victim of some sleeping sickness? Nothing of the kind had ever been mentioned in Sivart's reports. Perhaps her exhaustion had simply overtaken her. But what could have made her so tired?

He watched her lying on the bed—her breaths came slowly, as though her sleep were a deep one. He wondered whether he should cover her with the sheet or remove her shoes. Miss Greenwood had seemed, for a moment, generous with him. He would have to wait for her to wake up, and hope she would still be willing to talk.

He sat beside her and, without thinking, drew *The Manual of Detection* from his briefcase and opened it on his lap. He found the section Detective Pith had recommended to him that morning at Central Terminal, on page ninety-six.

If the detective does not maintain secrets of his own—if he does not learn firsthand the discipline required to keep a thing hidden from everyone he knows, and pay the personal costs incurred by such an endeavor—then he will never succeed in learning the secrets of others, nor does he deserve to. It is a long road that stretches from what a person says to what a person hides by saying it. He who has not mapped the way for himself will be forever lost upon it.

Unwin could picture himself on that road: a narrow avenue between tall rows of tenements, just a few lights on in each building, and all the doors locked. In both directions the road went all the way down to the horizon.

Did Unwin have any secrets of his own? Only that he was not really a detective, that he had been making unofficial trips for unofficial reasons—that he had considered, for a moment long enough to buy the ticket, abandoning everything he knew. But those secrets were liabilities.

When he glanced from the book, he was startled to find Miss Greenwood sitting up in bed. She carefully smoothed the front of her dress with her hands.

"You're awake," he said.

She did not reply. Her eyes were open, but she did not seem to see him as she rose from the bed. She went across the room without speaking.

"Miss Greenwood," he said, getting up again. He put the *Manual* back in his briefcase.

Ignoring him, she went to the window and unlatched it. Before he could reach her, she had thrown the window open. The chill autumn air pervaded the room immediately, and rain blew in from the alley, dampening everything.

EIGHT

On Surveillance

**It is the most obvious of mandates, to keep one's eyes
open, but the wakefulness required of the detective is not
of the common sort. He must see without seeming
to see, and watch even when he is looking away.**

Miss Greenwood climbed out onto the fire escape and balanced
on the toes of her high-heeled shoes as she descended the pre-
cipitous steps. Unwin was about to call her name again when he remembered something he had heard about the dangers of waking a
sleepwalker. He imagined her eyes popping open, a moment of confusion, a foreshortened cry. . . .

He dreaded the thought of going back into the rain, but he gathered
his things and followed her down two flights of steps, past the dark
windows of other hotel rooms. At the bottom he found his bicycle
chained to the base of the fire escape. He did not have time to unlock
it and bring it with him—Miss Greenwood was already on her way
out of the alley. He caught up with her on the sidewalk and opened
his umbrella over both their heads.

Was this what she had in mind when she said she wanted to hire
him? On the next block he followed her past the sweeping limestone

facade of the Municipal Museum as the rain dampened the cuffs of his slacks and the wind wrestled with his umbrella. She turned right at the next corner and led them away from City Park, then headed north. On that block a man came out of an apartment building with a sack over his shoulder. He drew up alongside them, and Unwin saw he was dressed only in his bathrobe. His eyes, like Miss Greenwood's, were unreadable. From within his sack—nothing more than a pillowcase—came the ticking of clocks, maybe a hundred of them.

Other sleepers joined them as they walked, women and men of varying ages in varying states of disarray, pajamaed, underdrawered, dripping. All bore sacks of alarm clocks over their shoulders, and all seemed to know where they were going.

Unwin felt he had stumbled into the mystery he was supposed to be solving, the one to which Lamech had planned to assign him. He suddenly hated that smug, silent corpse on the thirty-sixth floor. He wanted nothing to do with this mystery, but all he could do was allow himself to be dragged along by its current.

They walked ten, twelve, fifteen blocks. At the north end of town, they came to a part of the city that did not seem to belong to the city at all. Here a broad stone wall girded a wide, hilly expanse. A pair of iron gates, two stories tall, had been left open to allow the sleeping congregation through. The sycamores lining the drive beyond dropped samaras that spun in the rain as they fell.

At the top of the hill crouched a grand, high-gabled house. Lights shone in every window, illuminating stretches of wild gardens all around. The place seemed familiar to Unwin—had Sivart described it in one of his reports? Above the door was a sign depicting a fat black cat seated with the moon at his back, a cigar in one paw and a cocktail glass in the other. Written in an arc over the moon were the words CAT & TONIC. Unwin was sure he had never heard of it.

Beneath the portico a line of sleepers awaited admittance into the club. Unwin's group joined the line, and others gathered behind them.

A butler ushered them inside, welcoming each guest with a sleepy nod.

"What is this?" Unwin asked him, collapsing his umbrella. "What's going on?"

The butler did not seem to understand the question. He blinked a few times, then squinted at Unwin as though from a great distance.

The crowd pushed forward, and Unwin was driven into the club. The entry hall was dominated by a wide staircase. Most of the guests proceeded into a room on the right. It was a gambling parlor, and attendants and players alike were sleeping. There were no chips. Instead the players pushed heaps of alarm clocks over the tables. When the house had won enough of the clocks, butlers carted them away in wheelbarrows.

Emily was here among the players, dressed in yellow pajamas. Her face looked smaller without her glasses, and the rain had turned her hair a dark copper color. She had her own sack of alarm clocks, and for the moment she seemed to be winning. She laughed aloud, revealing her small crooked teeth. Others in the room, after a delay, laughed with her. Unwin felt as though he were looking into an aquarium: everyone in it breathed the same water, but sound and sense moved slowly among them.

Emily rolled the dice, won again, and a shirtless man with thick eyebrows put his arm around her shoulder. Unwin went toward them, thinking to shake Emily awake if he had to, but Miss Greenwood was suddenly at his side, her arm linked with his. She drew him away, back into the entry hall and through a curtained doorway opposite the gaming room.

Here dozens of guests were seated at tables, some smoking, some muttering, some laughing, all of them asleep. Sleepwalking waiters went among them, bringing fresh drinks and cigars. On a tasseled stage was a quartet of washboard, jug, rubber-band bass, and accordion. Unwin recognized the accordion player. It was Arthur, the custodian he had seen that morning. He had been sleeping when Unwin and Detective Pith were with him at Central Terminal, and he was still sleeping, still dressed in his gray coveralls.

Miss Greenwood did not search for an empty seat; instead she went toward a door at the right of the stage. Guarding it were Jasper and Josiah Rook. The twins were not asleep. They stood with their hands in their pockets, scrutinizing the crowd with their trapdoor eyes. Unwin half closed his own eyes to blend in, and let go of Miss Greenwood's arm.

Jasper (or was it Josiah?) opened the door for her, and Josiah (Jasper?) greeted her by name. They went with her through the door and closed it behind them.

Unwin wandered back to the tables. The guests went on with their dream-party, and he was invisible to them. He looked for an empty seat, thinking he should conceal himself in case the Rooks returned.

Then he saw her. The woman in the plaid coat was seated alone at a table in the center of the room. Beneath her coat she wore a blue nightgown. She tapped her glass of milk and stared toward the stage with glassy gray eyes.

What was she doing here? First she had taken his place on the fourteenth floor, and now she was ensnared by whatever madness had claimed Emily and Miss Greenwood. Could it be that the fault was Unwin's, that his unofficial trips had embroiled her in this dilemma of his? Detective Pith must have seen him watching her at Central Terminal, must have thought she was a secret contact. Perhaps the Agency had hired her to keep her close, promoted him to keep him closer.

Unwin went toward her, thinking that he had to explain, had to apologize for all the trouble. Assure her that everything would be set right again, as soon as he found Sivart. He stood to her side and took off his hat. "Are you waiting for someone?" he asked.

She perked one ear, though she did not look at him. "Someone," she said.

"Of course. I can't imagine you'd be here alone."

"Alone," she echoed.

Unwin checked his watch. It was nearly two o'clock. On a normal day, in only a matter of hours, he would be at Central Terminal. She would be there, too, and he would watch her and say nothing.

"I still remember the first day I saw you," he told her. "I got out of bed and took a bath, ate oatmeal with raisins. I put my shoes on in the hallway because they squeak if I wear them in the house and that bothers the neighbors. I don't blame them, really."

He could not tell if she understood what he was saying, but she did seem to hear. So he sat with her and laid his umbrella on his lap. "I ride my bicycle to work," he said. "I've perfected a technique to keep my umbrella open while riding. The weather . . . well, you know how it is. Sometimes I think it will never stop. The rain will fill up the bay, and one day the city will be gone, just like that. The sea will take it."

He looked around; no one was listening. He was the only person awake, but he might as well have been alone and dreaming. He wanted, suddenly, to tell her everything.

"That morning," he said, "the morning I first saw you. Something was different. No one was on the streets. At first I couldn't understand why. Then I realized that I hadn't turned off my alarm clock. I hadn't needed to. I'd woken hours before it was set to ring, hours before I should have been awake. The day hadn't started yet, and there I was, ready for work.

"I didn't know what to do with myself. I'd already made it halfway to the office by the time I figured out what had happened. I was standing outside Central Terminal. I've never had to take the train anywhere, because I've lived in this city my entire life. But suddenly I knew I could never go to work again. I really don't know why."

"Why," said the woman in the plaid coat.

"Well, because Enoch Hoffmann was gone," Unwin said. "The

Rook brothers, Cleopatra Greenwood, they'd all left. Sivart's reports were—only reports. I could tell he didn't care about the work anymore. What was the point?"

"The point."

"Yes, I'm coming to it. I went into the terminal. I bought a cup of coffee and drank most of it. It was awful. I took a schedule of trains from the information booth, and I even bought a ticket. I was going to go into the country, and I was never coming back. Sivart had imagined his cottage in the woods—why shouldn't I have mine? By then it was twenty-six minutes after seven in the morning. That's when I saw you. You came through the revolving doors at the east end of the terminal, and you went to Gate Fourteen and waited. I watched you. I pretended to look at my train schedule, but all I could do was watch you. And when the train arrived, and no one came to meet you, and you turned around and went back into the city, I knew—just as certainly as I had known a moment before that I could never go back to work—that I *would* go back to work, that I could not leave the city. Not while you were in it, left alone to wait."

"Wait," said the woman in the plaid coat.

"I will," Unwin said. "I have a bicycle that I clean and oil every day, and I have a hat that I'll never part with. My umbrella does everything it's supposed to do. I have a train ticket, and I keep it in my pocket, just in case that person you're waiting for ever gets back. But what am I supposed to do in the meantime? I still don't know your name."

The woman in the plaid coat was applauding—all the guests were. Unwin turned to look at the stage. Miss Greenwood had joined the musicians. She went to the microphone, and the music struck up, slow and somber. Arthur leaned into his accordion as he played, and in his hands it breathed like a living thing. The words Miss Greenwood sang were unfamiliar to Unwin, except for the refrain, which he knew from somewhere. Maybe he had heard it on the radio. Yes, it might have been the song that was playing in Zlatari's kitchen, behind the curtain in the Forty Winks.

> *Still I hear that old song*
> *And I'm sure I belong*
> *In my dream of your dream of me.*

Applause rose up again, and several guests threw long-stemmed roses onto the stage. She caught a few of the flowers and let the others fall at her feet. Unwin clapped, too.

"Mr. Charles Unwin?"

He turned in his seat. Detective Pith, very much awake and still in his herringbone suit, stood at his shoulder. "You," growled Pith. "Outside. Now."

Unwin rose from his chair and followed the detective from the room. They went outside and stood under the portico, where a few sleepwalkers were quietly puffing on cigars and mumbling insensibly to one another. Pith swung his hat as though he were going to hit him. "Damn it, Unwin, are you trying to get us both killed? What are you doing here? You came with Greenwood, didn't you? This is no good, Unwin, no good at all. Screed's trying to pin a murder on you, and now you're hanging around with Greenwood."

"I'm trying to find Sivart," Unwin said. "I thought she might know where he went."

"The Agency's through with the guy. If word gets out that you're looking for him, it could bother people high up, and I mean very high up. People you don't want to bother."

Unwin fiddled with his umbrella; he could not get the clasp buttoned.

"Now, I didn't expect to see you out in the field yet. That takes guts, Unwin, I'll give you that. But it doesn't take brains. You should have spent a day or two with your copy of the *Manual.* Have you read a word of it yet? If you want my advice, you'll get out of here and forget about the Cat & Tonic, forget about Cleo Greenwood. Talking the way you were in there! Do you know how long it took to set up this sting?"

The door burst open, and the Rook brothers stepped outside. Unwin immediately closed his eyes, then opened them enough to see what was happening. Pith was doing the same. But Jasper and Josiah went straight to him.

"My brother," Jasper said to Detective Pith, "has advised me to advise you to quit the somnambulism act."

Pith opened his eyes, and Unwin sidled over to where the others were smoking cigars. A sleepwalker offered him one, and he took it.

"Good evening, gents," said Pith. "I thought I was having a bad dream. Looks like I'm having two at once."

Jasper pointed toward the sycamores, and Pith started walking. They went two dozen paces from the house, and then Jasper told him to stop. Pith looked directly at Unwin and said loudly enough for him to hear, "You're done for, you louts. We have our best people working on this. Our very best."

Josiah drew a pistol from his coat, and Detective Pith took off his hat and held it over his heart. Josiah put the gun against the hat and fired once. Pith fell face-up in the rain.

AT THE SOUND OF THE SHOT, the cigar smokers started walking in circles and muttering but did not wake. The Rooks carried Pith's body to where their steam truck was parked. The bed was loaded with ticking clocks, and the alarm bells clinked sullenly under Pith's weight.

The Rooks had Edwin Moore, too. He was still in his gray museum attendant's uniform and lay beside Pith, bound at the wrists and ankles. The old man was unconscious and shivering. How long had they kept him out in the rain?

The Rooks were coming back up the drive now. Unwin ran inside.

A crowd of sleepwalkers was streaming through the curtained door, troubled and confused by the sound of the gunshot. He pushed through them and climbed the stairs, looking for a place to hide. He opened the first door he saw and went through it.

The room was wallpapered in a dark red pattern. A fire burned in the hearth, crackling and warm. On the back wall was hung an array of antique weapons, swords and sidearms rivaling the collection at the Municipal Museum. Now he understood why he had recognized this place. It was the mansion that had once belonged to Colonel Sherbrooke Baker, and this the very room where he had murdered his brother. Here was the precious hoard, complete and perfectly maintained. Had his son Leopold kept it through the years?

No: one object did not belong with the Baker estate. In a glass case on its own table, small and shriveled and yellow, lay the Oldest Murdered Man, the real one. Unwin had stumbled upon the trophy room of Enoch Hoffmann.

Two wingback chairs were angled toward the hearth. In one of them sat a short man in blue pajamas with red trim. He turned his squarish face toward Unwin and with lidded eyes seemed to see. He held a brandy snifter in one hand and gestured for Unwin to sit, then poured a second glass and set it on the pedestal table.

What a fool Unwin had been, mourning for all those years the disappearance of the nefarious biloquist. No report could be worth this encounter.

Hoffmann offered him a cigar cutter, and Unwin realized he was still holding the cigar the sleepwalker had given him outside. He set it down on the table. "Mr. Hoffmann," he said, "I really don't want to be your rival."

Hoffmann chuckled to himself, or maybe snored. He picked up a cigar and clipped it.

"I don't want to know if you killed Edward Lamech," Unwin went on. "Or whose body is in the museum, or what you want with Edwin

Moore. I don't even want to know what you're planning to do with all those alarm clocks. I just want to find Detective Sivart so I can have my old job back."

Hoffmann shrugged. He lit the cigar and puffed at it. Then he raised his glass as though in toast and waited until Unwin raised his own. The glasses met, and they drank. The brandy was hot on Unwin's lips.

"If you can't tell me where he is," Unwin said, "then maybe you can tell me something about one of your guests. She always wears a plaid coat."

Hoffmann leapt out of his chair and threw his brandy snifter into the fire. The glass exploded, and the flames burst from the hearth. Then Hoffmann leaned against the mantelpiece, head cradled in his arms, shoulders heaving.

Unwin rose and went to him. He wanted to stop himself but found he could not. He put one hand on the magician's shoulder. Hoffmann spun and glared at him with unopen eyes.

The brandy was still burning its way toward Unwin's stomach. "Please," he said, and what he wanted to say was, *Please, don't wake up,* but the words were stuck in his throat and the brandy erased them. Unwin stumbled backward, and the fire leapt again, and the music of accordion and rubber band swelled from below.

Gagging on brandy and smoke, Unwin fled from the room, following the music.

Downstairs everyone was dressed so well. He loosened his collar and took a few deep breaths, feeling his pulse slow. He was glad he had finally joined the party. Emily Doppel came from the gaming room, and the man who accompanied her was no longer shirtless; in fact, he wore a double-breasted suit of a very fine cut. When she saw Unwin, she pushed her escort away and came up to him. "What do you think of the dress?" she asked.

It was black, cut low in the front, and reached nearly to the floor. It was, Unwin meant to say, very flattering. The words failed him, but she smiled, took his hand, and led him to the dance floor. He still had his umbrella, so he hooked it over his wrist while they waltzed.

Emily laughed at him. "Admit it," she said. "You need me. You wouldn't be able to do any of this without me. You don't have to lie, Detective Unwin. You can trust me with your innermost thoughts and musings." She laughed again and added, "I'm a trustworthy gal!"

"I wouldn't lie to you," Unwin lied.

"I'm so glad we can finally say these things. It's different here, don't you think? Different from the office? And the car?" She was leading him in the dance, and he was thankful for it, because he was no better at dancing than he was at driving.

"Do you come here often?" he asked.

She looked around. "I'm really not sure."

"We're dreaming," he said. "I wasn't before, but now I am. We both are."

"You're sweet," Emily said. "Listen. Why don't you tell me why you're so interested in Cleopatra Greenwood? What's she got that's so special? Is she in on it, do you think? How do you know I'm not in on it? Don't ignore me, Detective Unwin."

He had caught sight of the woman in the plaid coat, still alone at her table. Unlike everyone else in the room, she wore the same clothes as before: a plain blue nightgown, blue slippers. Unwin noticed these kinds of things. He was a meticulous dreamer. "Excuse me," he said to Emily, and walked off the dance floor.

"Hey!" his assistant called after him.

He went up to the woman in the plaid coat. She was sitting with her legs crossed, watching the dancers. Her eyes were open now, gray and cool. They took Unwin in as he approached, and he struggled to keep balanced. It felt as though he were walking on sand while waves crashed about his legs.

"I don't remember inviting you," said the woman in the plaid coat.

"Isn't this Hoffmann's party?"

She sipped her milk. "Is that what he told you?"

The woman in the plaid coat seemed to know more than he knew. The revelation left him feeling helpless and strangely betrayed. "I thought I'd dragged you into something dangerous," he said, steadying himself with his umbrella. "But it's the other way around, isn't it? Who are you?"

She was starting to look annoyed with him. "It's too soon for us to speak," she said. "You haven't finished your report."

"My report?"

She sighed and looked at one of her slippered feet. "I am your clerk, you know."

The music had climbed to a new pitch, and the dancers swerved wildly over the floor. Arthur, the accordionist, bellowed while he played. Unwin turned to see the bassist's rubber band snap and fly across the room—with that, the set was over.

When he looked back, the woman in the plaid coat was gone. The party was ending, everyone was saying goodbye. What had happened to Emily? He had been rude to leave her on the dance floor alone.

Miss Greenwood found him and took his arm. "A few of us are headed back to my place," she said.

The butler nodded to them as they went out the door, and a dozen people congratulated Miss Greenwood on her performance. The man in the double-breasted suit was among them, but Emily was not. They went down among the sycamores together, and a bald man in a tuxedo grabbed a handful of fallen samaras and threw them into the air. They spun down around their heads, and he shouted, "Crazy little propellers!"

They returned to the Gilbert Hotel and climbed the fire escape to Miss Greenwood's room. The man in the tuxedo popped open a bottle of champagne, and they drank. Miss Greenwood laughed and dropped long-stemmed roses everywhere. Then the man in the tuxedo and the man in the double-breasted suit started fighting about which of them had given Miss Greenwood more flowers. After the first sloppy punches were thrown, she kicked them both out.

"I'm going to forget all of this," she said to Unwin. "He uses me, uses my voice, but keeps me in the dark. So you'll have to remember for both of us. That's why I hired you. To remember."

Unwin left. It was cold outside, and the walk was a long one. He could not tell if he was awake or asleep now—shadows fell at the wrong angles, and the streets curved where they should have been straight. The cold was real enough, however. His hand was a ball of ice around the handle of his umbrella. At last he found the narrow green door of his own apartment building and went upstairs.

A trail of red and orange leaves led from the door all the way into the bathroom.

Detective Sivart was in the tub. The water looked cold and was covered with leaves: a dark little pond. "This channel's closed to us now, Charlie. That woman, I was wrong about her. She broke my heart. Look." He pulled a torn leaf out of the water and slapped it onto his chest. It stuck fast.

When Unwin woke, he was on his bed, still wearing his clothes. His head throbbed, his alarm clock was missing, and someone was in the kitchen, making breakfast.

NINE

On Documentation

It is not enough to say that you have had a hunch.
Once written down, most such inklings reveal
themselves for what they are: something to be
tossed into a wishing well, not into a file.

The theft of November twelfth: who can think upon that black patch of the mind, lingering where a memory might be, and not feel cold, lost to it? It seeps like ink along the grooves of the fingertips. Who has not tried to scrub it away?

I was like the rest of you, Sivart wrote in his report. *Hoodwinked. Taken in. But then I had a hunch that morning, over breakfast. So what if hunches are against policy? I had one, clerk, and I acted on it. Lucky thing, too—for all of us.*

No one hired the Agency to solve the crime, because no one knew that it had been committed. Unwin went to sleep on Monday, November eleventh, and woke up on Wednesday, November thirteenth. He rode his bicycle the seven blocks to the Agency offices. He had been a faithful employee for eleven years, four months, and some-odd days, and it had never occurred to him, at this point in his career, to make unofficial trips for unofficial reasons.

On the fourteenth floor, the messengers brought no new assignment for him, so he passed the morning putting the finishing touches on a case from the previous week. It still needed a title. Unwin liked titles, even though the Agency filing system did not require them. Each case was numbered, and only the numbers were used in the official logs. Still, naming cases was a small and harmless pleasure, and occasionally useful, too. If a fellow clerk had a question about one case or another, using the name could save them both time.

Unwin was still pondering the possibilities over lunch. He had brought a sandwich with him in his briefcase. It was turkey and cheese on rye, his Wednesday sandwich. No better way to pass a Wednesday, he thought, than pondering titles over turkey and cheese on rye.

Nothing about this case had made it into the papers, so the clerks at neighboring desks had their eyes on Unwin's work whenever they thought he was not paying attention. He was always paying attention, though. Only when the file was completed, and for Unwin that meant titled, would his colleagues become privy to its contents.

As he finished his lunch, he became aware of an unusual number of telephone conversations taking place on the floor. Most of the other clerks were hunched over mouthpieces, mumbling. He sensed in their voices a mixture of fear and incredulity.

Were the families and friends of his colleagues calling to find out about his case? This was unprecedented. Unwin crushed his lunch bag and dropped it into the wastepaper basket. He knew by then what he was going to call the file—The Episode of the Facing Mirrors, after the case's most significant clue—but this show of discourtesy convinced him to delay the final processing for at least another hour.

More telephone calls came in while Unwin sorted papers and vetted old notes. Those who received the calls began to confer with one another, leaning over the aisles to whisper. If he had been deep in a case, Unwin would have found this immensely distracting.

The noise reached a crescendo when Lorraine, one of the most recent hires on the floor, slammed her receiver onto its cradle, flung back her head, and emitted a long, thin wail. As though in response, other clerks knocked stacks of pages off their own desks, rattled drawers, slammed typewriter keys, or went to the windows for air. Unwin, appalled and bewildered, threw himself over his files to protect them.

What had happened?

The overclerk's door opened, and Mr. Duden materialized for the first time that week. He jogged between the desks toward the center of the room, clutching his hair. "Stop!" he cried.

Unwin could see in the overclerk's eyes the same panic that had seized the others. Mr. Duden had not come to calm them; he had come to join them. "Stop everything you're doing!" he cried. "Everything is wrong! It isn't Wednesday, it's Tuesday!"

Unwin clutched his files more tightly. Mr. Duden was right—it *was* Tuesday, only two days since Unwin had woken to the ringing of the city's church bells. Yesterday's lunch had been cucumber and horseradish: his Monday sandwich.

He counted the number of times he had written the date since arriving that morning. *November thirteenth:* it was everywhere, in his notes, in memoranda, entries of at least four indices, the master log, the ancillary log, in the final sections of The Episode of the Facing Mirrors. He tried to multiply in his mind the number of errors he alone had committed by the number of people on the floor, and that by the number of floors in the Agency office building, but his calculative powers failed him. It would take weeks to undo the damage, and traces of the calamity were sure to abide indefinitely.

The story trickled in over the course of the afternoon, and the clerks gathered in circles at one desk or another, sharing new tidbits of information. Calls came in from people out of town who had noticed the discrepancy—Wednesday in the city and Tuesday everywhere else. There was chaos in the harbor: ships held in port or turned away by bewildered customs officials, goods piled on the wharf with no one to accept them, longshoremen brawling with sailors, radio officers trading insults on every frequency. Traffic on the major bridges halted as delivery trucks choked both lanes and drivers left their vehicles to huddle confused and indignant amid the mayhem. Appointment desks at beauty salons, employment bureaus, doctors' offices, and the courts were overwhelmed. At the schools children wept over examinations for which they had not studied.

Unwin remained in his own seat, trying not to listen to this news, working instead to list the corrections he would have to make. (He lost the list by the end of the day and would have to start over the next morning.)

That Hoffmann was responsible came as no surprise to anyone on the fourteenth floor, though it added to Unwin's dread the weight of impending responsibility. Evidently, the magician's criminal network extended well beyond the rickety sprawl of the Travels-No-More Carnival. His agents had somehow infiltrated all the major newspaper offices, radio stations, and civic departments, just to set the calendars ahead one day. But that did not explain how an additional X appeared on wall calendars in homes throughout the city. The biloquist might imitate any one of us, Unwin thought, but surely we are not all working for him.

Though the effects of the disruption were pervasive, it was at the Central Bank that the true purpose of Hoffmann's gambit was discovered. There a convoy of armored cars with a cargo of gold was slated to arrive midmorning. But because it was expected on Tuesday, and not Wednesday, no members of the bank staff were there to greet them. Hoffmann's own agents, dressed for the part, were ready to fill in. The gold went from one set of cars to another and would have left in them had Sivart not intervened.

It was all in the early edition the next day, the second issue of the city paper to bear the date of Wednesday, November thirteenth. Unwin skimmed the article in the elevator and went quickly to his desk. He had come to the office early and was the first to arrive on the fourteenth floor, except for Mr. Duden, who peeked through his office door and nodded gratefully. From the circles beneath the overclerk's eyes, Unwin guessed he had stayed through the night.

Sivart's report was already on Unwin's desk. It was improbably thin and, according to the cover page, the first and last in the series.

I don't think I really have to file a report on this one, Sivart began, *because I wasn't working on the Agency's dime. Call it a sick day if you like. Still, I'll give you a few of the details, and you can do what you want with them.*

There was little in the report that had not already appeared in the papers. Sivart said he had no idea how Hoffmann managed the trick; furthermore, he did not intend to find out. Unwin was dizzied by the implication—to file a case with no true solution!—but he read on.

Sivart, acting on that hunch of his, had alerted several other detectives from his floor and called them all down to the parking lot behind Central Bank. They staked out the place and waited for an hour. Hoffmann's agents arrived, not in their usual carnival remainders but driving a column of black trucks and dressed as bank staff. Sivart paid attention to one of them in particular.

The limp, he wrote, *was familiar.*

I had my men circle the place, just to be safe. Then I shimmied up to the lead vehicle and opened the door. The driver was picking his teeth in the mirror. I hit him as hard as was necessary and rolled him under the cab. Then I took his place and waited.

They were quick about their work. They had rehearsed. The one in charge got in beside me and let the hair out of her hat. "Okay," she said, "that's all of it."

"Not by a long shot," I said.

Greenwood wasn't happy to see me. And I saw a look on her face, one I'd never seen there before. I think it was surprise, but we might need a new name for it, just because it was hers.

"That's a lot of gold, honey. What's your cut?"

"I'll show you," she said, but I was ready for the dagger and got hold of the wrist on the other side of it.

I told her about my friends outside. I told her the game was up, goose cooked, et cetera. Eventually she came around, though neither of us was feeling good about it.

Listen, clerk. I wasn't on the job. Nobody assigned me to this case. What I did next I did as a citizen of this unfair land. I think I broke a law or two. If someone wants to come and arrest me for it, fine. I'm too tired to care.

I said, "We're going to round up your helpers, here, and we're going to bring the shiny stuff inside. But you, lady, you're going to leave. I don't ever want to see you in this town again."

"After this," she said, "you won't be the only one."

I left with her and let the others clean up. They're a decent bunch of yahoos, and none of them tried to stop me. I walked her to Central Terminal. We had pretzels on the way, just like old times, except we didn't have any old times, so we had to make them up. The whole town had gone mad, but the trains were still running. I paid for her ticket, one way, and we stood together awhile down on the platform. I won't tell you what we talked about. I won't tell you what happened just before I put her on the train. What business is it of yours, what we said?

I watched the train until the tunnel ate it.

Now I'm in my office. It's dark in here, and I'm choking on my own smoke. I'm starting to wonder about early retirement. I was wrong about her, clerk. As per usual. All wrong.

Unwin scoured the report again, searching for some better explanation. How did Sivart know what had happened that morning, when everyone else was fooled? The best explanation he could find, and the only conclusion the file would ever have, was Sivart's assertion that he had simply *remembered*.

UNWIN'S UMBRELLA WAS FOLDED on the bed beside him, droplets of water clinging to the black fabric. The bed was made, though the blankets were soggy and rumpled, as were his clothes. His briefcase was on the floor by the bed. From the kitchen came the sound of the icebox door clinking open and closed. A woman was humming to herself, and Unwin recognized the tune from Miss Greenwood's performance the night before.

It hurt too much to move his head, so he raised his wristwatch to his eyes. Six thirty-two—still early. But early for what? For work? They would apprehend him as soon as he brought his bicycle through the lobby door. For coffee at Central Terminal? They could be waiting for him anywhere: in line at the breakfast cart, next to the information booth, beneath the arch of Gate Fourteen. Even the woman in the plaid coat, it seemed, was in on it.

Then he remembered Edwin Moore, remembered how he had looked in the back of the steam truck, shivering among all those alarm clocks. *They will find me,* Moore had told him in the museum store-room, and he was right—they had found him. Would the Rooks murder him, as they murdered Detective Pith?

"Breakfast is ready," Emily called from the kitchen.

He sat up slowly. What was his assistant doing in his apartment? The sleep drained out of his head and pooled sickeningly in his stomach. He peeled the damp socks off his feet and dropped them onto the floor next to his shoes. He would have to find Edwin Moore, and quickly.

He rose shakily and went to the kitchen. Buttered toast was piled at the center of the table, and a pair of eggs, sunny side up, were set on a plate for him. Emily was swirling more butter over the hot surface of a skillet. It had been a late night for her, but she appeared rested, dressed now in a gray skirt and pinstripe blouse. The pencils in her hair were freshly sharpened.

"I hope you don't mind that I let myself in," she said. "I found the spare key in your desk yesterday. And since I couldn't go back to the office, I came right here. I figured you'd want to start on your case first thing."

"You stole my spare key?"

" 'Stole' is unfair," she said. She selected an egg from the open carton, cracked its shell, and spilled it into the skillet, all with one hand.

"Emily, we don't have time for breakfast. One of my . . . primary contacts. He's been kidnapped."

"Kidnapped? Who is he?"

Unwin wondered whether her question was genuine. Emily always seemed to know more than she let on. Still, she had only helped him thus far, so he would have to trust her for now. "He's a museum attendant. He—"

"Eat while you talk, Detective. I won't consider it rude."

It was more a command than a suggestion. Unwin helped himself to his plate from the table, took some toast, and ate standing up. He was hungrier than he thought, and the eggs were perfect, the whites cooked through but the yolks still runny. "His name's Edwin Moore," he said between bites. "He told me he used to work for the Agency."

She thought that over for a moment. "He could be valuable, then— if he's telling the truth. Where is he?"

"The Rook brothers took him."

She stood still, running the tip of her tongue along her crooked teeth. Then she sprinkled pepper over the eggs in the pan. "Nobody's seen the Rooks since Hoffmann went into hiding," she said.

"Emily, do you remember anything about last night? About the Cat & Tonic?"

He saw a twitch at the corner of her eye, magnified by her glasses. Some part of her knew what he was talking about, but she said, "I went straight home after I dropped you off at the Gilbert. I worked on a crossword puzzle and went to sleep. Cat, tonic. It *sounds* familiar. Did you do the same puzzle? I think maybe 'cat' was one of the answers, and so was 'tonic.' They might have shared their letter *t*. I'm not sure, though. I don't remember what the clues were."

She would not remember their dance, then, or anything else she had seen.

Unwin sat down. "Enoch Hoffmann's back," he told her. "The Rooks are working for him again, and they're up to something. Something big, I think. If we're ever going to find Sivart, we'll have to figure out what he was investigating when he disappeared."

She was quiet a moment. Then she flipped her eggs onto a plate and said, "In that case, you'll have to go to the Travels-No-More."

Unwin knew she was right. The Rooks had always operated out of the carnival—they arrived in the city with it thirteen years before. They would not have taken Moore to the Forty Winks: too many questions to answer there. But in the lightless center of Caligari's, they could carry on with their plans undisturbed.

Emily brought her plate to the table and sat down, then unfolded a napkin on her lap. "I just hope he's worth it," she said.

THEY WALKED TOGETHER UNDER Unwin's umbrella. Neither of them had seen the morning papers yet, but they knew that Unwin's photograph would likely have made front page by now. They kept to the alleyways and side streets, and Emily went ahead to peer around the corners. She took his hand, pulling him along while he kept the umbrella low over his face.

"Aren't we going the wrong way?" he asked.

"I think the closest entry point is a block north of here."

He knew better than to ask what she meant, and besides, Emily was doing a good job of keeping them out of sight. They passed no one on the sidewalks, and no vehicles moved on the streets. Still, Unwin felt they were being watched. He tried to remind himself that Sivart considered that a good thing. *Means I'm doing my job,* he often wrote.

She waved him into a subway station and produced a pair of tokens from her skirt pocket. As she passed through the turnstile, she raised her lunch box in the air. Unwin did the same with his umbrella. He had left his briefcase in his apartment: safer there than with him.

When the train arrived, Emily ushered him into an empty car. He moved to take a seat, but she grabbed his arm and pulled him over to a door on the opposite side. With a swift movement, she snatched the umbrella out of his hand and wedged it between the doors, forcing them open. Then she gave the umbrella back and led him onto the platform beyond. They went along the narrow walkway to a gate at its end—the entrance, Unwin thought, to a place only the city's transit workers could ever need to access. Emily lifted the padlock in her hand. "I know a few of the codes," she said, and added bashfully, "in case of emergencies."

She turned the dial a few times, and the lock popped open. Once they were in, she closed the gate and reached through the bars to lock it again. The air was cold and musty here, and Unwin could hear a low electrical hum. They took a flight of stairs downward, switching back at a landing, moving slowly until their eyes adjusted to the dimness of the place.

They had come to a second subway platform below the first. Water dripped from leaky pipes in the ceiling and formed grimy puddles amid bits of trash. Emily took only a few steps before turning to face the tracks. She grabbed hold of his left arm, lifting it to bring his wristwatch close to her face. The scent of her lavender perfume nearly blocked out the stench of the place.

"The eight train always arrives on time," she said.

"You mean the A train?"

Emily pursed her lips, then said, "I mean the *eight* train. I suppose they didn't cover that in your orientation. It's an old line, decommissioned by the city years ago. The Agency made arrangements. Only detectives are allowed to ride it."

He nodded as though to say that yes, of course, he remembered all that now.

"Not even assistants are permitted on board," she went on. "Really, we're not even supposed to know about it."

Unwin refrained from asking the obvious question.

The rails began to warble, and then the light of the approaching train appeared in the tunnel. Unlike the station, the train itself looked clean and well maintained. It glided into place alongside the platform, and the doors hissed open. Unwin got on, then turned to face his assistant.

"They say every detective has a dagger-sharp understanding of the human mind," she said to him. "Do you have a dagger-sharp understanding of the human mind, Detective Unwin? Can you tell me what I have in my lunch box?"

He had tested her; now she was testing him. Unwin wondered whether some part of *The Manual of Detection* might have prepared him for a question like this. Looking at the lunch box, he could not even tell if it was a detail or a clue. Finally he made his guess. "Your lunch?"

The doors closed. Through the window, behind her thick glasses, Emily's eyes were unreadable. She stood unmoving at the platform's edge as the train left the station.

He was the only passenger in the car—maybe the only passenger in the train. He took a seat and watched the tunnel walls slide past the windows.

It was seven o'clock now, and on a normal day he would already be on his way to Central Terminal. He thought of the woman in the plaid coat. Had she gone to wait at Gate Fourteen as usual? What if the person she was waiting for chose this day to arrive? Unwin would never see her there again, never know what happened. Who was she, to have taken his job on the fourteenth floor? To have sipped milk at the Cat & Tonic? Enoch Hoffmann was enraged at the mention of her. Did they know each other?

The train screeched as it rounded a bend. Unwin saw abandoned stations go by—not real places anymore, just forgotten hollows, decaying in the dark under the city. The train halted at one of them and opened its doors. It was not his stop.

All this was happening, he imagined, not because Sivart was gone, or because Lamech promoted him, or because Hoffmann was stealing the city's alarm clocks. It was happening because the woman in the plaid coat had dropped her umbrella and he failed to pick it up. If he *had* picked it up, she would have spoken to him. They might have left the terminal together, before Detective Pith could find him. They might have walked side by side and talked, he pushing his bicycle along the sidewalk.

His bicycle! It was still chained to the fire escape outside the Gilbert Hotel. Its chain would rust badly in this weather.

The door at the back of the car opened, and a gray, coveralled figure shuffled in, pushing a wheeled bucket in front of him. It was Arthur, the custodian. The man seemed to be everywhere—first in Central Terminal, then on the stage of the Cat & Tonic, and now in the subway. The train rounded another bend, and he stumbled. Unwin rose to offer assistance, but Arthur hopped to keep his balance, then resumed his advance.

The custodian's eyes were closed; he was still snoring. Yet he came toward Unwin as though with conscious design, squeezing the handle of the mop with his big hands, his knuckles white with the effort. They were very clean, those hands, and his fingernails were wide and flat.

The lights went out, and the darkness was total. Unwin could hear the creaking of the bucket's wheels draw closer. When the lights came back on, Arthur was only a few paces away, his teeth clenched behind parted lips.

Unwin backed away and knocked into a pole, nearly falling, then spun himself around to the other side of it. What did Arthur want with him? He blamed Unwin for Samuel Pith's death, perhaps; or worse, he was in league with those who had murdered the detective. Unwin fled, but this was the lead car—he had nowhere to go. The window at the front offered a view onto the tunnel, tracks gleaming in the train's single headlight.

Arthur drew closer, his face set in a rictus. Unwin could not make out the words he was muttering, but they sounded disagreeable at best. He pounded a fist against the door to the motorman's compartment. The only reply was the static from a two-way radio, and he thought he heard in it those familiar sounds—the rustling of paper, the cooing of pigeons.

The train slowed as it entered another station. Unwin brandished his umbrella in front of him as he circled the custodian and went to the door. For a moment he could see into Arthur's bucket. It was full of red and orange leaves.

When the train stopped, he ran along the platform toward the exit. The walls of the station were decorated with a tile mosaic depicting carousels and tents with pennants at their peaks. This was the stop he wanted. At a row of broken turnstiles, he paused to look back.

The train was leaving the station. The custodian had not followed.

TEN

On Infiltration

The hideout, the safe house, the base of operations:
you may assume that your enemy has one, but not
that it is to your advantage to find it.

An enormous plaster clown stood bowlegged at the entrance of the
Travels-No-More Carnival. The colors of its face and suit were
chipped and faded to shades of brown and purple, and the arch of its
legs were the gates through which visitors were compelled to pass. The
clown's smile was welcoming, but in a hungry sort of way.

Beyond was the flooded labyrinth of the Travels-No-More. Planks
of wood lay over wide pools of muddy water between the remaining
attractions—though "attractions" was hardly the word. Great machines
that had once swayed and wheeled and swerved now lay rusting, their
broken arms sprawled amid collapsed tents and decrepit booths. The
place was full of lost things, and Edwin Moore was one of them now.
Looking at it, Unwin felt lost himself. He knew he could not leave the
old clerk to this place.

He had gone no more than a few steps beyond the gate when the window of a nearby booth shot open. A man with a cigarette clenched in his teeth peered at him through a cloud of yellow smoke. He had a thick white mustache, stringy shoulder-length hair, and he wore an oilskin duster buttoned tight at his throat. From out of the collar, angular black tattoos like the roots of an overturned tree spread up his leathery neck to his jawline.

"Tickets," he said.

Unwin approached the booth, and the man folded his hands in front of him. The same tattoos extended from under his sleeves and down to his knuckles.

"How much?" Unwin asked him.

"Exactly," he said.

"Exactly what?"

"It'll cost you."

"Yes, but how much?"

"That's right," the man said, disclosing a yellow grin.

Unwin felt he had gotten himself into some kind of trouble, but he could not tell what kind.

The man was puffing at his cigarette, saying nothing. Then he squinted and looked past Unwin toward the entrance.

Someone else was walking under the legs of the enormous clown. She held a newspaper over her head as she limped toward them through the rain. It was Miss Greenwood, wrapped in a red raincoat. She insinuated herself beneath Unwin's umbrella and tossed aside the sopping newspaper. She looked more tired than ever—the revelries of the night before had deepened her exhaustion.

The man in the booth unbuttoned the front of his jacket. He had on a shoulder belt of worn leather, lined by a dozen or more gleaming daggers. He removed one and held it lightly by the blade end. Unwin checked its appearance against his memory of the Agency's index of weapons: small, slim, with a pommel weighted for balance. It was a throwing knife.

"Mr. Brock," Miss Greenwood said, "surely you're not troubling anyone for tickets on a day like this."

Unwin recognized the name from Sivart's reports. This was Theodore Brock, who had arrived in the city as Caligari's knife thrower and remained in it as one of Hoffmann's lieutenants. It was his stray throw, all those years ago, that had left Cleo with her limp. He spit his cigarette at their feet and said, "Well, if it isn't the enchantress Cleopatra Greenwood, come down to visit her old friends."

"I'm not here for a reunion, just a little outing with my new friend, who seems to have gotten ahead of me somehow." She shot Unwin a playfully angry look.

"And that's why you need a ticket. It costs money to see the freaks." He smiled again. "But you ought to know that, Cleo. How's the leg doing? Still hurt when it rains?"

She drew close to the window. "My guest is an Agency Eye," she said. "It's on business of his that we've come here. I think I can convince him not to see too much while we stroll the grounds, but for that you'll have to be nice."

"Agency?" Brock said. "But the hat's all wrong."

Miss Greenwood raised one hand, cupping it to her lips as though to whisper something in his ear. He leaned forward, then started and brandished his dagger, eyes going wide. She said something Unwin could not make out, and Brock's eyelids fluttered closed. The dagger fell from his hand and embedded itself in the ticket table; his head dropped hard beside it. The knife thrower was asleep.

Miss Greenwood looked around, then pulled the window shut. "Quickly," she said.

They went along paths strewn with broken bottles and toys, feathers, illegible playbills. The old fairground pavilions along the midway were constructed to look like the heads of giant animals, their mouths agape to allow access to the exhibits installed in the domes of their skulls. A pig's snout was a tunnel into fetid darkness, the eyes of a fish served as bulging windows, a cat's fangs were stalactites.

They passed them by and came to a causeway of wooden planks set on cinder blocks. Miss Greenwood went first, and Unwin followed.

"What did you do to Brock?"

"I told him to go to sleep," she said.

In some of his reports, Sivart had hinted that Cleo Greenwood possessed certain strange talents, picked up during her days with the Traveling Carnival. Unwin had assumed that the detective was being fanciful, or even poetic (*truly,* he had once written, *the lady is a knockout*), so Unwin cut those details. Perhaps he had been wrong to do so.

They stepped off the plank and walked along a row of junk stalls and shooting galleries. Mechanical ducks were perched on rusted rails, punched through with holes from real bullets. The rain pattering on abandoned popcorn carts and unmoving carousels made for a melancholy kind of music. "So different from the carnival I arrived with," Miss Greenwood said.

It was true: sixteen years ago Unwin had seen the sputtering caravan of red, orange, and yellow trucks passing through his neighborhood on their way to the fairgrounds. A west-side bridge had been closed that morning, to allow for the safe conduct of the elephants, and the newspapers ran photographs of the animals rearing on their hind legs. Posters were everywhere in the city, promising strange and stirring delights: Nikolai the mind reader, the giantess Hildegard, and Isidoro "The Man of Memory." But the show's main attraction was the biloquist Enoch Hoffmann.

Unwin never saw his performance, but he heard plenty about it in those weeks. The Man of a Thousand and One Voices was an unlikely magician, eschewing cape and hat in favor of the baggy, ill-fitting gray suit he wore with sleeves rolled. He gestured indifferently with little fingers while performing his feats and was quickly upstaged by his own illusions, the magic working almost in spite of him. Those who saw the show described the impossible—phantoms onstage, or animals, or inanimate objects, speaking to them in the voices of people they knew: relatives and friends, living and deceased. Those specters were privy to secret knowledge, and some who heard fainted at the revelations.

"The trick I used on Brock just now came in handy while I worked here," Miss Greenwood said. "Enoch and I had our own sideshow. Hypnosis, fortunetelling—that kind of thing. Of course, all that's changed. The remnants are no longer in the habit of entertaining."

The remnants of Caligari's were mentioned in numerous reports that Unwin had filed over the years. They were a crooked cabal, the progeny of a crooked line—plotters, scoundrels, and thieves, each one. Without them Hoffmann could not have seized control of the city's underworld. Unwin had seen them spying since the moment he and Miss Greenwood left the ticket booth. They stood in tattered coats beneath the eaves of game booths or skulked in the shadows of defunct rides, cooking breakfast over open fires: scowling roustabouts, disgruntled clowns, arthritic acrobats. They spoke together in whispers and guffaws or paced alone and spit. Unwin could smell sausage frying, could see the smoke of it threading the rain.

"They hate the Agency," Miss Greenwood said. "But you're safe with me, so long as I want you to be."

She had scarcely bothered to veil the threat—she was Unwin's captor as much as his guide. And here, in the den from which Hoffmann had recruited his every agent and thug, he knew he would need her. How many of the remnants had been apprehended due to the Agency's work? More than he cared to count. He clenched his teeth and tried not to sound bitter as he said, "That story you told me, about the open windows and the roses. You knew the cause from the beginning."

"I wasn't the only one playing tricks, Detective Unwin. It was Ed Lamech I'd wanted to see, remember?"

"But you meant for me to be there, at the Cat & Tonic."

"I needed someone to be my eyes."

"What did you expect me to see?"

"Strange things," she said. "The beginnings of a great and terrible crime. Hoffmann himself, maybe."

"And a murder."

Miss Greenwood lost her balance a moment, and Unwin put his hand under her elbow to steady her. She was flexing her bad leg. "Murder?" she said.

"Samuel Pith. The Rooks shot him."

She looked away. "That's horrid. Don't get me wrong. Sam was always a bit of a stuffed shirt. And he knew the risks. But he was an innocent, when it comes down to it. The rules must be changing."

"There are rules?"

"The Agency isn't the only organization requiring discipline, Detective Unwin. Now, tell me what else happened last night."

"You sang a song or two," Unwin said.

She stopped and turned, her face close to his under the umbrella. "You're sounding like a detective," she said. "Just when I was beginning to like you."

Some of the remnants had followed and were lurking now at the edge of the hall of mirrors. There were a dozen of them, maybe, or just a few, accompanied by their distorted reflections. They stood with their arms crossed in front of them, watching.

"What do you want to know?" Unwin asked her.

"What you're doing here, to begin with."

"I want to see the Rooks."

"No one *wants* to see the Rooks, Detective Unwin. They were sweet little boys when they came here with the carnival. But they were still attached then. After Enoch paid for the operation, they got to walk on their own, but it changed them in other ways, too."

"What do you mean?"

"They lost something," Miss Greenwood said. "I don't know what to call it. 'Conscience' isn't quite the word. Some people do cruel things, but the Rooks are cruelty itself, monsters under any moon. And they never sleep."

"Never?"

"Not in seventeen years."

Unwin thought that explained something, but he was not sure what. "You haven't slept in a long time either," he said.

"That's a very different story. The Rooks are no more than their master's hands. Now, I want you to tell me what happened last night."

When he hesitated, she turned to signal to the men by the fun house. They took a few steps forward, their reflections multiplying. Sivart might have seen a way out of this, but Unwin did not.

"I'll tell you what I saw," he said, and she signaled again for the remnants to wait.

Unwin described the gambling tables, the alarm clocks, her own performance, which seemed somehow to draw the sleepwalkers to the party. He told her how the Rooks were overseeing the operation and how the custodian had played accordion while she sang.

All of it interested her, but he could tell she was after something else. "I want us to be honest with each other," she said. "I must seem like a bully to you. The truth is, I only came back to the city because I'm trying to help someone. You were wrong when you accused me of showing your friend the truth about the Oldest Murdered Man. That must have been my daughter."

Unwin did not have to think long about the Agency's files on Cleopatra Greenwood to assure himself that there was nothing in them about a daughter. Either Miss Greenwood was lying to him or she was revealing something Sivart had failed to discover.

"I'm afraid she's gotten herself into some kind of trouble," Miss Greenwood went on. "She's turned out too much like her mother, that's the problem."

"You think she's wrapped up in Hoffmann's plans."

She glanced over her shoulder to make sure the remnants could not hear, then said quietly, "I'll help you stop him."

"Miss Greenwood, I don't want to stop Enoch Hoffmann."

Her exhaustion was showing again. A strong, sea-smelling wind hurled rain from the direction of the bay, and she squinted against it. "Hasn't it occurred to you that Travis might be dead by now?" she asked, her voice rising as the wind picked up. "Your only way out of this thing is to do what he failed to do."

A sound like thunder caused them both to turn. It was the clattering rumble of a heavy vehicle on a pitted road. Unwin looked for it, but a row of ragged sideshow tents blocked his view. The remnants were coming toward them now. Even with their reflections left behind, there were still a lot of them.

"Sivart was too stupid to see he'd been beaten," Miss Greenwood said. "Don't make the same mistake."

Unwin collapsed his umbrella and ran. In a moment the remnants were only a few strides behind him; they whooped into the rain, thrilling to the pursuit. Unwin headed for the nearest tent and slipped inside. The air smelled thickly of mold, and rainwater poured in through tears in the canvas. He ran to the back and swung his umbrella, rending the fabric, then split it to the ground with one downward stroke.

The Rooks' steam truck was approaching on the road beyond. It bounced over potholes and tossed black clouds from its smokestack, its headlights throwing twin yellow beams into the rain. He ran along behind until the truck slowed to round a corner. Then he hopped onto the rear bumper, opening his umbrella and swinging it over his head. He kept hold of the tailgate with his free hand.

Behind him Miss Greenwood stood in the middle of the road with the remnants, her raincoat bright amid those drab, disheveled men. She watched him go until the truck turned again, passing a row of old theaters on its way into the heart of the Travels-No-More.

———

DETECTIVE SIVART'S FIRST BRUSH with Caligari's occurred soon after the carnival arrived, months before the events surrounding the Oldest Murdered Man case. Reports coming into the Agency at the time indicated that the ringmaster might have represented a threat to the city. He was wanted in over a dozen states for crimes ranging from robbery to smuggling, blackmail to fraud. It was said that even his name was stolen—from a forebear in the trade, one who retired in infamy.

Sivart was one of several information gatherers assigned to investigate. He had taken a leisurely stroll along the midway, then slipped into a small pavilion in a remote corner of the fairgrounds. There an eight-foot-tall woman was bent over a worktable, measuring and mixing foul-smelling powders from barrels and bowls.

They need to get this gal a bigger room, Sivart wrote in his report. Hildegard, he discovered, oversaw the troupe's pyrotechnic displays and also served as the resident giantess. *We got along like old pals, and after a while we were sharing a drink. Well, "sharing" isn't the right word, since she emptied my flask with one swig. I went to find something more and brought back a cask of fancy stuff, paid for with Agency funds, thank you. If I have to drink on the job, I'm not going to pay for it.*

The two sat together for hours. She seemed to know what he was doing there but did not mind telling him about her time with the carnival, where they had traveled, the sights she had seen. While they talked, she poured her black-powder mixtures into the tubes of rockets and fixed fuses to them. When Sivart got too close to her work, she just pushed him back with one huge hand.

Nicest girl I've talked to in months, Sivart wrote. *The air must be clearer up there.*

Only when Sivart tried to turn the conversation to Caligari himself did the giantess grow reticent. The cask was almost empty, so he had to try a more direct approach. Was it true that the carnival served as a haven for criminals and outlaws? That Caligari was responsible for corruption and ruination wherever he went?

The giantess was silent. She went back to work, ignoring him.

That's when I put a cigar in my mouth, tore the end with my teeth, and raised a lighter to the tip. Before I could spark the flint, she had my fist closed up in hers. I showed her my best grin and said, "I can understand your not wanting to talk about it, angel. So maybe I should speak to the man himself?"

Though Sivart's report from this investigation belonged to no particular case, it was significant as the only documented account of an agent's meeting with Caligari. The ringmaster was in the tent where the elephants were stabled. According to the detective's description, he was a quick-moving, gray-bearded man in an ancient, moth-eaten suit, his eyes blue behind round, wire-rimmed spectacles. He told Sivart he had come just in time to help with the cleaning.

A little girl, about seven years old, handed the detective a brush and said, "They like it when you scrub them behind the ears."

From the report:

Apparently, Caligari and his young assistant do the dirty work themselves, almost every day. It is not fun and does not leave you smelling wholesome. If I'm ever feeling down, clerk, remind me not to run away and join the circus.

"The ears," the girl reminded me. I'd been sudsing the big guy's back, and she held my ladder steady while I worked, which was a good thing, what with my belly full of swill.

"Yeah, sure," I said to her. "The ears."

The three of us talked, and Caligari fed me a nonsense sandwich or two. He told me he took special care of the elephants because their dreams were so expansive, and clear as crystal.

That got a chuckle out of me. "What do you do," I said, "peel back their eyelids and shine a light in there?"

"Everything I tell you is true," he said, "and everything you see is as real as you are."

I'd read that on one of the posters they'd pasted around town. It was this fellow's catchphrase, and I didn't need it. Later, while we were getting fresh water from the cistern, I finally got him to say something interesting. "The people who stay put don't trust the people who don't," he said. "My carnival's been the subject of many wild accusations over the years, all of which have proved groundless. I'm getting tired of having to listen to the same old stories."

"Stories are what I'm here for," I told him. "Are you saying we have nothing to worry about?"

Clerk, you should have seen the sparkle in his eye. "You have plenty to worry about, Detective. Make no mistake, I am your enemy. You think you can control what is known and what is unknown? I tell you the unknown will always be boundless. This place thrives on mystery; we revel in it here. All the world's a rube, and he who tries to prove otherwise will be the first to wake onstage, victim of our just ridicule."

He'd worked himself up a bit and had to sit down and catch his breath. The little girl ran off and came back a minute later with a cup of cocoa. He sipped, watching the elephants. The animals were eating now, fetching clumps of hay with their trunks.

"They remember everything," Caligari said quietly. "I don't know what I'd do without them. And their dreams, Detective. A minute in one of their dreams is a month on the open plain, unfettered, unchartable."

I don't know what he meant by that, or whether he meant anything at all. But this much I know: we need to keep an eye on this character.

The carnival had closed up by then, and lights were going off all around us. The girl took my hand and led me away, back to the front gate. There she turned my hand over and looked at the palm. "You'll live a long life," she said, "but a long part of it won't be your own. Good night, Travis."

That bugged me some—not the fortune, which is malarkey. But the fact that she knew my first name. I hadn't mentioned it, not to anyone in the place.

Five months later Caligari vanished. His employees never left the city, and in the end the carnival was shut down by force. But the workers, despite numerous arrests, refused to go. They found other ways to provide for themselves, and like-minded souls were welcomed into their gang. The gates were shut against all others, and the Traveling Carnival became the Travels-No-More.

Many wondered: What about the elephants? What happened to them?

For years some reported hearing, on especially quiet nights, a trumpeting call out there in the dark, like a reminder, or an omen.

What troubled Unwin now was that little girl, Caligari's assistant, who had known Sivart's name and had spoken like some kind of sibyl. Could she have been the daughter of Cleopatra Greenwood?

IN THE BED OF the Rooks' steam truck, the ticking of the alarm clocks was the hum of a thousand insects. They jangled and buzzed when the truck went over bumps, and Unwin imagined they were about to burst free in a great tick-tocking swarm. Peering under the canvas, he saw that Moore was not in there, and neither was Pith's body. How many truckloads of clocks had the sleepwalkers stolen?

In time they came to the farthest corner of the carnival. Here at the edge of the bay, the tents were still striped with color, and electric lights along the waterfront shone red, blue, and orange. Most of the little makeshift structures had been converted into cottages, and shacks had sprung up among them. It looked less like a carnival here and more like a shantytown into which a carnival had erupted. The truck halted beside the largest of the pavilions, and almost immediately a group of men with shovels emerged.

Unwin hopped off the bumper and went around the passenger side. The men went straight to work, shoveling the alarm clocks into the tent, where thousands more were already piled. The noise of them was a second storm. Down at the docks, tractors swept heaps of clocks onto the deck of a waiting barge.

The steam engine of the truck spluttered and halted, and one of the Rooks climbed from the cab, a clipboard in his hand. Unwin knelt behind the rear tire. Looking beneath the truck, he saw a dockworker's shoes draw up to the big, uneven boots—Josiah's.

"What's Hoffmann want with it all anyway?"

"I believe there was something in your contract about questions and whether they ought to be asked," said Josiah.

"Right, right," the dockworker said. He flipped open a cigarette lighter and followed Josiah in the direction of the tent. "So long as I get paid."

The truck was parked not far from a row of cottages. They were built close to one another, some leaning nearly to the point of touching. Unwin took to the paths between them, crouching low under the windows, though all were dark. He moved as quickly as he could, keeping his umbrella closed in his hand, searching for some sign of Edwin Moore.

Rounding a corner, he nearly collided with an enormous animal—a real one, not one of those plaster simulacra. It was an elephant, gray and wild-looking in the rain, its eyes bright yellow in their dark, wrinkled sockets. Unwin slipped and fell in the mud at its feet. Startled, the elephant reared on its hind legs and raised its trunk in the air.

Unwin froze as the beast's forelegs churned over his head. He could smell the musky scent of the animal, could hear its wheezing breath. Finally the elephant held still, then slowly returned the columns of its legs gently to the ground.

Unwin got to his feet and picked up his umbrella. There were two other elephants here in a makeshift pen. These were older and lay with their bellies flattened to the muck. All three were chained to the same post, and their tethers had become tangled and knotted. The largest elephant, its hide sagging with age, raised its head and spread its ears but was otherwise still. The other rolled its eyes in Unwin's direction and lifted its trunk from the mud. Its searching snout moved toward him through the rain, issuing steam as it sniffed the air. The youngest began to rock impatiently, its great round feet squelching in the soft earth.

The beasts must have been evicted from their pavilion to make way for the alarm clocks. Unwin remembered the affection with which Caligari had spoken of the beasts, and he felt sick at the sight of them now. He would have liked to set them free, but even if he were able to remove the stake, it seemed unlikely that the elephants' condition would be improved. If those in charge cared little enough about the animals to leave them here, would they hesitate to kill them if they were set loose into the carnival? Unwin would have to return for them later; for now he had to concentrate on finding Edwin Moore.

The windows of one nearby cottage were lit with a flickering, rosy glow. Smoke streamed from a crooked length of stovepipe at the back, and Unwin thought he heard music playing within. He went to the window and peered through. Inside was a coal-burning stove, a table covered with books, and buckets of dirty plates and cups. A phonograph was on, and Unwin recognized the song. It was the same one Cleopatra Greenwood had sung the night before, at the Cat & Tonic.

At the back of the single room were two beds, perfectly made and barely an inch apart. More books were scattered over the beds, and the pillows were undented. Propped against the foot of the bed on the right was Edwin Moore. He was bound at the wrists and ankles by lengths of tough-looking rope, and his uniform was dirty.

The elephants seemed to have lost interest in Unwin. The youngest had gone to huddle against the eldest, and the other laid its trunk on the ground again.

Unwin tried the door and found it unlocked. The air inside was warm and smelled faintly of grease. He set his umbrella by the door, then opened his coat to rid himself of the chill he had carried with him all morning. On the table was a backgammon board, abandoned in midgame. White and brown playing pieces were grouped in sets of twos and threes, and the dice revealed the last roll as a double three. From what Unwin knew of the game, it looked as though each player had the other in a deadlock, with pieces captured and escape routes blocked.

Unwin knelt beside Moore and shook him. The old clerk mumbled in his sleep but did not waken.

Outside, the elephants were moving again; one of them sent up an aggrieved lament. Unwin moved around the beds, thinking to hide beneath one of them, but he stubbed his foot against a tin bucket and sent it clattering over the floor, strewing coal briquettes in a wide arc.

The door opened, and one of the Rooks came into the room. It was Jasper: left boot smaller than the right. He looked at Unwin, looked at the toppled bucket, then blinked once and closed the door behind him. He went to the phonograph and shut it off.

Unwin stepped over the coal, upsetting a stack of books in the process. He mumbled an apology and quickly began to gather them, blowing coal dust off the covers as he set them in a pile.

Jasper reached into his coat and withdrew a pocketwatch, checked the time, and put the watch away. His hand came back with a pistol in it. Even with the gun in his hand, Jasper seemed only vaguely interested in the fact that Unwin was there.

Unwin set the last few books into place and stood up. He thought of his own pistol, still in his desk drawer in Room 2919, but knew it would not have been of any help to him. Pith surely carried a pistol, and he had not even bothered to draw.

Talk. He had read that in the *Manual* somewhere. *When all seems*

*lost, start talking, keep talking. People do not kill people they think have
something useful to say.*

"Is it true?" Unwin said. "Seventeen years without a minute of
sleep?"

Jasper's face was a dull mask, his eyes green stones. He raised the
pistol, pointing it at Unwin's heart.

What would the shot feel like? Like a hole punch, Unwin thought,
when it punctured a small stack of pages. He took a step toward the
gun and said, "That's a tiredness beyond tiredness. Everything must
seem like a dream." He glanced at the pair of identical beds at the back
of the room. "When was the last time you even bothered to try?"

Jasper blinked again, and Unwin waited for the blast.

It did not come. "I wonder how it happened," Unwin said. "Did
you even want the operation? Or was that Hoffmann's idea? He needed
the two of you to be in different places at the same time, I suppose. But
he didn't know how much he was cutting. You weren't really two people
to begin with. There was a time when you could see each other's dreams,
hear each other's thoughts. But they were the same dreams, the same
thoughts."

He was guessing now, imagining a role for them in the earlier days
of Caligari's carnival: those boys Cleo Greenwood had described,
clothed in a single wide coat and set on a double stool, put onstage to
sing a duet, maybe. He must have come close to the truth, because
Jasper slowly lowered his pistol.

"One plus one does not equal one," Jasper said.

"No," Unwin agreed. "That man you have there, Edwin Moore, is
a lot like me. Or I'm a lot like him, maybe. We don't know each other
very well, but I understand him, I think. We were both clerks once. So
you see why I had to come looking for him."

Jasper seemed to consider this.

"I'm going to carry him out of here," Unwin said. "I won't ask you to help me. I won't ask you to open the door. I won't even ask you not to shoot me, but if you don't, I'll take it to mean that you understand, and I'll thank you for that."

Unwin lifted Moore by the arms. Taking care not to upset any of the books or to look at Jasper, Unwin dragged the man slowly toward the door. There he set Moore down and picked up his umbrella. It was shaking in his hands.

Just then the door opened and Josiah came in, still carrying his clipboard. He did not take his hat off, did not even blink. He looked at Unwin, looked at Moore, and looked at his brother. Then he set his clipboard on the table and whispered something in Jasper's ear.

The fire in the coal stove brightened, and Unwin felt the room grow suddenly hotter. Moore began to mumble in his sleep. The muscles of his skinny arms convulsed, and he slid back to the floor as Unwin lost his grip on him.

Jasper drew close and said, "My brother has advised me to advise you to hold very still." He raised the gun over his head and brought it down hard. With it came sleep—sleep, and a very strange dream.

IN THE DREAM, Unwin stood with his head against a tree, hands cupped around his face, counting out loud. When he finished counting, he had to go find some people who were hiding from him. His socks were wet, because he had been running around in the grass without any shoes on.

He stood on a hill near a little cottage, and at the bottom of the hill was a pond. The cottage was the one Sivart had written about in his reports, the one he wanted to retire to.

"Ready or not," Unwin called, but the words dropped like stones into the pond and fell to the bottom. A tire swing moved back and forth over the water, spinning as though someone had only just climbed off it. That, Unwin thought, was not a detail. It was a clue.

At the bottom of the hill, past a tangle of blackberry briars, he found footprints in the mud. He followed them around the edge of the pond, then down a trail leading into the woods, kicking red and orange leaves as he walked. In the middle of a clearing, the leaves were piled higher than everywhere else, just high enough to conceal a small person.

Unwin smelled something burning. A thin stream of smoke rose up from the leaves. Poking out of them was the tip of a lit cigar. He knelt beside it and cleared away some of the leaves, revealing the face of a young boy. The boy blinked at Unwin, then took the cigar out of his mouth and said, "Okay, Charlie. You got me."

The boy sat up and brushed the rest of the leaves off his body, off his gray raincoat. Then he stood and put his hat on. "I'll help you get the others," he said.

Unwin followed the boy back down the trail. His feet were getting cold. "Detective Sivart?" he said.

"Yeah, Charlie," said the boy.

"I can't remember the name of this game."

"It's an old game," the boy said. "Older than chess. Older than curse words and shoeshine. Doesn't matter what you call it, so long as you know how to play. Everyone's in on it, except one guy, and that guy's 'it.' Okay?"

"Detective Sivart?"

"Yeah, Charlie."

"I'm 'it,' aren't I?"

"And quick, too," the boy said.

They stood together at the edge of the pond, the boy puffing at his cigar. Up in the cottage, someone had turned the radio on. Unwin could hear the music, but he could not make out the words. The sun was going down behind the hill.

"Some birthday." The boy sighed. "So who's next?"

"We have to find the magician," Unwin said.

"They hired a magician? What kinds of tricks can he do?"

"All kinds," Unwin said.

"Then how do you know you haven't found him already?"

Unwin looked down. The boy's face had changed. It was squarish now, and his eyes had turned a dull brown color. He still had the cigar in his hand, but both his sleeves were rolled up, and the coat looked too big on him.

Enoch Hoffmann grinned. "See?" he said. "He could be anyone."

ELEVEN

On Bluffing

Answer questions with questions. If you are caught
in a lie, lie again. You do not need to know the
truth to trick another into speaking it.

Unwin waited for the world to stop swaying, but it did not stop
swaying, because the world was a barge, and the barge was out
on the rolling waters of the bay. He tried to check the time, but his
arms were tied behind his back. Anyway, he did not need his watch.
He was surrounded by alarm clocks—hills, mountains of them. On a
dozen of their rain-spattered faces, he read the same time. It was only
ten of eight.

Curled at his feet was Edwin Moore, still bound, still sleeping. In
this light, Unwin could see the lump at the top of the old man's forehead. He knew from the throbbing at his own temple that he had one
to match.

Next to Moore was the plump body of Detective Pith, his suit wa-
terlogged and bloodstained. Unwin glimpsed the ashen, jowly face
above the collar of the herringbone suit. He looked away.

Unwin's hat was still on his head, and his umbrella was open above him, fixed in place by the same ropes that bound his aching arms. He wondered which of the Rooks had afforded him this kindness. There was no sign of the twins here. In every direction he could see nothing but piles of alarm clocks. All the alarm clocks in the city, maybe even his.

"Wake up," he said to Moore. "Wake up, will you?"

He slid himself forward, bringing his feet close to the other man's, and tapped the sole of one of his shoes. "Wake up!" he shouted.

"Hush," said someone behind him. "The Rooks will hear you. You're lucky they prefer to watch their victims drown."

Unwin recognized Miss Greenwood's voice. "How did *you* get here?"

She knelt behind him and tugged at the ropes. "More easily than you did," she said. She reached into her coat, and Unwin looked over his shoulder to see a dagger appear in her hand. It was identical to those that Brock carried—it must have been the one that pierced her leg during his knife-throwing act, all those years ago.

"I don't like being left in the rain without an umbrella, Mr. Unwin."

"Those elephants back there," he said. "Something ought to be done about them, too."

She sighed. "Caligari would be furious."

Unwin waited, listening. He felt the edge of the blade against his spine. Then a sudden pressure, and the fibers of the rope started snapping. He held the umbrella over Miss Greenwood while she cut the cords around his ankles. When they both were standing, she said, "I know you're not a detective."

That passage from page ninety-six of the *Manual* returned to his mind. Without any secrets he was lost forever. But what was he now, if not lost already? "No," he admitted. "I'm not a detective."

"Not a watcher either. Something else, some new kind of puppet. I know you're working for him. I know he sent you to taunt me."

"Working for whom?"

She narrowed her eyes at him. "That phonograph record, those sounds. You have no idea what it's like, Mr. Unwin. To always find him there waiting for you. To have his eyes in the back of your skull."

"Whose eyes? What are you talking about?"

She stared at him, still disbelieving. "The Agency's overseer," she said. "Your boss."

It had never occurred to Unwin that the Agency had an overseer, that one person could be in charge. Where, he wondered, was that man's office?

Miss Greenwood must have seen that his surprise was real. "He and I . . . we know one another," she said. "Hoffmann is dangerous, Mr. Unwin. But you ought to know that your employer is something worse. Whatever happens, he can't find out about my daughter." The barge shifted, and she stumbled on her bad leg. Unwin moved to steady her, but she pushed him away. "There's a boat tied up on the starboard side," she said. "Go, take it."

He gestured at Moore. "Will you cut him free?"

"There's no time," she said. "The Rooks aren't far."

He held out his hand. "Give me the dagger, then. I'll do it myself."

Miss Greenwood hesitated, then turned the handle over to him. "I hope this rescue goes better than your first," she said.

Unwin knelt and started cutting. These ropes were thicker, and he made slow progress.

"I didn't want to come back to the city," Miss Greenwood said. "I was through with all of this. With the Agency, with Hoffmann; I can hardly tell the difference between them anymore. But I had to come back."

Unwin cut through the last cord around Moore's wrists and started working to free his ankles.

"These clocks remind me of a story I used to read to my daughter," she said. "It was in her favorite book, an old one with a checkered cover. It was the story of a princess who'd been cursed by an old witch—or was it a fairy? In any case, the curse meant she would fall asleep—forever, maybe—if she were pricked by a spinning needle. So the king and queen did what any good parents would do, and piled up all the spindles in the land and burned them, and everyone had to wear worn-out old clothes for a very long time."

The last of the ropes fell away. He swung Moore's arms up over his shoulders and with Miss Greenwood's help lifted him onto his back. She put the umbrella into his hand, and for a moment they stood looking at one another.

"How did the story end?" he asked.

It was not a question she had expected. "They missed one of the spindles, of course."

UNWIN TRUDGED TOWARD THE starboard side of the barge, following a narrow trail between mounds of alarm clocks. His shoes squeaked with every labored step over the slick metal deck. He would have taken them off, but shards of glass from the broken faces of clocks were everywhere.

He paused often to catch his breath and to reposition Moore's limp body over his back. Finally he saw the edge of the barge. Bobbing over the green-gray swells was the little rowboat Miss Greenwood had promised. But one of the Rooks was nearby, leaning over the water with his big left boot on the rail: Josiah. He gazed across the bay at the mist-shrouded city, smoking a cigarette while the rain poured over the brim of his hat, which was nearly the size of Unwin's umbrella.

Unwin thought he could reach the boat without Josiah's seeing, but not without his shoes betraying him. So he crouched and waited for Josiah to finish smoking.

Somewhere amid the hills of clocks, a bell began to ring, a futile attempt to wake some sleeper a mile or more away. To Unwin the sound was a hook in his heart: the world goes to shambles in the murky corners of night, and we trust a little bell to set it right again. A spring is released, a gear is spun, a clapper is set fluttering, and here is the cup of water you keep at your bedside, here the shoes you will wear to work today. But if a soul and its alarms are parted, one from the other? If the body is left alone to its somnolent watches? When it rises—if it rises—it may not recognize itself, nor any of brief day's trappings. A hat is a snake is a lamp is a child is an insect is a clothesline hung with telephones. That was the world into which Unwin had woken.

While he listened, the one bell was joined by another, and then another, and soon a thousand or more clocks were sounding all at once, a chorus fit to rouse the deepest sleeper. He glanced at his watch. It was eight o'clock; many in the city had meant to wake up now. Instead they had given him a chance to reach the rowboat undetected. The squeaking of his shoes was nothing compared to that thunderous proclamation of morning.

His sleeping companion's feet dragged bumping behind him as he ran, and the umbrella wobbled above. He leaned against the rails, heaving Edwin Moore up and over. The old man landed hard and the rowboat shuddered beneath him. One of his arms flopped into the water, and his bruised face turned up to the rain.

Josiah looked over—he had felt the rail shift under Unwin's weight. He flicked his cigarette into the water and came toward Unwin, an expression of mild disappointment on his face.

Unwin clambered up onto the rail, collapsing his umbrella. In his haste he caught the handle on the sleeve of his jacket, and the umbrella popped open again. The wind pulled at it, and Unwin pitched back onto the barge.

Josiah took him by the collar and swung him to the deck, his coat flapping in the rain as he fell upon Unwin. The heat coming off the man was incredible—Unwin thought he saw steam rising from the Rook's back. Josiah put one enormous hand behind Unwin's head, as though to cushion it, and the other flat over his face. His hand was dry.

He covered Unwin's nose and mouth and did not take it away. "Let's both be very quiet now," he said.

The bells were ringing all around them—some stopping as others started. The ringing joined with the ringing in Unwin's ears, and a darkness rose up as though from the sea. It seemed to him that he stood on a street in the dark. Children had left chalk drawings on the pavement, but there were no children here. It was the avenue of the lost and secretless: empty tenement buildings all the way to the bottom of the world.

Detective Pith emerged from the shadows and stood in the cone of light from a streetlamp. "Papers and pigeons, Unwin. It's all papers and pigeons. We'll have to rewrite the goddamn manual."

"Detective Pith," he said, "I saw them shoot you."

"Aw, nuts," said Pith. He took off his hat and held it over his chest. There was a bullet hole in the top of it. "Damn it, Unwin. Do something!" he said, and when he moved the hat away his shirt was covered with blood.

Unwin tried to hold the wound shut, but it was no use; the blood seeped between his fingers and spilled everywhere.

When the darkness receded, the blood was still there, pouring down Unwin's arms and over his chest. Not Detective Pith's, though. Miss Greenwood's dagger was in his hands again—he had slipped it into his pocket without thinking—and now the blade was stuck deep in Josiah's chest. Unwin had stabbed him.

Josiah took his hand from Unwin's face and sat down next to him, staring at the handle there between the third and fourth buttons of his shirt.

Unwin got to his knees. He reached to take the knife but stopped himself. Had he read in the *Manual* that removing the weapon will worsen the wound? "Don't move," he said.

Josiah closed his eyes. From below came the whirring of machinery, and the deck of the barge began suddenly to lift. Unwin grabbed Josiah's hand and tried to pull him toward the rowboat but could not budge him. The deck angled higher, and Unwin's shoes slipped. It was too late. He let go of Josiah and grabbed his umbrella, then scrambled under the rail and into the rowboat. He swiftly undid the knot securing them to the barge and started to paddle.

Josiah Rook tipped, then tumbled across the tilting barge. The hills of alarm clocks collapsed and slid with him. Many were still ringing as they spilled into the bay, going mute as the water took them.

Edwin Moore sat up and blinked. "I don't know any songs for this," he said.

Unwin did not know any either. He was thinking of the backgammon board he had seen in the Rooks' cottage, of the game left unfinished there.

UNWIN ROWED WHILE Edwin Moore held the umbrella over their heads. It swayed and bobbed above them while the boat bobbed beneath. They sat close to keep dry, facing one another with knees nearly touching. Someone had left a tin can under the seat, and Moore used it to bail water. Sometimes the wind dragged the umbrella sideways and they both were drenched.

Moore shivered and said, "I tried to forget as much as I could, but I couldn't forget enough. They knew me the instant I fell asleep."

The world was two kinds of gray—the heavy gray of the rain and the heavier, heaving gray of the water. Unwin could barely tell them apart. Reaching through both was the yellow arm of a lighthouse beacon. He rowed toward it as best he could.

"Who knew you?" he asked.

"The watchers, of course." Moore squinted, and drops of water fell from his thick eyebrows. "They watch more than the detectives, Mr. Unwin. They are detectives themselves, in a manner of speaking. Of course, I didn't know who would catch me first: Hoffmann's people or the Agency's. Some of your colleagues must still be using the old channels, the ones the magician knows to monitor."

Unwin understood that no better than he understood how to keep the boat pointed in the right direction. It veered as soon as he rowed on one side, then spun the other way when he tried to compensate.

Moore set the tin can on the seat between them and wiped his face with his hand. "I owe you an apology," he said. "I lied when I told you there is no Chapter Eighteen in *The Manual of Detection.*"

"But I saw for myself," Unwin said. "It ends with Chapter Seventeen."

Moore shook his head. "Only in the later printings. In the original, unexpurgated edition, there are eighteen chapters. The last chapter is the most important. Especially to the watchers. And to the Agency's overseer." He set his elbows on his knees, looked down, and sighed. "I thought you knew all this. That you were a watcher yourself, maybe, and had been sent to toy with me. I'm the architect of an ancient tomb, Mr. Unwin. I was to be buried inside my own creation, the better to keep its secrets. I will not tell you more, for your sake. But if you ask, I will answer."

The rain drummed on the umbrella as water splashed against the sides of the boat. Unwin's arms were sore, but he kept rowing. Their little craft was taking on water. He watched it swirl around his shoes, around Moore's shoes. The water was red. There was a stain on his shirt, and his hands had stained the oars.

"I killed a man," Unwin said.

Moore leaned close and set his hand on Unwin's shoulder. "You killed half of a man," he said. "It's the other half you have to worry about."

Unwin rowed faster. He was getting the hang of it now. The trick was to play each side off the other, but gently. Still, it would take a long time to reach the shore.

"Tell me about Chapter Eighteen," Unwin said.

—————

WHEN THEY REACHED THE harbor, it was far from the pier of the Travels-No-More. Unwin rowed in the shadows of cargo ships, and each splash of the oar echoed in the vastness between the towering hulls. It was dark, and the air smelled of rust and brine. They landed in a small cove at the base of the lighthouse, where bits of junk had collected among the rocks and seaweed. Together they dragged the boat out of the water.

Unwin noticed something gleaming at the fore of the craft as the light swept past. It was an alarm clock, and it looked a lot like the one that had vanished from his own bedside. Unwin put the clock to his ear, heard its machinery still at work, and wound it. The clock just fit inside his coat pocket.

They walked together through abandoned dockyards. What Unwin understood of Moore's description of Chapter Eighteen he would have disbelieved entirely if not for the events of the last two days. *Oneiric detection,* Moore had whispered to him. *In layman's terms: dream surveillance.*

This is was what Miss Greenwood must have meant when she spoke of another's eyes in the back of her skull. Dream spies. Had the Agency's overseer done this to her? Hounded her through her sleep so she never rested? She said she did not want him to know about her daughter. Would a dream of the girl be enough to betray Miss Greenwood's secret? Unwin wondered whether he himself could ever sleep easily again.

Edwin Moore, his feet back on solid ground, seemed to have discovered new stores of vitality. He walked with a jaunty step, his cheeks reddening from the exertion. He was still trying to explain how dream detection worked. "You've heard the story of the old man who dreamed he was a butterfly," he said. "And how, when he woke, he wasn't sure if he really was an old man who had dreamed he was a butterfly or if he was a butterfly dreaming it was an old man."

"You'd say there's truth to it?"

"I'd say it's a lot of nonsense," Moore snapped. "But the mind struggles with the question nonetheless. How often have you tried to recall a specific memory—a conversation with an acquaintance, maybe—only to determine that the memory was a delusion, spawned in dream? And how often have you dreamed a thing, then found that it spoke some truth about your waking life? You solved a problem that had been impenetrable the day before, perhaps, or perceived the hidden sentiments of someone whose motivations had baffled you.

"Real and unreal, actual and imagined. Our failure to distinguish one from the other, or rather our willingness to believe they may be one and the same, is the chink through which the Agency operatives conduct their work."

"But what do they do, exactly?" Unwin asked. "Lie down next to someone who's sleeping? Rest with their heads touching?"

"Don't be ridiculous. You don't have to be near your subject; you only need to isolate that person's frequency. It's work a watcher can do from the comfort of an office chair." Moore winced and touched the lump on his forehead, which had assumed a purple hue. He sighed and went on. "You know of course that signals from the brain may be measured, even charted. There are electrical waves, devices to read them, people who study these things. Different states have been identified, cataloged, analyzed. What our people figured out is that one brain may be entrained to another, 'tuned in,' so to speak. The result is a kind of sensory transduction. Not so different, really, from listening to the radio.

"That's my metaphor, at least. Those who practice dream detection describe it as a kind of shadowing, only they tail their suspect through his own unconscious mind rather than through the city. If they are after some specific piece of information, they may even influence the dreamer in subtle ways, nudging him toward the evidence they need."

They left the dockyards a few blocks from the cemetery. They would have to keep to the shoreline now—Unwin did not wish to draw too close to the Forty Winks and be spotted by someone who might inform Jasper Rook of his whereabouts. He led his companion north, and Moore seemed content to carry on with his lecture, following wherever Unwin directed his umbrella.

"Some in the Agency believe that this technique has been practiced for a long time but called different things through the centuries. It was easier to do, they say, when people lived in small tribes spread over the earth. Fewer signals to sift through then, and a greater willingness to allow them to mingle. The omens, visions, and prophecies of shamans and witch doctors: these might have been rooted in what we call dream detection.

"But I don't care much for the history, and in any case things are different now. In our city, each night is an enormous puzzle of sensation, desire, fear. Only those who have trained extensively can distinguish one mind from another. At the Agency their training is put to use on behalf of the organization's clients. The watchers, whose work is coordinated by the overseer himself, investigate the unconscious minds of suspects while the detectives seek out clues of a more tangible nature. It is this technique that gives Agency operatives their unprecedented insight."

"What if someone tried to use the technique with only a little training?" Unwin asked.

Moore glared at him. "Assuming he succeeded at all, he would put himself and others in danger. There are reservoirs of malevolence in the sleeping city, and you would not want to tap them accidentally." He paused, then added quietly, "There are, however, some who can assist in the process. Who can induce the focused states necessary to employ oneiric detection—or be more easily subjected to it. Their talents, when used, might appear as hypnosis to the uninformed."

Unwin recalled what Miss Greenwood had done to Brock that morning, at the carnival ticket booth. Something whispered in his ear and the man had fallen immediately into a kind of trance. "Cleopatra Greenwood is one of those people," he said.

Moore grunted. "The power of Greenwood's voice has been observed on several occasions. Sivart knew of it, though he didn't know what it was. You remember she had a brief career as a singer? When I left the Agency, the overseer was experimenting with recordings of her music, to see if they could help expand the uses of dream detection. To what end I'm not entirely certain. But Hoffmann, of course, is also aware of her talent. In fact, I no longer consider it a coincidence that one of Cleo Greenwood's songs was first played on the radio almost eight years ago, on the night of November eleventh."

Of course: Unwin had heard it, too. That was why he recognized the tune when he heard it performed at the Cat & Tonic the night before. The questions that Sivart had left unanswered in his report on The Man Who Stole November Twelfth returned to Unwin's mind: the day skipped on calendars across the city, the mysterious operatives—never identified or apprehended—who changed the date at all the government offices and news agencies. But maybe there had been no operatives, at least not conscious ones.

"Could Hoffmann have influenced us somehow?" Unwin asked. "Infiltrated our dreams and made agents out of us while we slept? We might have altered the calendars ourselves."

Moore frowned, his lips disappearing behind his whiskers. "He knows the technique of dream detection. Years ago the secret was leaked to him—the work of a double agent, probably. And he is more powerful by far than any of the watchers, because his mastery of disguise and ventriloquism makes him untraceable as he moves from one dream to another. But how he could have planted suggestions, fooled us into stealing a day from ourselves—that I cannot imagine. And if he had done it once, wouldn't he have done it again? Why stop with one day if he could take so much more? Every night, his sleeper agents would be doing his work."

"Last night the alarm clocks were stolen by a gang of sleepwalkers," Unwin said. "I saw one or two people emerge from every building we passed—they must have broken in to each apartment and taken the clocks. They thought they were going to a party to drink and gamble, but really they were delivering their plunder to the Rooks. Miss Greenwood was there, singing to them, and Detective Pith was shot because he discovered the operation."

Moore shook his head. "There's something we're missing, then. Some tool the enemy has acquired. A battle is under way, Mr. Unwin. The last, maybe, in a long and quiet war. I don't understand the meaning of the maneuvers, only the stakes. Hoffmann's desire for vengeance has grown in the years since his defeat on November twelfth. The gambling parlors, the protection rackets, the black markets—these have always been means to an end, a web from which to feed through the long years of his preparations. His true goal is the destruction of the boundary between the city's rational mind and the violent delirium of its lunatic dreams. His ideal world is a carnival, everything illusory, everything in flux. We'd all be butterflies dreaming we were people if he had his way. Only the Agency's rigorous adherence to the principles of order and reason have held him in check. Your work, Mr. Unwin, and mine."

From the north came the sounds of traffic, of the city awakening. Unwin's clothes were torn and bloodstained. How many people would have seen his name in the papers by now? It would not be good for his defense, he thought, to be found covered in another man's blood. He wondered whether there was a subway station nearby, one with access to the eight train.

"You realize by now that your search for Sivart is hopeless," Moore said. "He is probably dead."

"He contacted me," Unwin said.

"What? How?"

"He appeared in my sleep two nights ago. And again, I think, last night. He told me about Chapter Eighteen."

"Impossible. Sivart knows nothing about dream infiltration. None of the detectives do; they're given expurgated editions of the *Manual*, like yours."

"But the watchers—"

"The watchers never reveal the true source of their knowledge. It is disguised as intelligence gleaned from mundane informants. This is standard protocol; it's all in the Agency bylaws. The unabridged edition, of course."

"Someone told him, then. Zlatari saw him reading at the Forty Winks, just before he disappeared. It must have been a complete version of the *Manual*."

"Who would have given it to him?"

"The same person who showed you the gold tooth in the mouth of the Oldest Murdered Man," Unwin said. He stopped and took Moore's shoulder. "I thought you were only being forgetful when you said you dreamed her. But maybe it really did happen in your sleep."

Moore appeared suddenly dazed. He closed his eyes, and Unwin saw them darting back and forth under the lids. "It was Cleopatra Greenwood, I think."

"Are you sure?" Unwin said. "Describe her."

"You're right," Moore said, his eyes still closed. "She was younger than Miss Greenwood. Just as pretty, though. And very quiet, as if she thought someone else might be listening. Brown hair under her gray cap. Eyes gray, almost silver, like mirrors. She was dressed for bad weather. She was wearing, I think, a plaid coat."

The act of remembrance had left Moore in a stupor. Unwin stood with his hand still on his shoulder. The woman in the plaid coat had broken in to the old clerk's dream and shown him the thing he could not forget. She had unveiled Sivart's gravest of errors.

Little surprise that Moore had mistaken her for Cleopatra Greenwood. The resemblance, now that Unwin considered it, was obvious. The woman in the plaid coat was Miss Greenwood's daughter. And she was most certainly "in on it." But what did she have to gain from revealing the fake in the Municipal Museum? Or from stealing a copy of the *Manual* and giving it to Sivart?

Moore's eyes popped open. "We have a ride," he said.

A taxicab was approaching from a narrow side street farther up the block. Moore stepped out from under the umbrella to signal it with both hands. The taxicab lurched to the curb and idled there, its checkered chassis shuddering.

"We'll go to my place," Moore said to Unwin, "and plan our next move."

The driver of the cab was a slouched, thin-faced man. He lowered his window a few inches and watched them cross the street. Unwin drew his coat tighter over his shirt, trying to conceal the stains.

"You're available?" Moore called.

The driver took this in slowly, refusing to meet Moore's gaze. At last he muttered, "Available."

Moore nodded sharply and reached for the handle of the door. He tugged at it a few times, but the door held fast. "It's locked," he said.

The driver ran his tongue over his teeth and said, "Locked."

"Will you take us?" Moore demanded. "Yes or no?"

"No," the driver said.

Unwin lowered his umbrella over his face and searched for an escape route. Had the cabbie recognized him? He wondered if the newspapers had used the photo on his clerk's badge.

Moore was insistent, however. "Why did you stop when I waved for you if you did not plan to take on a fare?"

The driver mumbled inaudibly, then reached back, found the lock with his hand, and unfastened it. Moore threw the door open and slid across the seat. Unwin hesitated, but Moore beckoned for him to follow, so he closed up his umbrella and got in.

Moore gave an address just a few blocks from Unwin's own, then settled back into the seat. "Soon after I completed the *Manual*," he said, "it was decided that only a few specially trained agents would be privy to the secrets of Chapter Eighteen, and a shorter edition was quickly printed for general use. Enormous changes were under way at the Agency at this time: a new building, the construction of the archives. Controls had to be tightened. Every copy of the original edition was cataloged and accounted for. But what the overseer and I both knew was that one copy of the book could not be so easily repressed."

Moore tapped his own head and gave Unwin a meaningful look.

"But you would not have betrayed the Agency's trust."

"Of course not. I had been with the organization from the beginning, when fourteen of us shared one office heated by a coal stove. But the world had changed since then. The enemy had changed. Caligari's Traveling Carnival had arrived, and with it the nefarious biloquist Enoch Hoffmann. The old boundaries were already eroding, and to know a thing was to put it in jeopardy. The overseer had dictated to me his profoundest secrets, and he knew that Hoffmann, if he chose, could break the lock on my brain as easily as a child tears the wrapping from a birthday present. I was a danger to the Agency, loyal or not."

"The overseer threatened you?"

"He didn't have to."

"So you left. Made yourself forget everything."

"It was easier than you might think. I had been the Agency's first clerk. For years, I was its only clerk. I had developed memory exercises to retain all the information entrusted to me. Imaginary palaces, archives of the mind. They were structural; I could feel their weight in my head. The supports had been bending and groaning for a long time. I had only to loosen a brick or two, and let the rest collapse." Moore leaned forward and said to the driver, "You there, can't you go a bit faster?"

Unwin peered through the window. The streets were uncrowded, but despite Moore's insistence the driver maintained his pace, keeping always to one lane, never hurrying to beat a traffic signal.

Moore fell back into the seat, shaking his head. "I can't pretend to understand your role in all this, Mr. Unwin. But I think whoever has you on this case put you there because you know so little. How else to explain it? The enemy would not suspect your importance, even were he to search every corner of your mind."

"That's changing, though."

Moore nodded. "You know the dangers, but the dangers know you, too. We will have to act swiftly, now. Our investigation depends upon it."

"Investigation": it was just the word Unwin had been trying to avoid. How long now had he been doing the work of a detective, in spite of himself? Ever since he had stolen the phonograph record from Lamech's office. Or longer: since he first began to shadow the woman in the plaid coat.

"There's a document," Unwin said. "A phonograph record. I've played it, but I can't understand the recording—it's just a lot of garbled noises. I think Lamech intended to give it to me before he was killed."

Moore's face darkened. "It must have come from the Agency archives. That's where the overseer was experimenting with the new methodologies. You'll have to bring the record down there if you want to learn what it is."

Moore stopped talking and turned to rub condensation from the window with his sleeve. He gazed out at the street, frowning. Unwin saw the problem, too: their driver was headed the wrong way. Where was the man taking them? Perhaps a reward had been posted for Unwin's capture, and the cabbie meant to collect.

"I'm not paying you to take the scenic route," Moore said. "Left, man. Turn left!"

The driver turned right. On the next block, they saw a car that had swerved off the road and struck a fire hydrant. Water shot in torrents into the air, cascading over the vehicle, flooding the gutter and part of the street. A man in a suit sat on the crumpled hood of the car, scratching his head and trying to speak, but his mouth kept filling with water and he could only gurgle and spit. People walking by did not even look at him.

"This is outrageous," Moore said. "Has someone alerted the authorities? You," he said to the driver, "use your two-way radio, would you?"

The cabbie ignored him and drove slowly past the scene. Moore's face went red, and the bruise on his forehead grew a darker shade of purple. He seemed too angry to speak.

A police cruiser was parked at the next corner. Moore rolled down his window, and Unwin sank deeper into his seat as the old man shouted into the rain, "Officer! Officer!"

The driver's door was open. Seated behind the wheel with her feet on the dashboard was a girl of twelve or thirteen, dressed in her school uniform, twirling a billy club in her left hand. Imprisoned in the back of the car were seven or eight people, packed so tightly that one man— a policeman to judge from his hat, and maybe the rightful owner of the car—was stuck with his face pressed up against the glass.

Moore gasped. "The wicked truant!" he said to Unwin.

At the next block, the cabbie parked in front of a flower shop, where a few people stood beneath a blue-striped awning. He took the car out of gear and let the engine idle.

"I won't pay you a dime," Moore said. "Furthermore, I demand your registration number."

"Quiet," Unwin said to him.

Moore touched the lump on his head and looked at Unwin as though he had been struck.

"He's asleep," Unwin said. "They're all asleep. The whole city—everyone."

The people under the awning of the flower shop had noticed the taxicab. Moore peered through the window as they approached, then looked at Unwin. "You're right," he whispered.

A woman wearing a yellow housecoat opened the front passenger-side door. She leaned down and said to the driver, "Something to do."

The driver tapped his palm against the gear stick. "Someplace to be."

This was apparently the reply the woman was looking for, because she got in beside him and shut the door.

Unwin leaned close to Edwin Moore. "How could Hoffmann have done it?"

Moore was shaking his head and rubbing the white bristles on his chin. Quietly he said, "The alarm clocks."

Unwin thought again of the nighttime parade he had marched with, of that strange troupe with their thieves' sacks over their shoulders. Hoffmann had needed the help of only a few to steal the clocks. But then what? The entire city oversleeps and is susceptible to his influence?

"There is still something we're missing," Moore said. "But the clocks were implements of order, ones we've long taken for granted, and Hoffmann drowned them in the bay. These people outside, they may have dreamed of waking to phantom alarms, when in truth they were waking into a second sleep, one that Hoffmann had prepared for them. The city nearly fell to pieces on November twelfth. Now Hoffmann's cracked open the madness in its heart and spilled it into the streets."

"I don't see what he gains."

"Anything he wants," Moore said. "The dissolution of the Agency. The gold he thought was his on November twelfth, with interest. Who knows what he'll demand? We are beaten—and he has left us awake so that we may witness the manner of our defeat."

A sleepwalking boy in a green poncho opened the rear door and looked into the cab, his eyes dull behind drooping lids. Startled, Moore scooted across the seat, closer to Unwin. The boy climbed in and said to no one, "Have to get there soon."

Without turning, the driver of the taxi said, "Have to get it done."

Others were gathering around the vehicle now. They stood silent in the rain, swaying a little while they waited to take their places inside.

"There's more than plain madness here," Unwin said.

Moore pursed his lips. His eyes for a moment were those that Unwin had seen at the museum the morning before—blank in the dark caves of his eye sockets—and Unwin wondered how long the rebuilt frame of the man's mind would hold. But light quickly returned to them, and Moore said, "Yes, this group of sleepwalkers is different from those others. Special operatives of some kind, perhaps. It's as though they've been recruited for a particular task."

Unwin opened his door. "I don't think we want to be in this taxi," he said.

Moore shook his head. "One of us should stay with them, see what they're up to. And you already have a burden of your own. Get that record to the archives, Mr. Unwin. Let no one take it from you."

Unwin climbed out of the car. As soon as he was on his feet, a man in a red union suit slipped by and took his place. Now Moore was sandwiched between two sleepwalkers. For him there was no turning back.

Unwin reached in and handed him his umbrella. "You may need this."

Moore took it. "We have a good team here," he said.

Before Unwin could reply, the sleepwalker in the red union suit closed the door, and the taxicab rolled slowly away down the block.

Moore turned in his seat to gaze out the rear window, one hand open in grim salute.

"And the truth is our business," Unwin said quietly.

It was dark as midnight now, though according to Unwin's watch it was barely eleven in the morning. The storm had worsened, and inky clouds blotted out every trace of the sun. He pulled his jacket tight over his chest as he walked, though it meant baring one hand to the cold.

Sleepwalkers, dozens of them on every block, ignored him as he passed. Some, like the girl who had stolen the police car, were enacting their strange whims in the streets, transforming the city into a kind of open-air madhouse. One man had dragged his furniture onto the sidewalk and was seated on a soggy couch, tugging anxiously at his beard while listening to the news from a silent, unplugged radio. A woman nearby shouted up at an apartment building, arguing with no one Unwin could see or hear—there was a disagreement, it seemed, about who was to blame for ruining the pot roast.

Other sleepwalkers moved in small groups, stepping around Unwin as he passed. They were silent, their eyes open but unfathomable. They were headed east, the same direction Moore had been taken.

By the time Unwin drew near to his apartment, his clothes were soaked through but his hands were clean. A black Agency car was parked at the end of the block. He cupped his hands against the glass to peer through, expecting to find Screed's scowling face, but the car was empty. He returned to his building and went inside, climbed the stairs to the fifth floor.

His apartment door was open, his spare key still in the lock. He put that in his pocket and went in, closing the door behind him. In the kitchen he found himself again at the barrel end of a gun—his own this time. Emily Doppel's eyes were half closed, but her aim seemed true enough. She carried her lunch box in her other hand.

Testing her, Unwin walked toward his bedroom. Emily followed, keeping the pistol trained on her target. He considered going into the bathroom to change, but Emily would probably have followed him there, too. So he undressed in front of her, leaving the damp and bloody clothes in a heap on the floor. Naked, he wondered if there were Agency bylaws regarding detectives and their assistants and whether this violated any of them.

Once he had put on dry clothes, he set the alarm clock he'd taken from the rowboat on his nightstand, then changed his mind and tucked it into his jacket. "I'm sure I was wrong about your lunch box," he said to Emily. "This might be my last chance to learn the truth."

After a moment she seemed to understand. She shook the pistol at him, directing him into the kitchen, then put the lunch box on the table and flipped it open.

Inside were dozens of tin figurines. Unwin set them on the table, lining them up like soldiers. They were not soldiers, though—they were detectives. One crouched with a magnifying glass in his hand, another spoke into a telephone, another held out his badge. One stood as Emily stood now, arm outstretched with pistol in hand. Another resembled Unwin in his current stance, bent over with his hands on his knees, an expression of mild astonishment on his face.

Only flecks of paint remained on the figurines; they had seen a lot of use through the years. Unwin imagined a little red-haired girl, alone at the playground, sitting cross-legged in the grass, surrounded by her dreamed-up operatives. What adventures they must have had under her authority! Now the game had become real for her.

"You understand that the memo I asked you to type was not a ruse," Unwin said. "You deserve better. You deserve a real detective."

Emily swept the figurines back into her lunch box. She kept the gun pointed at him and gestured toward his briefcase, which was lying on the floor near the door. He picked it up and she directed him out of the apartment and back down the stairs.

No one was on the street to witness the sleepwalker conduct him at gunpoint to the black car at the end of the block. He got in on the passenger side and set his briefcase between his feet.

"Are you sure you can drive?" Unwin asked.

For answer, Emily put the car into gear and turned out onto the street. She drove very carefully the seven blocks to the Agency office building, though no one else was on the road now. They parked right outside the lobby, and when Unwin got out of the car, he saw that lights were on in all forty-six floors.

TWELVE

On Interrogation

*The process begins long before you are alone in
a room together. By the time you ask the suspect your
questions, you should already know the answers.*

T he fortieth floor, like the fourteenth, was a single enormous room,
but it was empty except for a square metal table and two chairs
at its center. Emily stood to one side, at the edge of the bright yellow
light aimed at the table from above. She still held the gun but had left
her lunch box in the car and taken Unwin's briefcase instead.

The man with the pointy blond beard was seated opposite Unwin.
Of all the people who lived in the city, this man was one who Unwin
wished were among the sleeping. But it seemed that Hoffmann had left
the Agency's employees to go about their work unhindered—Emily's
sleep was probably just a result of her condition. Whatever the magician was up to, he did not want anyone from the Agency's ranks involved. Or was it simply as Moore had said, that Hoffmann wanted
them to see how he had triumphed?

If so, the man with the blond beard revealed no concern for what
was happening outside. Without looking at Unwin, he set his portable

typewriter on the table. He snapped his fingers at Emily, and she gave him the briefcase. He began removing its contents.

"Two pencils," he said, and put them side by side. "In need of sharpening."

Next he took out Unwin's copy of *The Manual of Detection.* "Standard issue," he said, and sneered as he flipped it open to the title page. "Fourth edition, utterly useless."

Next were some file folders, all empty—Unwin liked to keep a few spares handy.

Last was the phonograph record. This he examined more carefully, holding it up to the light and gazing at its grooves, as though he could hear it if he looked closely enough. "A watcher-class file, Sivart-related. Recorded by the late Mr. Lamech, pressed by Miss Palsgrave on Agency premises. Not logged in any official registry. Most suspect." He slipped it back into its cover and set it on the table, then turned the briefcase upside down and shook it. It was empty.

"I think the Agency has bigger worries than what I keep in my briefcase," Unwin said.

"Quiet," snapped the man with the blond beard. He put everything back, set the briefcase aside, and loaded a sheet of paper into his typewriter. "It took me hours to polish the keys after your accomplice spilled water on them." He sat very straight in his chair and closed his eyes, then rubbed his temples with the tips of his fingers. Next he stretched out his arms and flexed his hands. He seemed to be getting ready for some kind of performance.

"Maybe you should take notes about what's going on outside," Unwin said.

The man with the blond beard said to Emily, "If he speaks again, shoot him."

Unwin sighed and looked at the table while the man went through his stretching routine again. Then, with his eyes partly closed, he began to type. He worked quickly, just as he had done at the museum café.

He seemed to be drawing words out of the air, typing them as he breathed them in.

He reached the bottom of the first page, set the sheet aside, and loaded another. Unwin looked at his watch to time the man's progress. He finished the second page in just under three minutes.

When the third page was done, the man with the blond beard stacked them together, folded them, and slid them into an envelope. He put the envelope inside his jacket, then closed the typewriter case and stood.

"That's it?" Unwin asked.

The man picked up Unwin's briefcase and went toward the door.

"Sir," Unwin said, getting to his feet, "I'd like my briefcase now."

"We have what we need," the man said to Emily. "And you have your orders."

Emily frowned in her sleep. It would not be easy for her to shoot him, Unwin thought. But she was angry. He had deceived her, disappointed her, made her believe he was something he was not. She must have drifted off to sleep sometime after she put him on the eight train that morning. Then she fell victim to the same plague that had infected the rest of the city, and her anger was shaken awake.

She pushed her glasses back on her nose and took aim. Did the *Manual* include advice appropriate to situations like these? No, Unwin thought, it was not *The Manual of Detection* he needed. It was his assistant's own good planning.

"Emily," he said. "The devil's in the details."

Her aim faltered a little.

He repeated the phrase, and Emily swayed on her feet as though the ground had shifted beneath her. "And doubly in the bubbly," she said, opening her eyes. She looked with alarm at the gun in her hand.

Unwin gestured to the man with the blond beard. "There," he said. "There!"

Emily swung the gun around, and the man with the blond beard stopped walking.

"Sir," Unwin said again. "My briefcase."

The man gave Emily a withering look and returned to the table. He dropped the case in front of Unwin.

"Your typewriter as well," Unwin said.

He set the typewriter down.

"Now sit."

Audibly grinding his teeth, the man with the blond beard sat. Emily kept the gun trained on him while Unwin removed the man's necktie and used it to bind his hands behind his back. It would not hold for long, Unwin thought, but it was the best he could do for now.

"Quickly," he said to Emily. "I need you to write a memo."

She put the pistol away, then sat and opened the typewriter, loaded a fresh sheet of paper.

The man with the blond beard snorted at all this but said nothing. Indeed, as Unwin began to dictate, he leaned forward a little, listening with apparent interest.

"To colon Benjamin Screed comma Detective comma floor twenty-nine return from colon Charles Unwin comma capital D capital E capital T capital E capital C capital T capital I capital V capital E comma floor twenty-nine comma temporarily floor forty return.

He took a deep breath and continued. "Sir comma despite the unhappy beginning of our association comma it is my hope that we may still find a way to work together as colleagues to our mutual satisfaction point. To that end comma I offer you the opportunity to assist me—"

But here Unwin frowned and said, "Emily, strike that. Resume: To that end comma I offer to assist you in solving a very important case comma or rather several important cases all at once point. In addition to delivering to you the killer of Edward Lamech comma I intend also to shed new light on cases now at rest in the Agency archives comma including The Oldest Murdered Man comma The Three Deaths of

Colonel Baker comma and The Man Who Stole November Twelfth point. I trust this will be of interest to you comma as you arc no doubt aware that our organization is in need of a new star detective comma and I can tell you I have no interest in the job point. If you find this satisfactory comma I leave it to you to choose our place of meeting point. I will come unarmed full stop."

Emily snatched out the page, quickly typed a final draft, and said, "I'll go and find a messenger."

"No messengers, Emily. I don't think they can be trusted. This remains, as you once put it, an internal affair."

The man with the blond beard was grinning now. Straining against the bonds, he turned in his seat to watch them go. Unwin avoided the man's eyes, glancing back only once while he and Emily waited for the elevator to arrive. He had not even bothered to look at the document the man with the blond beard had typed. Whatever it contained—a false confession, a memory somehow plucked from his brain—it could not possibly matter after this. They believed he was a renegade, and now he was acting like one.

Unwin had worried that the elevator attendant might recognize him, that even he might have been notified of Unwin's fugitive status. But the white-haired little man only hummed to himself as the car descended, seemingly oblivious to his passengers.

Emily drew close to Unwin and whispered, "Do you really know who killed Lamech?"

"No," he said. "But if I don't find out soon, I think it won't matter anyway."

Emily looked at her shoes. "I haven't been a very good assistant," she said.

They both were quiet, and the only sounds in the car were the elevator attendant's tuneless humming and the grating of the machinery above. Unwin knew that it was he, not Emily, who had failed. She had saved him from Detective Screed, had chosen the secret signal that saved him a second time. But outside the Gilbert Hotel, when she asked him what would happen to her once they found Sivart, he had failed to give her an answer.

Maybe he should have told her that he would remain a detective, that she would still be his assistant. Better yet, they could act as partners: the meticulous dreamer and his somnolent sidekick. Together they would untangle the knots Enoch Hoffmann and his villainous cohorts had tied in the city, in its dreams. Their suspects would be disarmed by his clerkly demeanor; she would ask the tough questions and do most of the driving. They would track down every error Sivart had committed, re-solve all the great cases, set the record straight. Their reports would be precise, complete, and timely: the envy of every clerk on the fourteenth floor.

But he had not even cleared his name yet, and Emily now would also be hunted.

She was still looking at her shoes when Unwin put a hand on her shoulder. "You are the finest assistant a detective could wish for," he said.

With a swift movement, as though the floor had tilted or the elevator slipped its cable, Emily fell fully into him and laid her head against his chest, wrapping her arms around his middle. Unwin stifled a gasp at the sudden and complete materialization of this young woman in his arms. He could smell her lavender perfume again, and beneath that the sharpness of her sweat.

Emily raised her lips close to his ear and said, "It's really something, don't you think? We have so much work to do, but we can't trust anyone. And when you get right down to it, we can barely trust each other. But it's better that way, I suppose. It keeps us thinking, keeps us guessing. Just a couple of shadows, that's what we are. Turn the light on and that's the end of us."

The elevator attendant had stopped humming, and Unwin caught himself wondering about bylaws again.

"Emily," he said, "do you remember anything of the dream you were having earlier?"

She moved back an inch and adjusted her glasses. "I remember birds, lots of them. Pigeons, I think. And a breeze. Open windows. There were papers everywhere."

The elevator attendant cleared his throat. "Floor twenty-nine," he said.

Emily slowly let go of Unwin, then stepped out onto the polished wood floor. The custodian had cleaned it to a shine—not a trace of black paint remained.

"Emily?" Unwin said.

"Sir?"

"Do try to stay awake."

The attendant closed the door, and Unwin told him to take him to the archives. Clerks, and even detectives, were technically prohibited from entering, but the little man made no protest. He threw the lever and sat on his stool. "The archives," he said. "The long-term memory of our esteemed organization. Without it we are nothing but a jumble of trivialities, delusions, and windblown stratagems."

A bulb on the attendant's panel lit yellow, and he brought the car to a halt. Unwin found himself looking into the broad office of the fourteenth floor. His overclerk, Mr. Duden, stood in front of him. The round-faced man took a step back when he saw Unwin. "I'll get the next one," he said.

THAT ONLY UNDERCLERKS were permitted access to the Agency archives had instilled in Unwin a simmering resentment of his inferiors. He sometimes daydreamed about catching one of the affable little men on his way to lunch and accompanying him to the booth of a local eatery. There he would buy the man a sandwich, pickles, a glass of what-have-you, and gradually turn the conversation to the topic of their work—forbidden, of course, between employees of different departments. In time the underclerk's caginess would give way to happy disclosure; he was as proud of his work as Unwin was of his, after all. And so Unwin would come to learn the secrets of that place to which his completed case files, and the files of a hundred other clerks, were delivered each day, to be housed in perpetuity. All for the price of a roast beef on rye.

Of course Unwin never did anything of the sort. He was not a faker, not a sneak. At least he had been neither of those things until recently.

The elevator attendant had left him in a corridor one level below the subbasement. It ended at a small wooden door. Slowly, but not so slowly he would appear to be trespassing, Unwin opened it and stepped through.

The heart of the archives (for what else could this be?) smelled of cologne, of dust, of the withered-flower sweetness of old paper. Its ceiling, high as Central Terminal's sweeping vaults, was hung with clusters of electric lamps shaded in green glass, and the walls were made entirely of file drawers. The drawers were of the older sort, with bronze handles and paneling of dark wood. Rolling library ladders, each seven times the height of a man, provided access throughout. Eight massive columns spanned the room, and these, too, were lined with file drawers and equipped with ladders.

Dozens of underclerks were at work here, browsing open drawers, jotting notes on index cards, ascending and descending ladders, wheeling them into new positions. They went back and forth between the files and a squat booth at the center of the room. Meanwhile, messengers in yellow suspenders appeared and disappeared through doors disguised to look like stacks of file drawers, some of them high in the walls. To access one of these, the messenger would climb a ladder, open the door with a telescoping pole he drew from his sack, then leap through the opening.

Unwin closed the door behind him—it, too, was disguised as a stack of file drawers—and walked along the wall searching for some indication of an organizational scheme. But the drawers were not labeled, nor were they divided into sections, alphabetical or otherwise. He chose one at waist height and opened it. The files were all dark blue, not the light brown he was accustomed to seeing. He removed one and found a card pasted to its front. Typed on the card were a series of phrases:

Stolen Journal
Jilted Lover
Vague Threats
Long-Lost Sister
Mysterious Double

The documents inside were formatted according to some method that was wholly unfamiliar to him. Pages of handwritten notes identified a client, described his meeting with an Agency representative, and gave an account of his suspicions and fears. But where were the clues? Who was the detective assigned to the case? How had the matter been resolved?

A nearby drawer slid open, and Unwin looked up to see an underclerk just a few steps away. The man grinned at him. He had round cheeks and wore a bowler hat and a scarlet cravat. Unwin returned the file and ran his fingers over the folder tabs, pretending to search for another.

But the underclerk came closer and bowed, and when Unwin did not look up at him, he bowed again, more deeply this time, and with the third bow he made a dispirited little huffing sound. Finally the underclerk spoke. "You must be the new fellow, yes, the new fellow?"

Unwin avoided answering by patting his palms against the folders and smiling.

"Why don't you tell me what you're looking for?" The underclerk's cheeks reddened. Apparently, the prospect of assisting someone else was a great embarrassment to him.

"You're too kind." Unwin did not want to ask this man about the phonograph record, but he had to tell him something, so he said, "I'm looking for the Sivart case files. The Colonel Baker case would be a good start."

The underclerk frowned at that. "Sounds like you've got too many modifiers. What's the primary correlative?"

Unwin considered. "Faked death," he said.

The underclerk tapped one finger against his round, clean-shaven chin. "Now, I've been here almost two years, and I don't recall . . ." His cheeks went redder, until they matched the color of his cravat. "What did you say your name was?" he asked.

Unwin coughed and waved his hand, and pretended to study the files again. The underclerk went away very quietly and quietly closed the drawer he had opened a minute before. Then he started off toward the center of the room with a quick, resolute pace, more like a messenger than an underclerk.

Unwin closed the drawer and followed. The underclerk saw him pursuing and walked faster, so Unwin began to run. The underclerk ran, too, and by this time most everyone in the archive was watching them. Unwin could see the booth more clearly now. At its peak was a four-faced clock, nearly identical to the one at Central Terminal. Unwin checked his watch and saw that it matched to the very second the clock at the heart of the Agency archives. It was seventeen minutes after one o'clock in the afternoon. The underclerk drew up to the booth, pushing others aside to reach the front. There was a lot of jostling and grumbling, but the others went quiet as he began to speak to someone inside the booth. Then they all turned to watch Unwin's approach. Some removed their hats and started fidgeting with the brims. They parted to let him through, and the one in the red cravat stood aside.

A woman was seated in the booth, surrounded by card catalogs. She was younger than Unwin, though older than Emily. She had straight brown hair and a wide, frowning mouth. She looked him over carefully, paying special attention to his hat.

"You're not an underclerk," she said.

"My apologies," said Unwin. "It is not my intention to deceive. I am a clerk of the fourteenth floor."

Now the underclerks began to chatter all at once. "Clerk!" they said, and, "Fourteenth floor!" They repeated the words until the woman hushed them with a wave of her hand.

"No," Unwin said, shaking his head, "I *was* a clerk. I am hardly accustomed to the change myself. Just yesterday I was promoted to the rank of detective. In fact, I'm here on business of a detectorial nature." He showed her his badge.

Again the underclerks started talking, their voices rising higher as they pushed and pulled at their hats, nearly tearing them in half. "Detective!" they said, and one among them wailed, "What's a detective?"

"Quiet!" the woman shouted. She glared at Unwin. "This is highly irregular. You'd better come in."

She opened a door to the side of her window and ushered Unwin into the booth; some of the underclerks made as though to follow, but the woman closed it before any could slip through. Then she closed green shutters over her window. Unwin could still hear the pleas of the underclerks outside: "What's a detective?" they cried, and then, "What's *promoted*?" The few near the window scratched at the shutters with their fingernails; one was brazen enough to tap his knuckles against the door.

Unwin now saw that the card catalogs replicated in miniature the archives themselves. Each stack of file drawers outside had a corresponding stack within the booth; even the columns were represented by eight freestanding pillars. This explained the lack of references to content or indexing in the archive proper. The only key was here.

The woman reached under her desk, took a silver flask from its hiding place, and set out two tin cups. She poured a little brown liquid into each and pressed one into Unwin's hand. She drank. Unwin was unaccustomed to drinking whiskey straight, from a flask or otherwise. And though he did not find it altogether unpleasant, each sip was a keen surprise to his tongue.

The underclerks were silent now. They had either dispersed or agreed to stay quiet and listen in.

"You must forgive them," the woman said. "They've had a very trying week. We all have." She offered him her hand; her palm was cool and papery against his own. "Eleanor Benjamin," she said, "Chief Clerk of Mysteries."

"Charles Unwin, Detective."

"And, I suppose, the reason I lost my best staffer to the fourteenth floor yesterday. To promote someone from one department to another is atypical. To promote two people at once is absurd. I'm afraid we're all a little rattled down here."

"The woman who has taken my place used to work for you?" Unwin asked.

"Yes," said Miss Benjamin. "Only two months into the job and she was already the best underclerk I had."

This was a surprise even sharper than the whiskey. The woman in the plaid coat, Cleo Greenwood's daughter, had started working at the Agency long before the first time Unwin saw her at Central Terminal. She must have used the time to find and steal an unabridged copy of the *Manual*. But what else had she been up to?

"I hardly know what to do without her," Miss Benjamin went on. "She went about her work so calmly that she kept everyone else calm, too. I'm certain one of these twittering old men will fall from his ladder someday. And they haven't even assigned a replacement yet. The whole archive could fall into ruin."

She paused and looked up at the shutters, seeming to see through them and into an archive in flames, sheets of burning paper falling out of the sky, columns of file drawers collapsing under their own weight. Unwin wondered if she knew that the world outside the Agency office was already in the process of disintegrating.

"Why was she promoted?" Unwin asked. "Did anyone inform you?"

Miss Benjamin blinked away her vision. "I hardly see the relevance of that," she said, and poured more whiskey into their cups. "You know perfectly well that detectives are barred from the archives, Mr. Unwin. Only messengers are permitted to move freely from one floor to another. And under no circumstances should a detective be caught drinking whiskey with a chief clerk. So what are you doing down here?"

Answer questions with questions, he reminded himself—he had read that in the *Manual.* "How many chief clerks are there?"

Miss Benjamin smiled. "I'm not unwilling to help you, Detective. I'm just saying that there's a price. Now, what were you looking for out there in my archive?"

Unwin found that he liked this chief clerk's plainspokenness, but he was not yet sure if he could trust her. "I was looking for my old case files," he said. This was not completely a lie—seeing those files would have been of interest, especially after all he learned since his first meeting with Edwin Moore.

Miss Benjamin laughed, and from outside the booth came the sound of shuffling feet.

"Are you surprised?" Unwin asked. "I've done plenty of case files. The Oldest Murdered Man, The Three Deaths of Colonel Baker."

"Yes, yes," said Miss Benjamin. "But you're talking post-detection, Mr. Unwin. Solutions. This"—she gestured to the card catalogs around her and, by extension, the file drawers beyond—"is Mysteries."

"Only Mysteries?"

"*Only* Mysteries! What did you expect, everything jammed into one archive? That would be an organizational nightmare. I am Chief Clerk of Mysteries, and the underclerks out there are familiar only with mysteries. It's why they don't know what a detective is—they don't need to. The vicissitudes of detection aren't part of their work. As far as they know, mysteries come here and stay here. It's why they're so nervous. Imagine having all the questions but none of the answers."

"I don't have to imagine it," Unwin said.

"Three."

"What?"

"You asked me how many chief clerks there are. There are three. Miss Burgrave, Miss Palsgrave, and myself. Miss Burgrave is Chief Clerk of Solutions. It's her archive you meant to infiltrate, not mine." She lowered her eyelids and added, "Though it isn't a terrible thing, having someone to talk to. Your average underclerk doesn't know a woman from a pile of paper clips."

Unwin sipped from his whiskey—just as little as he could, because he already felt dizzy from it. "What about Miss Palsgrave's archive?" he asked. "What is kept there?"

"What I want to know is why a clerk, promoted though he may be, would want to see his own files. Don't you fellows know your cases back to front?"

"Yes," Unwin said. "But it's less a matter of content than of cross-referencing."

She was silent. He would have to give her at least part of the truth. "The case files are categorized as solutions, and rightly so. They are the finest, most thorough solutions imaginable. But what if an error, a purposeful error conceived for some dark purpose, had been inserted into one of those files? What if an aspect of a solution were thus rendered a mystery? What then, Miss Benjamin?"

"You would not have done such a thing."

"I have, Miss Benjamin. Many times, perhaps, though without realizing it. I believe that a man was murdered to keep it a secret. Somewhere in these archives are mysteries that have been passed off as solutions, so they belong here, Miss Benjamin, in your archive. And they are deliberately being kept from you.

"Under normal circumstances, I could work through the messengers, calling up one file after another, checking references, piecing the puzzle together. But that would take time. And I don't know if I can trust the usual channels. Will you help me, Miss Benjamin? Will you tell me the way to the Archive of Solutions?"

He was not sure what he was getting himself into, but Moore had told him that the key to understanding the phonograph record was here in the archives. If not in the first, then maybe in the second.

Miss Benjamin stood, and Unwin saw that she was tall, perhaps a foot taller than he was. She crossed her arms and looked worried. "There are several paths to the Archive of Solutions," she said, "but most will be too dangerous." She pushed her chair aside and lifted an edge of the frayed blue rug. A trapdoor was beneath. "This passage is reserved for the use of the chief clerks. I don't think anyone but the three of us remembers it's here."

She lifted a brass ring and pulled the trapdoor open. A stairwell spiraled downward into the gloom.

"Thank you," he said.

Miss Benjamin took a step closer to him. With the shutters over the window, the air in the booth had grown warmer, and now Unwin found it difficult to breathe, especially when each breath carried with it the sweet aroma of the whiskey on Miss Benjamin's lips.

She said, "I do know a thing or two about detectives, Mr. Unwin. I know that with a few words you could have won my heart. But you're one of the noble ones, aren't you?"

Unwin did not contradict her, though he doubted that even the *Manual* would contain the few words—whatever they were—to which Miss Benjamin was referring.

"What about the third archive?" he said. "You didn't tell me about Miss Palsgrave."

Miss Benjamin stepped back. "I won't," she said. "This is Mysteries, after all, and Miss Palsgrave's work is her own."

Unwin put on his hat and started down the stairs. Miss Benjamin had seemed tall to him, and now, waist-deep in the floor, he looked up and found her terrible and magnificent, a towering, sulky idol in a brown wool skirt. "Good-bye, Miss Benjamin."

She capped her silver flask and sighed. "Watch out for the ninth step," she said, and Unwin had to duck as she kicked the trapdoor closed over his head.

THE STAIRS WERE LIT only by dim lamps that flickered as though to relay a coded message. There was no banister. The wooden steps creaked underfoot, and Unwin felt each with the toe of his shoe before stepping down. Was it a trick of the whiskey, that the walls of the passage seemed to narrow as Unwin descended? Or had he always been a claustrophobe and only needed an experience like this to find out?

The ninth step appeared as sturdy as the others, but he skipped it as Miss Benjamin advised. Unwin found it difficult to stop counting anything once he had begun. Counting sheep, in fact, was his surest route to insomnia—by morning he could fill whole pastures with a vast and clamorous flock. Now he counted steps, and by the twentieth he felt certain the walls really were narrowing, and the ceiling was getting lower, too. How deep did the stairway go? Maybe Miss Benjamin had tricked him into an oubliette. She could have locked the trapdoor and sent a message to Detective Screed by now—but then, perhaps Mr. Duden already had.

The lamps were fewer in number here, and dimmer. He hoped Edwin Moore had known what he was talking about. Could the old man's memory be trusted at all? Unwin had to bend low to take the last several steps. The fifty-second was the last.

Here was a plain wooden door no more than four feet tall. From beyond it came a sound—a wild, incessant clattering, as of many people typing without pause. Unwin felt for a doorknob but could not find one. When he pushed, the door swung open on silent hinges. He ducked through and had to remain crouched on the other side because the ceiling was so low.

The room was barely larger than the desk in his own office, though finished all in dark wood that gleamed in the light from a chandelier. Where Unwin had expected a legion of underclerks, he saw one tiny woman, her silvery hair pinned in a mound atop her head, seated at a desk at the center of the room. He stooped over her, an uncouth giant in a too-small cave, but she did nothing to acknowledge his presence. Her typing was the quickest Unwin had ever seen—quicker than Emily's, quicker, even, than the man with the blond beard's. The sound of one key-clap was indiscernible from the next, and the carrier bell never ceased to reverberate, chiming the end of each line in rapid succession.

"Miss Burgrave?" Unwin said.

The woman stopped typing and peered at him, the wrinkles at the edges of her mouth and eyes fixed in severe concentration. She wore red lipstick, and her cheeks, soft and sagging, were the pink of pink roses. "Oh, it's you," she said, then went back to her work.

Her little hands were a hundred-fingered blur. The paper went into her typewriter from a single great roll that had been mounted to the front of her desk, then onto a second roll mounted just above the first. This system freed her of the need to pause and insert fresh sheets.

Unwin bent over to read what she was typing, but Miss Burgrave stopped again and stared at him, causing him to withdraw so quickly that he bumped his head against the ceiling.

"This will not do," Miss Burgrave said. "You know what it means to be on a schedule, of course, so I will not rebuke you unnecessarily, as that would be tantamount to redundancy, which I already risk by speaking to you at all, and risk again by observing the risk, and so again by observing the observation. In this we could proceed endlessly. Will you not relent? Are you really so stubborn? I ask these questions rhetorically, and thus degrade further the value of my speech."

"I'm not sure I follow you, Miss Burgrave, but if perhaps you'd allow me into the archives—"

"*If perhaps,*" she repeated, her wrinkles deepening. "Mr. Unwin, we shall brook no degree of mysteriousness on this floor. So that weak-kneed naïf allowed you entrance through the trapdoor, and you believe that entitles you to further transgression—and with my assistance, at that."

Unwin kept quiet now. In spite of himself, he glanced again at the typescript mounted to the desk.

"Facts," Miss Burgrave explained. "Dead facts, all questions beaten out of them, all lines of inquiry followed to their termini. Answers and answers to answers, the end of the road, of the world, maybe. Yes, that is how I feel sometimes, as though the world has already ended, the shades drawn over every window, the stars burned down to little black beads, the moon waned beyond waning, all life a dollop of ash, and still I remain at work, trying to explain what happened."

"Explain to whom?"

"Ah, now we come to something." Miss Burgrave rose from her chair, and Unwin saw that she stood no taller than a child. She waved Unwin out of her way and opened a panel hidden in the wall. From there she drew a book about the size of *The Manual of Detection* but bound in red rather than green. She turned to a certain page and, without having to search, read aloud a single paragraph:

Solutions, as distilled by the clerks so Entrusted, from the Reports of detectives so Assigned, and borne by messengers to the aforementioned Dominions, are there to be studied and Linked each to the other according to common significance, and so prepared for Review by the

Overseer. It is solely to the Chief Clerk of Solutions to whom this Task falls, so let him work alone, unhindered by his subordinates in their Courses and his Seniors in their many Doings.

"Where are your underclerks, then?" Unwin asked.

Miss Burgrave sighed. She seemed to have abandoned something: a conviction, maybe, or a hope. She replaced the book and closed the panel, then gestured for Unwin to follow her through a door behind her desk. In the passage beyond, Unwin was able to stand straight again. He heard the quiet commotion of clerkly work: the whisperings, the pen scratchings, the hurried footfalls. But those who made these sounds were nowhere visible in the long hall, nor in the many branches extending from it. Out of the walls protruded two rows of file drawers, one near the floor and the other at waist height, situated so that all their contents were visible. Now and then these drawers would disappear into the walls, only to return a moment later.

As they walked, Miss Burgrave explained, "We are now between the walls of the Archive of Solutions. My underclerks are without, accessing what files they require, according to the instructions I give them by various means, including notes, bellpulls, and color-coded signals. They do not know me, nor would I recognize them, except by the way each clears his throat."

She took a stepstool from a shadow, climbed it, and switched on a light that extended over one of the drawers. She squinted and adjusted the glasses on her nose. "This is what you are here for, no doubt."

Unwin perused the titles quickly. There they were, in chronological order—all the work he had done in his twenty years, seven months, and some-odd days at the Agency, every word of every case file, the great works and the lesser-known, the grand capers and the minor mysteries. They barely filled the single drawer.

Miss Burgrave watched attentively as Unwin drew out the file for The Oldest Murdered Man. A long card was fixed to the back of the file, covered with typed references to files elsewhere in the archives. Here was the original mystery, upstairs with Miss Benjamin, here the case files of other detectives overlapping with this one. And below them references to another archive, a third.

He said to Miss Burgrave, "These refer to files kept by Miss Palsgrave. What are they?"

Miss Burgrave winced. "For a Chief Clerk of Mysteries," she said, "that Miss Benjamin has a great deal to say. How I long for the days of Miss Margrave, who preceded her in the position. Now, there was a woman who knew how to keep a thing to herself. She died just a few days after she retired. Nothing unusual in that. Some people have little in them except the work. But it's something of a syndrome here at the Agency. Clerks and underclerks are immune, mind you. But anyone who knows anything about anything is granted a very short retirement. I will have my own before long, I suppose. And if laws of proportion apply, then my retirement shall be very short indeed. And your own watcher—which is to say your detective's watcher—is due to retire soon. A nice man, Ed Lamech. I'll miss him."

Unwin understood then that Miss Burgrave knew nothing about his recent promotion. And why would she? His promotion was a mystery even to him, and Miss Burgrave knew only the solutions. So she had not heard of Lamech's murder either.

"You hesitate to speak," Miss Burgrave said, "and I warned you once about our tolerance for mysteriousness on this floor."

He chose his words carefully. "It was the discovery of Lamech's death, among other mysteries, Miss Burgrave, that brought me here."

She covered her mouth with one small hand, steadying herself against the file drawer with the other. After a moment she said, "Now, Ed Lamech, he and I used to play cards together. That was before all this, of course. Miss Margrave and I shared a desk, and the archive was just two cardboard boxes at the back of the room: one for mysteries, one for solutions. Edwin Moore kept the files in order. There was a big table at the center of the room where the detectives would lay out mug shots and maps of the city. They smoked and talked big and planned stings; Ed was the loudest of the bunch, but he always had something nice to say. He knew how to make a person feel a little taller. Some nights we'd clear off the table and play a few hands, all of us together. Yes, I always thought Ed Lamech and I might sit down and play cards again, when we found the time."

She switched off the light and said, "Help me down the stepladder, Mr. Unwin," and he did, but when she reached the floor, she did not let go of his hand. "This way."

Unwin's eyes did not have time to adjust as Miss Burgrave pulled him more and more quickly through the darkness between the walls. When a drawer opened or closed, a band of light from the archive swept momentarily across the floor, but that was all, and Unwin knew he would not find his way back on his own. They came to a corridor that was almost entirely dark, from the walls of which no file drawers extended.

"You go that way," Miss Burgrave said, "and you tell Miss Palsgrave that I sent you, though I doubt she cares anymore about what I have to say."

She took her hand back and added, "She works here, but she's never been like the rest of us; not really. Her curriculum vitae is a curious one, to say the least. Be wary of her. Be polite."

Unwin said, "I will, Miss Burgrave. But please, tell me one thing. If you know your underclerks only by their coughs, how did you know me?"

"Oh, Mr. Unwin, don't you know you're one of my own children? Your work has given me some pleasure through the years. When you leave a thing, you leave it where no doubt can touch it. I will not wish you luck. Of your success or failure I will hear in due course."

Unwin heard her footsteps receding, glimpsed the silver of her hair as it passed an open file drawer. And then Miss Burgrave was gone.

He went alone into the dark. The passage sloped downward and curved to the left, tracing a spiral through the earth. Sometimes he kept his eyes open and sometimes he shut them; it made little difference. Miss Burgrave had been right about him: he left matters where no doubt could touch them. But that had been his flaw, to bind mystery so tightly, to obscure his detective's missteps with perfect files. Somehow Unwin had made false things true.

At last his hands found something solid. He felt around the wall, found there the cool roundness of a doorknob and beneath it the gap of a keyhole. He knelt and peered through.

At the center of a vast, dark room were two velvet chairs set on a round blue rug. A blue-shaded floor lamp was set between them, and in its light a phonograph was playing. The music was all drowsy strings and horns, and then a woman began to sing. He knew the melody.

It may be a crime,
But I'm sure that you're mine
In my dream of your dream of me.

The doorknob turned in his hand, and Unwin entered the third archive of the Agency offices.

THIRTEEN

On Cryptography

**The coded message is a lifeless thing, mummified and
entombed. To the would-be cryptologist we must
offer the same advice we would give the grave
robber, the spelunker, and the sorcerer of legend:
beware what you dig up; it is yours.**

A distance of perhaps fifty paces separated him from the chairs, one
pink, the other pale green. Unwin felt drawn to the warmth of
the electric light, to the languid music playing there, to the voice that
could only have been Miss Greenwood's. It looked to him as though a
cozy parlor had been set down in the middle of a cavern. He went
toward it, feeling alone and insubstantial. He could not see his arms or
his legs, could not see his own shoes. All he could see were the chairs,
the lamp, and the phonograph. All he could hear was the music.

The floor was flat and smooth. A floor like that should have set his
shoes squeaking, but they were muffled—by the darkness itself, Unwin
thought. He kept his mouth shut tight. He did not want to let any of
the darkness in.

He stopped at the edge of the blue rug and stood very still. Here
was a boundary between worlds. In the one were chairs, and music, and

light. In the other there were none of these things, nor even the words for chair, or music, or light.

He did not cross over, only observed from the safety of his wordless dark. Phonograph records were stacked in a cabinet near the green chair, and on top of the cabinet stood a row of books. One of the books looked exactly like the red volume that Miss Burgrave had taken from the secret panel in her office. But everything in the parlor was subjugated to that pink chair. It was nearly three times as large as the green one. Anyone sitting in it would seem a child in proportion. It was the most sinister piece of furniture Unwin had ever seen. He could not imagine sitting in it. He could not imagine sitting in the one that faced it.

He took a step back. The chair would spring upon him if he gave it the chance, devour him whole. If only he could call it by name, he thought, then it might be tamed. Or if he had not given his umbrella to Edwin Moore, he could open it and shield himself from the sight.

From the farthest recesses of the room came a flash of light, bright and brief as the death of a little sun, and for the moment in which it burned, Unwin saw the walls in that region of the archive—saw that they were lined, not with filing cabinets but with shelves of phonograph records. The source of the light was a gigantic machine, a labyrinth of valves and pipes and pistons. It hissed and coughed steam into the air, resembling nothing so much as an oversize waffle iron. The light burst from the space between two great plates, pressed together by the machine's operator. She had wide shoulders and thick forearms, and it might have been a trick of light or perspective, but she appeared impossibly large, a titanic blacksmith at her infernal forge.

Unwin knew that this was the chief clerk Miss Palsgrave. The pink chair could only have been hers.

By the time the vision faded, the song on the phonograph had come to an end. The needle reached the lead-out and rose by itself, and the record stopped turning.

The darkness was no longer oppressive to him, nor was Miss Palsgrave's colossal chair. Worse was the thought that Miss Palsgrave herself would come closer, to put on a new record.

He retreated farther into the darkness, and the air grew warmer as he walked. There was a stale, burning odor in the air, like electrical discharge or the breath of the oversleeping. From all around came coughing sounds, rasps, weird mumblings. Unwin was not alone. But did those who made the sounds know that he was among them?

Something snagged his foot, nearly tripping him. He knelt and searched with his hand, found a rubberized cord stretched over the floor. This he followed several feet to the leg of a table. The table was knee-high, and there was a lamp on top of it. He found the switch and flipped it.

The shaded bulb cast its dim yellow light over a low, narrow bed. Its occupant was an underclerk—he wore an unfashionable gray suit and lay with his bowler perched on his chest. The bed was made up with drab, olive-colored blankets, but the underclerk slept on top of them rather than beneath. His little mustache trembled with each softly whistled exhalation, and his feet were bare. On the floor beside the bed were a pair of furry brown slippers, like two rabbits.

A little machine whirred softly on the table beside the lamp. It was a phonograph, though of a simpler, more utilitarian design than the one at the center of the archive. A ghost-white record, like the one Unwin had found in Lamech's office, revolved under the needle. The phonograph produced no sound that he could hear; it had no amplifying bell. Instead it was equipped with a pair of bulbous headphones, which the underclerk wore as he slept.

Other beds nearby were arranged, like the desks of the fourteenth floor, in three long rows. In each of them an underclerk lay sleeping. Some made use of their blankets, some did not. Some slept in their suits, some in pajamas, and some had black sleeping masks strapped over their eyes. All wore identical headphones plugged in to quietly humming phonographs.

Unwin leaned close to the underclerk's head, gently lifted the earpiece, and listened. All he heard was static, but the static was richly patterned, rising and falling in waves, cresting, breaking, receding. In time other sounds became apparent. He heard a muted honking, like traffic at a distance of several city blocks or birds circling over the sea. He heard animals calling from the depths of that sea and smaller animals scuttling over the sand at its bottom. He heard someone turning the pages of a book.

The underclerk opened his eyes and looked at him. "They've sent extra help, have they? Not a moment too soon."

Unwin let go of the earpiece and stood straight.

The underclerk's eyes closed, and for a moment it seemed he might fall asleep again, but then he shook his head and removed the headphones. "It's unprecedented," he said. "What is it, almost two in the afternoon? And they're still sending fresh recordings."

He sat up and rubbed his face with both hands. "It's as though no one is waking up. But the subjects lack culpability modulations of any kind, and the delineations are too vivid to be self-generated. And then there's the smaller bunch, all sharing the same image array—a whole subset with nearly identical eidetic representations, and it's a juvenile construct to boot." He raised the arm of the phonograph and switched off the machine.

"What is it?" Unwin asked.

"What is what?"

"The repeated . . . eidetic representation," Unwin managed.

"Oh. It's a carnival." The underclerk smirked and rolled his eyes.

There was another flash of light from Miss Palsgrave's machine, and both men turned to look at it.

"At first I thought it was a transduction error," the underclerk said,

whispering now. "But try telling that to *her*." He removed the phonograph record and slid it into its slipcase, slid his feet into the slippers
beside the bed. Then he stood, tightened the blankets over the edges of
the mattress, and fluffed the pillow. "Well," he said, "it's all yours. Feel
free to recycle my report if you get one from the circus crowd. You'll
grow tired of hearing it: 'Something to do, someplace to go.' What kind
of liminal directive is that?"

The underclerk clapped Unwin on the shoulder, then shuffled away
into the dark. A minute later Unwin heard a door open and close, and
he was alone again with the sleeping underclerks.

Unwin sat on the edge of the bed. He should have been exhausted,
but his brain was moving as quickly as his feet had been. The underclerk had repeated the phrases the taxi driver and his passengers had
used to identify one another. They were swimming in the same strange
dream—but for what purpose had Hoffmann devised it? Hopefully,
Moore had made progress with his investigation.

Unwin looked back toward the center of the archive and saw Miss
Palsgrave seated in her pink chair. She wore a lavender dress, and her
hair was all soft brown curls. From this distance her eyes appeared as
dark hollows. She seemed to be watching him.

Unwin stood and began to speak over the distance. "Miss Palsgrave,
I—" but she immediately put a finger to her lips.

The nearest underclerks turned in their beds, and some mumbled
in their sleep. One adjusted his headphones and said, "Trying to
work here."

Miss Palsgrave began to turn the crank on her phonograph. When
she finished, she set the needle down and Cleo Greenwood's voice, accompanied by an accordion, filled the archive again. Those underclerks
who had been disturbed were perfectly quiet now, and Unwin, too, felt
the effects of the music.

He set down his briefcase, switched off the light, and settled back
onto the bed. It was comfortable despite its small size. He kicked off

his shoes without bothering to untie them and swung his legs up onto the mattress. The pillow was very soft, and the blanket, once he had slipped beneath it, was the finest, most luxurious blanket in the world. It might have been made of silk, he thought.

He took off his hat and dropped it beside his shoes. He would never need any of those things again. He would stay down here where no one knew him and sleep through the rest of his days, and when he died, they could tuck him away into a long file drawer, write his name on the label, and close it up forever. His mind lingered for a time in the hinterlands of sleep, words drifting over the border as though on a warm wind, unfastened from their meanings. He had almost let the wind take him when a few of the words appeared in boldface and he woke himself by speaking aloud.

"Papers and pigeons," he said, and knew he had forgotten something important.

Fighting the effects of Miss Greenwood's mesmeric voice, he reached over the side of the bed and undid the clasp on his briefcase, found the record from Lamech's office, and drew it from its sleeve. He fitted it onto the turntable of the electric phonograph by the bed, fumbled with the machine's controls, and set it playing. Then he found the headphones and put them on.

Miss Greenwood's voice faded, and with it the somber strains of the accordion music. He heard the familiar static, the shushing, the cadenced crackling. It was a language of sorts, but Unwin understood none of it. Then he stopped hearing the sounds and began instead to see them. The static had shape to it, dimensions; it rose like a waterfall in reverse and then froze in place. More walls leapt up, and in the one before him was a window, in the one behind him a door, and lining the other two were rows of books with blue and brown spines. The static spilled over the floor and made a carpet, made shadows of chairs and then made chairs.

The crackling sound was rain tapping against the window. The shushing was the shushing of secrets in a desk, and on the desk were a green-shaded lamp and a typewriter. A man was seated behind it with his eyes closed, breathing very slowly.

"Hello, Mr. Unwin," Edward Lamech said.

"Sir," said Unwin, but Lamech raised his hand.

"Do not bother speaking," he said. "I cannot hear you. Nor, for that matter, can I be certain that it's you, Mr. Unwin, to whom I am speaking. In recording this session, I am merely preparing for one of many contingencies. I hope that I'll have the opportunity to place this file directly into your hands. If I do not, or if it falls instead into the hands of our enemies, then . . ." Lamech wrinkled his considerable brow. "Then they will already have understood my intentions, I think, and none of it will matter anymore."

Lamech opened his eyes. How different they were from those Unwin saw the previous morning. They were watery and blue, and very much alive. But they were blind to his presence.

Lamech rose from his seat, and a hat appeared in his hand. When he put it on, a matching raincoat fell over his shoulders. "I don't know whether I've been able to explain very much to you," he said. "But since you're seeing this, then you've likely received my instructions and taken this file to the third archive. So you may understand a great deal. Time moves differently here, and that can be confusing to the uninitiated, but it will work to our advantage. I will tell you what more you need to know while we walk together. I have a few errands to run before I go to my appointment."

He walked toward the door, and Unwin jumped aside to avoid him.

"In case you're wondering," Lamech went on, "I almost always begin with my office. We watchers work best when we stick to certain patterns. Some prefer a childhood home for their starting point, others a wooded place. One woman uses a subway station with countless intersecting tracks. My office is familiar to me, and I can reconstruct it with relative ease. These are only details, though, meaningless unto themselves. If you are seated, I suggest you stand at this time."

Lamech opened the door. Instead of the hallway of the thirty-sixth floor, with its yellow light fixtures and bronze nameplates, Unwin saw a twisting alleyway, dark and full of rain. They stepped outside, and the door closed behind them. Unwin wished for his hat and found that he was wearing it. He wished for his umbrella, and that, too, was with him, in his hand and open. But as they walked the maze of high brick walls, he remained partly aware of the warmth of the blankets on the bed and of the softness of his pillow.

"All this is representational," Lamech said. "And arbitrary, for that matter. But it takes years of practice to achieve this degree of lucidity. Think of the alley as an organizational schematic. It's one I find especially useful. Here are as many doors as I need, and they serve logically as connecting principles. Some watchers work more quickly than I do, because they don't bother with such devices. But they have forgotten how to take pleasure in their vocation. There is something good about it, don't you think? The night, and the splash of the rain around us? We move unseen through the dark, along back ways and side streets. Forgive me if I indulge in the particulars, Mr. Unwin. A lot has happened very quickly, and I'm working this out as we go."

The moon emerged from behind the clouds, and Lamech gazed up at it, grinning a little. Then it was gone again, and he drew his coat more tightly about his body. "Miss Palsgrave's machine in the third archive is a wonder—we tell her when we're close to something important, something we may need to document, and she'll tune it to the correct frequency. She can even check in on you herself and follow you from one mind to another if necessary. The truth is, it's one of the few advantages we have over Hoffmann: the ability to record, review, correlate, compare. We don't always know what he's up to, but we can spot Hoffmannic patterns in the recordings of the city's dreams, then act to thwart his next move.

"This recording," he added, "may turn out to be especially valuable, and more than a little dangerous—to you as well as to me, I'm afraid."

In the shadow of a junk pile, they came to a shabby door, blue paint peeling from its worn wooden surface. Lamech leaned close to it and listened. "Here we are," he said.

He opened the door, and bright light shone into the alleyway, gilding the wet bricks. Over Lamech's shoulder Unwin saw the impossible: a broad beach, the sea deep and boundless, and the sun, high and bright at the top of the sky. He followed Lamech out onto the sand. On this side, the door served as the entrance to a rickety beach house.

The heat was terrible. Unwin removed his hat and wiped his brow with his sleeve. He kept his umbrella over his head, shielding himself from the sun as they trudged toward the water.

Near the edge of the waves' reach was a heap of smooth black rocks. A round woman in a ruffled blue bathing suit leaned against them, watching the sea. When she saw Lamech coming toward her, she turned and waved at him. She wore a string of imperfect-looking pearls around her neck, and a few strands of gray hair protruded from under her white bathing cap.

"Edward," she said. "When are you coming home? I polished the silverware while I waited. Twice. You know how tired I get when I polish. Did you unplug your telephone again?"

Unwin remembered the cord left disconnected on Lamech's desk. So it was the watcher himself who had been responsible for that. He had wanted to make sure nothing would wake him during the recording.

Lamech removed his hat and bent to kiss the woman on her cheek. "Working late tonight," he said.

"Can't you bring your work home?"

He shook his head. "I just came by to say good night."

She looked at the sea, a trace of a scowl on her face. Her cheeks were red from the sun and the wind. "The strange thing is," she said, "I don't even know if this is the real Edward I'm speaking to. I wanted so badly to see you that I may very well have dreamed you up."

"No, ladybug, it's me. I have an appointment, that's all."

"Ladybug?" she said. "You haven't called me that in years."

Lamech looked at his feet and tapped his hat against his leg. "Well, I've been thinking a lot about the old times. You know, a couple of kids in the big city, working bad jobs, dancing to the radio at night, drinks at the corner bar. What was that place called? Larry's? Harry's?"

The woman fingered the roughly formed pearls of her necklace.

"Sarah," he said, "there's something else. I just want you to know—"

"Stop. We'll talk about this in the morning."

"Sarah."

"I'll see you in the morning," she said, her voice firm.

Lamech frowned and took a deep breath through his nose. "All right," he said.

The wind was picking up; it made the ruffles of Sarah's bathing suit flutter and teased the gray curls at the edge of her cap. She was looking at the sea again. "This dream always ends the same way," she said.

"How's it end?" Lamech asked.

She was quiet for a while. "Edward, there are leftovers in the icebox. I have to go now." She stood straight and ran her hands down her sides. Then, without looking back, she jogged away toward the water, her pearls swinging back and forth around her neck. Clouds had risen up over the edge of the horizon, and the sea appeared choppy and dark.

"Come on," Lamech mumbled. He turned and starting walking back toward the beach house.

Unwin stayed where he was, watching as Sarah strode nimbly into the water. When she was in above her knees, she dove forward over a wave and began to swim.

"Come on," Lamech said again, as though he had known that Unwin would stay.

Unwin folded his umbrella to keep the wind from taking it and hurried up the beach after Lamech. He could feel the softness of the sand beneath his feet, but his shoes left no impression.

Lamech's raincoat billowed and snapped in the wind. He stuck his hands in his pockets and drew his coat close about him. His shoulders were hunched, his head down. He did not look back.

Unwin looked back. He could no longer see Sarah—she had vanished into the water. A great wave was forming on the horizon. It churned and swelled and boiled, gathering the sea to itself as it rolled toward the shore. Unwin quickened his pace, but he could not take his eyes off the wave. It was tall now as any building, its roaring louder than the traffic of citywide gridlock. Gulls flew over its crest and screamed. In the smooth window of its broad face Unwin could see animals swimming—fish, and starfish, and great heaving squid. They went about their business as though nothing strange were happening, as though they were still deep in the ocean instead of hurtling toward dry land. The wind was saturated with the stink of their briny world.

Lamech was at the faded blue door now. He opened it, and Unwin followed him back into the alleyway, opening his umbrella over his head. Lamech left the door open long enough to watch the wave's shadow blanket the beach. Then he closed it.

"I try not to peer too often into her sleeping mind," Lamech said. "It is an occupational hazard of ours, to learn too much about the people we love. But on those occasions when I have met my wife on her own territory, so to speak, I have always been amazed at the vastness of events under way there. I admit that it frightens me a little."

He stuck his hat back on his head and walked off down the alley. Unwin went after him, fighting the urge to stop and shake the sand out of his shoes.

FOURTEEN

On Nemeses

**There is no better way to understand your own
motives and dispositions than by finding
someone to act as your opposite.**

Their route along the worn brick pathways of Lamech's dreaming mind grew ever more strange and circuitous. They ducked beneath rusting fire escapes, passed through tunnels that smelled of algae and damp earth, hopped gutters brimming with filth. Twice they crossed deep ravines on makeshift bridges of steel grating. Down below, Unwin could see other alleyways, other tunnels, other gutters. The place was built in layers, one maze stacked upon another—a peculiar choice, Unwin thought, for an organizational system. Why not a house, or even an office building, if anything were indeed possible? If Lamech could use doors to travel from one dream to another, could he not also use file drawers?

But the watcher appeared perfectly at home here; he traversed the convoluted byways of his phantom city with a prowess that belied his age and his girth. How terrible that Unwin could not warn him of what was ahead. But even if he could speak to Lamech, even if he could bend time as these alleys bent space, he would not know what to say. The engine of the watcher's destruction was still veiled to Unwin. Could a dream kill a man? Could it strangle him where he sat sleeping?

Ventilating fans churned over their heads, drawing air into edifices housing unknowable visions. Or knowable, Unwin reminded himself. To Lamech and his fellow watchers, these dreams were as rooms to be entered, books to be opened and perused.

As though Unwin's own thoughts were before Lamech's eyes, the watcher said, "Not all surveillance is as easily accomplished as what you just witnessed, Mr. Unwin. My wife desired my presence, so I was granted passage. But some of these doors are shut tight or locked. Others are too well hidden to be found. And the minds of a certain few are simply too dangerous to enter. We watchers wield some influence in the dreams of ordinary sleepers, but the visions of one practiced in the arts of dream detection are entirely his own. You could stumble into such a place and be driven mad by the monstrosities lurking there, summoned with perfect lucidity to taunt and cajole.

"You know, I'm sure, of whose methods I speak."

Ahead, Unwin glimpsed a part of the landscape that was different from the rest: a patch of bright, sparkling light the size of several city blocks. The buildings nearby reflected its glow, and the entire thing swelled and flexed as though breathing. For a moment Unwin thought it was the sea—that the water had poured, still shining, straight from Sarah Lamech's dream to flood this part of the city. But Unwin could hear the thing as well as see it, and it was not the crash of waves that reached his ear. A droning music emanated from the place: a haunting, repetitive tune.

It was a carnival, and Lamech was leading them toward it.

"In most cases," the watcher went on, "the greatest challenge is to remain undetected by one's subject. In order to exist in another's dream—and that is different from observing a recording—one must be *part* of the dream. How, then, is the watcher to keep from revealing himself? The trick is to keep to the dreamer's own shadow, to the darker places of his mind, to the nooks and crawl spaces into which he dare not cast his gaze. There are usually plenty of such places."

In front of them, the alleyway split in two. Lamech stopped walking and peered down each passage. To Unwin they were perfect mirror images. His guide hesitated, then shrugged and chose the one on the left.

"But the watcher is limited in his investigations by what the suspect dreams," Lamech continued. "A man may dream of a closet door, but unless he opens it, the watcher cannot see inside the closet. That is why we learn to nudge our suspects a little. 'Don't you want to see what's in there?' we might whisper. And the suspect does wonder, and opens the door, and lo, there is the memory of the murder he committed just last Tuesday."

Unwin looked back the way they had come, troubled by the doubt Lamech had shown at the split in the alley. Until then the watcher had chosen his route without hesitation. If he was unfamiliar with a feature of his own creation, was he exposing himself to some risk? Could they have taken a wrong turn?

"Curiously," Lamech said, "Miss Palsgrave's device somehow pushes those boundaries a bit. When you review a recording, you can see outside the suspect's immediate perspective: peer around corners, open books, search under beds. The machine seems to pick up low registers emanating from deep in the subconscious. It has a kind of peripheral vision and sees things neither the dreamer nor the watcher thinks he can see. Another advantage we have over Hoffmann."

Unwin, still looking over his shoulder, saw something that astonished him. A door opened, and a woman slipped quietly into the alley. She followed after Lamech, keeping close to the walls, a shadow among shadows, quick as the rain. When a stray beam of moonlight caught her face, Unwin nearly startled awake. Back in the third archive, his legs twitched and his feet became tangled in the blanket.

It was Miss Greenwood's daughter, her plaid coat belted around her waist, her hair pinned tightly beneath her gray cap.

Lamech failed to notice that his dream had been infiltrated. Unwin shouted at him, tugged at his coat, pointed at their pursuer, all to no effect. The woman in the plaid coat trailed only a few steps behind them. Unwin was invisible to her—she was part of the recording—but she watched Lamech intently, pausing only to adjust the gray cap over her hair. Unwin thought, *She is asleep, it is the night before last, and hours from now she will go to Central Terminal and drop her umbrella, and I will fail to pick it up.*

They were drawing close to the carnival. The streets were suffused with hazy white light, and Unwin could hear the music clearly now— it was that of a hurdy-gurdy or a barrel organ. The watcher rounded a corner, wiping his eyes and blinking a little. Unwin followed him, and the woman in the plaid coat came after.

"For the first time since the Agency adopted dream detection as standard practice," Lamech said, "unauthorized operatives have learned the truth of what we watchers do. If you are indeed seeing this, Mr. Unwin, then you are one of two. I'm sure you can guess who the other is."

At the mention of Unwin's name, the woman in the plaid coat narrowed her eyes and looked around. Seeing no one else, she continued on, but at a greater distance than before. So the daughter of Cleopatra Greenwood knew his name. Had she known who he was when she dropped her umbrella at Central Terminal? Somehow she had contrived to be hired as an underclerk and then promoted to Unwin's own desk. But her talents were such that she could infiltrate even an experienced watcher's dream. Cleo may have been concerned for her daughter's well-being, but to Unwin she seemed able to take care of herself.

"A week ago," Lamech said, "someone stole my copy of *The Manual of Detection* and gave it to Detective Sivart. He had seen the book before, of course, knew it front to back. But there was something different about this edition. It included an eighteenth chapter, detailing the technique termed oneiric detection by its author. Sivart was furious. Why had this technique been denied to him all these years? Why hadn't someone told him? Why hadn't *I* told him? That's what he asked me when he stormed into my office first thing that morning.

"I had to tell him something. So I told him the truth. I told him oneiric detection was deemed too dangerous by the overseer to be included in editions beyond the first. Only watchers were to be trusted with its secrets. Detectives, while benefiting from its existence, would remain in the dark, if you will. Sivart didn't like being in the dark. He told me he was going to win the war.

" 'What war?' I asked him.

" 'The war against Enoch Hoffmann,' he said.

"He thought that by breaking in to the sleeping mind of his enemy he could somehow learn his secrets. Forget that Hoffmann had been in hiding for years, kept always in check by our efforts. And forget that none of our finest operatives would risk half a minute in that man's mind. Sivart felt there was something unfinished between them.

"I couldn't stop him from going, so I helped him break some rules instead. First, I told him who his clerk was. He's built up a lot of respect for you over the years, Mr. Unwin, and he thinks you're the one to help him. He said you know things no one else knows about him—details from his reports that didn't make it into the files because they weren't relevant to the case. Things you would have cut, but which matter now. He wouldn't tell me what they were, of course.

"Second, I notified Miss Palsgrave I'd need a new recording made and that I didn't want it cataloged in the third archive. I asked her to send it to me directly, so that I could give it to you. I just hope it's enough."

The carnival bore a likeness to Caligari's Travels-No-More, with buildings shaped like enormous animal heads, striped tents topped with pennants, and row upon row of gaming booths. This carnival, however, appeared to be in perfect working order: no flooded cause-ways, no broken rides, no collapsed pavilions. The place had an ethereal quality, its every part emanating that pale glow and seeming to swell and shiver as though touched by a wind Unwin could not feel on his own dreamed skin. The music came from everywhere at once, and the clouds above were lit like B-movie ghosts.

Lamech walked more slowly now, taking care with every step. "This place isn't what you think it is," he said. "At least not exactly. We've been unable to pinpoint the precise location of Hoffmann's mind, so each of these structures marks only one possibility. He leaves echoes of himself wherever he goes, to throw us off his trail. The people repre-sented here may be among the remnants of Caligari's. Or worse, they are ordinary folk who don't know they've been touched by the magi-cian's hand. In recent weeks, especially since Sivart's departure, this area has expanded dramatically."

They were nearing what must have been the center of the carnival. The cars of the nearby big wheel groaned on their axes as they slowly revolved. Lamech stopped walking and spun in a circle, surveying his surroundings. The woman in the plaid coat retreated around the edge of a ticket booth but kept the watcher in sight.

"I am loath to admit that its appearance is not of my choosing," he said. "Hoffmann's power is such that he determines his own semblance, even in the minds of others. Believe me, it's a damn annoyance. And I don't much care for the music either."

The warmth of the bed in the third archive was gone from Unwin's senses—only the cold light of the carnival was real to him now; that, and the rain thumping against his umbrella and spattering his shoes. His socks were getting wet. His socks were always getting wet, even in his sleep.

"There," Lamech said.

Unwin followed his gaze to a squat building with a wide set of stairs leading to a windowed gallery. Inside, the carnival landscape appeared reflected and fractured along seemingly endless corridors—a hall of mirrors. Lamech himself was replicated dozens of times over, his body distorted or broken into pieces: an arm here, a leg there, his gut over there. Unwin had no reflection, but for a moment he glimpsed another form moving among the panels: a hat, a gray raincoat, the ember of a cigar.

Lamech jogged quickly toward it, puffing a little, and Unwin was at his side. By the time they reached the building, the image was gone. Lamech put one foot up on the bottom step and leaned on his knee. They waited.

"Hoffmann probably caught him as soon as he set foot in there," Lamech said. "All he has to do now is stay asleep to keep him prisoner. But it's worse than that, much worse. The longer Sivart is trapped, the less his mind is his own. Hoffmann will learn all that he knows, subsuming his identity along with his thoughts. In the end, Sivart will be nothing, a vegetable. Or a witless pawn subject wholly to the magician's will."

Sivart reappeared. There were many copies of him, all tiny—he must have been deep inside the hall of mirrors, and what they saw was an image a dozen times reflected. He seemed to see them, too, because he crouched and tilted his hat back.

"Travis!" Lamech called. "Can you hear me?"

The miniature Sivarts all stood straight and took their cigars out of their mouths. Unwin thought he could see the mouths moving, but he heard nothing except the rain and the creaking of the big wheel. He and Lamech leaned closer. Something changed in the glass then, and Unwin's vision blurred. He closed his eyes and opened them, but the problem was not with his eyes.

The reflection of the carnival at their backs was moving, fading in some places as it brightened in others. Parts of the landscape receded into the distance, while other parts zoomed closer.

Unwin no longer heard the sound of the rain on his umbrella. The hall of mirrors had enclosed them. Lamech, in his confusion, spun around once and stepped backward into a transparent wall. "What?" he said, and then, as though he were on a telephone with a bad connection, "Hello?"

"Ed Lamech," the many Sivarts called, moving again, some of them disappearing as others materialized. "What brings you down here at this time of—" He stopped a moment. "Aw, heck, buddy. Is it day or night? I lose track."

"It's good to see you alive, Travis. I'm giving someone a tour, that's all."

"They'll pay you for anything, huh?" The Sivarts ducked around corners, and some of them grew. He was drawing closer. "Who you got with you?"

"Someone who can help us, I think. Help you, Travis—maybe get you out of here."

"That's great, Ed." Sivart's tone had turned suddenly sour. "I'm glad you've still got my back."

Lamech swept his hat off. "I told you not to go. You've put us all in jeopardy. Here in Hoffmann's mind, one of the Agency's top men!"

"Now you're just flattering."

"We made a good team, Travis. But I'm in some pretty deep water here. Deeper than you know. It's dangerous for me to be in this place." Lamech was feeling the walls with his hands, batting at them with his hat. He found an opening between two mirrors and moved through it; Unwin followed him.

"They call this a fun house," Sivart said. "But I tell you it's worse than anything we've sent the crooks to. He comes in now and then to check up on me. And when he does, it's like having the top of my skull screwed off and a flashlight shone in. It hurts, Ed. You should have told me what I was up against."

"I tried, Travis. I tried."

Several more of the Sivarts vanished. There were only a few of them now. He was close, but Lamech could not find his way to him.

Sivart and his reflections said, "You know how he did this? He learned it from Caligari, that crazy little guy who brought the carnival here. You remember: 'Everything I tell you is true, and everything you see is as real as you are.' What did that mean anyway?"

"No," Lamech said, "the technique came out of the Agency. Somebody stole the secret and brought it to Hoffmann. Greenwood, probably."

"That's just the story. Bunch of smoke. Truth is, we're dabbling in something a hell of a lot older. This goes back, back to the beginning, maybe. It came in with the carnival, and your boss got hold of it somehow. We'd all have been better off without it."

"How do you know this?"

"You don't think I got caught right away, do you? I saw it firsthand. Not the way the *Manual* said to, though. I jumped in at the deep end, went right for the spooky stuff. I wanted to know what makes him tick."

Lamech was out of breath. He stopped walking and put his hands on his knees. "Well?"

"Nobody taught him to do the voices," Sivart said. He was pacing back and forth, his reflections multiplying and converging while he spoke. "He was born like that. Grew up in a little village out in the country, immigrant family, hardworking folks. He stole bread by impersonating the baker's wife, calling him out of the shop with her voice. Clever boy, see? Later he hid in a church balcony and pretended to be an angel, tricked the minister into altering his sermons. Convinced him to put in strange things about overturning the order of the world, no salvation but in topsy-turvydom, et cetera. When they figured out what was going on, they put the kid down as some kind of devil. Probably would have killed him if the carnival hadn't taken him in."

Something was wrong. Sivart was shaking as he spoke, and when the face of one reflection was visible for a moment, Unwin thought he saw tears. Lamech noticed, too. "Travis," he said, "we don't have time for this."

Sivart tore the cigar out of his mouth and threw it on the floor. "It could be important, Ed. Will you listen to me for once? Hoffmann was just a boy when his mother gave him to the carnival. And that monster Caligari taught him but never taught him enough. So Hoffmann thought he'd figure it out on his own. He sneaked into the old man's mind one night, trying to learn his secrets. Caligari caught him and kept him there. Tortured him, wouldn't let him wake up. Worst of all, he knew that Caligari had kept something from him, would always keep something from him. He would never share the secret that made him powerful."

Lamech looked calm now, as though he had arrived at an understanding of some kind. "Sounds to me like Hoffmann needed a lesson, Travis. Sounds like he was getting ahead of himself."

There were only two Sivarts now. They both turned away and threw their hands in the air. "What do you know? You haven't seen what I've seen. Anyway, you better let me in on the plan. Who is it you're recruiting? I hope he's good."

"Under the circumstances," Lamech said, "it's probably better that I not tell you."

The Sivarts were quiet for a time. Then they stood straight, stretching to crack their necks. When they turned around, their eyes were closed and they were grinning. "What circumstances, exactly?"

"I know who you are," Lamech said.

The Sivarts took a deep breath. There was a squelching sound as the face of the nearer loosened and crinkled around the edges. It slid off and fell to the floor, folding like an omelette where it landed.

Unwin stepped back. Down in the third archive, he heard himself whimper into the pillow.

The face that had been masked was squarish, dull, bored-looking. Enoch Hoffmann opened his eyes and rolled up his sleeves. The biloquist was wearing his pajamas now, blue with red trim.

The real Sivart fell back against a transparent wall, a marionette whose strings had been cut. He looked groggy, exhausted, invisibly bruised. Had his mind already turned to dust? No: he coughed and grimaced at Lamech, managing a little wave.

"I ought to strangle you," Hoffmann said to the watcher. His regular voice was as Sivart had described it in his reports—high-pitched and whispery, barely a voice at all, empty of feeling even when it threatened.

"You'd have to wake up first," Lamech said. "And you're not going to do that, are you? Now that you've finally caught him, you can't bear to let him go. You're as much a prisoner as he is."

The magician was ignoring him; his gaze was fixed on the spot where Unwin stood. Hoffmann came toward him, and Unwin felt as though his damp clothes had frozen solid. The corridors stretched, so that the magician seemed to approach from a great distance, with the inevitability of a nightmare. The look on his face was unreadable—it might as well have been carved into a block of wood. "Who is it you've brought with you?" he asked.

Unwin stepped aside at the last moment, and Hoffmann walked past him. He reached around a mirrored wall and came back clutching the wrist of the woman in the plaid coat. Hoffmann yanked her to her feet; she let out a cry and stumbled forward, her cap coming loose. She regained her balance, then stood straight and straightened her coat.

"Hey, kiddo," Sivart said, getting to his feet.

Lamech put his hat back on. "Where did she come from?"

Sivart snorted. "She followed you, fancy-boots. Ed Lamech, meet Penelope Greenwood. She's better at what you do than you are, knows everything you're thinking, and can hurt your feelings without saying a word. Self-taught, too—a real wunderkind. Enoch, I believe you're already acquainted."

Hoffmann, for the first time since he made his presence known, appeared shaken. His lower lip was trembling as he gazed at the woman in the plaid coat.

"Dad," she said to him, "we need to talk."

Lamech was looking at Sivart. "Greenwood? She and Hoffmann? Travis, why didn't you ever report this?"

Hoffmann gestured vaguely toward Lamech. The watcher put up his hands and started to speak, but whatever he said was lost as his hat grew to twice its size and swallowed his head. He tore at it with both hands, but the brim was stuck under his chin and his shouts were muffled by the heavy felt.

Hoffmann took a step toward the woman in the plaid coat, arms outstretched. "I searched for you," he said. "I tried so hard to find you."

"Maybe I didn't want to be found." She picked a piece of lint off her coat, avoiding his eyes.

"Your mother took you from me."

"You let her get caught," Penelope said. "The job was more important to you."

Sivart knelt down to pick up his cigar, listening to their argument as though to a story he already knew. And Unwin realized that Sivart did know this story, because he had played a role in it. Hoffmann and his daughter were talking about November twelfth, about the day Sivart caught Cleopatra Greenwood at Central Bank and sent her out of the city. *I won't tell you what we talked about,* he had written. *I won't tell you what happened just before I put her on the train.* This is what they had talked about: Miss Greenwood's little girl. They were making arrangements that day in the terminal. They were deciding how to get Penelope out of the city, away from her father.

"That isn't what I came here to talk about," Penelope said. "I want to tell you about my new job. It's all underground, more than you know about. They have you beat, Dad. You remember Hilda Palsgrave? She used to do the fireworks for the carnival?"

Unwin drew a breath, a real one. Hilda, the giantess Hildegard: Sivart had met her the same day he met Caligari, had spoken to her while she mixed black powder for her rockets. Now she was chief clerk of the third archive. How had one of Caligari's old employees come to be with the Agency?

Hoffmann was incensed. "You're both working at the Agency? Working for *him*?"

The overseer, Unwin thought. The man Miss Greenwood had said was something worse than Enoch Hoffmann.

Though that was hard to imagine just now, as Lamech fell to the floor, rolling and twisting, beating at his hat with his fists. This, Unwin thought, was how Lamech's life was to end: suffocated by his own hat. He could not stop it from happening. And when Lamech died, the recording would end. He did not have much time.

"Penny, Penny," the biloquist whispered, almost singing her name. "We lost each other so long ago. Where have you been? Your eyes, when you were born, like little mirrors; terrifying! Caligari saw you and claimed you for his own. But you've come back to me just in time. I need your help. We'll work together, like we did before."

Sivart laughed. "Sure. We all know how well that went."

"November twelfth was a fluke," Hoffmann snapped.

Sivart waved his hand dismissively, but the woman in the plaid coat was listening with evident interest. She and Hoffmann stood looking at one another. He was nearly a foot shorter than she was, almost forlorn in his rumpled pajamas.

"Kiddo," Sivart said to her. "Don't listen to him."

Penny ignored him. "We need to talk," she said again to her father. "Alone."

With a nervous glance at Lamech, Sivart snatched his own hat off his head. But Hoffmann was not preparing any new tricks. "I'm not taking my eyes off him," he said.

"What do you think he'll do?" Penelope asked. "Rummage through the junk in the back of your brain? Find out you're one of the bad guys? Let him wander for a minute." She gave Sivart a meaningful look and added, "We'll have him back here soon enough."

Hoffmann was frowning, but he sighed and said, "All right." He snapped his fingers, and behind him a single mirror dissolved into mist. The stairs down to the carnival were just beyond.

Sivart shrugged and put his hat back on. Then he puffed at his cigar a few times, until the ember burned red again. "You kids have fun," he said, and with a last look at Lamech's writhing form he went briskly from the hall of mirrors.

Unwin followed him. Outside, the eldritch light of the carnival had grown brighter, almost fiery, and the rides were chugging and whirling at breakneck speeds. The air smelled of popcorn and fresh sawdust, and the music of the hurdy-gurdy roared. Sivart leapt onto the turning platform of a carousel, and Unwin hurried after him, grabbing hold of a horse's reins to steady himself. Sivart debarked on the other side and jogged away into the outer reaches of the carnival.

The detective was moving purposefully, as though according to some prearranged plan. Could he and Penelope Greenwood have conspired in advance to allow him this reprieve? Unwin did not know how far he could follow. He was already pushing at the boundaries of what Miss Palsgrave's machine had recorded, and he felt a tug at the back of his skull. This dream was nested like one of those dolls that contain themselves a dozen times over. But if the chief clerk of the third archive had been observing the dream, might she have shifted the focus from one mind to another, changing frequencies as Lamech said she could? Yes: the closer Unwin kept to Sivart, now, the better the recording maintained its coherence.

Sivart had reached the edge of the carnival. There at its border was a small, almost perfectly square building, its windows reflecting the fairground's glow. The detective went up to the steps and put his hand on the doorknob, then shut his eyes and wrinkled his brow. "Okay," he said to himself, "easy as spinning a radio dial." He turned the knob and threw the door open with a flourish.

On the other side was Unwin's bathroom.

Sivart went in and looked around. He yawned, stretched, then took his coat off and flung it over the shower curtain. "This is more like it," he said. He turned on the hot-water faucet and undressed, then reached up into his coat pocket and pulled out a small bottle of smoked glass. This he unstoppered, sniffed, and emptied into the water. The tub filled with bubbles. When the bath was ready, he tested the water with one toe and got in. With his hat down over his face, he began puffing on his cigar, dropping ashes into the tub. The only spot of color in the room was the ember of the cigar, and it burned so hot it made the steam over the tub glow red.

Unwin stretched his legs beneath the covers of an underclerk's bed in the third archive of the Agency offices. In his dream of Lamech's dream of Hoffmann's dream of Sivart's dream, a dreaming Unwin opened his bathroom door, a fresh towel over his arm, his robe cinched tight around his waist. Sivart scrubbed his feet with a long-handled brush, and the other Unwin said, "Sir, what are you doing in my bathtub?"

Sivart told the other Unwin not to use his name. Somebody could be listening in. He accused him of being forgetful. He said, "I'm going to tell you something that you're going to forget. Ready?"

"Ready," the other Unwin said.

"Okay, here it is. You're awfully worried about getting everything right. I've seen what you've done to my reports. I've read the files. You edit out the good parts. All you care about are details, and clues, and who did what and why. But I'm telling you, Unwin, there's more to it than that. There's a . . . I don't know"—he waved his cigar in the air—"there's a spirit to the whole enterprise. There's mystery. The worse it

gets, the better it is. It's like falling in love. Or falling out of love, I
forget which. Facts are nothing in comparison. So try, would you? Try
to leave the good parts alone?"

"Sorry," Unwin said, "what were you just saying? I was thinking of
something else."

"Never mind. Just remember this: Chapter Eighteen. Got it?"

"Yes."

"Say it back to me: Chapter Eighteen."

"Chapter Elephant," Unwin said.

FIFTEEN

On Skulduggery

**If you are not setting a trap, then you
are probably walking into one. It is the
mark of the master to do both at once.**

Somewhere an elephant trumpeted. Somewhere else an alarm clock rang. And back in Lamech's city, someone was screaming.

The cord that had tugged at the back of Unwin's brain grew taut and wrenched him from the nested dreams, out of his bathroom, out of the carnival, back into the hissing static of the rain. A dark shape rolled on the ground at his feet. It was Lamech, still pulling at his hat, which was shrunk tight over his face now, so that his nose and brow were visible through the felt. Unwin crouched over him, wanting to help somehow, trying to get hold of the hat, though he knew it was impossible.

Lamech kicked his shoes against the cobblestones and bellowed. He twisted and rolled, his shirt coming untucked. Finally the hat popped off. His face was red and sweaty, his mouth a perfect O as he gulped the air.

The hat had lost its shape and lay on the ground, a dead little animal. Lamech slapped it into the gutter, where the water carried it away. He rose slowly to his knees and watched it go, his breath coming in hoarse wheezes. Then he got to his feet, brushing himself off with his hands. So it was not Enoch Hoffman who had murdered the watcher.

He looked nowhere in particular and said, "All right, end of the tour. There's little else I can do to help you. We're pickles in our own jars, Mr. Unwin. That's how it has to be now."

He wiped his brow with his sleeve. He was breathing easier, but his voice was quiet. "I could have done better. I could have shown you more. We're in trouble, the whole lot of us. Read your copy of the *Manual*. Find Sivart if you can, and get him out of there before he makes things worse."

Lamech thrust his hands into his pockets and looked around. "Well?" he said. "Wake up, already."

Unwin woke up.

BENEATH THE HEAVY COTTON BLANKET, his feet were damp in their socks. His head was heavy, and the pillow felt heavy beneath it. He had the odd impression that his skull had been magnetized. There was an unpleasant metallic taste in his mouth.

No music played in the third archive, and Miss Palsgrave had left her machine. Hilda, the Giantess Hildegard, the Chief Clerk of—of all this, Unwin supposed—was nowhere to be seen. Around him her underclerks carried on with their slumberous labors. What strange visions had Hoffmann and his daughter contrived for their perusal? Only the ever-wakeful Jasper Rook could remain immune to them forever— and Jasper, Unwin reminded himself, was probably back in the city by now, searching for the man who killed his brother.

The phonograph needle had reached the lead-out on the record of Lamech's final dream and was traveling an endless, soundless loop.

Unwin stopped the machine and flipped the record over, found more grooves on the B-side. Lamech had told him there was nothing more to see, but the watcher did not seem to understand everything that was happening. Unwin needed more; he put the needle down and closed his eyes.

Again the sounds formed patterns, the patterns shapes, and this time he sank into the dream from above. For a moment he had a dizzying view of Lamech's city beneath him. He descended quickly, matching speed with the rain, so that each long drop appeared to hang unmoving in front of him. He looked up. More drops hovered like daggers over his eyes; he wished for his umbrella, had it, opened it. The umbrella parachuted over his head, and he swung below it like a pendulum while the rain drummed over his head.

Lamech was headed for the entrance of a building, the tallest in this part of the city, in all of the city, maybe. It stood a little apart from those nearby, a dark obelisk. There was something familiar about the place. Just as Unwin's feet touched the ground, he realized why. It was the Agency office building.

Unwin followed, slipping through the lobby doors before they closed behind Lamech, then collapsed his umbrella on his way toward the elevator, just as he had done many hundreds of times before in that other lobby, the real one. If Hoffmann's mind was represented by a hall of mirrors, whose dreaming thoughts were housed here?

Lamech went past the elevator doors, mumbling to himself as he walked. "Stupid, stupid," Unwin heard him say—to himself, apparently. Then he shook his head, as though to clear his thoughts. At the back of the lobby, he angled his watch in the dim light. Someone called out, "Come in, Ed, you're right on time." Unwin did not recognize the voice; it came from behind a door stenciled in black letters: CUSTODIAN.

When Lamech went in, Unwin heard a noise that was immediately familiar. It was the rustling of paper and the cooing of pigeons. The sounds froze him for a moment, and he barely had time to squeeze through, ducking under Lamech's arm as the watcher closed the door.

The room was small, and smaller for its contents. Piles of paper, some bundled into files, some floating free, were stacked floor to ceiling. Filing cabinets stood in rows and at odd angles, forming a kind of maze. A living breeze inhabited the place, lifting pages from one pile and dropping them onto another or discarding them on the floor. Some of the file drawers stood open, and in most of them pigeons had roosted, with nests of twigs and paper and bits of trash. The birds regarded Lamech familiarly, puffing with disdain when his coat brushed their drawers.

"Won't you ever clean this place up?" Lamech said. He rounded a filing cabinet and stood with his hands in his pockets. "Arthur, there used to be a chair here."

The custodian was seated at a little desk that had fallen to the same disarray plaguing the rest of the room. His accordion was hung on the wall behind him, over the wide basin sink from which a mop handle extended. Hanging beside it was a pistol in its holster. The place must have been a replica of the custodian's real-life office, though surely the original was not equipped with so many file drawers. And hopefully the custodian did not have all these pigeons, either—nor that gun.

Arthur looked up from the file he was studying, stared at Lamech a moment, then removed his spectacles. It was the first time Unwin had seen the man's eyes. They were pale and attentive. "Emily," he said. "Find our guest a place to sit, please."

Unwin had to stop himself from speaking her name aloud as Emily Doppel, wearing a yellow peignoir and blue slippers, emerged from behind a stack of papers at the back of the room. She stuck her pencil into her hair and came around the custodian's desk. Waving her arms, she evicted the pigeons nesting on a chair, then moved a pile of papers off it and onto the top of another pile.

"Elaborate," Lamech said, watching her.

"She's real," Arthur said. "I have her come in to keep things tidy, but mostly she does crossword puzzles. Imagine the devotion, to do crossword puzzles in your sleep."

Emily sniffed at this.

"I hope he pays you enough," Lamech said to her.

"He doesn't pay me," Emily said. "I have a condition. I fall asleep when I mean to be awake, and he takes advantage by bringing me here. Nights, too. I've always wanted to be an Agency operative, but this is not what I imagined."

"Tell him to get you a day shift," Lamech said.

"Get me a day shift," she said to Arthur.

"What, and have you nodding off on the job? Sweetie, you know it wouldn't work."

"I quit, then," she said. The two men watched as she gathered her things: black lunch box, newspaper, a pillow. She brushed past Lamech and went out of the room, slamming the door behind her. The pigeons fussed and warbled.

"She does this every day," the custodian assured Lamech. "It's the only way she knows how to leave. I do have plans for her, though. Just waiting for the right assignment to come along. Now sit, sit."

Lamech shrugged and sat down, letting his coat droop open. His face was still red from the struggle with his hat. He probably could have dreamed up a new one, but maybe he could not bear to.

Arthur ran his tongue along his teeth and looked at the ceiling. "Those memos of mine," he said.

Lamech waved his hand. "You know, Arthur, it gets hard to keep track of all the rules. It's getting to be like the bylaws need bylaws."

The custodian sat upright and tossed his spectacles onto the desk. He stared straight at Lamech, his face reddening. "These are the basics, Ed. You keep track of your copy of the *Manual*. You know that."

Lamech hung his head.

"Who took it?"

"I don't know."

"The whole thing makes me tired," Arthur said. "Imagine that: tired in your sleep."

Lamech said nothing for a moment. Then he asked, "What are you, three days in?"

"Three, four, maybe," Arthur said, shaking off a laugh. "Shows, does it? I'm trying to keep up on Cleo, that's all."

Unwin recalled what Miss Greenwood had told him, out on the barge, about the eyes in the back of her skull. Not just a watcher's eyes, but this man's. Who was the Agency custodian, that he should be conducting dream surveillance?

"Most I ever went was six hours," Lamech admitted, "and that was by accident. Strangest thing, too. My subject dreamed she woke up, and I thought she really was awake. Went about my day for a while, but it turned out I was still in her head."

"Hah," said Arthur.

"But listen, Greenwood's back in town, isn't she? Maybe she's the one who nabbed my book. I'll get after her myself. I'll—"

Arthur stopped him by slapping a sheaf of papers against the desk. He stacked the pages even, his big fingers moving with an accordionist's quickness. "You don't ever quit, do you, Ed? You could have retired—what, seven years ago? It's a dangerous job. I don't have to tell you that. You have a wife, children."

"A grandchild, too," Lamech added. "Little girl, four years old. Wants to be like her grandpa when she grows up."

Arthur clicked his tongue against his teeth, signaling approval. He set his hands down on the square of desk he had cleared. "But something has to go wrong, eventually."

"Eventually," Lamech agreed.

Just then a pigeon came in through a window, and Lamech ducked as it landed on the desk in an uproar of scattered feathers and paper.

Arthur steadied the bird with one hand and got hold of its leg with the other. A tiny canister was fixed to the pigeon's leg; Arthur opened it and withdrew a rolled slip of paper.

Carrier pigeons, Unwin thought. The dreamed equivalent of the Agency's messengers.

Relieved of its charge, the pigeon flapped off and found its nest among the file drawers.

"It's from your pal down the hall, Alice Cassidy," Arthur said, reading the note. "Her agent's been busy lately."

Lamech leaned closer. "Sam Pith? What's he up to?"

"Got him staking out the old Baker place. We think it might be where Hoffmann's holed up these days. Time we got to the bottom of whatever all the chatter's about." He set the note down, and it curled again. "How's the weather out there?"

Lamech sat back in his chair. "Clear skies and a balmy breeze," he lied. "Sunshine, warm on the face. Piles of red leaves. Children run, laugh at themselves. Laugh at the whole damn thing."

Arthur frowned and scratched the side of his face with one big fingernail. "What about your case, Ed?"

"Sivart," Lamech began.

"Taken a powder, has he?"

The watcher got to his feet. He moved his jaw from side to side, as though he wanted to spit. "Well, you already know. You always already know. Why do you bother with these appointments? I'll send a bird next time. I've got work to do."

"Sit down."

Lamech cursed under his breath and sat with his arms crossed.

Arthur smiled peaceably. "I wanted to hear about it, straight from the source. Was he angry? Was he furious? How furious was he? Tell me about it."

"Whoever took my copy of the *Manual* turned around and gave it to him. Unexpurgated edition."

A phone rang. Arthur dug through the papers on his desk while Lamech looked on, incredulous. The telephone was identical in appearance to every other telephone Unwin had seen in the Agency offices, but there was something different about the sound of this one's bell. It echoed as though from the far end of a tunnel.

Arthur snatched up the receiver. "Yes. . . . What? . . . No, listen. Listen to me. . . . Hey, listen! I don't care if he eats the same thing all next week, too. Keep on him, he's your man. Check your frequencies. . . . Recheck them, then. I'll do it myself next time." He hung up.

"Funny," Lamech said.

Arthur sucked his teeth and said, "That Miss Palsgrave is a wizard with the gadgetry. This is our latest development. Turns out the recording thingum can be plugged into the transmission gizmo, then spliced to a telephone's domajig. Means instant communication between the oneiric mind and a mundane pay phone. Connection's a little spotty, still."

Lamech shook his head at all this.

"Nikolai there," Arthur went on, nodding at the phone, "was at the Municipal Museum today. He thinks he's found Edwin Moore. And it looks like our old friend was in touch with Sivart just before he went AWOL."

"What, you think it's connected?"

"Listen, Ed, I need help here. If Hoffmann gets too deep into Sivart's head, it's trouble for all of us. We need to find him."

"Hoffmann's keeping himself checked out. Even if we found him, we wouldn't be able to wake him. Sivart's trapped."

"Who said anything about waking him?" Arthur said.

Lamech shifted uncomfortably in his chair. Then he looked around, as though something had startled him.

"What's wrong?" Arthur said.

"Thought I heard—"

"Focus, Ed."

Lamech grumbled. "Hoffmann's up to something, something big, November twelfth big. But it sounds like Cassidy and Pith know more than I do. I hear Sam's been working with you directly. With Sivart stuck where he is, we need to throw off the opposition, keep them guessing. So we do something we've never done before—and that means breaking some rules, Arthur. We promote someone. Someone completely incapable of solving a mystery. That should buy us the time we need to find Sivart. The harder their agents work to follow our guy, the farther off course they'll be."

Arthur looked at him like he thought he was kidding. Then his face went red and his whole body shook with his laughter. It was an angry, wheezing laugh. "I like it," Arthur said, crying a little.

"Good," said Lamech. "Because I've already sent the memo."

That got Arthur going again, and Lamech laughed, too. They went on like that until the custodian was wiping tears from his eyes. Then he sighed his whistling sigh and started playing with the papers on his desk.

"Strangest thing, though," Lamech said.

"Oh, yeah?"

"I saw Hoffmann just now."

"Just now?"

"Came from his place directly."

"No kidding. What'd he have to say?"

"A lot of nonsense, mostly. One thing that caught my ear, though. About our standard procedures. He said the Agency didn't come up with Chapter Eighteen. That dream detection predated our work. He said he didn't steal it from us but that we stole it from him."

Arthur put his spectacles back on.

"Got me thinking," Lamech said. "Maybe we're not just worried about Hoffmann getting too far into Sivart's head. Maybe we're worried about Sivart getting too far into his."

Arthur nodded slowly. "Well, Ed, you're no slouch. See, I met

Greenwood in the early days of the carnival, long before the Oldest Murdered Man case, when she and Hoffmann had their own little sideshow. You'd go into their tent expecting your fortune to be told, but then Cleo would put you to sleep and Hoffmann would hop in and see what you had on your mind."

"Sure, I see," Lamech said. "A little blackmail operation. You telling me they got you with that scam?"

"It was just after I took over this outfit. That's why I made all those changes, wrote all those rules—had to keep as much as I could hidden."

Lamech's jaw was clenched. "Hoffmann would have learned everything about our operations otherwise."

"I know I should have told you, Ed. But it's more personal than business. See, Cleo and I got to know each other after that. We were kids. We fell in love. But the only way we could see each other without Hoffmann catching on was if we met sleepside, in the old Land of Nod. What a courtship that was! I convinced her to teach me how it was done, so I could go over to her place, too, if you follow me.

"Hoffmann told you the truth, Ed. That Caligari fellow taught him dream detection, though he'd have called it something different. Then Hoffmann taught Cleo, and she's the one who brought it to me. To the Agency. She and I didn't last, of course. Too complicated, once we found ourselves in opposite trenches."

Lamech took all this in. "Must be strange for her now," he said. "Her old boyfriend on full-time surveillance duty."

"I'm wearing her down, Ed. She's hiding something from me. I don't know what it is, but she can't keep it up much longer. I've got the lights turned up bright, and she's getting tired."

Lamech looked around the room and said, "There it is again."

"What?"

"I heard something. Not here. In my office."

Arthur waved his hand. "That's just me."

Lamech gave him a careful look, and after a moment Arthur shrugged.

"Ed, I'm in your office." He looked put out by having to explain. "All the time I've been spending in here these days, I've had to work on my sleepwalking. There are a lot of places I have to be, you know."

"Just stopping in to empty the wastepaper basket, I guess?"

"That's right," Arthur said. "Coming by to clean things up a little."

"I may as well go, then," Lamech said. "I'll shake your hand topside, on my way out."

"Door's locked," Arthur said. "You don't wake up until I do."

Lamech was moving his jaw again, though he looked more thoughtful than angry.

"You've been like an uncle to me," Arthur said. "Showed me the ropes when I first came on staff. Remember me in my messenger's suspenders? I'd still be wearing them if it wasn't for you. You pretended like I knew what I was doing before I knew a damn thing. That's what makes it all so difficult."

"Makes what difficult?"

"The lying, Ed. I've lied to you. So much. But the best way to fool a monkey is to fool his trainer. Sivart's the monkey, Ed. You've always known that. I just want to come clean about the rest of it."

"Why bother?" Lamech said.

"Ed, listen to me. Sivart's cases were all bogus."

"His cases," Lamech said.

"Your cases. Bunkum. Hooey. Everything you solved, you solved wrong. The both of you, together. You made a good team. That's how we needed things. Kept the important stuff hidden that way. Except November Twelfth. He got that one right somehow."

"That your hand on my shoulder, Artie?"

"Listen to me. You've done great work, Ed. The most important work anyone in this outfit has done for me. Just not in the way you think. That night at the carnival, when I realized Hoffmann had me—had us all—I knew I had to make a deal. One hand washes the other."

"Dirties it, more like."

"Easy now, Ed."

"How's it work?" Lamech asked. "You let him get away with the crimes and you do cover-up? The Agency makes its dollar, your puppet looks like a hero, he gets anything he wants."

Unwin thought it over and was sickened when he saw how it fit together. The phony mummy, Colonel Baker alive and well—Hoffmann and Arthur must have orchestrated each of those cases in advance. Hoffmann kept the priceless trophy he wanted, kept Colonel Baker's inheritance as well. And the Agency had its star detective and its front-page stories. Sivart had been tricked every time, and Unwin along with him—the whole city, too.

"I had to come clean with you, Ed. Had to let you know how it was."

Lamech touched his own throat. He danced his fingers around his collar, grasping for something he could not get hold of. He was fighting the hands of a ghost. Unwin thought he could feel them, too.

"Could be something," Lamech said, gasping.

Arthur was calm as he watched the man opposite him. "Something you haven't told me yet? Something I need to know that I don't know already? Probably not, Ed. I'm the overseer. I'm the man who sees too much."

But there was something, Unwin knew. Penelope. Her existence was the thing Miss Greenwood was fighting to keep hidden from Arthur, and the fight had exhausted her. Would Lamech trade what he knew for his life?

"You were supposed to watch him," Arthur went on. "That was your job, Ed. But this isn't happening because you failed. It's happening because you've done so well."

Unwin went to Lamech, tried to feel for the hands that were choking him. His fingers blurred with the watcher's, passing through them as though through a mist. Unwin was seized by cold panic. He screamed and grabbed at the air, punched at it.

"I just have to clean your office," Arthur said. "Tidy up a little."

Unwin closed his dreaming eyes, but he could not occlude the vision of the man thrashing where he sat. The dream insisted. In the watcher's office on the thirty-sixth floor, Lamech had died as he died here. His convulsions formed a weird geometry amid the fluttering papers. The pigeons were mesmerized.

Lamech was still trying to speak, but Arthur had begun sorting papers again. Unwin's senses went gray as the watcher's body stilled.

He felt himself lifted from the bed, felt the blanket falling off his body. He tried to catch it, but something snatched him upward and away. The earphones landed on the pillow. He saw below him a great lavender dress and knew he lay in the arms of Miss Palsgrave. She cradled him like a child while she slipped his shoes onto his feet. Her breath was warm on his forehead. She put the record back in his briefcase and gave it to him; his arms were shaking as he took it.

At the far end of the archive, near the place where Unwin had entered, a pair of flashlight beams swept through the dark, casting broad ovals of light over the floor. Miss Palsgrave sighed to herself when she saw them, then tapped Unwin's hat back onto his head. She started walking. Underclerks slept undisturbed all around them.

How cold Unwin was! Through chattering teeth he said, "You used to work for the carnival. For Hoffmann."

Miss Palsgrave's voice sounded metallic and thin; it was a voice from a string-and-tin-can telephone. "For Caligari," she said. "Never for Hoffmann. After he staged his coup, I left."

"And defected to the Agency."

"The problem is not belonging to one or the other, Mr. Unwin— and there is always an Agency, always a Carnival to belong to. The problem is belonging for too long to either of them."

Unwin thought of the little square building that represented his own mind in Lamech's final dream. It had stood right at the edge of the carnival; might it be annexed in time? "Have I—" he said, but he did not know how to finish the question.

Miss Palsgrave looked down at him. In the dark he could see only the dull gleam of her eyes. "The sleeping king and the madman at the gates," she said. "On the one side a kind of order, on the other a kind of disorder. We need them both. That's how it's always been."

"But your boss—my boss. He's a murderer."

"The scales have tipped too far," Miss Palsgrave agreed. "When Hoffmann made a deal with the overseer, he stopped working for the carnival and started working for himself. Their deal fell apart on November twelfth because Sivart solved that case correctly and Hoffmann imagined he had been betrayed by his conspirator. Now the Agency oversteps its bounds while the carnival rots in the rain. Hoffmann's grown desperate over the years. He'll drown the city in nightmare just to have it for his own again."

They came to the enormous machine at the other end of the archive. Here the air smelled of wax and electricity. On a wheeled cart nearby was a row of freshly pressed phonograph records. Now that Unwin knew the truth of the Agency's overseer, he saw this place in a new light. A repository of the city's most private thoughts, fancies, and urges, all in the hands of a man who would coerce and torment to learn what he wanted to know, who would murder an old friend to keep his secrets safe. Unwin's own dreams were out there, he thought, along with those of anyone who had ever drawn the attention of the Agency's unblinking eye.

"How could you allow Arthur such . . ." He struggled to find the right word. ". . . such trespass?"

"There was a time when I thought it necessary," Miss Palsgrave said. "Hoffmann was too dangerous, and we needed every tool to fight him."

"And now?"

She seemed, for a moment, uncertain. "Now a lot of things must be changed."

The two detectives Unwin had seen on the elevator with Detective Screed—Peake and Crabtree—had arrived at the middle of the archive. They cast grim glances at the huge pink chair, the lamp, the rug. Peake smacked his flashlight against his palm and said, "Forgot my spare batteries."

"Hush up," said Crabtree, even louder.

The detectives were limping. Peake had cuts and bruises on his face, and Crabtree's green jacket was torn along one shoulder: Miss Benjamin must have neglected to warn them about the ninth step. They aimed their flashlights deeper into the archive. A few of the underclerks sat up, removed their headphones, and blinked into the light.

"Enoch and Arthur have both grown stupid and hungry," Miss Palsgrave said to Unwin. "Someone will have to see them unseated. Someone will have to restore the old balance."

"Not me," Unwin said.

Miss Palsgrave sighed. "No," she said. "I suppose not."

Behind the cart of phonographs was a caged platform—the dumbwaiter. Miss Palsgrave opened the wire mesh door with her free hand and gently set Unwin inside.

"Where do I go now?" Unwin asked.

She leaned close and said, "You go up."

She took hold of the rope that hung from the ceiling and began to pull. Unwin fell against the floor of the little car as it shot into the air. He was treated to a brief view of the archive from above, of the pink chair glowing under its lamp, of the underclerks waking and sitting up in their beds, and of Miss Palsgrave, formidable in her lavender dress, drawing him into the air by the force of her great arms as the detectives closed in on her.

Unwin had to remind himself to breathe as the pulley far above creaked under the strain. In that nothing-place between here and there, time slowed, hiccupped, leapt forward. He felt he was still separated from his body, an invisible specter in someone else's dream. Seams of light marking the secret doors into offices throughout the building flitted past. Unwin heard voices on the other sides of the walls, heard typewriters, footsteps. He was seeing the world from the other side now—from the center of mystery, out into the lighted place he had once inhabited.

The ascent ended abruptly, and his arrival was announced by the ringing of a little bell. Unwin tapped the wall in front of him, and a panel flew open. When he clambered out of the dumbwaiter, he found himself once again on the thirty-sixth floor, in the office of Edward Lamech.

The watcher's body was gone now, but Unwin was not alone. Detective Screed stood beside the desk, a few papers in his hands. When he saw Unwin, he stuffed the papers into his jacket pocket and drew his pistol, then shook his head as though to say that now, at last, he had seen it all.

"They always come back to the scene," he said.

SIXTEEN

On Apprehension

**Woe to he who checkmates his opponent at last,
only to discover they have been playing cribbage.**

Screed looked Unwin up and down, his thin mustache bending with
pleasure, or disdain, or both. "You look terrible," he said. "And
again that hat on the thirty-sixth floor."

Screed's suit, navy blue, was identical to the one Unwin first saw
him in. It had been cleaned and pressed, or exchanged for a pristine
duplicate. If Emily had succeeded in bringing him the memo, Screed
did nothing to acknowledge it. He patted Unwin down, keeping the
pistol trained on him. He was thorough in his search, but all he came
up with was the alarm clock from Unwin's jacket pocket. This he held
gently for a moment, as though he thought it might explode. He shook
it, put it to his ear, and stuffed it into his own pocket.

"I'm not much of a tough guy," he said, relaxing his grip on his
pistol. "And we're both gentlemen, as I see it. So I'm going to put this
away now, and we'll talk like gentlemen. Agreed?"

Without waiting for a reply, Screed put his pistol back in its shoulder holster. Then he closed his hand and struck Unwin in the jaw with a quick jab. Unwin fell back against the wall.

"That," Screed said, "was for getting into the wrong car yesterday."

Screed grabbed him by the shirt and pulled him out into the hall. The place was silent, the other watchers' doors all closed. They took the elevator to the lobby, and Screed led him around the corner to where his car was parked. With an unlit cigarette in his mouth, the detective drove them uptown, along the east side of City Park.

The somnambulists were all around them, on every block. They went insensibly through the streets, playing the lead roles in their own delirious dramas. A man in a business suit stood at the edge of the park throwing seeds over his head while a flock of pigeons descended upon him to feed. His face was covered with scratches, his suit soiled and torn. A nearby tree was full of young boys, all of them throwing paper airplanes made of newspaper pages. While Unwin watched, one of the boys leaned too far off his branch and fell.

Screed hit the horn and swerved to avoid an old woman crouched in the middle of the street, her hands covered in dirt. She had relocated a pile of soil onto the pavement and was planting flowers in it.

"People these days!" Screed said.

The detective seemed to think that nothing was out of the ordinary—that this was simply the chaos of the everyday. *An enemy to messiness in all its forms,* he had called himself. Maybe Hoffmann's version of the world was how Screed already imagined it to be. When they stopped at a traffic signal, he took the cigarette from his mouth and leaned forward to pick his teeth in the rearview mirror.

Unwin rubbed his jaw where Screed had struck it. He considered the many accounts he had read of the wild assertions made by suspects after they were apprehended. Protestations of his own would only sound like the pleas of a desperate man, but he had to try to convince Screed of his innocence. "I sent you a memo," he told him. "Part of it was about Sivart's cases."

"Uh-huh," Screed said.

"I found out he was wrong about a lot of things. That most of his cases have never been solved correctly. You could be the one to fix the record, Detective Screed. We can still help one another."

"Oh, we are going to help one another," he said, accelerating through the intersection.

Screed reached into his jacket pocket and removed the pad of paper he had taken from Lamech's office, holding it so Unwin could see the top sheet. It had been rubbed with the flat of a pencil to reveal the impression left by words written on the previous page. Unwin recognized his own handwriting. *The Gilbert, Room 202.*

They parked across the street from the hotel. Screed directed him through the lobby to the restaurant, a dim, high-ceilinged room, crystal chandeliers coated in dust. The wallpaper, patterned with curlicues of gold specks, was stained yellow from years of tobacco smoke. On each table was a vase of withering lilies. They sat themselves in the back of the room.

"Your accomplice," Screed said, "has been under surveillance since shortly after she returned to the city two weeks ago. We lost track of her for a day here and there, but we know it's become her habit to take her meals at the Gilbert, where, as you know, she is currently lodged."

The restaurant was all but empty. A few old, well-dressed men sat at a table near the center of the room, speaking quietly. When Unwin could hear what they were mumbling, he heard only numbers. They were arguing about an account of some kind, or the dream of an account. Seated to Unwin's left, alone with his napkin tucked into his shirt collar, was the man with the pointy blond beard. He scrutinized an omelette while cutting small bites from it and chewing with measured care. When he saw Unwin look in his direction, he flashed him a glance of smug triumph.

"We will wait here for Miss Greenwood's arrival," Screed went on, "and you will greet her without rising from your seat. When she sees you, you will urge her to join us. When you speak of me, you will speak of me—in whatever sly, insinuating terms with which the two of you are accustomed to communicating—as one who has been brought into your plot to infiltrate the Agency."

Unwin had no choice but to play along. "She'll suspect something," he said. "Even if she does sit with us, she won't tell us anything."

"That's in your hands," Screed said. "I'm giving you a chance to help, Unwin. You should be grateful. Now drink some more, your glass is too full."

Screed had insisted on whiskey sours for both of them. There was no waiter in the place, but a red-jacketed bellhop—or a boy dreaming he was a bellhop—had filled in, taking the order and returning with the drinks. Unwin sipped from his glass and winced.

"Yes," Screed said, answering a question he must have silently posed to himself, "my biggest case yet." He took the maraschino cherry from his drink and plucked it from its stem with his teeth.

Just then the bellhop came back into the restaurant. The boy was oddly alert, and his actions more precise than those of the other sleep-walkers Unwin had seen. He went to the man with the blond beard and gestured with his thumb and pinkie open over his ear: a telephone call. The man with the blond beard looked annoyed but set down his fork, a bit of omelette still stuck to it, and rose from his chair. His napkin was dangling from his collar when he followed the bellhop into the lobby.

Unwin wondered whether it was the overseer on the phone, impatient for an update from his agent.

A minute later the bellhop came back. This time he had on his arm an old man in a tattered frock coat. He directed him to a table nearby, and the old man was about to sit when he saw Screed. He looked at Unwin, then at Screed again, then nodded and closed his eyes in solemn resignation.

It was Colonel Sherbrooke Baker. Like them, he was perfectly awake.

"So you have me at last," he said. "Battered, world-weary, a lowly fugitive, and a threat to no one. But you have me, and now you demand my surrender."

Screed glowered at Unwin, as though he were somehow responsible and had better not try anything.

The colonel went on, "Once in the poor dregs of his life, the old wretch determines to take his meal in the company of his fellow men, and that is when you nab him. So be it. Better this than to die alone in my cell, wondering how long before I am found by room service, stiff in my chair, eyes gone to jelly."

Screed's mustache was twitching as Colonel Baker sat with them at their table.

"My name is Sherbrooke Thucydides Baker," he said. "I am eighty-nine years old. I am going to tell you the story of my first three deaths and how I was undone at last by the wiles of a madman and his treacherous agents."

Screed recognized the name—he knew Sivart's case files as well as anyone, if only out of envy. Slowly grasping the situation, he said, "You've made the smart choice, Baker. Why don't you start from the beginning?" He took the notepad from Lamech's office out of his pocket and gave it to Unwin. "You're a clerk," he said. "Write this down."

Unwin took a pencil from his briefcase and waited.

"She came late one night to my home," Baker began, "uninvited, unexpected. That Greenwood woman, from the carnival. I was busy at my polishing and would have shot her where she stood, if not for the plan she proposed. For a modest price, Enoch Hoffmann would oversee the faking of my death. It would be, she told me, the simplest of feats for the master illusionist. I saw immediately the advantages of such an arrangement."

Screed leaned forward, his elbows on the table. "Okay," he said, "so Hoffmann helped you with the phony funeral. I read the rest of it in the papers. All to fool your son."

The colonel took hold of the napkin and crushed it in his hand. His voice cracked as he said, "Leopold. My boy!"

"Easy now," Screed said, looking to make sure Unwin was getting it all down. "What about your second death?"

The colonel dropped the napkin onto his plate. "Hoffmann betrayed me. He was the one who contacted my brother, told him where I was, what I'd planned. Reginald came to stop me, to claim my treasures."

"You killed him," Screed said. "You stabbed him with that dagger, eight times."

"What a bore he was. How dreadful to see living boredom spilled from lips identical to yours. Forget the war, forget our childhood on the hilltop. Forget the hedgehog hunts; I despised them! Where was that, where?"

"You fled," Screed said, trying to keep him on track.

"I was dead again, and a murderer besides. I went to City Park, to that old fort. It pleased me to go there sometimes, in the autumn. I took my son, once, to show him the view from the battlements." The colonel chuckled to himself and drummed his hands against the edge of the table, as though to beat out the march of an approaching regiment.

Screed was at a loss. He sipped from his drink again, shaking his head.

"Sivart found you," Unwin tried. "You fled to the bridge."

"No, not to the bridge! To Hoffmann, to that carnival sideshow. He was in his tent at the fairgrounds, looking smug. There was a party going on. He invited me in, introduced me to the other guests. I remember there was a man who stood no taller than my knees, and some lascivious acrobats, and a woman with a hairless cat on a leash. I hated them all and showed them my teeth. He took me outside, sat me next to a fire, gave me a glass of brandy. I told him not to put on airs— anyone could see how lowly and mean were his circumstances. They say a magician never reveals his secrets, but out of spite he told me how he had encompassed my ruin."

"They found your coat in the river," Screed said.

"My son!" the colonel cried again, taking up the napkin and twisting it. "Greenwood found him. She was still working to finish Hoffmann's trick."

The man with the blond beard had come back into the restaurant, his napkin still tucked in his collar. He took in the scene instantly and came toward them with his beard thrust forward.

"Poor, poor Leopold," the colonel said. "He thought his father was dead. Everyone suspected him. Greenwood found him and told him he was done for, gave him my old coat to wear. There was no escape for him. A little lion, my son, he always was. He put the coat on. I should have been the one to go to the bridge. Not he!"

"Stop this!" cried the man with the blond beard. He grabbed Screed by the shoulder. "You must end your investigation, close the case. Orders from up top."

The three older gentlemen at the other table were looking around, troubled by all the noise but blind to its source. They spoke nervously in streams of inexplicable digits, their voices rising.

The colonel said, "Hoffmann would pose as my son, you see. It was the simplest of tricks for the master illusionist. I was dead, my brother was dead, and he would inherit everything. My collection, my home— he was going to throw nice parties there, he said. Not so lowly and mean anymore. He said he would drink brandy at my fireside."

The man with the blond beard circled the table and tried to snatch Unwin's pencil. Unwin kept hold of it until it snapped in two.

"He let me keep one thing," the colonel said. "Any one thing of my choosing." He withdrew the antique service revolver from his pocket. It shone from constant polishing and was worn to perfect smoothness, like an object come back from the sea. It was the brightest thing in the room.

"Cease, desist!" shouted the man with the blond beard, lunging at him.

The colonel responded to these words as though to a battle cry. He growled and locked arms with his adversary, spittle flying from his lips. Neither of the men was very strong; they circled one another in a jerky dance, the colonel straining backward to keep the beard from brushing his face. He fell, and the man with the blond beard fell with him. Then came the shot.

Colonel Baker rose to his knees. He took hold of the edge of the table and pulled himself up. The man with the blond beard remained on the floor. His teeth were chattering. It sounded, Unwin thought, like coins falling through a pay phone.

"Just the one thing," the colonel said. The old service revolver was still in his hand. He looked surprised to see it there. "I took only what I needed."

Screed had his pistol out, but there was nothing he could do to stop the colonel from turning the gun on himself. Unwin looked away just before the shot that signaled the fourth and final death of Colonel Baker.

Screed dropped his pistol on the table and picked up the napkin. He put it to his face and breathed quickly, making little sounds into the fabric. A minute later he put the napkin down and drank his whiskey sour. When that was gone, he started drinking Unwin's.

Unwin stood with his back against the restaurant's dappled green wallpaper. He could not remember when he had risen from his chair. Screed was saying something to him, but Unwin could only see the detective's lips moving. Gradually his hearing returned.

"You were telling the truth," Screed said. "About Sivart's cases."

On the floor the man with the blond beard had stopped chattering. "Yes."

"I don't want the cases," Screed said. "I want Enoch Hoffmann."

Unwin allowed himself a few more breaths, taking time to think that over. "And in exchange you'll let me go."

Screed's mustache twitched, but he said, "Yes, I'll let you go."

A plan was forming in Unwin's mind. It was full of holes, and he did not have time to check it against the recommendations of the *Manual*. Still, it was all he had. "Okay," he said. "I'll make the arrangements."

"What do you need?" Screed asked.

"I need my alarm clock."

Screed fished it out of his jacket and thrust it at him, its alarm bell jangling.

"Go to the Cat & Tonic at six tomorrow morning," Unwin said. "Go to the room that was Colonel Baker's study and wait."

"Why?" Screed asked.

"Hoffmann will be there, and he won't be ready for you. You have to wait for the right moment, though. You'll know it when it comes." It was the sort of bold statement Sivart would have made in order to buy himself more time. Sometimes the detective delivered, sometimes he changed the rules enough that his promise no longer mattered. Unwin would be lucky, he thought, if he managed to survive the night.

He put the alarm clock in his briefcase and left through the front door. In the alley he found his bicycle chained to the fire escape, right where he had left it the night before. He had been correct about one thing. The chain would need a good deal of oiling.

SEVENTEEN

On Solutions

A good detective tries to know
everything. But a great detective knows
just enough to see him through to the end.

U nwin walked his bicycle toward the street but found the Gilbert's
bellhop at the entrance of the alley, blocking his way. The boy
stood under a broad black umbrella. He held it out to Unwin and said,
"This was in lost and found. I thought you might need it." The boy's
voice was perfectly clear, but his eyes were half closed and unfocused.

Unwin approached slowly, then ducked under the umbrella with
him. "Tom," he said, reading the name tag on his red jacket, "what
makes you think I need this more than anyone else?"

Without looking at him, the bellhop said, "It's a long ride from here
to the Cat & Tonic."

Unwin felt suddenly colder. In spite of himself, he stepped back into
the rain, rolling his bicycle with him. He remembered his vision of that
morning—the game at the cottage, Hoffmann's blank stare: *The magician could be anyone.*

"Tom, how do you know about the Cat & Tonic?"

The bellhop frowned and shook his head, struggling with the words. "I don't," he said. "I'm just the bellhop. But Dad says I might get promoted to desk clerk if I keep my head screwed on straight."

While the bellhop was talking, Unwin began to circle slowly around him. But Tom grabbed his wrist and held him there. The boy's grip was strong. "I don't know anything about the Cat & Tonic," he said. "But I'm good at getting messages to people."

"You have a message for me? From whom?"

Unwin could see the boy's breath as he spoke. "She's on the fourteenth floor right now, asleep with her head on your old desk. Mr. Duden is trying to wake her, and he might succeed soon. In the meantime she and I are in . . ." Tom trailed off, frowning again. "We're in direct communication."

Unwin looked around. He saw no one on the street, no one looking down from the windows above. He moved back under the umbrella and whispered, "Direct communication? With Penelope Greenwood, you mean."

"No names," Tom said. "Don't know who—"

"Don't know who might be listening in," Unwin said. "That's fine, Tom. But what's the message?"

"She and her dad are in the mist. No, the midst. Of a contest of wills. She's trying to stop him. She says she's on your side."

"But I saw their reunion," Unwin said. "Her father said they would work together. He said it wasn't the first time."

Tom tilted his head, as though his ears were antennae and he was trying to improve reception. "She was eleven years old on November twelfth. He . . . conscripted her."

"Into what, exactly?"

Tom closed his eyes and breathed slowly, swaying a little. A minute passed, and Unwin thought that he had lost him, that the connection to Penelope—whatever its nature—was broken. Then the bellhop said quietly, "Her father is no puppeteer. But she had another teacher.

From him she learned to . . . to let herself in, but also to leave things behind."

"What sorts of things, Tom?"

"Instructions," he said.

This was the part of Hoffmann's scheme that had boggled Edwin Moore that morning. The magician did not know how to plant suggestions into a sleeping mind—but his daughter did. Caligari had taught her how.

"Instructions," Unwin repeated. "To get up in the night and cross tomorrow off your calendar. Or to steal your neighbors' alarm clocks. Or worse, to abandon all sense and help turn the world upside down." Unwin gestured toward a man who had exited the hotel with a suitcase. He was going along the sidewalk, leaving his clothes draped over everything he saw. He had already dressed a letterbox and a fire hydrant. Now he was trying to button a jacket around a lamppost.

"She says that's not her doing," Tom replied. "They went together through the sleeping minds of the city last night, and she did what he asked. She opened up their deepest selves and jammed them open. But she made sure you and everyone at the Agency were left alone. And in some people she planted the . . . seeds of resistance. A limin . . . a liminal . . ."

"A liminal directive," Unwin said, recalling the words of the underclerk in the third archive: *something to do, someplace to go.* So the sleepwalkers Moore had gone off with *were* special operatives. But they were working for Penelope Greenwood, not Enoch Hoffmann. "She tricked him, then. But what was the directive? What were her instructions?"

Tom tightened his grip and shook Unwin's arm. "You have to stop him, Charles. Her father's onto her, and she doesn't have much time."

"What about Sivart?"

"There's barely anything left of him." Tom was looking directly at Unwin now, his eyes nearly open. "He's been broken. None of us can help him."

"I have a plan—"

"There isn't time. Get back to the Cat & Tonic, quickly. Finish this."

The bellhop thrust the umbrella at him, and Unwin took it, but Tom left his arm extended, hand palm up. A moment passed before Unwin realized that the boy was waiting for a tip. He fished a quarter out of his pocket and gave it to him.

They turned at a chugging, rattling sound, just audible over the patter of rain on the umbrella. To Unwin the sound was unmistakable—it was the Rooks' steam truck. The vehicle was not far off, and running hot, to judge from the high-pitched whine that accompanied the thunderous clamor of its engine. Jasper was coming for him.

"Charles," the bellhop said. "Go!"

Unwin collapsed the umbrella and tucked it under his arm. He turned his bicycle onto the street, pedaling hard despite the stiffness in his legs. He rode north along the park, following as best he could the route Miss Greenwood and the other sleepwalkers had taken the night before. Cold water dripped off his hat brim and trickled past his collar, down his spine. His pants were flecked with grime from the street, and his socks squelched in his shoes.

No one drove on the avenue. Some cars and taxicabs were left in the middle of the road or driven up onto the curb and abandoned. In that strange quiet, the sounds of the steam truck grew steadily louder. The rumbling seemed to come from every direction at once, echoing off the facades of buildings and through the twilit park.

Unwin braked in front of the Municipal Museum. Edwin Moore was seated on the bottom step, shivering beneath the umbrella Unwin had given him. The old clerk saw Unwin's reflection in the puddle he was staring at and looked up, squinting under his thick white eyebrows.

"Mr. Moore," Unwin said. "What happened?"

"Do I know you?" Moore said. He studied Unwin's face, shaking his head. "I can't recall. I know that I knew, and yet . . . Mr. Unwin, that's your name, isn't it? Did we work together?"

"I'm Charles Unwin. We were in the rowboat together, and then the taxi—"

"The taxi," Moore said, his eyes brightening a little. "Yes, I was a passenger in one of many taxis, and we joined others who had walked the whole way. They were bound for the fairgrounds, Mr. Unwin—an army of somnambulists, all set to one great task. We have been beaten, I'm certain of it now. Hoffmann has won."

"Why?" Unwin asked. "What did they do?"

"They gathered tools. They brought ladders and saws and drills. The remnants of Caligari's were terrified at first and tried to keep them out, tried to wake them. But once the old carnies comprehended the invaders' objective, they let them be, and then they joined them, even helped to direct their work. I had to pitch in, too, or be found out!" Moore was trembling harder now. "Caligari's Carnival is remade, Mr. Unwin, in all its iniquity. Hoffmann's lair of old is restored. He is laughing at us—laughing."

Unwin set his bicycle down and knelt beside the old clerk. He put a hand on Moore's knee and said, "Mr. Moore, I'm not sure it was Hoffmann who did this."

"Who then?"

"The woman in the plaid coat. The same woman who showed you the gold tooth of the Oldest Murdered Man, that night in your sleep."

Moore stood and moved back a step. "Who are you, to have seen into my dreams?"

"No, it's nothing like that," Unwin said. "We have a good team here. Remember?"

Moore was moving farther up the steps. He surveyed the street as the sound of the approaching steam truck grew louder. "You're one of *them,*" he said. "I remember nothing. Nothing! You may put that in your report if you like." He threw the umbrella to the ground and hurried back up the steps. Unwin watched him go, hoping he would stop, but the old clerk scurried between the massive columns and through the revolving door of the museum.

What good would it do to go after him? Moore would walk the halls of the museum alone, keeping to his usual route. There would be no guests today, no tearful children seeking their parents. After a while he might come to the chamber where the Oldest Murdered Man was housed. There, he would notice the glinting of a gold tooth at the back of the corpse's mouth. And then he would telephone the Agency, to let Detective Sivart know that he had been tricked, that he had better come see for himself and fix his mistake.

The discarded umbrella was already filling with rainwater. Unwin left it and pedaled on.

IN THE LIGHT of day, Unwin saw that the wall of the Baker estate was in disrepair; stones had long ago come loose in places and lay in mounds over the sidewalk. The iron gates, which he had thought left open for Hoffmann's sleeping guests the night before, were simply rusted open on their hinges. He pedaled up the long drive, his legs aching, the bicycle tires scattering wet sycamore seeds behind him.

At the top of the hill, the mansion lay in partial ruin. It had appeared stately the night before, lit from within and shining like a magic lantern. Now Unwin saw its sickly old face, its slumping porches and teetering balconies, its broken windowpanes and gapped shingles. He dismounted and walked his bicycle the rest of the way up the hill, left it leaning against a column of the portico.

The front door was unlocked. He went into the foyer, his clothes dripping on the hardwood. In the room where Miss Greenwood had performed the night before, highball glasses crusted with milk lay strewn over the tables and ashtrays overflowed with cigarette butts and stubbed cigars. The floors were covered with muddy footprints, most from bare feet.

He took to the stairs, and the creaking of the steps was the only sound in the place, aside from the rain pattering on the roof. He went down the hall to Hoffmann's room and opened the door.

The hearth was cold. A draft from the chimney played with the ashes, tracing small spirals over the floor. Hoffmann was still in his chair, asleep. Someone had left him with a blanket, but it had fallen off him and lay twisted around his ankles. He mumbled and shook, his hands trembling in his lap. He looked like nothing more than a harmless old man in blue pajamas.

Penelope had given up on Sivart, but Unwin could not. *You're the best chance I've got,* the detective had told him in the dream Unwin twice dreamed, first in his own bed and then in the third archive. *Try this time, would you?* And so he would try. It was possible that Penelope had underestimated Sivart's stubbornness.

Unwin took the alarm clock from his briefcase, wound it, and turned the hands to match those on his wristwatch. It was six o'clock exactly. He set the alarm as far in advance as he could and carefully placed the clock on the table, next to the near-empty bottle of brandy.

Eleven hours, fifty-nine minutes: that was how long he had to set everything in place. It was just a matter of timing now. If his plan worked, it would be like Miss Greenwood's story about all those spindles, and the one the king had missed. Only in this version of the story, instead of someone falling asleep, someone was going to wake up. A few people, actually.

A shadow moved over the floor. Unwin turned to see Cleo Greenwood standing by the window, her red raincoat dripping on the rug. She had been watching from a corner of the room—had come in, maybe, through one of Colonel Baker's old secret passages. The pistol in her hand was steady in spite of her exhaustion. It was another one of Baker's antiques; she had taken it from the wall.

"You're standing in my way," she said.

Unwin stood straight and kept himself in front of the magician. "Hoffmann is already spoken for, Miss Greenwood. And anyway, he's only half of the problem. If you'll give me the chance, I can deliver the overseer to you." Unwin was making bold promises again. He knew that it was more likely he would soon find the overseer's fingers at his own throat the next time he slept—if he ever slept again. But he went on talking.

"Those eyes at the back of your skull," he said. "You've had to work hard to keep your secret hidden from them. I understand now why you don't want him to know about your daughter. He would torment her as he's tormented you. And if she were turned to his side, nothing would be safe from the Agency's eye. Arthur thinks he's close to breaking you."

"He is," she said.

"Then let me help you."

"What do you get out of it?"

"Sivart. My old job back, maybe."

She held still a moment, then covered her face with her free hand. "You're a clerk," she said, her shoulders shaking. "Oh, God, you were his clerk."

"Not a very good one," Unwin said. "My files are full of errors. I'm just trying to make corrections now."

Hoffmann mumbled in his sleep again. On the table beside the magician, Unwin's alarm clock ticked faintly.

"All those years you played the magician's assistant," Unwin said. "I know how you tricked Colonel Baker out of his fortune. And you were there that night on *The Wonderly*, to make sure Sivart took the wrong corpse back to the museum." He gestured toward the display case at the back of the room. "There's the real Oldest Murdered Man there. And it's Caligari's corpse in the museum, isn't it?"

She did not deny it, and Unwin knew that his guess was right.

Hoffmann would have needed the old man's carnival to seize control of the city's underworld. And he needed it more after striking his deal with the Agency: where else to find so dependable a supply of performers to act as the agents, goons, and spies who would be thwarted by Travis T. Sivart? Getting Caligari out of the way, and hiding his body in plain sight, must have been the first scheme on which the magician and the overseer colluded.

"I got out when I could," Miss Greenwood said at last.

"But now you're back in. Hoffmann needed you to make everyone sleep. Just as he did on November twelfth. Your song was on the radio that time. We all heard it, we all slept. But putting people to sleep wasn't enough. He could get into their dreams, but that wasn't enough either. He needed to plant a single suggestion in all their minds, all *our* minds: cross that one day off the calendar. That's where your daughter came in."

"It was Caligari who realized what she could do," Miss Greenwood said. "He took an interest in her from the beginning. He said that she was a natural hypnotist, that it would be dangerous to allow her talents to develop unschooled. Once, when she was only six or seven, I caught her watching me in my own dreams—just standing there, staring. Those eyes of hers, Mr. Unwin. When I saw them, I knew that my daughter no longer belonged to me, would never belong to me again. I was frightened. So was Enoch."

"Not too frightened to put her talents to use."

A sound from outside: the Rooks' steam truck had arrived. It spluttered to a halt, and the door opened and slammed closed.

Miss Greenwood heard it, too. She squeezed the handle of the gun. "I would have stopped him if I'd known how he intended to use her. It's why I'm here now."

"And why is Penelope here?" Unwin asked. "Why would she want to rebuild Caligari's Carnival?"

The ancient pistol shook in her hand. Unwin could not tell if she was surprised by the question or by the fact that Unwin knew her daughter's name. "To give it back to her father," she said, "or to take it from him." Miss Greenwood swayed slightly, struggling to stay awake even as she stood there. The front door opened, and heavy footsteps sounded on the stairs.

Unwin glanced down at Hoffmann, saw the magician's eyes darting behind their lids. A fever rose up from him, and Unwin thought he detected the sickly burning odor of kettle corn. Sivart was still in there—trapped in that other carnival, the spectral one Hoffmann had built in the dream of the city. What would happen to Sivart if Miss Greenwood pulled the trigger?

"Cleo," Unwin said. "Please."

The door slammed open, and Jasper Rook burst in, his green eyes feverish under the brim of his immense hat. With every step he seemed to grow in size, until they were all gathered up in the great black heat of his shadow. Unwin opened his umbrella to shield himself, but Jasper flung it aside, and Unwin stumbled backward, landing hard on the floor.

Jasper reached for him with those enormous, suffocating hands. They filled Unwin's vision, and he felt himself drowning in the monster's shadow, which was bottomless and the color of headache.

Then Miss Greenwood was there, her arms around Jasper's shoulders. She had her lips to his ear as she embraced him. Jasper's eyelids fluttered, his body slackened, and he staggered back. Miss Greenwood eased him down, until finally he lay across the rug with his head in her lap. She took off his hat and smoothed his hair with her hand, still whispering sleep into his ear.

"He's tired," Miss Greenwood said to Unwin. "He'll sleep for a very long time, I think."

Unwin stood and found his umbrella, then leaned himself against the back of Hoffmann's chair. The air in the room was cooling again. "I will too, when this is over."

Miss Greenwood said nothing, but through her exhaustion Unwin saw something else, something she could not speak of, even now. She had loved those two men, and both had tried to destroy her—Hoffmann when he let her take the fall for November twelfth, Arthur when he began to besiege her dreams. *A kind of order and a kind of disorder:* Miss Greenwood had suffered in the tempest between the two.

In the refuge of her lap, Jasper Rook started to snore.

TOGETHER THEY dragged the sleeping body out of the room and down the stairs. Nothing woke Jasper—not the steps striking the back of his head when Unwin lost his grip for a moment, not the rain falling full on his face outside. With much effort they managed to get him up into the bed of his truck. Miss Greenwood found an oilcloth tarp and laid it over him. It was just after seven o'clock when they left the grounds of the Baker estate.

Miss Greenwood was familiar with the peculiar controls of the steam truck. She kept her eye on a row of gauges over the dashboard while regulating the engine with a row of levers under the wheel, which was enormous and had the spokes of a ship's wheel. The boiler thumped and hissed at their backs.

Unwin gazed silently out the passenger window. On one corner a young boy was shaking a woman's arm and crying, "Wake up, Mom! Wake up!" Lights were on in some apartment buildings, and Unwin glimpsed nervous, confused faces in the windows. Some people had woken and gone home. Was Hoffmann's grip beginning to loosen?

"It will come in waves now," Miss Greenwood said. "He can't keep them asleep all the time, so some will get a reprieve. But most who do will doubt whether they're really awake."

It was hot inside the cab, and sometimes the needles on the dials strayed into the red. Miss Greenwood drove south past the Agency office building and into the old port town. They left Jasper and his truck in front of the Forty Winks, where someone from the carnival was sure to find them. At eight twenty-seven, Unwin and Miss Greenwood went together into the cemetery.

Unwin read the names on tombstones they passed: Two-Toe Charlie, Theda Verdigris, Father Jack, Ricky Shortchange. Saints' Hill had always been the place where criminals went to bury their own, and these were the outlaws, thieves, and grifters of an earlier era. It ended with the rise of Enoch Hoffmann and was familiar to Unwin only through the oldest of the Agency's files.

"Caligari took Hoffmann in when he was a boy," Unwin said. "It couldn't have been easy for him to plot the old man's murder."

"They always disagreed on how the carnival should be used," Miss Greenwood said. "I think Caligari saw it as a tool for stirring up trouble—but only for those he felt deserved it. He would go ahead to each town we visited, get a room somewhere, and 'scout things out,' as he used to say. He was delving into the dreams of the people there."

"Looking for what?"

"He never really explained, and there wasn't always a logic to it. But most of time he found people who had something to hide. Caligari could be ruthless once he'd chosen his subject. Sometimes, though . . ." She paused and rested with one hand against a tombstone, catching her breath.

Unwin waited, and for the first time since he had met her, Miss Greenwood smiled. "Sometimes the carnival was just a carnival," she said.

She led him through the door of one of the mausoleums. Together they strained against the lid and moved it aside, revealing a set of tiled stairs where a cadaver should have been. There were lights on down there. Miss Greenwood climbed in first, and Unwin followed after her, sliding the lid back into place behind them.

At the bottom of the stairs was a dank subway platform. Roots grew through the cracked and dripping ceiling. The eight train was already in the station, its doors open. Unwin and Miss Greenwood were its only passengers. Once the train was moving, he said, "What about Hoffmann? He saw the carnival as a means for profit?"

"That's what he saw when he met Arthur: the potential for profit, for control. What Enoch's doing now resembles a plan he used to talk about sometimes. A way to seize the city entirely if his deal with the Agency ever went sour. The understanding he'd had with Arthur fell apart on November twelfth. Then, when Sivart bumbled into his head, he must have assumed the worst."

"Which is what your daughter expected," Unwin said. "That's why she gave Sivart the stolen copy of the *Manual.*"

"I understand now what she's doing. She always considered Caligari her true father and wanted to follow in his footsteps. There was a saying of his she liked to repeat, about those who belong to the carnival. 'We're just some people who lost their house keys, and everyone who loses their house keys are neighbors.'

"You see, Mr. Unwin, she intends to give the carnival back to the remnants. To steal it from the man who bent it from its true purpose."

The train squealed on its tracks and swayed as it rounded a corner, and they both held tightly to the straps.

If Penelope succeeded, Unwin thought, then part of Miss Palsgrave's changing of the guard would be complete.

"Well," Miss Greenwood said after a while, "don't you think it's time you told me your plan?"

Unwin was figuring parts of it out as he described it to her, but Miss Greenwood listened patiently. When he was finished, they were both quiet a moment.

"It's not a very good plan," she said.

THEY GOT OFF at Central Terminal and went up the stairs to the concourse. Some of the trains from Central Terminal were still running on time. The one they boarded moved into the tunnels a few minutes after ten o'clock: less than eight hours, now, before the alarm at Hoffmann's side would ring. When the conductor reached their booth, Miss Greenwood paid for her ticket and Unwin handed him the one he purchased nine days before, on the morning he first saw the woman in the plaid coat. The conductor punched it without looking and moved on.

It was dark, but Unwin did his best to memorize everything he saw outside the windows: the city thinning and then giving way to trees, the bridges spanning the river, the rise and fall of the mountains on the far side. He tried to imagine what it would look like in the daytime.

Miss Greenwood read magazines to stay awake. Whenever Unwin caught her drifting off, he reached under the sleeve of her red raincoat and pinched her. She swore at him, though they both knew that even a momentary slip could cost them everything.

They reached the end of the line with less than five hours left. No one met them at the station. The town was just as Unwin had imagined, and seeing it was like remembering. Maybe he *was* remembering. Maybe this was where he had come once, as a boy, to play that game with the other children. Seek-and-find? Call-and-hide?

They walked north along the town's only street, and Unwin counted his steps, noting everything: the gray cat moving between the slats of a picket fence, the colors of the mailboxes, the breeze coming off the river. They followed a dirt path into the woods. It was cooler here, and Unwin paused to button his jacket. He smelled the pond before he saw it.

"I cut all mention of this place from Sivart's reports," he said. "I'd always assumed he made it up."

"You overestimate his imagination," Miss Greenwood said.

The water, patched with oak leaves, was dark and cold-looking in the moonlight. A tire swing hung from a tree at its edge. Anyone kicking hard enough could swing far over the water. He could let go if he wanted; he could let himself fall right in.

Beyond the swing a slope covered with blackberry briars and, at the top of the slope, the cottage where Miss Greenwood and her daughter had lived for the seven years of her exile. A rubberized electrical cord snaked down from one of the windows. They followed it east into the woods, away from the water. Unwin recalled his dream of footprints in the mud, of the meeting with the boy who had been Enoch Hoffmann, and shivered.

The clearing was just as Sivart had described it. But there at its center a narrow brass bed instead of a pile of leaves, and on a table beside it a green-shaded lamp and a typewriter. The lamp was plugged in, and the bulb glowed yellow. Sivart was asleep under a yellow cotton blanket, on top of which was spread a second blanket of leaves. He snored with his hat down over his eyes, and his face was stubbled.

A dozen open umbrellas were hung in the tree above the bed, forming a makeshift canopy. He must have used to stepladder to get them arranged that way.

"I told him he could use the place but that I didn't want him sleeping in my room," Miss Greenwood said. "I thought he'd understood I meant for him to use the couch, or the spare room in the back. Instead he drags my bed all the way out here."

Unwin recalled what Sivart had written about this spot: *A nice place to take a nap.* He removed Sivart's hat from his head and peered at the man's eyelids. They were purple and bruised-looking. "Wake up," he said quietly. "Wake up."

Miss Greenwood already had hold of the detective's ankles. "You get his wrists," she said.

They lifted Sivart off the bed and carried him across the clearing, where they leaned him against the trunk of an oak tree. Unwin put the detective's hat back on his head, then returned to the bed. The sheets were still warm from Sivart's body. He settled into the pillow and closed his eyes, listening to the sound of the rain on the umbrellas above.

"Four hours and a half," Miss Greenwood said. "You'll be able to keep track of the time?"

"I'm more worried about falling asleep," he said. "I should be tired, but I'm not."

Miss Greenwood leaned close and whispered something into Unwin's ear. The words fit like a key into a lock he had not known was there, and he fell asleep so quickly he had forgotten what the words were by the time he started dreaming.

EIGHTEEN

On Dream Detection

Among the many dangers associated with this technique—
if it may be so characterized—is the possibility that its
practitioner, upon waking, may wonder whether
everything he has seen was real or simply a construct
of his own fancy. Indeed, the author of this manual
cannot claim with certainty that the technique
described in these pages actually exists.

Unwin dreamed that he woke in his own bed, that he got up and put on his robe. He dreamed himself a nice hot shower (no time for a bath), and because he was a meticulous dreamer, he took care to tie the right tie this morning and to turn off the stove before his oatmeal burned. He did not want to be late. He carried his shoes to the door and put them on in the hall, just as he always did. He almost picked up his umbrella, then remembered that he had dreamed the sun out and the clouds gone.

Outside, the streetlights were still on, and the only vehicles moving were delivery trucks bringing bottles of milk and soda water. The bakery across the street had its door open, and he could smell the bread on the cool air.

Everything was pretty much the way it was supposed to be, but his bicycle was still at the Cat & Tonic, so he walked. At the corner he felt for a moment that someone was watching him. Had he glimpsed a figure standing in the bakery door? He tried to recall what advice *The Manual of Detection* had for those who suspected they were being tailed. Something, he thought, about being friendly to your shadow. Well, it hardly mattered—he was going only a few blocks.

At Central Terminal there was no line at the breakfast cart, but he did not need a cup of coffee. If someone asked him why he came to Central Terminal, he would tell the truth—that he was taking the first train out of town, all the way to the end of the line.

The old schedule was still in his pocket. He checked it against the four-faced clock above the information booth. His train would board in just a few minutes.

He dreamed he still had the ticket he purchased the morning he first saw the woman in the plaid coat, then dreamed he sat at the front of the train. As the conductor punched his ticket, he turned in his seat, fighting the feeling that someone was watching him. He was one of only a few passengers in the car, and everyone else was either reading a newspaper or napping.

The train began to move. Unwin settled back in his seat as it emerged from the tunnels into a brightening morning. The city rose up on either side of the tracks, then gradually thinned. They passed under a bridge and veered north along the river. In the valley the leaves on all the trees had turned red and yellow. The colors reflected on the surface of the water made him dizzy. He closed his eyes against them and dozed.

He took the train as far into the country as it would go. The terminal at the other end of the line was small and made of red brick, with a door painted green. Seeing it all reminded him again of that game he had played with the other children.

Hide-and-seek: that is what the game was called. It had been somebody's birthday, he thought.

He walked north on the town's one road. A gray cat moved between the slats of a picket fence, following him without looking like it was following him. Beyond the last mailbox, he found the dirt path leading into the woods. It was cool in the shade there, and he buttoned his jacket. The ground was soft but not too damp.

Again the feeling that made him turn, expecting a pair of eyes in the shadow. There was no one there, just a small animal darting into the ferns. Two days as a detective and already he was suspicious of everything.

He came to the pond, to the tire swing. Unwin followed the electric cord into the woods, to the clearing where Sivart had moved the narrow brass bed. The lamp was on, and some leaves had fallen onto the typewriter. Sivart was under the covers, his hat down over his eyes.

Unwin stood at the foot of the bed and shook it. Sivart did not stir, not even a little. Back at the Cat & Tonic, the magician was still asleep, still keeping him prisoner. Unwin checked his watch. He had just a few minutes before the alarm would ring.

"Move away, Mr. Unwin."

Arthur, still in his gray coveralls, appeared at the end of the path. He had a pistol in his hand. "I knew I'd have to take care of this myself eventually."

Unwin stepped aside. "You knew I'd come here."

"I didn't know where 'here' was, but I knew you had nowhere left to go. And I understood the same thing Lamech did, when he promoted you. That if anyone knew where Sivart had gone, it was you."

The overseer walked up to the foot of the bed. A breeze stirred the leaves on the blanket and brought a few more down out of the trees. Unwin could just hear the creaking of the tire swing over the pond.

Arthur said, "I was trying to tell you something yesterday morning, when I saw you on the eight train. I was trying to tell you that I got your memo. The one you sent to Lamech, knowing it would reach someone in charge. Your request is granted, Mr. Unwin. You're not a detective anymore. Which means you don't have to watch this."

"I'll stay," Unwin said.

"Suit yourself." Arthur raised the pistol and closed one eye to aim.

"You're going to miss," Unwin said. "Are you sure it's even loaded?"

Arthur's arm shook a little. He opened the cylinder to check and gave Unwin a weary look. Then he snapped it closed and readied himself.

"You're going to miss," Unwin said again. "You aren't even pointing the gun at Sivart. You're pointing it at me."

"You're an odd one, Mr. Unwin." He let out his breath and dropped his arm. "Why is this gun so damn heavy?"

"I don't think it's a gun," Unwin said. "I think it's your accordion. You must have grabbed the wrong thing on your way out of your office."

Arthur whistled through his teeth. "A total loon."

"It's nothing to be ashamed of," Unwin said. "It would be easy to mix them up while you were sleepwalking."

"I didn't sleepwalk," Arthur said. "I waited for you outside your apartment building. I was hiding in the bakery across the street. I followed you those few blocks to Central Terminal. I bought a ticket and rode one car behind you, all the way to the last stop. I've been awake the entire time."

"But I'm still asleep, sir, so you are, too. That's the way it works, isn't it? Door's locked. You don't wake up until I do."

Arthur leveled the gun. "You're talking nonsense."

"Actually, I got the idea from something Lamech said, in his last dream. The one he was having when you killed him."

Arthur moved his jaw while he thought about that. "Oh, yeah? What did he say that gave you this idea of yours?"

"He said that once, during an investigation, his subject dreamed she woke up, and Lamech thought she really had. He went about his day for a long time before he figured out he was still asleep, still in the dream he had infiltrated."

"What makes you think I'd fall for a thing like that?"

"I'm a meticulous dreamer, sir. Always have been. I took a train out of town last night, and Miss Greenwood came with me. I made note of everything I saw on the way. I knew I'd have to dream it later, make it perfect. I came out here and found Sivart asleep in this bed, in the moonlight with that lamp on. I dragged him out and took his place.

"Miss Greenwood helped me sleep. I dreamed that I was home, that I woke up there. I dreamed that I went down to the street and smelled the bread baking, and that's when you started following me. I went to Central Terminal and took the first train into the country. I dreamed it well enough for you to follow me. You've been asleep for so long, I think you don't remember what it feels like to be awake. I'm still asleep. You're asleep, too. And I'm pretty sure that's just your accordion in your hand. With your eyes closed, you must have taken the wrong thing off the wall. Still, I wish you'd stop pointing it at me."

Arthur had grown more agitated while he listened, and his whole body was shaking now. "I don't believe any of this," he said.

"I saw you murder Lamech," Unwin said. "Miss Palsgrave recorded the dream—she knows you killed him, too. Do you think she'll stay loyal to you after this? Do you think any of your watchers will?"

With a growl Arthur pulled the trigger, and the gun leapt in his hand. The shot shook the bed, shook more leaves out of the trees. It was so loud it woke Unwin and Arthur both.

Unwin sat up and felt his chest—no wound, only wet leaves. He brushed them away and checked his watch: it was just after six o'clock. Back at the Cat & Tonic, the alarm clock he left had woken Enoch Hoffmann.

Woken Sivart, too. The detective was standing beside the bed, hat low over his brow, his gun aimed at the overseer. Arthur looked down at his accordion. He was holding it by the bass strap with the bellows unlatched and dangling, so that the other end nearly touched the ground.

"I don't know any songs for this," Arthur said.

Sivart rubbed the back of his neck. "I am so tender. Charlie, couldn't you at least have given me a pillow?"

Miss Greenwood stepped into the clearing, limping badly on her bad leg. She went to stand next to Sivart. Her exhaustion had developed into something else, something hard and cracked. The look in her shadowed eyes, when she saw Arthur, was full of a strange fire.

Unwin leaned over the edge of the bed and started putting on his shoes.

"Idiots," Arthur said. "You know what that madman's doing to my city. To our city. You need me."

"Like hell," Sivart said.

"Mr. Unwin, you saw the third archive. What the Agency always needed was an honest-to-goodness record, not just of our work but of the city's work. Its secrets, its thoughts, its dreams—good and bad. They're down there in our basement, the whole shebang. It's only because of Hoffmann that any of it's necessary. He'll twist the world out of whack if we don't keep a watch on things."

For a moment Unwin found himself wanting to be convinced. It would be safer for everyone, he thought, to keep those records, to make more of them, to document everything they could see, to possess forever the solutions to those mysteries for which each person was treasury, keeper, and key.

But if everything is knowable, then nothing is safe, and the sentinels are unwelcome guests, mere trespassers. Not an antidote to the enemy— only his mirror.

"Hoffmann's taken care of," Unwin said. "Screed has him by now."

Sivart looked furious when he heard that. He came over to Unwin and said, "Ben Screed? That jokester? It isn't his case, Charlie, never was. You shouldn't have done that."

Arthur seemed to have given up on them and was watching Miss

Greenwood attentively. He righted his accordion and held it with
both hands. "How's that one go, darling?" he said, running his
fingers over the keys. "The one we used to play when it was almost
time to go?"

She drew a gun from the pocket of her red raincoat. It was the antique pistol she had taken from Hoffmann's trophy room. "Almost time
to go," she said.

Arthur filled the bellows and played a few chords. "Wait, wait," he
said. "I've almost got it."

He and the others turned at the sound of another person coming
up the path. Something glinted in the shade—a pair of eyeglasses,
Emily Doppel's. She must have followed the sleepwalking overseer,
maybe even sat next to him on the train. She had Unwin's pistol in one
hand and her lunch box in the other.

She took a long look at everyone in the clearing. Unwin wondered
whether she could have created the same scenario with those figurines
in her lunch box. Investigator, suspect, informant, criminal: there were
only so many ways to arrange them.

Unwin stood and went to her. "We did it, Emily. We found
Sivart."

"Did we?" she said, her voice flat. "And what now?"

"Now—well, I was thinking about it. I was thinking we should keep
working together. I don't know what the rules are, exactly, but what's
to stop us from solving more mysteries together? I think I'm getting the
hang of this. And I think I can't do it without you."

She met his gaze, but only for a moment. "You know, Detective
Unwin, I applied three times to work at the Agency. I was twelve the
first time. I wanted to be a messenger, but I fell asleep in the middle
of the interview. A year later I tried again, but they remembered who
I was and they didn't even ask me to come in. The last time was about
a year ago. I thought maybe I'd ask for a spot at a clerk's desk. But I
changed my mind at the last minute and told them I wanted to be a

detective, that I wouldn't be happy with anything less. They still remembered me. And they knew, somehow, what I had in my lunch box. 'Little girl,' they said, 'why don't you just go home and play with your toys.'

"I was so mad I almost went down to the carnival, to see if the remnants would take me in. But before I could, Arthur visited me in my sleep." She was looking at the overseer now. "He gave me a chance when nobody else would. He said, 'Come and be my assistant. I'll teach you everything.' I thought maybe it was just a delusion, something I'd invented to make myself feel better. But it wasn't. Every time I drifted off, I was back in his office. And cases I heard about there would show up in the papers a few days later. It was real. And the head of the Agency was teaching me everything."

Emily's gaze had settled on Cleo. "Miss Greenwood," she said, "you have to drop that gun now."

Arthur wheezed until his wheezing became laughter. "Attagirl," he said, still teasing a tune from the bellows. "I knew I could count on you."

Miss Greenwood showed no indication that she had heard any of this, and Emily took a step closer to her.

"Lady," Sivart said to Emily, "put the gun down."

Emily pointed the gun at Miss Greenwood as Sivart took aim at Emily. Did the *Manual* contain a name for this, for what was happening? These three could stand that way forever, no one making a move, because there was no good move to make. Miss Greenwood shook her head—barely conscious, it seemed, of what was going on around her. She knew the gun, knew the man at whom she aimed. That was all, maybe.

The overseer was still wheezing. He looked at Emily and said, "What are you waiting for?"

She ignored him and said to Unwin, "I convinced Arthur to assign me to you, after your promotion. The plan was to keep an eye on you. Make sure you stayed on track. Make sure you found Sivart for us."

Unwin felt cold as he recalled one of the first assignments he had given his assistant—to contact the Agency's custodian and ask him to clean the paint spilled in the hall. But they had discussed more than spilled paint—as they must have every time she fell asleep.

"You did a good job of it, then," Unwin said.

"Not good enough," she said. She was shaking her lunch box as she spoke, rattling the tin figurines inside. "It shouldn't be like this. . . ."

Arthur had stopped laughing. "That's right, Emily," he said. "There are protocols."

Emily did not seem to hear him. "I stole Lamech's copy of *The Manual of Detection*," she said.

The accordion sagged in Arthur's hands, emitting a dissonant sigh. "Emily," he said quietly.

"At first I just wanted it for myself," she said. "But once I'd read the whole thing, I saw what it could do, what it could . . . incite a person to do. So I left it in Sivart's office, where he was sure to find it. I couldn't stand the waiting anymore. I wanted someone to make a move, a real one. I wanted Hoffmann back, and the Agency ready to fight him."

Unwin took a step away from her, closing his eyes as he considered his mistake. Penelope Greenwood was not the thief of the unexpurgated copy of *The Manual of Detection*. Though in revealing the gold tooth of the Oldest Murdered Man, she had worked in concert with Emily, and toward the same end. The two of them, without apparent knowledge of one another, had together rekindled the old war between the Agency and the carnival.

The leaves, when the breeze took them, rustled like paper. Emily looked at the ground, shaking her head. "What a mess I've made. I could have done a better job."

"Don't be too hard on yourself," Sivart said.

She half closed her eyes, then recited, " 'To the modern detective, truth is rarely its own reward; usually it is its own punishment. And if you cannot track mystery to the back of its ugly cave, then be content to stand at the edge of the dark and call it by name.' "

She looked at Arthur as she lowered her gun.

The overseer, as though a spring in him were suddenly loosed, leaned into his accordion and began to play. The bellows strained and crumpled between his hands, and his big fingernails danced over the keys. "That's how it goes, isn't it, darling?" he said.

Miss Greenwood went closer to him. "Stop calling me that," she said.

Arthur's song was the opposite of a lullaby, thunderous and brash. "Sure," he said, stamping the time with his foot. "That's it. What are the words? 'Between you and me, All the way to the sea, In my dream of your dream—' "

Miss Greenwood's shot sent him tumbling backward. He tripped over the roots of the old oak and fell cradled against its trunk. His arms were still moving as he lay there, but the air went in and out through the two holes the bullet had made in the bellows, and the notes were just ragged whispers now.

Detective Sivart took his hat off and sat on the edge of the bed. He looked at the ground and waited until it was quiet again. Then he switched off the light.

THE DINING TABLE was big for the cottage, and Unwin had to walk with his back against the wall to reach his seat. He looked around while Sivart fussed in the kitchen. There were shelves of old books and photographs on the walls. The pictures were hung with their frames nearly touching, so that the wallpaper—a faded pattern of carts and haystacks—was all but obscured. In one yellowing image, the giantess Hildegard sat on a tree stump, boxes of fireworks open all around her. Aloof and queenly on her bower throne, she regarded the camera with her chin raised and her eyes downturned.

In another picture a young Miss Greenwood was seated at a dime-store counter, straw in her soda glass. Her smile was careful. A little girl sat on the stool beside her, legs dangling with her ankles crossed. Penelope, her hair tied back in a braid, gazed mistrustfully at the camera.

"Be there in a minute," Sivart called from the kitchen.

Unwin realized he had been drumming his fingers against the table and stopped himself. Through the window he had a view of the pond at the bottom of the hill. Emily and Miss Greenwood were walking around the water together, talking.

Sivart came into the room with a blue dish towel draped over his shoulder. He had taken off his jacket and shirt, leaving his black suspenders strapped over his undershirt. "Hope you're hungry," he said. He set down a tray covered with strips of bacon and fried eggs, most of the yolks broken. He went away and came back with plates and forks, a pile of toast, pancakes, a bowl of blackberries, butter.

The detective looked at everything, frowning. He left again and came back with a pot of coffee and a creamer. "Haven't eaten in days," he said, tucking a napkin into his collar.

Unwin was hungry, too. He helped himself to pancakes and a handful of blackberries. Sivart forked a stack of bacon onto his plate and said, "It took you long enough to figure out where I was."

"You could have told me right from the start."

"Nah, you would have screwed it up if I'd done that. Like today, except our friend out there would've been awake, and he would've remembered to bring his gun."

Outside, Emily and Miss Greenwood had arrived at the tire swing. They were still speaking, and they seemed to have come to an agreement of some kind. Miss Greenwood was nodding, her arms crossed over her belly, while Emily stood with one foot up on the tire.

"That Emily's a firecracker," Sivart said as he ate. "Reminds me a little of Cleo's girl. Now, Penny, she was an odd kid. Barely ever talked, listened to everything like she was taking notes. I used to see her down there on the swing. It never seemed like she was playing, really. More like she was just—I don't know—*waiting*."

Unwin spread butter over his pancakes. "Hoffmann looked almost afraid of her when I saw them together in Lamech's dream."

Sivart grinned and stabbed another piece of bacon. "He should've been. I wish you'd seen him when he realized what she was doing with *his* sleepwalkers. I thought his skull would break open and we'd both fall out.

"You know, Penny caught me at Central Terminal the day I was headed out here. We talked it all through in advance, about you being our agent in the field. We needed radio silence through the whole thing after that. Between Arthur and Enoch, there were no safe channels."

"That's why she's at Central Terminal every morning," Unwin said. "She's waiting for you to come back and let her know it's over."

Sivart chewed thoughtfully, washed it down with coffee. "I'm not going back, Charlie," he said.

The two women came inside, and Miss Greenwood went straight for the coffee. Emily stood in the doorway until Sivart gestured at her and said, "Sit. Eat." Then she reluctantly found a chair and put her lunch box on the table.

Sivart looked at it and said, "Do you have one of an old detective, ready to retire, a respectable gut under his coat?"

"No," Emily said. "They're all active-duty."

"Well, those days are over for me," he agreed. Then he turned to Miss Greenwood. "How about you, honey?"

"I'm going to get some sleep," she said.

"Here? Or in the slammer?"

"Here," Emily said. "But that depends on Detective Unwin, really. He'll be the one writing the report."

Miss Greenwood looked at Unwin over the rim of her cup.

"I'll have to include everything I know," he said. "But I'm a clerk again, so it's my job to determine what's relevant and what isn't."

Sivart shook his head and snickered. "Spoken like a true-blue spook," he said.

For a while the only sounds were the clatter of forks on plates and spoons in coffee cups and the ticking of a clock in another room. Sivart, sated, leaned back in his chair and raised his arms over his head. "Still," he said, "I wish we all could have sat down and talked about it. The three of you, me, Hoffmann. Even Arthur down there."

Miss Greenwood had begun to doze in her chair, but now she was listening again. Her voice was cold when she spoke. "It would have been helpful for your memoirs," she said.

Sivart shifted uncomfortably in his chair. Unwin knew they were all thinking the same thing—that those memoirs, if Sivart ever wrote them, would have to tell the story as it was in the files, not as they knew it now. The detective was looking to Unwin for help, but it was Emily who spoke first.

"Maybe we can open the archive to you," she said. "For your research."

Sivart took the napkin out of his collar and said, "Fine. That would be fine." He got up and started gathering the dirty dishes.

Later Sivart and Miss Greenwood walked Unwin back to the station while Emily returned to the clearing. ("Someone has to start cleaning up," she said.) A cool breeze was blowing off the river, and Unwin noticed details he had failed to include in his dream of the place: the second church steeple at the south end of town, bits of trash floating along the shore, some old railroad ties in the weeds beside the tracks. If Arthur had not been asleep for so long, he might have sensed that something was wrong when he followed Unwin here. But waking and dreaming must have been a blur to him by the end.

One part of Unwin's dream had carried over to the real world some-how. The rain was gone, and the sun was rising into a clear sky. It was as though no one trusted it yet—all the people climbing into the train still wore raincoats and carried umbrellas.

The conductor called for them to board. Sivart, suddenly sheepish, rubbed the bristles on his chin and said, "I think I promised you a drink once, Charlie."

"Another time," Unwin said. "Maybe next month, for your birthday."

"What, you figured it out?"

What Unwin had figured out was that Sivart did not have a hunch on the morning of November twelfth, as he wrote in his report. It was just that Arthur and Hoffmann chose the one day of the year that the detective would notice had gone missing.

Sivart handed Unwin the typewriter that had been at his bedside, closed up in its case now. "It's just my old portable," he said. "I don't think I'll need it anymore. And there's no telling how the chips are going to fall, back at the home office. Might be good to keep a little nimble, you know?"

Unwin hefted the case to test its weight. It was lighter than he expected, but he noticed a keyhole by the latch. Sivart saw what he was looking at.

"Let's see," the detective said. Then, with a swift, graceful movement, he reached behind Unwin's ear. The key was in his hand when he brought it back.

Sivart's grin fell away, and his face went pale. "I didn't even mean to do that," he said. "A week ago I didn't know how. More Hoffmann's style, really. You don't think there are side effects, from all that time we spent cooped up together? Like maybe there's a bit of old twiddle-fingers still left in here?"

Unwin recalled what young Penny Greenwood, all those years ago, had said to Sivart when she read his palm. That he would live a long life but part of it would not be his own. Unwin took the key. "Thank you," he said. "The typewriter is perfect."

The detective, something like fear on his face, stared at his own shaking hand. Miss Greenwood took it in her own and held it. "Don't worry," she said to Unwin. "I'll take care of him."

Unwin boarded and chose a seat on the side facing the shore. As the train pulled away, he glimpsed Sivart trudging back up the road, toward the cottage. He and Miss Greenwood were walking arm in arm.

Unwin opened the typewriter on his lap. One of the oak leaves was stuck between the type bars. He put that in his pocket, loaded a fresh sheet of paper, and began to work on his report. "I," he decided, would have to be part of it after all.

Lest details be mistaken for clues, note that I ride my bicycle to work every day, even when it is raining. That's how I came to be at Central Terminal last Wednesday morning with my hands full and my umbrella under my arm. So encumbered, I found it impossible to recover the umbrella dropped to the floor by a certain party, whose role in all this I will, over the course of this report, attempt to explain. She was, as they say, "in on it" from the beginning, whereas I was merely "it," and I use the word as children do when playing games that involve running and hiding, and seeking those who are hidden.

We have been playing a game like that, a great many of us for a great many years. Some of us did not know we were playing, and some of us were not told all the rules.

Now that I have the opportunity to begin this report, I do not know how best to categorize it. I am both clerk and detective, but due to the circumstances of the case at hand I am also neither of those things. A train will bring you back to the place you came from, but it will not return you home.

Dozens more black raincoats boarded the train at each stop on its descent through the valley. The clattering of the wheels kept time with the rhythm of Unwin's typing, and newspapers rustled all around. He caught sight of one of the headlines: RETURN OF THE CARNIVAL THAT NEVER LEFT.

He wrote, *At least I know who I am writing this report for. Miss Greenwood's daughter is my clerk, after all, and she will want every detail, every clue, from top to bottom.*

The seven twenty-seven train arrived at Central Terminal one minute late as usual. Unwin put the typewriter away and slipped the pages of his first report into an empty folder from his briefcase. He waited for the last of the black raincoats to pour out the doors, then followed them through Gate Fourteen. The woman in the plaid coat stood on her toes. She stopped searching when she saw him, and he went to her. She had been waiting a long time.

HE DID NOT see Emily again for several days. When he did, it was on the Agency elevator. She was wearing the same blue woolen dress she had worn the day they started working together. At first it seemed as though she were going to ignore him. "I'm sorry," she finally said. "It's just that it's against policy for us to speak."

"You've been promoted."

"Yes."

"High up in the ranks, I hope."

"Very," she said, and touched the pencil in her hair. "Some of the watchers, I guess, have had their eyes on me. And then, you know, there was a vacancy."

Unwin recalled Miss Palsgrave's words about the changing of the guard and knew that it was not Edward Lamech's place Emily had taken. She had been the overseer's only assistant—no one knew the job better than she did. He wondered whether she kept those figurines on her desk while she worked: totems of the agents whose efforts she now directed. Better that, he supposed, than those blank-eyed pigeons.

"There must be a lot of changes under way," Unwin said.

Her gaze grew suddenly hard. "Well, change takes time. And there are only a few people who know as much about this place as you do, Mr. Unwin, so I'm trusting you to keep it that way. Do you follow me?"

"I'm not sure that I do."

"Please try, Mr. Unwin. You're very valuable to us." Her voice softened. "To me, I mean. It would be terrible, you know, if you put me in a difficult position."

"A difficult position," Unwin said.

She took his hand and pressed something into it. He recognized its shape against his palm: it was the figurine from her collection that he thought looked like him. The one with his hands on his knees and a look of astonishment on his face. She kept her hand in his until they reached the twenty-ninth floor. Then Unwin pocketed the figurine and stepped off the elevator, turning to say good-bye. Emily's smile was sad, and Unwin thought for a moment that the sight of her crooked teeth would break his heart—and then it did, a little. He could not even tell her why, not now, though she might understand once she received his report.

Emily looked away as the attendant closed the door.

He packed his things quickly: silver letter opener, magnifying glass, spare spools of typewriter ribbon. He took some typing paper, too. It could be a long time before he had fresh supplies at hand again.

He closed the office door behind him and found Screed waiting in the hall.

"I need your help getting this thing lit," Screed said. His right arm was in a cast, and he was fumbling with the lighter in his left hand. Unwin took it from him, struck the flint, and raised the flame to the cigarette dangling from the detective's lips. It was the first time Unwin had actually seen him smoking.

"Everything was just as you said it was," Screed said. "The Cat & Tonic was empty, and there was Hoffmann, asleep in his chair. Wasn't he surprised to see me, after your alarm went off! I had him, Unwin."

"You had him," Unwin repeated.

"I wanted to take my time, you know. Get in touch with the right people at the newspaper. I figured that everyone should know about the historic occasion. I left him locked in my closet while I made the arrangements."

"But you forgot about his voice," Unwin said.

Screed looked at the floor and coughed smoke through his nose. "I was only gone a minute. When I got back to my office, Peake and Crabtree were waiting in the dark. They jumped me. Hoffmann had called them over using my voice and convinced them that Hoffmann had stuck me in the closet and was coming back to kill me. By the time we'd figured out what happened, he was gone."

Screed would not look Unwin in the eyes. They both knew that Hoffmann might never be caught again, that he could already be anywhere, any*one*. But if Sivart really did have a bit of Hoffmann still in his brain, might the opposite also be true? It pleased Unwin to imagine a fragment of the detective in the magician's mind, shadowing his every move.

After a while Unwin said, "At least you got the Oldest Murdered Man."

Screed sighed. "There's one old museum attendant down there who was pretty pleased about it. Not sure anyone else cared. I think they're even going to keep the plaque with Sivart's name on it."

Screed was still smoking when Unwin left, flinching each time he had to move his arm.

The fourteenth floor was Unwin's next stop. The clerks pretended not to see him, which made the walk to his old desk a little easier. Even now the sounds of the place tugged at him. He would have liked to sit for a while with his eyes closed, just listening to those typewriters and file drawers.

Penelope Greenwood had packed her things into a cardboard box. When she saw Unwin, she tucked it under her arm and put on her gray cap. Mr. Duden was watching as they returned to the elevator together. Unwin glanced behind him and caught the overclerk wringing his hands.

Out on the sidewalk, Unwin stood with Penny in the sunlight and waited. After the third time he checked his watch, she took his wrist gently and said, "Charles, this isn't the kind of thing it's possible to be late for."

She had returned to the city to revenge the murder of Caligari—but revenge, Unwin had come to understand, was not her only motive. She felt it was her duty to reclaim the thing that was lost when the carnival passed to her father. "The unknown will always be boundless," Caligari had said, and Unwin believed that Penelope Greenwood meant to keep it that way.

Some at the Agency, he thought, would be pleased to hear that the organization had a proper adversary again.

Caligari's Carnival rounded the corner. It was restored in full and traveling again, the mud of the old fairgrounds washed away, its every part repainted red or green or yellow, flinging streamers and music in all directions. The remnants had taken to their trucks; they waved and honked horns at the children who shouted from the sidewalks. The parade heaved itself in starts and stutters up the avenue, and at the front were the elephants, walking trunk to tail. Penelope had cleaned and fed them and scrubbed them behind their ears. Even the oldest of the three looked lively again.

As the parade drew close, a series of deep thudding sounds shook the sidewalk. Unwin and Penny held each other's arms as cracks appeared in the cement at their feet and a gust of hot, acrid air erupted from the Agency lobby. They turned to see black smoke streaming out the door, and with it a crowd of bewildered, red-faced men clutching bowler hats to their heads. Whistling sounds and the cracks of explosives followed.

Unwin and Penny drew closer as the underclerks tumbled past them, shouting and coughing, some still pulling jackets over their pajamas. The crowd merged with the parade in the street, bringing the procession to a halt. Clowns and underclerks toppled over one another as drivers shouted from their seats and hats, pillows, and balloons flew into the air. Up and down the avenue, people huddled at open windows to watch the spectacle. The youngest elephant, out of delight or indignation, reared on its hind legs and trumpeted.

The tremors ceased as Hildegard Palsgrave ducked out through the lobby door, her arms and face covered in soot. She dragged her enormous pink chair behind her, and on it was her phonograph. "My first fireworks display in years," she said.

Penelope shook soot from the dress of the giantess. "You haven't lost your touch," she said.

Unwin gazed up the facade of the Agency office building and saw windows opening on every floor. Clerks looked down from the nearest rows, taking turns at the view. Detectives watched from their higher floors, shaking their heads at the scene. Farther up, so far that Unwin could not make out the expressions on their faces, the watchers observed everything from the comfort of their private offices, and above them, fewer in number, were operatives whose titles and functions he did not know.

Emily's first week on the job, and changes were under way more quickly than she had anticipated. The watchers would be asking their new overseer what to do, now that the chief clerk of the third archive had destroyed what she helped to create.

Edgar Zlatari was driving the Rooks' truck. He navigated slowly through the crowd and drew up to the curb with the steam engine sputtering. Theodore Brock, the knife thrower, was in the cab beside him, and Jasper was still in the back, still sleeping. Miss Palsgrave set her chair beside Jasper and climbed in.

"What about the Forty Winks?" Unwin asked Zlatari. "What about your work?"

"Show me a place where nobody's drinking and nobody's dying, and

I'll show you a man ready to stay put," he said. "Besides, there's an old crook in need of burying. Seems his funeral's been long delayed."

Unwin looked at Penelope, and she smiled. They must have smuggled Caligari's remains out of the museum somehow, after the real mummy was returned.

Miss Palsgrave smacked the roof of the cab to signal that she was ready. She had a traveling bag with her, and inside were more recordings of Miss Greenwood's songs, to make sure Jasper Rook stayed sleeping.

Unwin was tired, too. He had worn himself down—to nothing, nearly—with his cuts and corrections, his erasures and emendations. He was awake now, but was there still time for him? His mind had wearied of its appointed rounds, of the stream of typescript and transcript, and now he wondered what might have been different, what might still be different, if only the day would hold and not abandon him to sleep.

The carnival had disentangled itself from the knot of baffled underclerks and was preparing to move on. The elephants stamped impatiently, the drivers returned to their trucks, and Penny left Unwin's side to join the front of the line.

Zlatari offered him a ride. He turned down the offer but set his portable typewriter and his briefcase in the cab. He had found the time, that week, to oil the chain of his bicycle.

Maybe Penny was correct, and this was not the kind of thing he could be late for. He glimpsed Caligari's old motto emblazoned across the side of another truck: EVERYTHING I TELL YOU IS TRUE, AND EVERYTHING YOU SEE IS AS REAL AS YOU ARE.

If that was right, then nothing Unwin saw was real and the ticking of his watch was just another magician's trick. He had time, so much time. He had all the time he needed.

Some of the underclerks wrapped themselves in the blankets they had brought with them from the archive and stood watching the parade withdraw, dumbfounded. A few of them, confused by all the sights and sounds, or just because they had no place to go, went with it. Other people joined the carnival as it moved west between the office buildings—those who, no doubt, had been among Penelope's sleepwalkers, the members of her resistance. They had helped rebuild the carnival in their sleep and recalled enough that it mattered. The carnival was twice as large as it had been by the time it left the city.

He allowed himself a last glimpse of the Agency office building, and it appeared to him as it had many times before: a watchtower, a tomb. Not his, now, though someone there—the overseer herself, probably—would be expecting his report. If Unwin dispatched a copy from afar, would its recipient be surprised to find that it originated in the camp of the enemy? He smiled at the thought of it, and the smile surprised him into laughter. He was still laughing when a wind rose up from the river, nearly taking his hat. He held it to his head and steered his bicycle with one hand.

It would be hours at least before they halted long enough for him to set out his typewriter, so he carried on with his work as best he could, drafting in his mind the report that was the last of one series and the first of another.

I rode alongside the steam truck for a while, then overtook it and wove my way to the front of the column. Penelope Greenwood walked with the reins of the lead elephant in her hand, and the big beast flapped its ears in the wind. What frightens us about the carnival, I think, is not that it will come to town. Or that it will leave town, which it always does. What frightens us is the possibility that it will leave forever, and never come back, and take us with it when it goes.

It is taking me now, and I am frightened and alive and very much awake.

Where are we going next? With what purpose? Penny says she will carry on with Caligari's work, and whatever happens, someone is going to have to write it all down. So I have my job back, in a way, but the words mean nothing, all is mystery, and always there's room enough for more.

　　I'll try to record it as we go, but that's for another report. This one ends here, on a bridge over the river with the elephants leading us toward what routes they remember, and Hoffmann still out there with his thousand and one voices, and Agency operatives already on our tail, and the city waking, and the river waking, and the road waking under our feet, and every alarm clock ringing at the bottom of the sea.

Acknowledgments

Thanks first to my family: Sean, Caitlin, and Kellin Bliss, Kevin, Debbie, and Michael Berry, Michael Bliss, and Robert Boolukos. Cara Parravani, Dorothy Strachan, and Frank, Ellen, and Kyle Berry, each greatly missed, are everywhere in this novel. I am deeply indebted to Kelly Link, Gavin Grant, Sabina Murray, Mira Bartók, and Holly and Theo Black for their friendship and advice. Thanks also to Chris Bachelder, Brian Baldi, Robert N. Casper, Cecil Castellucci, Ellen Datlow, Miciah Bay Gault, Noy Holland, Shahrul Ladue, Leigh Newman, Jon Sequeira, and Terri Windling for all their help and sound criticism; to Esmond Harmsworth for his guidance and great insight; to Eamon Dolan for his encouragement and general brilliance; to Jason Arthur for his support, and for bringing this book to the UK in style; to Mimi Di-Novo for her generosity; to Deirdre d'Albertis for Chesterton, to William Weaver for Calvino, to Bradford Morrow for Carter and most everyone else; to Christa Parravani for lending me her dream of the sea.

This book is dedicated to my mother, Maureen Berry Bliss, who is always looking for a good mystery.